*To Janet*

# The Cost
# of
# Commitment

*Buckle your seatbelt for this one!*

## By
## Lynn Ames

*Lynn Ames*

THE COST OF COMMITMENT
© 2010 BY LYNN AMES
REVISED 2ND EDITION

ISBN: 978-0-9840521-5-8
Library of Congress Catalog Number: TXu001202263

This trade paperback original is published by

PHOENIX RISING PRESS
PHOENIX, ARIZONA
www.phoenixrisingpress.com

First Edition: October 2004

This is a work of fiction. Names, characters, places, and incidents are the product of the author's imagination or are used fictitiously, and any resemblance to actual persons, living or dead, businesses, companies, events, or locales is entirely coincidental.

CREDITS
EXECUTIVE EDITOR: LINDA LORENZO
AUTHOR PHOTO: JUDY FRANCESCONI
COVER DESIGN BY: PAM LAMBROS,
WWW.HANDSONGRAPHICDESIGN.COM

# *Dedication*

For Alex, whose smile lit my days

# Other Books in Print by Lynn Ames

### Outsiders

What happens when you take five beloved, powerhouse authors, each with a unique voice and style, give them one word to work with, and put them between the sheets together, no holds barred?

Magic!!

Brisk Press presents Lynn Ames, Georgia Beers, JD Glass, Susan X. Meagher and Susan Smith, all together under the same cover with the aim to satisfy your every literary taste. This incredible combination offers something for everyone — a smorgasbord of fiction unlike anything you'll find anywhere else.

A Native American raised on the Reservation ventures outside the comfort and familiarity of her own world to help a lost soul embrace the gifts that set her apart. * A reluctantly wealthy woman uses all of her resources anonymously to help those who cannot help themselves. * Three individuals, three aspects of the self, combine to create balance and harmony at last for a popular trio of characters. * Two nomadic women from very different walks of life discover common ground — and a lot more — during a blackout in New York City. * A traditional, old school butch must confront her community and her own belief system when she falls for a much younger transman.

Five authors — five novellas. *Outsiders* — one remarkable book.

### Heartsong

After three years spent mourning the death of her partner in a tragic climbing accident, Danica Warren has re-emerged in the public eye. With a best-selling memoir, a blockbuster movie about her heroic efforts to save three other climbers, and a successful career on the motivational speaking circuit, Danica has convinced herself that her life can be full without love.

When Chase Crosley walks into Danica's field of vision everything changes. Danica is suddenly faced with questions she's never pondered.

Is there really one love that transcends all concepts of space and time? One great love that joins two hearts so that they beat as one? One moment of recognition when twin flames join and burn together?

Will Danica and Chase be able to overcome the barriers standing between them and find forever? And can that love be sustained, even in the face of cruel circumstances and fate?

### One ~ Love, (formerly The Flip Side of Desire)

Trystan Lightfoot allowed herself to love once in her life; the experience broke her heart and strengthened her resolve never to fall in love again. At forty, however, she still longs for the comfort of a woman's arms. She finds temporary solace in meaningless, albeit adventuresome encounters, burying her pain and her emotions deep inside where no one can reach. No one, that is, until she meets C.J. Winslow.

C.J. Winslow is the model-pretty-but-aging professional tennis star the Women's Tennis Federation is counting on to dispel the image that all great female tennis players are lesbians. And her lesbianism isn't the only secret she's hiding. A traumatic event from her childhood is taking its toll both on and off the court.

Together Trystan and C.J. must find a way beyond their pasts to discover lasting love.


## Other Books in The Kate and Jay Trilogy

### *The Price of Fame*

When local television news anchor Katherine Kyle is thrust into the national spotlight, it sets in motion a chain of events that will change her life forever. Jamison "Jay" Parker is an intensely career-driven Time magazine reporter. The first time she saw Kate, she fell in love. The last time she saw her, Kate was rescuing her. That was five years earlier, and she never expected to see her again. Then circumstances and an assignment bring them back together.

Kate and Jay's lives intertwine, leading them on a journey to love and happiness, until fate and fame threaten to tear them apart. What is the price of fame? For Kate, the cost just might be everything. For Jay, it could be the other half of her soul.

### *The Value of Valor*

Katherine Kyle is the press secretary to the president of the United States. Her lover, Jamison Parker, is a respected writer for Time magazine. Separated by unthinkable tragedy, the two must struggle to survive against impossible odds...

A powerful, shadowy organization wants to advance its own global agenda. To succeed, the president must be eliminated. Only one person knows the truth and can put a stop to the scheme.

It will take every ounce of courage and strength Kate possesses to stay alive long enough to expose the plot. Meanwhile, Jay must cheat death and race across continents to be by her lover's side...

This hair-raising thriller will grip you from the start and won't let you go until the ride is over.

The Value of Valor—it's priceless.

# CHAPTER ONE

Bob, can you get a better fix on what caused the incident at Sing Sing? I've got reporters breathing down my neck and pretty soon they're gonna start making up their own version of events."

The uniformed correction officer struggled to match the long, graceful strides of the woman walking alongside him. "Sure thing, Kate. We're working on it. Should have an answer to you within the half hour. They're just interviewing the last inmate now." He continued down the corridor, and Kate peeled off to the left as they reached the door marked Katherine Kyle, Director of Public Information, New York State Department of Correctional Services.

"Kate?"

The tall, raven-haired woman turned inside the door to face her beleaguered assistant. "Yeah, Marisa, what is it?"

"The commissioner wants to see you."

"Great. Tell him I'll be right there." She continued moving through the suite and into her office, where the phone already was ringing. The readout on her phone said "incoming call." That meant the call originated outside the state government system. Although she couldn't be positive who it was, Kate felt confident. "Hi, beautiful."

There was a second's hesitation on the other end of the line, followed by a surprised chuckle. "What if it hadn't been me, love?"

"Ah, but it was."

"Yes, but..."

"Well, if it had been someone else, I guess I would've had to offer to take *her* to dinner and make mad, passionate love to her afterward."

"Grrr."

"So, I guess it's a good thing it was you, eh?"

"One of these days, Kyle...if you keep this up, I'm not gonna share the three rare Captain America comic books I found for you today."

"Oh, that is so far below the belt, Jamison Parker. You wouldn't dare—"

"Do you want to find out?"

Kate cleared her throat and sighed. "Um, Jay, honey, sweetheart?"

"Yes?"

"I've missed you so much today. Can I take you out to dinner someplace nice and then make mad, passionate love to you afterward?"

"I'll think about it and have my people get in touch with your people."

"Hey!"

"Well, Stretch, the offer sounds wonderful. It's your delivery that needs work."

"Everybody's a critic." Kate smiled. God, it felt so good to be able to tease each other without reservation again. It had taken nearly all of these past three months to reestablish their equilibrium and get beyond the hurts caused by both circumstance and each other.

As sometimes happened these days, Kate found herself mentally cataloguing the improbable events that got them to this point—the explosion at the capitol that brought Jay back into her life, the cover story in *Time* magazine, the tabloid pictures of her kissing Jay, getting fired from her anchor job at WCAP-TV, dropping out of sight to protect Jay's identity, Jay's anger and hurt, their reunion and, after they returned home, the media's incessant hounding of Kate in an attempt to uncover the identity of her lover.

*All things considered, Kyle, three months isn't so bad.*

"Earth to Kate, come in, Kate? You are still on the phone with me, right?"

"Sorry. Right here."

"How's your day going?"

"Not too bad. The usual mix of mayhem. Inmates beating each other over the head, officers breaking the law, reporters making up their own stories. You know. How's your day?"

"Better than that, I guess. I only have to contend with corporate officers who won't speak on the record."

"Ah. Which train are you catching to Albany? Will you be home tonight in time for dinner?"

"Looks like it right now. How about you?"

"I'm hopeful. It would be the first night this week and it's already Thursday." Kate got serious. "I really do miss you, Jay. We live in the same house, and still it feels like I haven't been able to spend any time with you lately."

"I know, honey. I miss you too, but we both knew when you took this job it wasn't going to be easy. Don't worry. We'll make it work."

"Thank you for being so patient and understanding. I promise I'll be home in time to take you to dinner at seven thirty, okay?"

"It's a date."

"See you then. Right now the commissioner is waiting to see me. Until tonight, babe. I love you."

"I love you too, Kate. Bye."

Kate tipped back in her chair and surveyed her surroundings. Governor Charles Hyland took a huge risk politically when he called to offer her the PIO job. After all, she had just been fired as WCAP-TV's lead anchorwoman after the *Enquirer* outed her as a lesbian. She would always be grateful to him for hiring her despite the media storm that ensued. It started with headlines ranging from factual to inflammatory: "Former TV Anchorwoman Turns Spin Doctor," "Hyland Hires Disgraced TV Personality," "Governor Goes for Gay Girl," and, in one ultraconservative newspaper, "Pervert to Speak for Prisons." Subsequent editorials called into question the governor's judgment, morals, ethics, and commitment to follow the will of his constituents. Still, the governor stood by Kate, even when she offered him a way out.

Yes, given everything that transpired, it was hard to believe she was sitting here.

�᷐᷑

"Kate, c'mon in."

"Good morning, sir. Something I can do for you?" She stood expectantly, notebook at the ready.

"Sit down, Kate. No need to be so formal."

She took the seat nearest the massive cherry desk, noting once again that, despite his lean physique, her new boss's presence pervaded the room. Brian Sampson was neither loud nor overbearing. Rather, he projected a quiet, calm confidence that indicated his comfort with the seat of power he held. "We've certainly been keeping you busy, haven't we?"

Kate smiled. She liked this man. He was both honest and honorable, rare qualities in a politician. "You could say that."

In fact, Kate's first ninety days as sole spokesperson for the third-largest prison system in the country had been a blur. With 67 prisons, 47,000 inmates, and 35,000 employees, there was never a dull moment. So far, she'd managed one full night's sleep in three months without being awakened by either a reporter writing a story or the command center letting her know about an incident.

It had taken her a while to get used to her phone ringing at all hours of the day and night, but it was customary for the officers in the command center to alert her any time an incident took place anywhere in the system. She needed to have that information so she could stay one step ahead of the media.

"Sir, this job makes being a journalist on deadline seem like a walk in the park."

Commissioner Sampson tipped his chair back and laughed. "As I recall, the governor warned you that being the DOCS public information officer would be a challenge."

"Yes, he did, and he was right." Kate smiled wistfully.

"I've been impressed with your work so far. You seem to have little trouble grasping the nuances of this business, and your ability to deflect negative publicity is uncanny. In short, you've caught on quickly and stopped our image from hemorrhaging any further. It's nice to have a spokesperson on board who can get along with the press." Here he smiled, and Kate could clearly hear the unspoken phrase, *unlike your predecessor.* "I just wanted you to know that I've noticed, and that I am awfully happy to have you here."

"Thank you, sir. I'm glad you feel that way." Kate was somewhat at a loss. She was pretty sure her boss hadn't called her in just to inflate her ego.

After a moment's hesitation, he went on. "Ah, Kate, I don't know if you're aware of this, but the governor's been under a lot of pressure lately." At her raised eyebrow, he explained, "Seems the boys from the DNC aren't crazy about some of his positions. They see him as their meal ticket to the White House next year and they're afraid of him alienating middle America." His tone was derisive.

"What you're saying is the Democratic National Committee wants him to take no real stand about anything meaningful, accomplish nothing, and just *pretend* like he's governing for the duration, right?"

"Charles is right about one thing—you are perceptive and not shy about telling it like it is in the appropriate company."

"Sir, I've never been one to subscribe to the 'tell them what they want to hear' theory. I believe people like you and the governor rely on me to offer the unvarnished truth. It's that kind of advice that has real value. I'm afraid I'll never be a good yes-person."

"Thank God, Kate. Thank God."

"Sir, I'm sure there's a reason why you're telling me this now."

He sighed. "Yes. I want you to know that there's going to be increased scrutiny of everything we do here. You know what a hot-button issue crime and corrections is for a Democrat. We're going to have to make sure we dot every *i* and cross every *t* for the next year. You, in particular, are going to be in the hot seat. Are you all right with that?"

Kate favored her boss with a cockeyed grin. "Respectfully, sir, been there, done that."

~∽⌢∾

In the luxurious private study at the exclusive Fort Orange Club in Albany, three Democratic power brokers were in a heated discussion. Robert Hawthorne had been selected the year before to take the helm of the Democratic National Committee. He recently retired from the U.S. Senate, where he had served four terms. Michael Vendetti, press secretary to Governor Charles Hyland of New York, was the most powerful spin doctor in the state. David Breathwaite, uber-PR person or "super flak" of all New York law enforcement agencies, had made himself indispensable over the years by unearthing all manner of damaging information on important figures on both sides of the political aisle.

"God damn it, David, you promised she wouldn't be able to handle the job."

The former director of public information for DOCS answered, "Relax, Michael, you know you're not supposed to get excited. Imagine what that's doing to your blood pressure."

Vendetti, impeccably dressed as always in a finely tailored suit, sat across the table from him and snarled. It was clear that he regarded Kate's predecessor and the current czar of criminal justice PR as the human personification of a weasel.

David continued mildly, "You're the governor's press secretary. It's not my fault he prefers her advice to yours."

Vendetti rose so quickly that his ornately appointed high-backed chair toppled over backward, landing with a resounding bang on the hardwood floor. "You little—"

"That's enough. Both of you." Hawthorne leaned forward in his seat. "It won't do us any good to fight amongst ourselves. We can't afford to lose sight of the objective here. We need our boy Charlie in the White House—"

Under his breath David mumbled, "That's only because you couldn't get yourself elected dog catcher last time around, *Mr.* Senator."

"And that Amazonian dyke is standing in our way." If Hawthorne had heard the cutting remark directed at him, he chose to ignore it. "She has entirely too much influence over our boy. She goes to dinner with him every few weeks and all of a sudden he's making dramatic policy announcements that have nothing to do with our agenda. Not only that, but we've got a wild card in the form of a commissioner we can't control. I don't like it."

"Bob, it's too early to be concerned. She's only been in the position three months. We said we'd get her out at six months." Breathwaite never looked up as he chewed on his cuticles. "Give her time, she's bound to screw up. If not, we'll help her."

"Yes, well, I'm not leaving anything to chance here, so I've asked an old friend of mine to join us." Hawthorne rose from his position at the head of the table and went to an inner door. "You can come in now, Willie." To the others in the room, he said, "Gentlemen, I'm sure you know my good friend William Redfield, executive deputy commissioner of DOCS."

David Breathwaite visibly blanched. "Bill. I didn't realize you and the senator were on such friendly terms."

Redfield smirked. "There are a lot of things you don't know, David. Bob and I went to college together. He called me recently and filled me in."

"Yes, I thought it was important that we have someone on the inside."

Breathwaite protested, "We have someone on the inside already."

"Yes, David, that's true, but so far I've been less than satisfied with the results we've been getting from our source. We need someone with a little more pull, someone who can make things happen, if you will." Hawthorne smiled thinly. "Please, Willie, have a seat."

Redfield selected the fourth and last available seat at the table.

"Michael, how did our boy Charlie take my discussion with him today?" Hawthorne asked.

"As you might expect, he was less than overjoyed at having you come in and dictate political strategy and policy positions to him."

The veins in his neck bulging, Hawthorne thundered, "For Christ's sake, he's running around like he's actually his own man. He belongs to this party. He belongs to *us*, and we're gonna make sure he gets elected president in spite of himself. I don't give a rat's ass whether or not he's happy as long as he sticks to our agenda!" Adjusting his tie, he added more quietly, "Michael, you'd better keep him in line. Will, I'm gonna need your help here. Kyle has got to be out the door in three months, no ifs, ands, or buts. Can you make that happen?"

"You've got nothing to worry about, Bob."

"Good. I knew I could count on you. David, for God's sake, try to stay the hell out of the newspapers and keep your head down. How are we going to reinstall you in Kyle's place if you keep creating controversy?"

In truth, Hawthorne hated Breathwaite as much as everybody else at the table, but the man had a remarkable knack for finding weak spots and exploiting them. He had certainly found Hawthorne's, blackmailing him when he discovered the chairman's scheme to use Governor Hyland as a puppet to gain control of 1600 Pennsylvania Avenue. He was a valuable asset to have...and a very bad enemy.

Unfortunately, when the idiot created a swirl of controversy and a host of enemies in the press, he nearly got himself fired as DOCS PIO by the governor. Hawthorne and company had to scramble to get him out of the line of fire for a time. Why he wanted to go back to DOCS so badly was a mystery, but Hawthorne didn't care. If that's what Breathwaite wanted, that's what he would get. They needed him on the team.

"That's all for now, gentlemen. Keep the contact and conversation to a bare minimum, and we'll meet back here in a month or two. I'll be in touch when it's time."

"Kate, sweetheart, are you home?" Before she had time to put her briefcase down, Jay was accosted by seventy-nine pounds of bouncing blonde fur. "Hey, buddy! Hey there, Fred. How was your day?" She bent over and scratched the golden retriever lovingly on the hindquarters as he marched in place between her legs. "Where's your mommy, huh, guy? Is she here yet?"

As if in answer to her query, Kate shouted from a distance, "Hey, Jay, I'm up here. C'mon up!"

"On my way, as soon as Fred is done practicing his marching band routine." Jay looked down again, "Let's go, big guy, I can't wait to see your mom."

She bounded up the stairs to the second floor of the house Kate designed prior to their relationship, impressed, as always, with how comfortable and how much at home she felt here. *Well, it is my home now.* The notion sent a thrill through her, as it never failed to do.

At the top of the stairs, Jay was enveloped in a strong, but sensual hug. She glanced up to find twinkling eyes gazing lovingly at her and a smile on her partner's face. Kate ducked her head and welcomed Jay home with a slow, sweet kiss.

"Mmm, I love coming home to this."

"And I love you."

"I love you too, Kate."

They stayed like that a few heartbeats more, just savoring the moment, until Fred made his presence known once again. They both smiled indulgently as Kate made eye contact with the spoiled beast.

"Yes, doll, we know you're here. No group hugs for you, though. Right now, this beautiful woman is all mine."

"Kate, we'd better hurry if our reservation is at seven thirty. Where are we going? What do I need to wear?"

"Dressy tonight, babe. Something elegant and strapless, I think."

"Oh, what's the occasion?"

"Does there have to be one? Now go on, get moving." Kate swatted Jay on the rear end, pushing her gently down the hall in the direction of what once had been the guest suite but now was Jay's personal space. The blonde affectionately referred to it as "the place where my clothes live in a world by themselves."

⊰⊱

Kate retreated to the master bedroom, where she hastily dabbed on some Shalimar, her perfume of choice, and finished dressing. She slipped into a pair of high heels that matched her dress perfectly and hurried down the stairs, calling, "You've got about ten minutes, Jay. I'll meet you downstairs."

She hustled to the side door and opened it to admit three men in waiter's uniforms. "Hurry, guys, we only have a few minutes."

Behind the servers came two women dressed in chef's outfits. The first one stopped and kissed Kate on the cheek. "Hiya, beautiful. Don't be so nervous. I promised you everything would be perfect, and so it shall."

"Barbara," Kate whispered urgently, "Jay's gonna walk down the stairs in less than ten minutes expecting me to take her out for an elegant evening. Everything has to be in place before that happens!"

"Tsk, woman, it's a wonder you don't have an ulcer already. Have I ever not delivered on a promise to you?"

Sighing in exasperation, Kate answered, "No."

"Right, and I'm not about to ruin my reputation now. I didn't get to be a world-renowned doctor by folding under pressure, toots."

Kate had to laugh. She was right. Barbara Jones was a well-recognized physician, a master gourmet chef, and a wonderful friend. Heaven knew she had seen Kate—then Kate and Jay together—through some rough patches.

Turning to the waiters, Barbara pointed past the kitchen. "Okay, boys, the dining room's that way. Work your magic."

At Kate's upturned eyebrow, Barbara laughed. "Honey, these boys know more about presentation and style than any woman I've ever met. What is it about gay men that gives them such a sense of panache? I assure you, you're in the best hands possible. In less than five minutes, your dining room is going to scream romance."

"You're the best, you know that?"

"Yeah, that's why you keep me around, I presume."

"That and the fact that I can't seem to keep myself out of harm's way." Kate winked as she made her way to the bottom of the staircase to await Jay's arrival.

It didn't take long. Five minutes later she looked up to see a vision that robbed her of breath and speech. Jay paused at the top landing, her short blonde hair shimmering in the light from the chandelier, the emerald green, strapless, knee-length dress accentuating her lithe form and toned muscles to perfection. As she descended, Kate watched Jay's smile grow wider in answer to her own.

"You are the most magnificent woman I have ever laid eyes on, Jamison Parker."

"And you, Katherine Ann Kyle, are the sexiest creature on the planet."

Kate wore a rich navy sheath that hugged her form, the material reaching over one shoulder, leaving the other, and most of her upper back, bare.

"May I?" Kate reached for Jay's hand, and guided her down the last steps and toward the dining room.

"Um, Kate? I may not have a great sense of direction, admittedly, but even I know that the garage is that way." Jay pointed in the opposite direction.

"It is? Damn, they must have moved it on me again." But she continued moving in the direction she intended.

"Okay, Kyle, what are you up to? Spill it."

"Oh, I love it when you get that authoritative tone in your voice."

"I mean it."

"Who says I have to be up to anything?"

"I know you've got something cooked up here. You've got that cat that ate the canary look on your face."

"Moi?"

"Yes, you, Miss Innocent."

They had reached the entrance to the dining room. Kate moved ahead slightly, wanting to block Jay's view in case everything wasn't ready yet. She needn't have worried; the room was transformed. Candlelight sent a warm glow throughout the spacious area, highlighting the dark richness of the mahogany table and chairs and painting interesting shadows on the Oriental rug. Fine china and silver glinted in the low lighting, while soft music played in the background. She stepped aside.

"Oh, Kate..." Jay looked up questioningly.

"I hope you like it, sweetheart."

"But...why? Am I missing something here?"

Kate took her lover's hands in her own and forced eye contact. "I know I've been really busy with the new job, but I want you to know that no matter what else is going on, every day, I thank whatever power exists in the universe that brought you back into my life. I love you, Jay, more than life itself, and I just wanted to find a special way to show you how I feel."

Tears flowed down Jay's face. She buried her face in Kate's chest. "Oh, sweetheart, that is so beautiful. You are the most incurable romantic. It's one of the most amazing things about you. And I love you so much."

Kate bent her head and kissed Jay reverently on the mouth. "C'mon, the food's getting cold."

"But—"

"You're wondering if I've learned to cook overnight. Nope."

"Then what...how..."

Kate smiled indulgently. "How about if you just sit down and all will be revealed to you."

Jay grinned sheepishly and accepted the seat Kate offered.

"Gentlemen, I think it's time."

The waiters, who had been standing at a discreet distance inside the doorway to the kitchen, moved with efficiency and grace into the room, carrying serving plates. The first server bowed slightly at Jay's side. "Would you care for some French onion soup?"

She smiled at him. "I'd love some, thank you." To Kate she said, "Um, should I ask how you pulled this off and who these fine gentlemen are? Or where, exactly, the delicious food is coming from? I mean, it smells like it's coming from our kitchen, but..."

"Very observant, my dear." Kate said nothing more.

"That's it? *That's it?* You're not going to tell me how dinner is getting to our table?"

"What does it matter as long as you like it?"

"Stretch, you know how I am when my curiosity is aroused."

Kate grinned evilly. "I know how you are when *you* are aroused." Her gaze dropped to Jay's breasts.

Jay blushed. "Don't change the topic. You know what I meant."

"Okay, if you must know, I brought in a master chef to cook for us this evening. Are you happy now? Satisfied, Miss Snoop? No wonder you make such a good reporter."

"Thank you for answering me." Jay leaned over and kissed Kate, a long, slow, sensuous joining of the lips that lasted for several moments.

"If I had known *that* would be your response, I would have answered you sooner."

"Brat."

Kate gazed deeply into Jay's eyes, which were accentuated by the combination of candlelight and the emerald color of her dress. "I will never tire of looking at you, you know that? You are the most beautiful

16

woman in the world, and I still have to pinch myself to make sure this isn't all a dream."

As Jay opened her mouth to respond, Kate's business phone rang.

Annoyed, Kate snapped, "*That*, on the other hand, is a nightmare. I'm sorry, love, I have to get that."

"I know. Go ahead, don't worry. I'll wait for you."

Picking up the phone in her office, Kate barked, "Kyle."

"Um, Kate, this is the command center. Sorry to bother you."

"That's okay, John." She made a conscious effort to take the bite out of her tone. "What's going on?" *After all, Kyle, it isn't his fault the job can be damned inconvenient at times.*

"Two inmates got into a fight in the mess hall at Auburn. One of 'em pulled a shank and stabbed the other. He's gone to the hospital. Last word was he was in critical condition. They don't think he's gonna make it."

Kate was taking notes. "Okay, I'm going to need names, crimes they're in for, sentences for each, whether they had any history together before tonight, race, how the officers responded, where the perp is now, and if this was just a one-on-one thing or part of something larger."

"Yes, ma'am."

"John, that was, what...the third incident at Auburn in the last week that involved a weapon? What's going on there? I need to know if there's any hint of a connection between the events. I'll tell you right now that the reporter for the paper out there is pretty sharp. It won't take him long to put two and two together and wonder if he's got four. Are we going to lock the place down and do a cell-by-cell? If so, word's going to get out in a hurry."

"I'll get right on it and get you answers ASAP, Kate."

"Thanks, John, I appreciate it."

Back in the dining room, Kate kissed Jay on the shoulder. "I'm sorry about that. Now, where were we before we were so rudely interrupted?"

"Everything okay?"

"Yeah, just murderers killing murderers. Another day in paradise."

"So it's going to be a long night for you."

"Only if the reporters find out about it. For now, I'd much rather concentrate on you."

"Mmm, that's okay with me."

The rest of dinner was uninterrupted. They managed to eat their way through the salad for two, the petit filet mignon, lobster tails, asparagus tips with hollandaise sauce, and twice-baked potatoes without much difficulty. Except, that is, when Jay missed while trying to feed Kate some of the potatoes. To make up for her gaffe, she licked the overflow from Kate's chin. The transgression was quickly forgotten.

Apparently unable to decide between the fresh apple cobbler and the homemade strawberry cheesecake, Jay opted to sample both. When she had polished off both desserts, she pushed back from the table.

"Sure you've had enough?"

"Well..."

"Ugh. It's a wonder you don't weigh three hundred pounds. I can't fathom where you put it all."

"You're just jealous, that's all."

"Yep, you're right. How did you know?"

"I've seen the type before."

Again, the business phone forestalled further conversation. "I'll be right back, sweetheart. I'm really sorry about this. I wanted tonight to be perfect."

"It is perfect, Kate. Don't worry about it...it's not as if it's something you can control."

Actually, at the moment Kate was contemplating how long it would take her to fly out to Auburn to finish both inmates off herself. However, recognizing the impracticality of that solution, she opted to answer the phone instead. "Kyle."

"Hi, Kate, it's John again, in the command center. I've got your answers for you. Unfortunately, the poor slob died a half hour ago. Here are the particulars..."

She listened and asked more questions for the better part of a half hour, taking notes and formulating strategy. Then she hung up and glanced at the clock over her desk—10:02 p.m. Jay was right—it was likely to be yet another long night. Sighing, she made her way out of her office and stopped in the kitchen long enough to thank Barbara again for her services.

"Oh, you know me, Kate, I'm a sucker for a good romance."

"And I'm grateful, my friend. Good night."

"You better get going before she goes to bed without you." Barbara turned and made her way out into the night, the waiters and sous chef having preceded her.

Kate found Jay in the family room picking out music. Sneaking up behind her, she tilted her head and nibbled on the side of Jay's neck. She felt the shiver even as Jay's head tipped back to give her better access.

Given the invitation, Kate wrapped her long arms around Jay from behind and pulled their bodies into close contact. She continued to taste and lick her way up to Jay's earlobe, sucked it into her mouth and bit down lightly.

Jay groaned, and Kate could feel compact abdominal muscles contracting beneath her hands. Jay turned in the circle of Kate's arms, placing feather-light kisses on her collarbones and chest.

"Um, sweetheart, before we get too carried away here, I have something for you."

"Love, you *are* something for me," Jay purred as she licked her way across to Kate's bare shoulder.

Kate pushed away just enough to give herself room to maneuver. Reaching inside her bra, she extracted something shiny.

"Hey, I could've done that."

"Yes, and I hope you will...later." Again, Kate had to still Jay's wandering hands.

"This is for you, because you are the most brilliant gem in my life." She gently grasped her lover's arm, turning it over so that the palm faced up. She kissed the sensitive skin there before concentrating on the task at hand. Stepping back slightly, she waited as Jay examined her wrist.

"My God, Kate, you didn't have to do this. It's gorgeous!" On her right wrist sparkled a three-carat diamond tennis bracelet.

"I love you, Jamison."

"I love you too, sweetheart."

Kate kissed the top of the fair head she cherished so much, then eyelids, nose, cheeks, and finally, the perfect lips that beckoned her. She felt Jay's nipples harden through the thin material of her dress as she deepened the kiss, sucking gently on Jay's tongue before releasing it.

They continued to kiss as Kate guided them up the stairs to their bedroom, with Fred trailing behind, used to this behavior from his humans. She slowly lowered the zipper on Jay's dress, kissed and caressed every inch of newly exposed flesh, let the material slide to the floor, and helped Jay step out of it. Slip and pantyhose followed close behind, until finally, the only remaining barriers were a strapless bra and very sexy, lace bikini underwear.

Kate returned to Jay's mouth momentarily as she released the catches on the bra, freeing creamy white breasts and painfully erect nipples. She kissed and licked along the underside of the left breast and then the right while sliding her hands up the inside of Jay's thighs.

"Argh, please. I need you so much." Jay tried to back up to the bed, but Kate held her fast.

"No, babe. I want you to stand." This she said as she ran her tongue around the rim of one nipple.

"Sweetheart, I'll fall over."

"No, you won't. I've got you. Just hang on to me."

"Ah!"

Kate's hand was following the outline of Jay's panties as her other hand traced a line up Jay's body from her abdomen to her breasts.

"God, I'm so wet for you. Please, I can't take it anymore."

Kate knelt and slowly removed Jay's panties. Kate quickly swirled her tongue in the warm wetness that awaited her. She closed her eyes and savored the taste with the same sense of wonder she felt every time they were together this way. She wasn't quite ready to linger there, though. There was so much more that she wanted to do. She continued on her journey, her mouth tracing her lover's bikini line, stopping to nibble on the insides of her thighs as her hands caressed the soft, but firm flesh in place after place. "You are so, so very beautiful."

Jay was barely able to stay upright, and her cries of urgency increased with every stroke of Kate's tongue. She clutched at Kate's shoulders in an obvious effort to ground herself. "Please."

Hearing the desperation in her cry, Kate relented and returned to Jay's center, gently stroking her first, exploring her folds, tasting her clitoris, slowly drawing the moisture from her, before increasing the pressure and driving Jay over the top.

Kate held on tight as Jay trembled, aftershocks rolling through her body like waves to the ocean's shore. When they passed, Kate guided Jay onto the bed, and removed her own clothes before joining her. She wrapped Jay in her arms and softly stroked her skin.

"My God, woman, I think you just tried to kill me!"

"Nah," Kate smiled, "If I was trying, I'd have succeeded."

"Hmm. I'm tough to kill, ya know."

"Oh, yeah, I would suspect as mu—"

Kate's words were cut off when Jay inserted a leg between her thighs, rolled her over and pinned her to the bed. She brushed lips and fingers over Kate's ribs, then up her breastbone to her shoulders, and finally back down to her aching breasts, all the while rocking against her wet center.

Kate arched up off the bed as Jay ran one hand down into her moist curls, entering her slowly while continuing to exert pressure with her thigh. When Jay bit down lightly on her nipple, Kate came with a sharp cry.

The two women spent long, languorous hours loving each other before pulling up the covers and falling into a blissful slumber.

# CHAPTER TWO

K ate's peaceful sleep was shattered at exactly 2:14 a.m., when the somewhat muted but insistent ringing of her bedside business telephone combined with the vibration of her pager as it danced its way across the wooden surface and onto the floor.

"Kyle." Her voice was rough with sleep, which made perfect sense considering she and Jay finally drifted off only two hours earlier.

"Hello, Ms. Kyle, this is Danny Wenger from the *Auburn Citizen*. I'm sorry to wake you..." Kate thought he sounded about as convincing as a three-day-old dead toad, which is to say not very.

"Hang on, will you? I've got to change phones." She put him on hold. Next to her, Jay stirred briefly and mumbled in her sleep before she settled back down. Kate regarded her lovingly. She looked so much like an angel. Sighing, Kate kissed her gently on the forehead, grabbed a robe from the bathroom, and headed downstairs to her office where Jay's rest wouldn't be disturbed by conversation.

"Okay Mr. Wenger, what can I do for you?"

"I understand an inmate died tonight at the Auburn Correctional Facility. Is that right?"

"Yes, that's correct."

"According to my sources, his name was Nathaniel Diggs, a guy doing time for murdering his girlfriend after she told him she was pregnant."

"The next of kin hasn't been notified yet, so I cannot confirm or release any information about the deceased at this time."

"C'mon, Ms. Kyle, just tell me if I'm right or not. You know I am, all you have to do is confirm it."

"When's your deadline, Danny?"

"It was two hours ago. They're holding a few inches of space for me for the next half hour."

"Tell you what. I'll try everything within my power to get you a yes or no before that time."

"Thanks."

"But if I can't give you something either way by your deadline, you leave any supposition or unconfirmed rumor out of the piece."

"How am I supposed to scoop the early TV news if you don't help me here?" He sounded like a petulant child.

"Danny, ever hear the expression 'it's better to be right than first'? I think that applies here, okay?" In fact, Kate already knew the name of the deceased and that of the inmate who killed him. It just so happened that she was trying to save Danny's ass—Nathaniel Diggs was actually the murderer, not the victim, although she couldn't tell the reporter that until the dead man's family had been notified. The only question now was whether or not this eager, young journalist was smart enough to listen between the words. Guess she'd find out later that day when the *Auburn Citizen* was published. Since the victim's family was in Ghana, West Africa, she seriously doubted she'd be able to give the press anything before the late editions in the afternoon.

She had barely placed the receiver back in the cradle when it rang again.

"Kate? This is Wendy Ashton from the Associated Press. How've you been?"

"Great, Wendy, how's life treating you?"

"Can't complain. My girlfriend does plenty of that for both of us."

"Ah, hates that you work the night beat, eh?"

"You've got that right."

"Well, I'm pretty sure you didn't call me at two forty a.m. to commiserate about your love life."

"Nah. Heard about the dead dude out at Auburn. Sounds like he got sliced up pretty good."

Ah, now here was a smart reporter. She stated her supposition as fact, expecting Kate simply to acknowledge her statement. Very slick.

"I'm sorry, Wendy, I don't have anything for you on cause of death or weapon yet. Wish I could help you there. I can tell you that a suspect is in custody."

"Very cute, Kate. Aren't they *all* in custody inside a prison?"

Oh, she was good. "Yes, but this one is in the SHU."

"He's in the special housing unit?"

"Yes."

"Was he there before this incident put him there? You know, already in isolation?"

"Yes."

"Well, that narrows it down, now doesn't it? Why, there must be only eighty-three or so guys in twenty-three-hour-a-day lockdown, right?"

"Look on the bright side, Wendy—that's better than the one thousand seven hundred eighty-five that are in the general population."

"Gee, thanks. I hear from reliable sources that this isn't the first dustup at Auburn this week. Any chance they're connected?"

There was no sense denying that there had been other incidents. It was a matter of public record. "It's a little too early in the investigation to tell, Wendy. They're still sorting it out."

"When will you know?"

"Hard to say. I'd tell you to try back early next week. I might have something for you then."

And so the rest of the short night went. At a little after 3:45 a.m., Kate sneaked back up the stairs to their bedroom. Quietly, she slipped back under the covers, and Jay immediately molded herself to her side. Kate savored the feeling of warmth and love that suffused her for the fifteen minutes left before the alarm was set to go off. Reaching over, she shut it off before it buzzed, preferring a more personal method of awakening her partner.

"Mmm." Jay rolled over on top of Kate, who was busy peppering her bare shoulder with gentle kisses. "Now this is the way to wake up in the morning." She smiled down at Kate, her expression morphing into a frown when she noticed the obvious dark circles under Kate's normally sharp eyes. "Did you get any sleep at all?"

"A little."

"Maybe we should skip the workout and run this morning. You could sleep in a little longer."

"Nah, I'm okay. Besides, today is Friday. I'll rest over the weekend, I promise."

"Where have I heard that before, Katherine?"

In one smooth motion, Kate rose from the bed, carrying Jay with her and standing them both upright. "Let's get a move on, Scoop. I've got to be in the office early and you've got a six thirty train to catch."

"Killjoy," Jay groused affectionately.

Within minutes, having donned cutoff sleeveless T-shirts and short gym shorts, both women were in the basement. They selected Nautilus machines at opposite ends of the circuit and began their morning workout routine. For the next hour, they sweated and grunted in relative silence, the only sounds in the room emanating from a television mounted strategically on the wall where it was visible from every angle.

"Do you really think Jaclyn should have married Dennis Cole? I mean, he's certainly a handsome guy, but look at what a lousy actor he was."

"Face it, Jamison, you're just jealous of him."

"Heck yeah."

They moved over to the side-by-side treadmills Kate had installed to prevent overzealous paparazzi from snapping pictures of her and Jay as they went out on their daily five-mile run. They both hated having to run indoors, but for the moment, it seemed like the best solution.

"I remember when I first started watching *Charlie's Angels*. I always felt like it was a guilty pleasure. You know, so many scantily clad, beautiful women, so little time."

"Now look at you, Kate, every episode on tape, fast-forwarding through the commercials to get more time with your girls. You've turned into a complete letch."

"I don't hear you complaining, Parker."

"Nope. No complaints here."

Their treadmills chalked up the first mile.

"What's going on with your story? You don't seem too enthusiastic about it."

"I don't know, lately it feels like all I've been writing about is corporate sludge. I'm just a bit restless, I think."

"Okay." Kate thought about it. "Why don't you pitch Trish a story that you really want to write?" When Jay looked at her with a raised eyebrow, she continued, "Well, why not? You've got the clout now. She's got you writing a cover story every other week. Maybe it's time to leverage your value a little."

Jay pondered the idea. "What would I want to write, if I had my choice?"

"It seems to me you most enjoy the stories that have a human angle. Something with depth."

"That's true."

"You know, when I was traveling through the Navajo and Hopi reservations near Four Corners..." Kate glanced sideways when she heard the pained sigh. Even all these months later, Jay studiously avoided any mention of their brief separation. Kate reached over, brushing her fingers lightly along Jay's arm. "I had an opportunity to talk with their healers. Their approaches to medicine are so spiritual, so different from our scientific bent." *It was as if they could feel my emotional pain and wanted to heal it.*

"More holistic, you mean."

"Yeah. It's like they treat the mind and spirit as well as the body. I think we here in the 'civilized' world could learn a lot from our Native American brothers and sisters."

"I thought they were pretty secretive about their customs, though, aren't they?"

"Yeah, to an extent, but I've seen you in action, love. I have no doubt you could get them to share some of their ways with you for a story. Heck, you could talk a mother hen off her nest."

"Thanks for the vote of confidence, sweetheart. I'll give it some thought. Besides, it's beautiful country out there."

"That it is, Jay, that it is."

∽◈∾

Kate pored over the faxes that had been arriving in a steady stream from the superintendent's office at Auburn for the past hour. So far, the coverage of the murder had been relatively evenhanded. The young buck at the *Citizen* wisely withheld the name of the victim pending notification of next of kin, Wendy from the Associated Press had refrained from any wild speculation linking the murder to other recent incidents at the prison, and the transcripts of the television coverage seemed rather benign.

"Yeah, I think she's down meeting with the commissioner. No, so far she seems to have it under control. No, I tried to keep her from seeing that, but she got a hold of it by herself. David, I'm doing my best here..."

Curious about the whispered conversation her assistant was having about her, Kate set the papers aside and focused her acute hearing outside her door. It was abundantly clear that Marisa didn't know she was in her office.

"Christ, David, I don't want to be too obvious here. She's bound to figure it out...Hey, it's not my fault she's sharp. You're the one who told me this would be easy and you'd be back here soo—" Her voice trailed off as Kate strode purposely past her desk. "Oh God, I've got to go." She didn't wait for an answer before hanging up.

Apparently unsure what to do, her face burning red with embarrassment at having been caught, Marisa chased her boss down the corridor.

"Are you quite finished with your report to Mr. Breathwaite?"

"I—"

"Because if you are, I believe there is plenty of real work sitting on your desk waiting for your attention."

"Kate—"

"No." Kate rounded on her assistant. "I don't want to talk about this right now, nor do I think you would want me to. I suggest you go back to the office and think about how important your job is to you and just who it is you work for."

Without another word, Kate resumed her course, leaving her deflated assistant behind. In truth, she wasn't sure where she was going, nor was she sure what she wanted to do about what she had just heard.

She sorted through her dealings with Marisa over the past three months. At first she had wondered why her predecessor hadn't simply taken his assistant with him when he left—after all, that was standard procedure. Although she could have hired someone of her own choosing, Kate decided to give Marisa a chance, reasoning that it would be wise to retain someone familiar with the workings of the office. Now she faced the ugly possibility that her assistant had stayed behind only to monitor and undermine her. In any event, keeping Marisa seemed an untenable option at this point.

Having made up her mind, Kate directed her steps to the executive deputy commissioner's office. He was the one charged with handling staff matters, and she knew that she would need his blessing to have the woman reassigned.

Through his closed door, she could hear him screaming at some poor soul on the other end of the phone. "What? You idiot! All right, don't worry, I'll take care of it...Never mind. I'll fix your little mess...*this* time."

Kate knocked when she heard him slam the phone back into its cradle.

"Come."

She poked her head around the door. "Bad time?"

Bill Redfield smiled. "Never for you, Kate. What can I do for you?"

"I hate to bother you with this, but I'm having a problem with my assistant. There are some trust issues and I just don't think I can continue to work with her. I'd like to have her reassigned to another department."

"I'm sorry to hear that, Kate. Unfortunately, there are no openings right now, so I'm afraid you're going to have to work through whatever it is. I'm really pressed for time, I apologize." He looked at his watch as if to emphasize the point. "Don't sweat it, Kate. I have faith that you'll find a way to make it work."

With that she was dismissed. *That was odd.* Walking deliberately back down the hall to her office, she made a couple of decisions.

"Hey, Technowiz, how the heck are you?" She was on the phone in her office with her door shut, having passed by Marisa's desk without so much as a glance in the woman's direction.

"Well, if it isn't the all-important Ms. Kyle. To what do I owe the pleasure?"

"Actually, Peter, I was wondering if you had plans for dinner tonight." Other than Jay, Peter Enright was Kate's closest friend. A security, tactical weapons, and technology expert, he had retired recently from DOCS to start his own consulting firm. At the moment, he was under contract to the feds to try to determine the origin of the bombs that ripped through the state capitol several months earlier.

"Why do I get the feeling this isn't just a social invitation?"

"It's not. There's something rotten in Denmark and I need to pick your brain. Are you game?"

"Me, turn down an intriguing opportunity like this? Never. Tell me what time and I'll be there. Not only that, but I believe it's my turn to bring the Chinese takeout."

"I knew I could count on you, buddy. See you at eight p.m."

Kate hung up the phone and redialed.

"Parker."

"Jay, you've got to work on your phone etiquette. You're sounding a little gruff there."

"Hello, sweetheart. I wasn't expecting you. How are you?"

"I've had better days."

"What's going on?"

"I can't go into it all right now, but I've invited Peter to dinner. I hope you don't mind?"

"No, of course not. If you've called in the big guns it must be serious. Are you okay? You sound a little shook up."

"I'm not sure. I don't want to sound paranoid."

"You? Paranoid? You've got to be kidding. What happened, Kate?"

"I'll explain it all later. Right now I've got some ass to chew."

"Okay. Glad it's not mine."

"Never yours, love...although taking a nibble out of those cute buns now and then..."

"Katherine..."

"Okay, okay. I told Peter eight o'clock. Will you even be out of the Big Apple by then?"

"You bet. I should be home by seven fifteen."

"Good. I could use a good hug and some alone time before he gets there."

"You've got it, sweetheart. See you in a few hours. Don't take any prisoners."

"Can you hear me groaning from here, Parker? That was a terrible pun."

"Well, I never said I was going to quit my day job."

"It's a good thing. Later, Jay."

Kate took a minute to gather herself and put on her game face before opening the door.

"Marisa, get in here."

The assistant appeared almost before Kate finished the sentence.

"Shut the door and sit down."

"Kate, I'm really sorr—"

"You know, there are four qualities I value above all others—trust, honesty, loyalty, and respect. You have managed to violate all of those things."

"I didn't know you were in your office," Marisa said quietly.

"You think that was your transgression? Let me see if I understand you—if I hadn't been in my office, it would have been all right for you to be reporting to your former boss on my handling of the job? It would have been acceptable for you to withhold vital information from me in, what—an attempt to make me screw up?"

Marisa wisely chose to stay silent and avoid Kate's eyes, which were flashing dangerously.

"I have to tell you that my first inclination was to toss you out of here so fast your head would spin."

Marisa's head shot up and her eyes showed real fear for the first time.

"However," Kate paused here, content to let her victim sweat, "I have reconsidered my position and I'm willing, God help me, to give you another chance."

"Thank you, Kate."

"I'm not finished yet." She waited until the young woman's eyes were on her. "You need to know that you only get two strikes with me. If I note so much as a comma out of place, you're history. Do you understand me? That means no phone contact—in fact, no contact of any kind with David Breathwaite about anything related to this office or its business. It means I had better see everything that is meant for my eyes as soon as it hits your desk."

"Yes, ma'am."

"You've got a long road ahead of you to try to prove yourself worthy of my trust again, Marisa. I strongly suggest you don't squander the opportunity I'm giving you. You won't get another chance, I assure you."

"Yes, ma'am."

"Now get out of my sight."

◈◈

As it turned out, Jay walked through the door only seconds before Peter's arrival.

"I'm so sorry, baby. I really tried to get here sooner. Unfortunately, I haven't learned how to drive the damn train yet."

"It's not your fault."

Jay stepped back and took stock of her lover. "You look like you've been through the wringer today. What the heck happened?"

"I'll tell you when Peter gets here. For now, I just want to hold you."

Jay moved into Kate's arms once again, wrapping herself around her and bringing them into contact all along their bodies. She could feel the tension in the strong shoulders and back. Just as she began a light massage, the doorbell rang.

Jay, who was standing with her back to the door, turned and opened it to admit Peter.

"If it isn't my two favorite ladies."

"Flattery will get you nowhere in this crowd."

"Don't I know it," Peter mumbled good-naturedly.

"Hi." Jay hugged Peter around the waist. At six foot four, he was a full foot taller than she was.

"Hi, Half-pint, it's good to see you."

"Just what do I have to do to gain full pint status around here?"

"Grow!" Kate and Peter answered simultaneously.

"Easy for you two to say. Have you ever tried being vertically challenged?"

"Not since before puberty," Kate said. She took the food from Peter and headed for the kitchen.

Jay shook her head in mock disgust as she and Peter followed.

Never one to waste time, Peter started right in as soon as they were seated. "Okay, now that we've got the niceties out of the way, let's have it. Kate, you look like crap, and that never happens. What the heck's going on over there? Place go to hell after I left?"

"Can you try to be a little less subtle next time? I'm not sure I know how you really feel." Running her hands through her unruly mane, Kate sighed heavily. "I'm not totally sure what the real story is, but it definitely smells." She laid out in detail the events with Marisa and Redfield. "Frankly, two things about the whole sequence really stuck out in my mind."

"Only two? I can think of a bunch." Jay was outraged.

Kate put a restraining hand on her arm and continued, "The first was Marisa's remark to Breathwaite about him promising he'd be back, or at least that's what she started to say before she saw me. The second was the fact that Redfield never even asked me what it was Marisa had done to prompt me to want to fire her. It was as if he already knew."

Peter was silent throughout Kate's recitation, but his expression bespoke his deep concern.

Kate went on, "You know, I've been over this a hundred times in my mind, and I still can't come up with an explanation or scenario that makes any sense to me. Why on earth would Breathwaite want to take a demotion to come back? And what the blazes does that have to do with Redfield? Are they connected in some way? Am I just being paranoid here?"

Jay started to jump in, but Peter interrupted quietly, "I don't think you're imagining this, my friend. I'm just having trouble putting the pieces together right now. Redfield was never a Breathwaite fan, to be sure. So that's a tough one to reconcile. I'll have to think about that and get back to you. As for Marisa, well, she's not the sharpest crayon in the box, so I can't say I'm surprised that she would be doing her ex-boss's bidding. At the time they created the new position for him, Breathwaite had managed to draw too much heat. I think the governor actually was getting set to fire his ass. The 'promotion' was a way to keep him out of trouble while allowing him to save face."

"Do you know whose idea the new job for him was, Peter? Who conceived it and who created it?"

"I don't know, Jay, but I suspect that if we find the answers to those questions, we might have a better handle on what's really behind all this. I know the governor had to sign off on the new spot, but I'm pretty sure it wasn't his idea."

The three friends finished their meal in contemplative silence. At a quarter past ten, Peter bid Kate and Jay good night with a promise to keep in touch and an admonition for his best friend. "Katherine, you be careful. Redfield and Breathwaite don't play nice, and they sure as shooting don't play by the rules. If there is something going on, it looks like you'll be right in the thick of it. I want you to keep track of everything and anything that looks suspicious. Collect any evidence if there's any to be had, and make me copies. Don't overlook anything. The devil may truly be in the details here."

When he had gone, Jay took Kate in her arms. "Sweetheart, it's going to be okay. With Peter's help, we'll get to the bottom of this. I have to tell you, though, my first reaction is to go down there and bash some heads."

"Have I told you lately just how much I love you?"

"I never tire of hearing it, babe."

Jay ran her fingers up Kate's abdomen, brushing gently over her firm breasts before resting her hands on her broad shoulders. Their kiss was equal parts passion and tenderness.

"Mmm, can I interest you in a little ice cream?"

"Nope." Jay continued to nibble on Kate's lower lip.

"Um, how about some cheesecake?"

30

"Negatory."

"Jamison Parker turning down dessert? I don't believe it!"

Jay waggled her eyebrows suggestively. "Who said anything about turning down dessert?"

# CHAPTER THREE

I'm only going to say this once. Either you do what I say, or I tell your wife about your little girlfriend. The choice is yours, but I suggest you make it quickly. If that editorial doesn't go to print on Sunday, you might be finding your clothes in your front yard."

On the other end of the line, the receiver went dead.

"Heh. This is even more fun than I thought it would be."

His gloating was cut short by the ringing of the phone.

"Breathwaite."

"David, we have to meet. Lunchtime at the club. Be there."

෯෯

"Enright."

"Hey, Technowiz. Hungry?"

"When and where?"

"Now, Lombardo's."

"See you in fifteen."

"Right."

෯෯

"What do you think you're doing, Breathwaite?"

"Bob wanted results, I'm getting him results, Bill. What part of that don't you understand?"

"You're being so heavy-handed, it's starting to raise eyebrows. The commissioner wants to know what the hell's going on, and so do I. What have you done?"

"Just using a little leverage. Putting a little pressure in the right places."

William Redfield wanted nothing more at that moment than to wipe the smug expression off the little weasel's face. "If this backfires and one of your 'projects' talks, you're on your own," he snapped.

"Bill, has anyone ever told you, you worry too much?"

Redfield stormed out of the room.

࿓

"Okay, Spinmeister, what's going on?"

Kate and Peter were settled into a high-backed booth at the back of Lombardo's, a family-style Italian restaurant at the lower end of downtown Albany.

"Nothing good." Kate pulled a blue manila file folder from the briefcase at her feet and placed it in front of Peter. Inside was a series of newspaper clippings.

After reading the first five clips, he looked up, both eyebrows hiked into his hairline. "Huh," he whistled softly. "If I didn't know any better, I'd have to say somebody gave these folks a little help with their stories."

"My thought exactly. But that's not the worst. Keep reading." Kate reached over and located a clipping halfway down in the pile. It was dated September 21, 1987—two days earlier.

Peter uttered a string of expletives as his eyes scanned the top of the page. The editorial headline read, "The Woman Behind the Deceptions at DOCS."

> Just four months into the job, it seems that the State Department of Correctional Services' lead spokeswoman has settled in quite nicely, thank you. In instance after instance, Katherine Kyle, the governor's controversial choice as public information officer for the nation's third largest prison system, has buried the truth, misleading the public and abusing her position. When an inmate was murdered last month at the Auburn Correctional Facility, Ms. Kyle told our Daniel Wenger that the incident was unrelated to a series of violent outbursts earlier that same week. Reliable sources and further investigation prove that Ms. Kyle lied: the victim and the killer belonged to rival gangs that had been involved in several scuffles over the course of a two-week period. It is our considered opinion that Ms. Kyle should either resign or be fired: she can no longer be trusted to tell the truth about anything.

When Peter's eyes met Kate's, they held fire. "There aren't too many ways that ace reporter and his editors could have gotten that little tidbit, now, are there?"

"No. But what bothers me more is that they're questioning my credibility in ways that are difficult to combat." Kate's wounded eyes met Peter's. "In this business credibility is everything. Without it, I can't do my job effectively."

He put his hand over hers in sympathy.

"The sad thing is, I told the truth. That inmate wasn't killed as a result of anything gang related, he just happened to be in the wrong place at the wrong time. Unfortunately, the newspaper has just enough of the basic facts right—there *were* members of rival gangs planning a turf war, there *were* several violent incidents during those two weeks, and the perp and the vic *were* members of opposing gangs. Since nobody ever asked me those questions in that way, the information was never made public. But the way the editorial is worded, why should anyone believe me now?"

Peter's jaw muscles stood out in bold relief. "None of the line staff would be stupid enough to talk to the newspaper. Hell, none of them would've been able to supply all of that information. No, it had to be someone much higher up. My guess would be Breathwaite. But speculation and proof are two different things."

"Not to mention motive," Kate added dejectedly. "What the blazes is his game, anyway?"

"I'd say it's pretty obvious he wants to discredit you and shove you out the door. The question in my mind is the same one it was a month ago—why?"

"I've been puzzling over that one myself. Why would he want to take what many would consider a demotion to come back to DOCS? What's in it for him?"

"If we can figure that out, we may be able to stop the train before it runs over you. Where are the governor and the commissioner on this? I'm assuming you've heard from them, right?"

"I had a meeting with the commissioner this morning. He wanted me to know that the DNC wants me fired because I'm a...quote liability end quote."

"Hmm."

"There's more. I offered to step aside."

"This isn't your fault, Kate."

"I know that and you know that, but..." Kate sighed.

"What was the commissioner's response to your offer?"

"He said, and I quote, 'Kate, I appreciate your willingness to take one for the team, but you and I both know that this whole thing is bullshit. Whatever's going on, it has nothing to do with your competence. You've been doing an extraordinary job, and scathing editorials to the contrary, I have no intention whatsoever of either asking for, or accepting, your resignation.'"

"He's a good man."

"Yes, he is. He also told me he talked to the governor, and the governor agrees. I have their full support."

"Good," Peter said. "I'm assuming you didn't share your suspicions with him about the root of this whole mess."

"Right. First of all, I didn't want to sound as if I was making excuses, and, second, I didn't want to come off as some paranoid wacko. Not to mention the fact that we don't really know yet what's going on."

"No, we don't, but we will. I swear to you we will."

"I know you're right, Technowiz. I just hope it doesn't take too long."

"What's going on with you and Jay?"

Kate acknowledged Peter's deliberate change of topic. "Everything's great, except that we don't seem to have nearly enough time for each other. I never thought I could feel this way about someone. The second she's out of my sight I miss her."

"She's clearly just as crazy about you, you know."

"Yeah," Kate sighed dreamily. "I know."

"Have you guys talked any more about when the wedding is going to be, or where, for that matter?"

"We made a date to talk about it tonight, in fact. I can't wait."

"Well, just make sure you give me enough warning so that I can rent a tux."

"A man-about-town like you doesn't own a tux? Why, Peter Enright, I'm shocked and appalled!" She slapped him playfully as they made their way out the back door of the restaurant.

"Yeah, yeah, tell it to somebody who believes you, Kyle." After a pause he added, "Hey, Kate, make sure you keep in close contact with me about this, okay? Don't second-guess yourself. I want to know everything that looks even remotely suspicious."

"I promise, you'll be the second to know."

"See ya."

"Yeah, try to keep your hands off things that go boom and stay out of trouble in the meantime."

"Right." Peter winked as he got in his standard-issue blue Ford sedan.

∽⌒⌒

"My God, Jay, you are the most beautiful woman in the world. How did I ever get so lucky?" Kate stood with her arms around Jay's waist from behind. A brilliant shaft of moonlight shone down on them as they stood outside on the deck overlooking the backyard.

The moon was bright and full, and as they gazed up at the profusion of stars overhead, Jay sighed contentedly. "Sweetheart," she rotated her head and kissed the corner of Kate's mouth, "I'm the lucky one." She turned fully to nuzzle the expanse of neck and shoulder that were within easy reach. "What happened today..." She trailed off as slender, graceful fingers covered her lips.

"I don't want to talk about work right now, babe. I just want to be here with you, okay?" Kate replaced her fingers with lips, punctuating her words with a long, slow kiss.

"Mmm. You won't get any arguments here." Breathless, Jay pulled back in the circle of Kate's arms and regarded her. "Shall we talk about the future, love?"

"As long as it involves you, me, and a lifetime of togetherness, I'm easy."

"Sounds wonderful to me. Well, then, I guess there's nothing more to say." Jay made as if to go inside.

"Hey, wait a minute!"

"What?" Jay batted her eyes innocently.

"Get back here, you."

"Something you want?"

"Mmm-hmm. You. I can't wait to make you mine."

"I *am* yours, sweetheart."

"I know, but I really want to formalize it, sooner rather than later." She looked into Jay's eyes. "Jay, you mean everything to me, and I want something tangible to reflect how I feel about you. I want to marry you, even though it's not legally binding."

For several heartbeats, they both were lost in bittersweet memory. The moment Kate first proposed marriage and Jay accepted had been the happiest of their lives. That was just before all hell broke loose and the future seemed lost.

The shadows receded just as quickly as they came. Lightly brushing her fingers over Kate's chiseled cheekbones, Jay smiled up at the woman with whom she wanted to spend the rest of her life. "Darling, I would marry you right here, tonight, if you wanted."

"This might surprise you, but I'm a pretty old-fashioned kind of gal. No elopements here."

Jay laughed. "No kidding."

"I would prefer a traditional kind of ceremony." Kate glanced down at Jay. "What do you want?"

"When I was a little girl and my father was abusing me," Jay began, squeezing Kate's hands reassuringly when she stiffened, "I would escape in my mind into fantasies. In one of them, it was my wedding day, and I was dressed in a beautiful, flowing gown with a long train. I felt like a princess in a fairy tale."

"I want to give you everything you've ever dreamed of, Jay, including a fairy-tale wedding."

"You don't have to do that, Kate."

"That's what I want too."

Jay bit her lower lip in thought. "What do you think about going back where it all started? The chaplain at college was a good friend of mine. I think she might agree to perform some kind of ceremony for us."

"That sounds perfect. I'd love that."

"I'll get in touch with her to see whether she's willing to officiate, and if so, when she and the chapel might be available. Oh, darling, I can't wait." She snuggled into Kate's embrace, the safety and security of those arms the only home her soul would ever need.

# CHAPTER FOUR

It was shortly after 7:00 a.m. on a mid-October morning, and Jay sat in her customary seat on the Amtrak train headed from Albany to Grand Central Station in New York City. Although she held a book open in her lap, she barely glanced at it, her mind wandering as she regarded the passing landscape. The ride along the Hudson River was always scenic, but never more so than at this time of year, when the leaves were changing colors in preparation for their winter shedding. The riots of red, orange, yellow, and green were a sight to behold.

She sighed. Despite the beauty of her surroundings, she was troubled. It was hard to remember the last time Kate had gotten a full night's sleep. Ruefully, Jay thought, *It was probably just before she took this job, which is to say,* way *too long ago.* The hours alone were clearly taking a toll on her partner, but even more disconcerting were the suspicious circumstances and innuendo swirling just beneath the surface at DOCS.

Had it been *her* integrity or credibility being called into question, Jay would have been far less concerned. But to have the media, and by extension the general public, attack Kate made Jay's blood boil. It was all so absurdly ridiculous. Anyone who knew Kate knew she was the most upright, fair, scrupulously honest person on the planet, didn't they? The hardest part, though, was that there wasn't a thing Jay could do to help except to be supportive, offer an ear and a different perspective, and express her outrage at the situation.

As for her own job, perhaps Kate was right—maybe what Jay needed to do was to try pitching her editor a story of her own. Heaven knew the ones she'd been covering lately had been less than groundbreaking.

By the time the train pulled into the station, she had made up her mind. She would talk to Trish first thing.

When Jay got to Trish's office, the editor had the phone to one ear, an assistant talking in the other, papers strewn across the surface of her sizable, modern workspace, and her head resting in the palm of one hand, fingers splayed through already disheveled light brown hair. Trish rolled her eyes and mimed to her ace reporter to sit in one of the visitors' chairs in front of the desk. She dismissed the assistant with a wave.

"No, Chad, I don't care if he has to crawl in here, I'm not gonna accept another lame excuse. I want that story on my desk by noon today, got it? Good." She slammed the receiver down without waiting for a response.

"Have you ever noticed, Trish, that your New York accent gets more pronounced the louder you yell?"

"Can't say as I've paid that little tidbit any mind, Jamison. But now that you mention it, I'll be sure to keep an eye on the situation." Sharing the usual banter with her favorite writer always managed to calm her considerable temper. Jay had that effect on everyone, Trish suspected. "What can I do for you, other than provide your amusement for the day?"

Jay shifted in her chair. "Um, you know I'm grateful for the way you've supported me these past few months, right?" When Jay, of her own accord, revealed to Trish that she was the other woman in the *National Enquirer* picture, the editor stood by her without hesitation.

"Yeah." Trish drew the word out. She couldn't remember ever seeing Jay this uncomfortable, not even when she outed herself earlier in the year. "It sure sounds like there's a 'but' in there somewhere."

"It does?"

"Mmm-hmm. Out with it, Parker. You can't even look me in the eye."

Jay peeked up from where she had been staring at the hands in her lap.

"Ohmigod." Trish knew a moment of sudden panic. "Please don't tell me you're leaving."

"What? No, of course not. Why on earth would you think that?"

"I don't know. It's just that I've only ever seen you look this uncomfortable once before, and I can't imagine what could be bigger than that, except maybe a new job. So please, tell me whatever it is already before I have a heart attack."

"It's nothing like that, Trish. It's just..." Jay paused. "The stories I've been doing lately have been less than inspiring. I guess I'm just getting a bit restless. I know it sounds stupid, but—"

"Oh, Jay, I'm sorry." Relief coursed through the editor. "I didn't realize you felt that way. Truth is, I've been trying to keep you close to home so you and that gorgeous woman of yours could have some time to get used to living together and establish a sense of normalcy."

"Really?"

"Yeah, really. Guess I shoulda talked to you about it first, huh?"

"That's all right. I didn't understand. I thought maybe I did something to get on your bad side and that's why I was getting all the lousy assignments."

Trish laughed and Jay joined in. "Nah, kiddo, if you were on my bad side, believe me, you wouldn't have to wonder—you'd know it. Here I was trying to do you a favor, and all you can do is bitch about it."

Jay's trademark smile was back. "I'm not complaining, Trish, just looking for an upgrade, that's all."

"Does Kate know you're tired of spending every night with her already?" Trish was thankful that the problem wasn't anything serious and overjoyed to yank Jay's chain about it.

"Actually, she kicked me out the door this morning—wanted to know when you were going to get me out of her hair." Jay winked.

"Well, far be it from me to disappoint that woman. After all, I hear she has connections in dark and dreary places." Trish consulted her ever-present storyboard. "Okay. It's action you want, eh? I think we can do something about that..."

࿇࿇

"Hi, baby. The honeymoon's over."

"Um, Jay? Don't we have to be married before you can say that?"

"Well, normally I'd say yes, but in this case..."

"Have I done something wrong?"

"Quite to the contrary you beautiful, sexy woman."

"Okay, now I'm really lost."

"Katherine Kyle, you're a genius, and if I were there, I'd give you a big, wet kiss."

"I can live with that, but what does all this have to do with our honeymoon?"

"You were right pushing me to talk to Trish. Seems she's been intentionally keeping me close to home so you and I would have more time together."

"I knew I liked that woman."

"Ahem. But now that she knows I'm itching for good stories..."

Kate sighed. "I've shot myself in the foot, haven't I?"

Jay laughed. "Pretty much."

"Where're you headed, Scoop?"

"There's an upstart AIDS awareness political action group called the AIDS Coalition to Unleash Power."

"That's a mouthful."

"Right, smart girl, which is why they go by the name ACT UP. They're just starting to make some serious waves and Trish wants someone on the inside to chronicle their rise."

"Cool acronym. You're going undercover? As an activist? Oh, that could be fun. Jay as a zealot. Very sexy."

"Very funny. Keep it up and I might just have to cut you off."

"C-cut me off? You wouldn't. You couldn't."

"Do you really want to find out, hot stuff?"

"Jay, sweetheart, honey, doll? This assignment sounds perfect for you."

"That's better." Jay's laughter faded. "Actually, I'm not going undercover at all, I'm just going to shadow the group and its leaders—learn about their tactics and philosophy—talk to them."

"That sounds like it should be really interesting."

"I think so too. The downside is that I'm going to have to stay here in New York for a little while."

Kate tried to hide her disappointment. In the past few months, Jay's talents had been wasted on second-rate stories that didn't challenge her considerable intellect, leaving her restless and frustrated. The assignment was just what she needed to get her out of her funk. "Well, sweetheart, that's why you kept your apartment in New York. At least you'll be comfortable while you're working and not stuck in some generic hotel room."

"Thank you for understanding, Kate. I wish you could be here with me."

"That would be fun, but there are pressing matters here I have to attend to." Kate thought about the cryptic phone call she got from Wendy Ashton of the Associated Press half an hour ago. She was scheduled to meet her in a parking garage downtown after dark, and she didn't have a clue why. The reporter refused to say over the phone and sounded downright panicked when Kate tried to push her on the matter. She returned her attention to Jay. "Do you want me to send Fred down to keep you company?"

"No, Kate. He'll be much happier up there with you. I'll be fine. Call you tonight?"

"Absolutely. I'll tuck you in and put you to sleep."

"Don't forget the warm milk and cookies, Mom." Jay's chuckle echoed down the phone line as she hung up.

༻❦༺

"Hello, Wendy." Kate considered making a joke about reporters having clandestine meetings with sources in dark parking garages when she got a good look at the woman approaching her. She was gaunt, her razor-sharp features made even more pronounced by stress. Her navy slacks and tan blazer were rumpled, and her salt-and-pepper hair was in disarray. While Wendy Ashton wasn't the sharpest dresser or the neatest person she knew, Kate recognized her disheveled appearance as being out of character.

"Kate. Thanks for meeting me here like this." The reporter's eyes darted around the garage.

"What's going on, Wendy? You look out of sorts."

"Yeah, well, I don't usually have assholes threatening to toss me out of the closet."

"Who?" Kate was instantly alert.

"Your lovely predecessor, that's who," she spat out.

"Breathwaite threatened to out you as a lesbian?"

"Yep." The reporter took a deep breath, apparently satisfied that they were alone. "It was the strangest thing. I get a call at my desk at around two thirty this afternoon and it's him. He starts off wanting to know what I think about the job you're doing at DOCS."

Kate tried to look surprised for propriety's sake, but the truth was that Breathwaite blackmailing reporters into writing damaging stories was exactly the scenario she and Peter had surmised. Perhaps now they would get closer to finding out the rest of his game.

The reporter continued, "I thought that was pretty odd, so I pulled out my tape recorder and plugged it into the line. I figured he's always up to something, and whatever he had up his sleeve this time, I wanted to be prepared."

"Good thinking."

Wendy smiled weakly. "Thanks, but there was no way I was ready for this." She pulled a small microcassette recorder out of her blazer pocket and pressed the "play" button.

"So, ah, here's the thing." Breathwaite's nasal twang filled the air between Kate and Wendy. "What if I told you Kyle wasn't telling you everything about what happened yesterday with that officer at Coxsackie?"

"I'm listening."

"What if I told you she regularly leaves out facts, the net result being that you look like a fool, your ass hanging in the breeze."

"If that were true, why in the world would you tell me? Aren't you and Kate on the same side of the equation?"

"Perhaps I just want to help you."

The reporter's taped laughter echoed loudly in the stillness of the dark concrete structure.

"David, you've never cared about anyone but yourself. So why don't you get to the point and tell me what this is really about and stop wasting both of our time."

"Listen to me, you two-bit dyke," he spat, "I can end your career in less than the time it takes you to turn on your tape recorder."

"What do you want, you slimebag?"

"I want you to write a story that will be carried wide  every major daily in the state, and radio too. I want you to discredit Kyle."

"Or?"

"Or I will out you in spectacular fashion to your bosses, your peers, every news outlet worldwide. I'll get you so much ink you won't be able to find a job taking out the trash. Oh, and your lovely girlfriend? I'm sure all of the attention will sit well with her father the ultraconservative congressman."

"You prick."

"I love it when you talk dirty."

"What kind of story are you looking for?"

"It has to be something that will end her fledgling career as a PIO."

"It will take me time to put something like that together."

"You have seventy-two hours. Good-bye, Wendy. I'll be in touch."

"Wait!"

"Yes?"

"What's in it for you, Breathwaite?"

"That's of no concern to you, Ms. Ashton. Just take care of business."

The dial tone turned to a faint hiss.

"My, isn't he just the charmer." Kate forced a smile. "Why are you sharing this with me?"

"Because you've always dealt fairly with me. Because I know what you went through, and I would be the last one on earth to put you through yet another undeserved professional hardship. Because I like you. But most of all because it pisses me off to be blackmailed, especially by a twerp like Breathwaite."

"Fair enough. What are you going to do?"

"I haven't figured out a game plan yet. But I'm going to take him down if it's the last thing I do."

"I can't say I'd shed a tear if that happened, but I'm not sure that's the best course of action for the immediate future."

"What? Kate, I like what I do. If I don't take him down, I either have to go along with him, which puts you in jeopardy, or I get outed and lose my job."

"Wendy, if you take him down now, he'll out you anyway. While exposing him might make you feel better in the short term, it won't solve your problem."

"You're awfully cool for someone whose neck is on the line."

Kate laughed humorlessly. "He can't take away from me the things that really matter. He can ruin my career." She looked pointedly at the reporter. "Don't get me wrong, that would pain me greatly. I've worked very hard to get where I am in life, and I like to think I do a damn good job. But my professional life pales in comparison to what I have personally, and he can't touch that."

"Okay, I can understand that. So what do you suggest?"

"You've got another two days to work with, right?"

"Yes. Tick tock."

"Give me until tomorrow night to come up with something, okay?"

"I guess." The reporter began to turn away.

"Wendy?"

"Yeah?"

"Thanks for coming to me with this. You're a good person."

"Don't tell my mother that. She thinks I'm the demon spawn from hell."

"By the way, did Breathwaite know you were taping him?"

"Probably not."

"Oh." Kate was disappointed, knowing that such evidence might never be admissible in a court, if it ever came to that.

"But Kate?"

"Yeah?"

"I don't ever pick up the phone until the caller hears my taped voice informing him that the conversation may be taped, and that by staying on the line, he is consenting to being taped."

"Wendy, I love you!"

The reporter smiled for the first time that evening. "Does your girlfriend know?"

"Very funny. Hey, can I borrow the tape? I promise to give it back to you."

"You know a good reporter never gives up a tape."

Kate blew out a breath. "I understand."

Wendy touched her on the arm to force eye contact.

"But I did make you a copy." She winked. "I'll call you at home tomorrow night."

"Better yet, let's meet at the Falcon at ten o'clock."

"Oh, *very* wicked, Ms. Kyle. The asshole would never think to look for us in a gay bar."

≪∂∂≫

Later that night Kate and Peter sat at his kitchen table, Fred at their feet and a speakerphone between them.

"What's going on, you two? You call me on speakerphone at eleven at night? You must be up to no good."

"Why, Half-pint, I believe I should be objecting to your insinuation."

"Oh, big word for you, Peter."

"Okay, you two, knock it off before I send you both to your rooms without supper."

"She's such a killjoy, Jay, isn't she?"

There was a snort on the other end of the line. "Um, Peter? Do you really want me to answer that?"

Peter blushed. "I suppose not," he mumbled.

"Right, then," Kate said. "I had a very interesting meeting this evening with Wendy Ashton, a reporter for the Associated Press. Seems our friend Mr. Breathwaite tried to blackmail her today."

"Now there's a surprise," Peter said.

"With what?" Jay chimed in.

"Her sexuality."

"Oh, *that's* original."

"It doesn't have to be original, Jay, it just has to be effective."

"I know, honey, it just galls me that living your life honestly makes you vulnerable."

Kate wondered if Jay would ever get past being angry about the circumstances surrounding Kate's dismissal from WCAP. "Me too, but it's a price I, for one, am happy to pay."

"Why is she telling you this?" Peter asked. "Why not just do what the asshole wants and save herself?"

"I asked her the same thing. She's clearly no fan of his, I've always given her a fair shake, and she'd love to nail his slimy butt to the wall."

"Fair enough."

"What does he want from her?" Jay asked, the indignation clear in her voice.

"He wants her to write a story for wide distribution that will force the governor and the commissioner to fire me."

Jay's growl echoed in Peter's kitchen, prompting a chuckle from Kate.

"Down, girl."

"I'd like to wring his scrawny little neck."

"I know the feeling, sweetheart, but I'm not sure that homicide would solve our problem."

"What do you mean?"

"She means," Peter said, "that Breathwaite can't reinstall himself as PIO, so he must be only part of the equation."

"Exactly. Which is why we need to carefully consider our next move. If we flush him out now, we're still going to be on the defensive, wondering who else is out there and reacting to whatever their game is."

"Kate's right, Jay. We need to let this play out further until we can identify whoever else is behind all this."

"So we're just supposed to sit here and watch him shred her publicly like this?"

"To some extent, yes."

"No way."

"Jay, I love your protective side, but Peter's got a point. And neither one of us is advocating that we let the jerk succeed, just that we let him keep trying."

"But what about Wendy? If she doesn't do his bidding, he'll go after her."

"Which is why we have to help her write a story that will satisfy Breathwaite, but not be sufficiently damaging to Kate to require her removal."

"Got any ideas, Jay?"

The line went quiet for several moments as all three contemplated the possibilities.

"We can't let him continue to attack your credibility, that's for sure. How about if we let her write something personal?"

"What do you have in mind?"

"Give her the story every tabloid's been clamoring for."

"No."

"Kate..."

"Absolutely not. Out of the question, Jay."

"Just hear me out."

"No. I've spent how many months protecting your identity, keeping the vultures away? Now you want me to let them have at you intentionally?"

"Well, Breathwaite could hardly argue that Wendy didn't give him something big, and it wouldn't weaken your standing on the job, since your sexuality is hardly a secret."

"Jay could be on to something here, Kate."

"Unacceptable. I won't do it."

"Honey." Jay's gentle tone touched Kate's heart, as it never failed to do. "Trish already knows, and she's stood by me. He can't hurt me, and I'd be damn proud to be identified as your lover. Heck, imagine the envy out there. I'd acquire a reputation as a stud overnight!"

"I don't want to give him the satisfaction."

"Kate, you know I'm right."

"You're correct that giving him something personal, rather than professional, might be the right thing to do. But not that. Tell you what," Kate sighed, "let's make the story about my parents' deaths."

"How does that satisfy Breathwaite?"

"The drunk who killed them never served time. We could slant the story to sound like my bitterness at the criminal justice system affects my performance in the job."

"That's professional."

"Not really. The focus would be on this orphaned eighteen-year-old with an axe to grind who schemed for years to get back at the system that abandoned her. Like all the other stories that have been written to date, it has elements of truth, but this time she gets extra points for bringing in a personal angle."

Peter considered. "I like it. It's different than what's being written now, which might satisfy Breathwaite temporarily, yet so far-fetched that it won't even raise the commissioner's eyebrow."

Kate added, "And we get the added bonus of controlling the story."

"Right."

"Kate, I know that was a painful time for you. Are you going to be all right with this?"

Kate tried to ignore the ache that always accompanied thoughts of her parents' deaths. This was an area that she held most private—even Jay didn't know the depth of her feelings or thoughts on the subject. As she had for years, she shut down the emotions that threatened to swallow her.

"Thanks, baby. It was a long time ago, and while I miss my parents every day, I don't waste a second of my time on the scumbag who ran them into that tree."

"Do you think Wendy will go along with it?"

"I think there's a good chance she might if I can convince her that the story will be enough to get Breathwaite off her back and out of her bedroom."

"What was she planning to do with the tape?"

Kate laughed. "I think it has something to do with proctology."

"Delicately put."

"Yeah."

"When will you talk to her next?"

"We're meeting at the Falcon tomorrow night."

"I do love your sense of humor. Don't be letting any strays follow you home."

"No worries, my love, you're the only one with a key."

"On that disgustingly mushy note," Peter intoned, "I'm kicking you both out so I can get some shuteye. Good night, Jay."

"Good night, Peter."

"Good night, John Boy."

"Good night, Mary Ellen."

"Ugh, you didn't actually watch that drivel, did you?"

"No, the credits were my favorite part."

"Get out of here. See you soon, Jay."

&#10086;&#10087;

The Falcon was crowded for the middle of the week. Bodies pulsed to the music. The clink-clink of glasses and beer bottles mixed with laughter and loud conversation. On the level slightly above the dance floor, a serious game of pool was in progress.

"Whoa, would you get a load of that one."

More than one set of eyes followed the sleek form of the woman in tight blue jeans and a button-down shirt as she surveyed the room.

"Put your tongue back in your mouth, Tess, I saw her first. She's mine."

"You can both forget it. You're not her type. She's far too sophisticated for the likes of you."

"Oh, and you think you're more her style, Robbie?"

Stepping down from the entranceway, Kate ignored the leering and the chatter and nodded to the bartender, who was serving someone at the other end of the Formica-topped bar.

"What can I get you, gorgeous?"

"Just a Diet Coke with lemon, thanks."

"Oh, big drinker, eh?"

"Yeah," Kate laughed. "I'll try not to guzzle it."

"Don't look now, but I think that woman over in the corner is trying to get your attention."

"Is that so? What's she drinking?"

"Killian's."

"Okay, give me one of those too."

"Huh, I wouldn't have picked her for your type."

Kate rolled her eyes, threw down a few bills, and picked up the beer bottle and her soda. "She's not," she said over her shoulder as she walked away.

"Hello, Ms. Ashton."

"Ms. Kyle." The reporter nodded. "Fancy meeting you here."

Kate made a show of looking around. "Nothing fancy about this place."

"Let's just say you class up the joint," Wendy rejoined. "You do realize that every woman in the bar is staring at you, right?"

"What, is my fly undone?"

"Very funny. How do you deal with that?"

"With what?"

"With the kind of attention and looks you get everywhere you go."

"My fiancée says I'm oblivious and obtuse. She's probably right."

"In that case, maybe I should be asking her how *she* deals with it."

Kate smiled. "I'd venture to say that she's the one who turns heads, not me."

"Well, you must make quite a couple."

"I think so." Kate shifted minutely in her chair, uncomfortable talking about Jay with a reporter, even one as friendly as Wendy. "Any more word from Breathwaite?"

"No. I'm not supposed to hear from him until Friday afternoon."

"Good." Kate leaned forward to be heard over the music without shouting. "I want you to give him his story."

"What?"

"I want you to write a story that will satisfy Breathwaite."

"But that could mean the end of your career."

"Not if you write the story I have in mind." Kate's eyes burned with intensity.

"Talk to me."

"My parents died when I was eighteen and away at college. They were killed by a drunk driver on the Hutchinson River Parkway in Westchester. The guy was found civilly liable, but never served time."

"And this is relevant exactly how?"

"What if, all these years, I've been carrying this chip on my shoulder? What if I've been plotting all this time to put myself in position to get back at the criminal justice system that denied me justice so long ago?"

The reporter considered. "Yeah, like you had yourself outed and fired from WCAP just so the governor would feel sorry for you and hire you as PIO at DOCS. As if you could have planned all that."

"Perhaps I was just biding my time, getting experience in the media and getting close to the governor in order to ingratiate myself to him until the appropriate opportunity arose."

"Nobody's gonna buy that."

"Probably not, but the story has elements of truth, and it gives you something Breathwaite will love."

"What's that?"

"A personal angle. Imagine how much he'll enjoy seeing my personal pain splashed across newspapers all around the state."

"That *would* appeal to the asshole."

Kate ticked off the points on her fingers. "He gets his story, you save yourself, I get to keep my job because the story isn't sufficient to warrant my dismissal. Everybody wins."

"What if it's not enough to get him off my back?"

"I'll give you enough details to make him happy. Wendy, I'm not going to let him take you down, I promise you."

The reporter still seemed unconvinced.

"Look, there's a much juicier story to be had here. This is not an isolated incident with Breathwaite. There's something much bigger going on."

"I've noticed that you've been under the gun in a bunch of papers lately. Why?"

"I'm not sure yet. All I know so far is that Breathwaite wants me out, and he wants to come back to DOCS as PIO. What I don't know is why or who else is involved. But I intend to find out. And when I do, the story is all yours, exclusively. Just work with me on this piece now. Deal?"

The reporter bit her lower lip and contemplated. "Deal. Let's get writing."

David Breathwaite hated Friday afternoons. They represented the slowest time in the news-making business. He knew that the best way to bury a story in the news cycle was to plant it on a Friday afternoon for release on Saturday. Conventional wisdom and detailed research showed that the general public paid less attention to the news on Saturday than on any other day of the week.

Likewise, the best way to get something out that would normally never be newsworthy was to announce it on a Friday afternoon. Since so few stories were available to cover, reporters were sure to gravitate to the story, which would likely get much wider play than it merited.

In this case, Friday afternoon was going to suit his purposes just perfectly. Breathwaite wanted Wendy Ashton's story to get attention without being overshadowed by other big stories. He also planned to have her embargo the story for release in the Sunday papers, not Saturday's. *So,* he thought smugly, *I get the best of both worlds.*

He picked up the phone and dialed.

"This is Wendy Ashton of the Associated Press. I'll be with you in just a few seconds. Please be patient. As always, your call may be recorded. If you don't mind that, please stay on the line and I'll be right with you."

Breathwaite listened with half an ear as he leafed through some papers on his desk.

"Ashton."

"Hello, Wendy. Are you enjoying your Friday?"

"I was."

Breathwaite laughed. "I'll get right to the point, then. Do you have my story?"

"What's my assurance that you won't double-cross me?"

"Wendy, Wendy, Wendy. I am a man of my word. I'm hurt that you wouldn't trust me."

"Excuse me if I'm a little skeptical. You know all reporters are born cynics."

"If you give me what I want, you have my promise that you can keep your dirty little secret—for now."

"I filed the story a half hour ago, for release in the Sunday editions. It should be on the wire even as we speak."

"Hold on a second and let me check. You'll excuse me, after all, if I don't take *your* word for it?"

Breathwaite swiveled in his chair and examined the AP wire as it spat out news items. He scanned the stories until he found the byline he was looking for. As he read it quickly, his eyes narrowed. He tapped his pen on his desk blotter as he considered. The story probably wasn't enough to force Kyle out. On the other hand, it did air her personal laundry publicly. He smiled a wicked smile. For a private person like that dyke bitch, that could be rather painful. Perhaps she would decide she's had enough and step aside on her own. While the story wasn't everything he hoped for, it might have the intended result, and he could continue to hold the threat of exposure over Ashton's head. He nodded.

"Okay, Ashton. I hoped you would come up with something a little more explosive than this." He could almost feel her squirm in her chair. "But I'm going to let you off the hook—for the moment."

"Breathwaite, I don't know what your game is, but I don't want any part of it. I'm done, do you hear? I've done what you asked me to, now lay off."

His voice exploded, echoing off the walls of his office, "You're done when I say you are, bitch!" He straightened his tie and collected himself. "Now be a good dyke and run along. Be grateful I've accepted your little offering." He severed the connection.

⋞⋟

On her way to a meeting with senior staff, Kate glanced down at her buzzing pager. There was a single number there—one. She breathed a sigh of relief. Wendy was telling her, through their prearranged signal, that Breathwaite had accepted the story.

# CHAPTER FIVE

Jay brushed the hair from her eyes. It had been a long day, but she felt invigorated by the prospect of writing a really important story. ACT UP was going to change the tenor of the debate on AIDS; she felt sure of it. She spent the better part of three days with Barry Kaplan, one of the masterminds behind the group's philosophy and strategies.

Although it was still months away, plans were underway to mark the group's first anniversary. The event, as Barry and his crew of volunteers envisioned it, would take place where it all started—on Wall Street, the financial capital of the world. It was there on March 24, 1987, that ACT UP first made its presence known, protesting profiteering by drug manufacturing companies.

"People need these drugs to have any chance at survival, and the pharmaceutical companies know they have us over a barrel," Barry said as he took Jay on a tour of the ACT UP headquarters in Manhattan. "They can charge outrageous sums and limit availability of things like AZT to control the market. It's shameless. We have to do something to make our voices heard."

"Do you think you can make a difference?"

"We have to believe that we can. I've lost dozens of friends to this dreadful disease. I too, will succumb someday in the not-too-distant future. We can't roll over and apologize for who we are anymore. They throw us a few crumbs and we bow and scrape and thank them for their generosity. Where is our pride? Where is our passion?"

"A lot of people will say you get more with honey than with vinegar. You have to work within the system to get what you want. What do you say to that?"

"I say that you have to have a seat at the table and a voice before you can have meaningful dialogue. What we are doing here is putting them on notice—we have power and we will use it in any way we have to until you treat us with respect and dignity."

"Until you are offered a seat at the table."

"Yes." He hesitated, looking Jay in the eye. "Ms. Parker, we are dying by the tens—no, hundreds of thousands. We have nothing to lose. Those who come after us have everything to gain. Desperate times breed desperate measures. We will do whatever it takes to win this war, and make no mistake about it, it is a war. It's a war waged on a disease, and a war against ignorance on one side. It's also a war waged on people who are different. For some, AIDS is an excuse to brazenly engage in homophobic behavior."

"You see it as a way to justify the marginalization of gays."

"Absolutely. It's the old, 'they're getting what they deserve, it's God's will,' argument. In fact, Ms. Parker, I think it rather remarkable that *Time* magazine is interested in us. Far more forward-thinking and progressive than I would have given you all credit for."

Jay's eyes twinkled. "I don't know, Mr. Kaplan, we just might surprise you."

❦

"I'm sorry, Kate. I wish I could get home tonight, but there are fewer trains on Saturdays, and I just missed the last one. Besides, I've got to get this story written for Monday morning." Jay pouted. "God, I miss you so much it hurts inside."

"I know the feeling, baby. Fred and I miss you too. It's all right. You'll probably get more done without us around to bother you, anyway."

"Sounds like you're pretty busy yourself. What's all that noise in the background?"

"You just focus on your story, there, Scoop. Don't worry about what I'm up to. Write fast so you can come home to us."

"You know you just obfuscated, right?"

"Oh, big word, there."

"You're doing it again, which tells me that you're up to something."

"Me? Nah."

"Argh. You're maddening, but I'm going to let you get away with it—this time."

"I love you, Jay."

"I love you too, Katherine Ann. Bye."

Jay hung up the phone, but held the receiver against her chin a moment longer. Five days. This was the longest separation from Kate since they returned together from Sedona. She sighed. "You can't have it both ways, Parker. You're the one who told Trish you were ready to get back to work in earnest. That means time away. Suck it up and get on with it."

A knock on the door halted her thoughts.

She looked at the clock. 10:35 p.m. "Who in the world?" When the knock came for the second time, she picked up the softball bat she kept near the door and moved to the peephole. How had someone gained access to the building? Putting her eye to the opening, she glanced around.

"Ah!"

She fumbled so quickly with the lock and chain that it took her three tries to get the door open. "Get in here!"

Fred barked exuberantly, throwing himself at Jay and weaving through her legs.

"Shh, buddy. The neighbors'll kill us." Kate's last word was swallowed as Jay pulled her inside, crushing their lips together in a passionate kiss.

When they parted several moments later, Jay said, "This is getting to be a habit with you. You have got to stop calling me from downstairs."

"Well, if you want us to go..." Kate made a move toward the door, but was stopped immediately.

"Don't you dare."

Kate chuckled. "Since you're the one with the baseball bat, I suppose I ought to do as you say."

Jay looked down sheepishly. "Oh, that. Hey, you never know what kind of scum might come knocking at your door in the middle of the night."

"Scum, is it? Fred, did you hear that? First she scolds us, then she calls us names. Are we gonna stand for that?"

The dog continued to dance between Jay's legs, talking like Chewbacca, the Wookiee from *Star Wars*.

"Sorry," Jay said, "looks like you're gonna have to be indignant on your own."

"Sure, buddy, one scratch and you change allegiances. Can't say as I blame you, though. You do have good taste." Kate claimed Jay's lips again, causing Jay to lose her balance as she stumbled over Fred.

They laughed at the same time, and Kate shooed her faithful companion away. "Sorry, Fred. This is my time." Taking a step forward, she pulled Jay into her arms. "I missed you so much I couldn't think straight. There I was, sitting in the house moping, and I thought, 'What am I doing here? It's the weekend, I have a beeper. Let's go!' You don't mind the company, do you?"

"Mind? Are you kidding? My God, Kate, I can't stand being away from you. In fact, when you knocked I was just giving myself a pep talk to keep myself from ditching the story, renting a car, and driving home tonight."

"Yeah?"

"Yeah." Jay's voice was a husky whisper as she ran her hands up and down Kate's sides, pausing to grasp the hem of her sweater and pull it over her head. She gasped audibly when she realized that Kate wore nothing underneath. "God, you are so very beautiful." Cupping Kate's perfect, white breasts in her hands, she lowered her mouth to take an erect nipple between her teeth.

Kate shuddered and reached down to grasp Jay's buttocks, bringing their bodies into full contact. "You feel so good, love."

"Mmm. I love the way your skin tastes," Jay murmured against the breast she was sampling.

Kate managed to insinuate her hands between them and began unzipping Jay's jeans.

"Um, honey?"

"Yes?"

Jay gripped Kate's wrist to stop her roaming hand. "Before we go any further, can we take this upstairs to the bedroom?"

"Where's the challenge in that? Besides, you're the one who started it." Kate maneuvered them into the living room, where the large plate-glass window overlooked the twinkling lights of the city below. "We should enjoy the view."

"I am enjoying the view," Jay said as her eyes feasted on her lover's bare upper torso.

"And I'm glad you are." Kate's voice lowered an octave. She took a step backward until she was just out of Jay's reach. "Sometimes I look at you, and I can't believe you're mine."

"I feel the same way."

They stood two steps away from each other, the air around them crackling with the intensity of their emotions.

"Thank you, Jay."

"For what?"

Kate's eyes brimmed with tears of gratitude. "For showing me how to live. For bringing me joy and laughter. For teaching me, maybe for the first time in my life, how to give of myself without reservation or fear."

"Do I do all that?"

"You sure do."

"Wow, maybe I should put in for a raise, huh?" Jay moved forward, using her thumbs to wipe the moisture from Kate's eyelashes. "Kate, before I met you, I *existed*, moving in my own little world. I never allowed anyone to touch me. Not really. Now, I can't imagine living like that. You've opened up a whole new universe to me. I'm the one who should be thanking you."

"I guess we're both pretty lucky then, huh?"

"I guess we are." Jay wrapped her arms around Kate's bare waist, hugging her tightly. After a minute she asked, "Now can we go upstairs?"

Kate laughed and tipped Jay's chin up so that she could claim her lips. "Mmm. Sweetheart, you can take me anywhere you want."

"In that case, come with me."

❧❦

Kate stirred and glanced at the digital clock on the nightstand. 7:22 a.m. Jay was sprawled on top of her, in exactly the same position she had fallen asleep after several rounds of lovemaking. Kate ran her fingers lightly over the soft skin of her lover's buttocks, delighting in the texture. She buried her nose in silky strands of hair, the smell reminding her of a fresh summer breeze. It was these moments, just before they started their day, that she cherished most.

"What are you thinking about, love? Your heart is fluttering."

"Just enjoying how wonderful it feels to hold you like this. I love you, Jamison Parker."

"I love you too, Katherine Kyle."

Just as Jay was about to kiss Kate, a stuffed angelfish was unceremoniously shoved between them.

Kate sighed. "Good morning to you too, Fred. I don't suppose you could wait another few minutes, could you?"

The canine wagged his tail furiously, his whole body wiggling from the effort.

"Didn't think so." To Jay, Kate said, "I'm sorry, baby. I've got to get him fed and out."

"That's all right. I've got to get the ACT UP story written anyway."

"Okay. Well, why don't I take him for a run around the Village. I need to pick up a newspaper on my way back too." Kate kissed Jay on the top of the head and slid out from underneath her. Immediately, Fred began dancing in circles, the stuffed fish clenched tightly between his jaws.

"C'mon, ya goofball." Kate scratched the dog on the head as she headed downstairs to the kitchen to feed him.

❧❦

As she and Fred rounded the corner on the way home, Kate stopped at a newsstand. She selected the *New York Post*, the *Daily News*, the *New*

*York Times,* and *Newsday.* She was about to head up the steps to Jay's apartment building when she thought better of it. Instead, she crossed the street, Fred following obediently on the leash, and went into the park.

"Jay needs to concentrate on her work, buddy. Let's enjoy the day for a bit, shall we?"

The fall air was chilly. The leaves were beginning to change, the maple trees showing hues of red, orange, and yellow. There was a quietness to this section of the city, a rhythm that differed from the hustle and bustle of midtown Manhattan. The sounds were more muted here, the pace of life a bit slower.

Kate settled down on a bench, and Fred lay down at her feet. She spread the papers out next to her, choosing to start with the *Post* first, figuring that paper would be likely to have the most inflammatory version of the story, and perhaps even a companion piece by one of its own reporters in addition to Wendy's piece.

Kate opened the paper to page two. "Prison PIO Has an Axe to Grind," the headline screamed.

"Now that's catchy." Noting the prominent placement of the story, she added, "Must be a slow news weekend. Just my luck."

> State prison spokeswoman Katherine Kyle may have more on her mind than handling the press, according to anonymous sources close to the situation. The Associated Press has confirmed that Kyle, on the job for a little more than three months, has a reason to be bitter at the very criminal justice system she purports to represent. As a freshman in college, Kyle lost both her parents to a drunk driver in a crash on the Hutchinson River Parkway just outside New York City. Although he paid a large amount in damages awarded in civil court, the man never served a day in jail.
>
> "There's no question Kate thought he should have done time. It made her very angry at the system. I'm not sure she's ever gotten over that," the source revealed.
>
> A review of Kyle's record on the job to date does not turn up any overt examples of sabotage, but several media outlets around the state have questioned her job performance of late.
>
> State Department of Correctional Services Commissioner Brian Sampson, reached by AP while touring several prisons in the western part of the state, said, "I have

complete confidence in Ms. Kyle. Her integrity and professionalism are beyond reproach."
AP's attempts to contact Kyle were futile.

With a sigh, Kate turned to the editorial page. Sure enough, the lead editorial headline was "Prison PIO Should Resign." Sitting on her bench in the quiet of a Greenwich Village Sunday morning, the subject of the attack shook her head sadly.

Predictably, the opinion piece questioned her objectivity, motives, and veracity. It demanded a review of any and all instances in which she had spoken on behalf of DOCS, questioning if the information she had provided news outlets could be trusted.

Kate set aside the *Post* and picked up the other three newspapers. To her great relief, the *Daily News* and *Newsday* simply carried Wendy's story. The *New York Times* didn't run the piece at all.

She closed her eyes, trying to stave off the tension headache that had been her constant companion for the past three months. Unbidden, long-dormant memories of her last conversation with her parents crept in. It was December 15, 1978, and her last exam for the semester was over.

She had just told them she didn't plan to come home for Christmas vacation. She was enjoying her freedom, experiencing life on her own for the first time. She was just about to start a new job with the ski patrol at the college ski area, and her new bosses had asked her to work over the holiday. Kate could have said no, but she didn't want to. Her father was angry, her mother just disappointed.

Kate promised to call them Christmas morning. But she never had the chance to talk to them, or to tell them she loved them, and never would again. Kate wiped tears from her face.

"I miss you guys. I'm sorry. If I had made a different choice, you might not have gone to that party and been on that parkway that night. Maybe you'd still be here with me. I was so selfish. If I had only known..." She bowed her head. She would never forgive herself for allowing angry words to be the last between them.

Fred, who must have sensed his mother's distress, sat up and put his chin on Kate's lap. Smiling through her tears, she reached down and scratched him on the head.

"C'mon, buddy. Enough of the maudlin for one day. Let's go see what Jay's up to."

As she stood up and gathered the newspapers, her beeper went off. She frowned at the number displayed on the readout.

"Figures, buddy." Kate led Fred at a jog across the street to Jay's apartment building.

When she opened the door, Jay emerged from her office.

"Honey, Commissioner Sampson is looking for you. He called here. I told him to try your beep—what's the matter?" Jay ran her fingers over Kate's tear-streaked face. "What happened?"

"Nothing, baby. I'm all right. I need to call the boss back." At her displeased expression, Kate added, "I'm not blowing you off, Jay. We can talk about it later. Right now, I don't want to keep the big man waiting."

"I'll accept that—for now—but we are going to address what's bothering you afterward, right?"

"Absolutely." Kate kissed Jay on the forehead before heading into the living room to make her phone call.

❦❦

"Kate? Have you seen the papers yet this morning?"

"Yes, sir, I have."

"I just want you to know, I am standing behind you one hundred percent on this thing. It's outrageous that some scumbag reporter would use something as personal as the death of your parents to try to disparage you. I've half a mind to call up the editors at AP and demand that she be fired."

"Sir, I don't think the story was her doing."

"What?"

Kate felt her way carefully, trying to decide how much to reveal. "I see a pattern here, and it goes much further than one reporter and one news outlet."

"What are you saying, Kate?"

"I'm saying there appears to be a concerted effort underway to discredit me."

The commissioner was quiet for a moment. "There has been an unusual amount of negative publicity directed specifically at you lately, hasn't there?"

"Yes, sir, there has. And if you want me to step aside in order to make that stop, I will."

"I've told you before, Kate. The governor and I have complete faith in you. I won't hear of it."

"Thank you, sir."

"Not at all, Kate. Who do you think is behind this?"

"I'm not really sure yet, sir." Technically, that was the truth, Kate thought. Breathwaite clearly had associates they'd yet to flush out, possibly even including Sampson's second in command.

"I intend to find out," Sampson stated.

"No, sir. This is my fight. I'll take care of it."

"Kate, if it affects my staff or my department, it's my business."

"Please, sir, I'd like the chance to investigate further without a lot of fanfare. I think it will be easier to operate under the radar that way."

"All right, Kate. But if you need anything, don't hesitate to ask. I want you to know my displeasure isn't with you…it's with whoever's pulling the strings on this thing."

"I understand, sir, and I appreciate that."

"Keep your chin up, Kate. Don't let them get the best of you."

"Thank you, sir. Enjoy the rest of your weekend."

Kate found Jay in the kitchen, where she was busy cooking them omelets, home fries, and toast for breakfast. "Mmm, something smells delicious." She wrapped her arms around Jay's waist, nuzzling her neck from behind.

"Keep that up and something's going to smell burnt."

Kate raised her hands in mock surrender, backing away several steps. "Far be it from me to spoil a wonderful meal."

Jay regarded her intently. "What's going on, sweetheart? Why were you so upset, and what did the commissioner want this early on a Sunday?"

"Have I told you how absolutely breathtaking you are?"

"Stop it, Kate. Changing the topic will not get you anywhere, and I'm not in the mood for your tricks. So give."

"You win. Wendy's story hit all the papers today. I was just having a nostalgic moment for my folks. That's what had me upset."

"Oh, honey." Jay closed the distance between them, taking Kate in her arms. "I'm so sorry. I wish you hadn't given her that kind of ammunition. I hate to see you in pain."

"I just let my guard down for a second. I'm fine now."

"What did the commissioner want?"

"He saw the stories and he was spitting mad at Wendy. Wanted to have her fired."

"Uh-oh. How'd you get around that?"

"I told him just enough of the truth to mollify him." At Jay's raised eyebrow, she continued, "I told him there was something fishy going on that was much bigger than her, but I hadn't figured all the angles yet."

"Did he accept that?"

"He wanted to bust heads. I told him I wanted to handle it myself. He's giving me the room to do that, provided I let him know if I need anything."

"Well, that's good, right?"

"Sure is."

Jay regarded her speculatively. "Honey?"

"Hmm?"

"I hate what all this is doing to you." Kate tried to pull away, but Jay held her fast. "Just hear me out. You're so stressed your jaw barely opens, you're not sleeping well, you have to think three steps ahead of everything all the time. This is crazy."

"I can handle it."

"I'm not arguing whether or not you can handle it. I'm just saying I wonder if this is all worth it."

"What are you driving at?"

"You don't need this. We don't need this. You could walk away and be well out of it."

Kate stiffened. "No."

"Don't you even want to think about it? Look at what this is doing to you."

"No way. Jay, first of all, I like what I do. Second of all, I'll be damned if I'm going to let these bastards, whoever they are, win. I won't do it."

Jay, sensing that her partner had her mind made up, relented. "Okay then. I'm with you. We'll get through this together."

"Thank you, Jay. Your support means everything to me."

"*You* mean everything to me, Katherine Ann Kyle. We'll do whatever it takes. Let's get the bastards."

"That's my girl."

# CHAPTER SIX

A s soon as they were seated around the table in their usual meeting spot, DNC Chairman Hawthorne began. "Okay, gentlemen. Where are we?" He looked meaningfully around the table. "So help you God if the news isn't good."

At the same time, the governor's press secretary and the DOCS executive deputy commissioner glared at Breathwaite.

"Well, David, it seems that all eyes are on you."

"So it does." Breathwaite barely glanced up from the notebook in which he was doodling.

"And?"

"I'm working on it, Bob."

"We're running out of time, and I'm running out of patience, you little—"

"Relax, Senator. I don't see anyone else in this room stepping up to the plate."

"You said you could handle it." Vendetti pointed his finger at Breathwaite. "I've been busy trying to do damage control to keep Governor Charlie from derailing this train. Every goddamned time our boy has dinner with Kyle, which is too often, he comes out with some bold policy initiative that's sure to draw fire. At this rate, I'll never get to the White House."

"Oh, stop your whining, pretty boy. My strategy is already in play. It's just a matter of time."

"Time, you maggot, is a luxury we don't have."

Breathwaite's ears began to turn red, the only visible sign of his anger. Before he could answer, however, Bill Redfield joined the conversation.

"For your information, genius, your 'strategy' is only making things worse. The commissioner called me this morning to tell me he's standing by Kyle, despite the sudden onslaught of negative publicity. He's figured out that these stories aren't random, and he's itching to find out who's at the root of this smear campaign, as he called it. The only thing that's saving us is that Kyle apparently convinced him not to intervene."

"She's probably ready to resign." Breathwaite appeared unconcerned about the development.

Redfield shook his head. "She's not going anywhere of her own volition, and he's not throwing her out. She told Sampson she wanted to take care of the situation herself."

"It's obvious they know there's something organized going on. I thought the idea here was to be subtle." Vendetti leaned forward in his chair.

Breathwaite sneered, "I thought the *idea* here was to get results."

"Either way, you've failed," Vendetti said.

Breathwaite jumped to his feet. "Listen, you sniveling ingrates. It's not over yet. You said six months, and it's only been four. Get off my back!"

"Sit down, David," Hawthorne ordered.

Reluctantly, he did.

"It appears we now have two problems. We still have to get Kyle out of the way, and, we may have to do something about Sampson before he starts to make noise to Charlie about his suspicions."

"Great. Just great."

"Michael, shut up. It's your job to keep tabs on any interactions between Charlie and Sampson. If it looks as if Sampson's brought the issue to Charlie's attention, then we've got to move."

"I'm not sure we can afford to wait for that to happen, Bob. Once the governor is made aware of the situation, it becomes far more complicated. I think it's time to pull out what we've got on Sampson now."

"*We* don't have anything on Sampson. I have it, and I'll take care of it."

"The same way you've taken care of Kyle, Breathwaite?"

"It seems to me, Willy, that it's in your best interest to be nice to me. After all, you do want to be the next DOCS commissioner, don't you?"

"Why you—"

"Gentlemen. Cool it. Baiting each other will get us nowhere. We're all in this together." Hawthorne stood. "I want Kyle and Sampson gone within the next two weeks, Breathwaite, do I make myself clear?"

"Don't worry."

"Right. Michael, I want you to clear the way with Charlie for Bill to take over at DOCS. Then, with Kyle gone, we can move David back in as PIO and be back on schedule before any more damage is done."

"I'll do my best."

"The next time I hear from you all, I want to know that everything has gone smoothly. Good day, gentlemen."

"What's that delicious smell?" Kate walked in from the garage, placed her briefcase on the floor, and hung her keys on the key rack just in time to stop Fred from running her over. "Hi, handsome. Is Jay home and cooking? Lucky us, huh, buddy?"

Jay stood in the doorway, watching her interact with the dog, glad beyond measure of the smile he always put on her face. "Hi there, beautiful. Do I get a scratch too?"

"If that's what you really want. I was thinking, though, that we both might enjoy this"—she kissed Jay sweetly on the lips—"a little more."

"Mmm. Definitely. If I'm really good, can I have another?"

"I don't know, how good are you?"

Jay purred, "You need to ask that question?"

"Um, never mind, I withdraw the question. What are you doing home so early? I thought you'd be coming in on a late train."

"I turned in my story early this morning, waited a few hours for Trish to get around to looking at it, cooled my heels for an hour or so waiting for the next assignment, then decided Trish could call me when she was ready. I wanted to be here when my fiancée got home from work."

"I love the way you think." Kate wrapped her arm around Jay's waist as they made their way to the kitchen. "What are we having? Whatever it is, it smells like heaven."

"I thought I'd get a bit creative tonight. I'm making duck a l'orange with wild rice, salad and, if you're really nice to me, chocolate mousse for dessert."

"Wow. What did I do to deserve all this?"

"You fell in love with the right girl."

"I sure did." Kate turned Jay in her arms, running her hands up her back while pulling her in close. "I love you, Jamison. So very, very much."

"And I love you, more than words can ever express."

After a moment lost in each other's gazes, they allowed their mouths to meet. It was not a passionate kiss, but one that bespoke a connection that ran deeper than either could put into words.

When they parted, Kate ran her finger along Jay's jaw, evidently unwilling to sever the physical link so soon. Her eyes lingered on Jay's face. Eventually, she broke the spell. "Let me just go change my clothes quickly. I'll be right back."

"Okay. Dinner will be on the table in five minutes, so no dawdling up there."

"Are you calling me a loafer?"

"Just get moving, you're wasting time. You're down to four minutes, twenty-eight seconds. Twenty-seven, twenty-six..."

"I get the idea. I'm going, already, I'm going."

True to her word, Kate was back in under five minutes. Jay was just putting the food on the table when she walked into the dining room.

"It looks as wonderful as it smells. Always a good sign."

"Keep it up and Fred will be eating your portion."

"Hey, that's a little extreme, don't you think?"

"I try not to."

"Very cute." Kate took Jay's hand, kissed the back of it, then turned it over and kissed the palm. "Thank you for making a lovely meal, honey."

"That's better." Jay winked. "Nice comeback."

"Glad to see I haven't lost my touch."

They enjoyed a leisurely dinner, feeding each other bits of duck along with forkfuls of rice. When it came time for dessert, by mutual consent they decided to move to the bedroom. Kate carried the bowl of mousse upstairs.

Jay ran one finger down Kate's fly, pausing before retracing her movements upward. Reaching the button at Kate's waist, she released it from its clasp, lowering the zipper with exaggerated slowness and easing the jeans down her long legs.

Kate stepped out of the pants, her eyes fixed on Jay's mouth. Without turning her head, she located the dessert bowl and spooned some of the fluffy chocolate onto her index finger. Carefully, she painted Jay's lips before ducking her head and spending a long time removing the confection.

"Mmm. Tasty dessert, love."

Jay bent down and relieved Kate of her panties. "I'll have to see for myself, now, won't I?" She scooped a generous helping of chocolate onto her fingers and slid them against Kate's wetness. Pausing to look up at her lover, she smiled wickedly just before dropping to her knees, immersing herself in Kate's sweet-tasting center.

"How's—oh God, right there, baby—the mousse?" Kate managed to choke out, seconds before a wave of pleasure swamped her senses.

When she was able, she pulled Jay to her feet, lifted her into her arms, and carried her to the bed. She took care in stripping Jay, applying chocolate to breasts, pelvic bones, navel, and clit. She sucked each chocolate-covered finger into her mouth, smiling when she felt Jay squirm in anticipation of what was to come.

Kate began with Jay's breasts, her palms caressing the outer curves, her mouth hovering over coated nipples. Gradually she lowered her head, her lips enveloping the sweet-tasting skin.

"Mmm, now this is the way to enjoy dessert."

Trying to think of a witty comeback, Jay murmured, "Sure saves on the dishes."

"That it does." Kate dipped her tongue into the well of Jay's belly button.

"Ugh. You're killing me, baby. Please."

"Patience. I'm trying to savor the flavor."

Jay growled in frustration, which only served to make her lover laugh.

Kate feasted on succulent pelvic bones, lingering over each one before succumbing to Jay's entreaties and pressing her mouth against her throbbing clit.

When the orgasm came, Jay felt more alive than she ever had in her life. As her breathing resumed its normal pattern, she buried her face in her hands.

Immediately, Kate was alongside her, her hands framing Jay's face. "What is it, love? Are you all right?"

"Never better. It's just...sometimes it's hard to fathom how much you mean to me. I am the luckiest woman on the planet."

"Honestly? I'm the lucky one."

"How about if we settle on the notion that we're both lucky and leave it at that?"

"Works for me."

Breathwaite paced the length of his office, turned around, and stalked the other way. "It's not working. I need something more. The stubborn bitch isn't budging."

The blockish man sitting in the corner continued to clean his teeth with a toothpick. "What do you want me to do, boss?"

"I want you to find me something—anything—that I can use to get Kyle out of that seat. Damn it all to hell, Kirk. If I don't make this happen, and soon, I'm out of the game."

"Maybe you haven't been looking in the right places."

Breathwaite narrowed his eyes. "What do you mean?"

Kirk looked supremely bored. "You've been trying to discredit her professionally, right? Shake her credibility?"

"Of course. If I can plant that seed of doubt—make her seem less trustworthy—I'll have her."

Kirk examined his nails. "Seems to me that hasn't been working too well for you so far."

Breathwaite rounded on him. "You got any other ideas?"

"Hey," Kirk held up his hands, "I'm just a stupid PI, remember?"

"Don't play games with me, you lazy son of a bitch. I pay you good money to dig up dirt, and so far, I have to say, you haven't proved to me that you're worth a dime."

Kirk snarled. "I was smart enough to uncover your con, little man, so you'd best watch your manners."

Breathwaite clamped his jaw shut with a resounding click. After collecting himself he said, "It's obvious to me that you've been giving this matter some thought. Care to share your ideas?"

Kirk smirked. "That's better." He went back to manicuring his nails. "As a matter of fact, I have been giving this considerable thought. What's the chink in this dyke's armor? What's her Achilles' heel? You've been going on the assumption that it's her pride, her professionalism. But that doesn't seem to be it, right, boss?"

"Right."

"So what else is there, I asked myself."

"Her girlfriend."

"Bingo."

"You know something."

Kirk smiled beatifically. "Could be."

"Spill it."

"Ah ah ah. Patience, little man. It's going to cost you."

The grinding of Breathwaite's teeth was audible in the silence.

Kirk chuckled. "You must be a dentist's dream. Relax, all I want—in addition to my money, of course—"

"Naturally," Breathwaite muttered.

"All I want," Kirk raised his voice slightly, "is a cut of the action when you get to D.C."

"What, exactly, do you have in mind?"

"I want a position as chief of security for the big man."

"Can't be done," Breathwaite dismissed him out of hand. "Chief of security has to be secret service. You might remember that there are a few black marks in your portfolio. You'd never get through the screening process."

"Okay then, expunge my record."

Breathwaite considered. "Done."

"Right, then." Kirk reached into the briefcase that was sitting at his feet. He walked across the room, and unceremoniously tossed a manila file folder on the desk.

Breathwaite scooped it up greedily and leafed through the contents. He stared hard at a glossy picture in the middle of the pile before returning to the top page. He began to read aloud. "Jamison Parker, age twenty-four, reporter for *Time* magazine." He glanced at the next series of pages—a *Time* magazine story from the previous May, making special note of the date at the top. Smiling evilly, he shut the folder with a snap.

"Kyle." Kate rolled over and answered the phone automatically, scowling at the bedside clock. 3:45 a.m.

"Good morning, Ms. Kyle. David Breathwaite here."

"How can I help you, David?"

"I'd like to meet with you at your earliest convenience."

*I'd rather eat rats for breakfast.* "Regarding?"

"I'd rather talk about it in person, Ms. Kyle. Let's just say it would be in your best interest to make it sooner rather than later. Perhaps I could buy you a cup of coffee before work this morning, for instance?"

Kate weighed her options. She could refuse the invitation, but there was no real advantage to doing so. She did, however, want to force Breathwaite to meet her on her own turf. "My office in one hour. I'll supply the coffee."

It was clear from the momentary silence on the other end of the phone that Breathwaite didn't like being dictated to, but he agreed to the terms of the meeting and rang off.

Jay rolled over sleepily and propped her chin on her lover's naked shoulder. "Who was that, sweetheart? You look like you swallowed a lemon."

"That was our good friend Mr. Breathwaite. Seems he wants to meet with me ASAP."

Jay's growl reverberated in the quiet of their bedroom, causing Fred to look up from his customary position next to Kate's side of the bed. "I strongly dislike that man."

Laughing, Kate hugged Jay. "Really? I couldn't tell."

"I take it you're going?"

"No, actually, he's coming. I wanted him on my home court."

"Oh. Good thinking, sweetheart. Put him at a disadvantage."

"As much as that's possible without knowing most of what's going on."

"Looks like you may be about to find out."

Kate looked pensive. "Maybe, but somehow I don't think he's likely to be very forthcoming."

✦✦

Kate walked into her quiet office, glad that, other than the two officers in the command center, there were no employees in the building at this early hour. She looked around at her cramped space, neat stacks of paper covering most of the sturdy, solid oak desk that dominated the room.

In addition to the desk and its accompanying executive's chair, there were two straight-backed visitors' chairs and a printer stand that held the AP Teletype machine. There were no windows and no personal effects anywhere to be seen.

Kate sat down and opened a steaming container of coffee. Within seconds she heard footsteps approaching from the outer office. At the knock on the doorframe, she looked up to see Breathwaite. She invited him in with a wave of her hand, beckoning him to sit.

"Good morning." She shoved the second cup of coffee across the wooden surface of the desk. She intentionally hadn't asked him how he liked his coffee, ordering it black and hoping like hell that wasn't the way he took it. Anything that made him more miserable was fine with Kate.

"Hello," Breathwaite chirped too cheerfully.

"What can I do for you, David?"

"It's not what you can do for me, Ms. Kyle, it's what you can do for yourself."

Kate folded her hands on the desk and waited.

Breathwaite cleared his throat. "I see you've been having quite a time of it lately in the media."

"Nothing I can't handle, I assure you, David." Kate noted that Breathwaite had yet to look her in the eye.

"The pressure must be getting pretty intense."

"Not really." Kate stared at him levelly.

"No? With so many news outlets questioning your credibility and the tabloids still so interested in the identity of your girlfriend..."

Kate tensed minutely in spite of herself, an action that she was sure was not lost on her visitor.

"I would have thought," Breathwaite continued, "a woman of independent means like you might have opted to give this endeavor up in exchange for a quieter, more private life."

"That's never been a consideration."

"Really? That's odd. You've gone to such extraordinary lengths to protect Ms. Parker to this point."

At the mention of Jay's name, Kate's eyes flashed.

Breathwaite leaned forward in his seat. "Yes, I know who she is, Ms. Kyle. There's very little I don't know or can't find out."

"Why exactly are you here, David? I'm assuming there's a purpose to your visit—other than to take up space in my office, I mean?"

Breathwaite rose and began to pace, seemingly inspecting the artwork on the walls. "I'll make this simple, Ms. Kyle. You resign, and your secret remains just that."

"And if I refuse?"

He turned to face her. "I'm sure the *National Enquirer* would be thrilled to know the identity of your lover." He spat the word. "And I'm equally certain that *Time* magazine would be pleased to know that your partner in perversity in the *Enquirer* photos is a woman who had just finished writing a glowing front-page article on you for them."

"What could you possibly gain by forcing me out, Breathwaite? Why is my leaving so damned important to you? What's your game?"

"What's your answer, Kyle? Are you willing to destroy your girlfriend's career?"

Kate took a sip of her coffee in order to allow herself time to think before responding. Her first instinct was to protect Jay from this ugliness at all costs. As soon as the thought crossed her mind, however, she dismissed it. She'd nearly lost Jay the very same way not six months earlier and had vowed then and there never to make decisions on her lover's behalf again without clear direction from her.

Kate thought about Jay's willingness to out herself to help her and their more recent discussion in which Jay explicitly told Kate they would stay and fight, together. She nodded to herself and rose to her full height. Towering over the much shorter Breathwaite, she snapped, "Go to hell, you two-bit scum."

Breathwaite planted his hands on the desk and leaned forward, bringing him to within a foot of Kate's face. "You have no idea what hell looks like, Kyle, but you're about to find out."

⋘⋙

After Breathwaite departed, Kate drummed her fingers on the desk, her mind working furiously. "That's it."

She rushed out of her office, downstairs to the first floor, out the door and hopped into her car. Within twenty minutes she was home.

She bolted through the front door. "Jay? Honey?"

"In here."

Kate followed Jay's voice, taking the stairs two at a time, practically colliding with her as she rounded the corner from her home office.

"What are you doing home, Kate?"

Kate gathered her in her arms, hugging her close.

Jay pulled back slightly, apparently in order to gauge the expression on Kate's face. "Did you have your meeting with Breathwaite? How'd it go? Are you all right?"

Without answering, Kate took Jay by the hand and led the way downstairs to the living room. She sank down on the couch and pulled Jay into her lap.

"You remember when you said you were willing to expose yourself as my lover for Wendy's story?"

"Yes." Jay drew out the word.

"And you remember that I was vehemently opposed to the idea?"

"Oh, yes."

"Let's just say it's out of our hands."

"Breathwaite knows?"

Kate nodded sadly. She gave Jay a rundown of the meeting, after which silence permeated the room.

Finally Jay murmured, "That son of a bitch."

Kate, easily able to feel her partner's agitation, rubbed her back gently. Seeing her suffer only strengthened her resolve. "Sweetheart?"

Jay sighed. "Yeah?"

"Let's get him."

Jay straightened up. "What do you have in mind?"

"I want to steal the story out from under Breathwaite's nose—beat him to it."

Jay raised her eyebrows.

"We need to make the announcement ourselves, honey, before he leaks it." Before Jay could say anything, Kate added, "That's the only way we can have any control over the story."

Jay thought for a moment. "Okay. That makes sense. Tell me, oh great spinmeister, how do you propose to go about this?"

"Jay," regret was etched in every line of Kate's face, "this could get really ugly. I think it's entirely possible that he'll try to attack your journalistic integrity."

"I will not apologize for the story I wrote about you." Jay was defiant. "I disclosed everything to my editor at the time, and Trish stood by me then. I suspect she'll stand by me now. In any event, you and I both know that the piece was as objective as it would have been had a stranger written it."

Kate ran her fingers along the fine jawbone that she loved so much. "I'm so sorry you're getting dragged into this, sweetheart. I never meant for this to happen."

"Shh, I know that. I told you before, I'm proud to be your fiancée, and it will be a relief not to have to hide that anymore. Breathwaite has no idea what he's in for."

Kate chuckled. "That's my tough girl."

Jay kissed Kate lightly on the lips. "That's me. I say bring it on!"

"I'm sure that's exactly what the asshole will do."

"So, what's our plan?"

"Let's start by bringing Peter and Barbara up to speed."

"Barbara?" Jay asked, a little surprised.

"Yep. She may be 'just' a doctor, but she's also got a brilliant mind and a gift for seeing all the angles."

"Okay."

"We've got to hurry, Jay. We don't have much time."

Less than half an hour later, the four met in Barbara's nearby office. It was not yet 6:45 a.m.

"Now you know what I know," Kate said. "I wish like hell I could've gotten some hint of the scope of this thing, but Breathwaite didn't bite. So we're no closer to finding out the rest of the pieces of the puzzle than we were before, and Breathwaite has new ammunition that he's gleefully willing to use."

Peter weighed in, "No. You're wrong. We know that he's getting more desperate by the minute, which tells us a lot."

"Peter's right," Barbara chipped in. "For one thing, the escalation might indicate that he's on a timetable—that he has to have you out by a certain date. For another, it seems to me as though the timetable is not his and he's not the boss here. I know that might have been obvious to you before, but, as with all scientists, I like to see corroborating evidence. Finally, I'll go out on a limb here and say that whoever it is, it's someone who wields a significant amount of power if it can make an essentially arrogant, self-important imp feel fear."

Jay muttered, "You're right. It *is* almost as if he's running scared of something."

"There's certainly nothing subtle about his approach, that's for sure," Kate added. "Okay, I take it back. We did find out some things of value. Still, there's too much we don't know yet. We have to find a way to flush out the other players. We think Redfield might be one, but he's not powerful enough to scare Breathwaite."

"How do you suggest we go about finding the others?" Barbara asked.

Jay jumped in before Kate could answer. "Wait. Before you consider that, we need to focus on the here and now. What's staring us in the face this morning is the immediate threat. We can turn our attention to Breathwaite's cohorts after we deal with this."

"Right, Jay." Kate spared a loving look for her partner. "Within the next three to three and a half hours, Breathwaite will have had a chance to give the story to the tabloids, not to mention the *Post* and the *News*."

"What do you recommend, Kate?"

She considered her options as she had any number of times over the course of the past couple of hours. "First, I want to call Wendy Ashton and give her a half-hour jump on the story. Then I think we should call a press conference, introduce Jay as my partner, explain that we are making the announcement at this time because we are proud of our relationship, tired of being hounded incessantly by the media, and because we wish to get this out of the way so that we can have some peace and move on with our lives without having to endure the type of scrutiny normally reserved for heads of state."

Heads nodded around the room.

"What about timing?" Barbara asked.

"Talk to Wendy now, ask her to embargo the story until nine, then do the media circus at nine thirty."

"Explain the purpose of doing it that way, please? For those of us who don't do this for a living."

"Talk to Wendy first because she's a lesbian, will handle the story with class, and because I owe her. Nine thirty a.m. for the press conference because it gives assignment editors, who come in an hour in advance of their reporters, just enough time to get their folks scrambled out the door before any other events take place. Also, we beat the magic ten a.m. hour, which is when most print journalists in this town start their day. Breathwaite will likely wait until then to make his phone calls, since he knows it's mostly a waste of time trying to reach anyone in their office before then. Assignment editors, on the other hand, won't wait—they'll call their guys at home and tell them to get their asses in gear *now*. Not only that, but having Wendy's story on the wire will make covering our press conference a must, since every other reporter already will be behind the eight ball."

"And," Jay chimed in checking her watch, "the timing still gives us a couple of hours to put everything in place."

"Why not just put out a statement? Why do you want to face that media circus?" Barbara asked.

All eyes turned once again to Kate.

"Good question. If we put out a statement and don't give the vultures an opportunity for photos, they'll just keep hounding us everywhere we go until they get the shot they want. If we let them snap away at the press conference, that should satisfy them. I hope."

"I'm sure you two have thought of this," Peter piped up, "but you both have bosses that you ought to fill in before you go any further."

The lovers looked at each other. Finally, Jay said, "You're right. I better let Trish know what's about to come down." She sounded less than thrilled at the prospect, and Kate moved closer to wrap an arm around her.

"I'm so sorry, love."

"No," Jay said fiercely. "Don't you dare apologize. This is not your fault. The blame lies squarely with that two-bit troll."

"She's right, Kate," Barbara added gently.

Looking at his friend, Peter said, "And you, my dear Katherine, have a commissioner to face. Better get him up to speed."

Jay looked dubiously from her lover to Peter.

Kate explained, "Honey, if the commissioner was involved, I'd already have been fired. Peter and I are as sure as we can be about anything that he's clean."

"Okay, I'll have to take your word on that."

Peter said, "Kate, why don't you draft an advisory with the details of the press conference, and Barbara and I can fax it from her machine. Just give us your media contact sheet and we'll send it out to the news outlets."

Barbara added, "Then you and Jay will be free to take care of your respective bosses."

"Thanks guys. That makes good sense." She looked at her best friends and summoned her cockiest grin. "Well, this ought to be fun. See you in a bit."

"Trish? It's Jay. I hate to bother you at home, but I thought I'd better not wait."

"What's up? Are you so anxious for your next assignment that you couldn't wait until I got into the office? You know I love your initiative and drive, but..."

"Very funny. You know I wouldn't bother you unless it was really important."

"I know that, kiddo, I was just trying to lighten you up a bit. You sound pretty strung out."

"Well, it's not every day that my relationship gets splashed all over the headlines and my professionalism called into question."

"Slow down, Jamison. You lost me. What are you talking about?"

Jay explained everything that she and Kate had been through since Kate took the job with the prison system, including Breathwaite's visit that morning.

"I wish you'd told me what was going on. No wonder you've seemed a little on edge lately."

"Yeah, well, I didn't really think it was your problem. Now, though, it seems more than likely that he'll go after me professionally. He probably figures if he can push Kate's buttons he can make her quit."

"Will it work?"

"No," Jay said quietly, knowing that Trish was thinking about Kate's innate tendency to protect Jay without consulting her. "Kate told him to go to hell, came right home to tell me everything, and we planned the strategy together."

"Okay. I just don't want to see you get hurt again."

"I may well get hurt," Jay said grimly, "but not by Kate. We're going to take our relationship public before the jerk has a chance to do it for us."

Trish whistled. "Wow. Gutsy move." There was a pause on the line. "Smart, I think. It prevents him from having a role at the outset."

"Right."

"But I think you're right. It doesn't sound to me like he's the kind of guy who's gonna let that stand for very long."

"Exactly. If the first day's story is my identity, you can bet that day two's headlines will be the timing of the cover story last May."

"Mmm. Makes sense."

"Trish, I know you stood by me then, and I really appreciate it, but I don't want to do anything to damage the magazine's reputation." The note of dejection was clear in Jay's voice.

"I know that, Jay. Your integrity is one of the things I admire most about you. Let's cross that bridge when we get to it. For now, you just focus on what you have to do this morning. I'll have a conversation with the managing editor and we'll come up with a plan."

"Okay."

"Chin up, kiddo. I'll be rooting for you."

"Thanks, Trish. You're the best."

Kate walked into Commissioner Sampson's office and closed the door.

"You needed to see me, Kate?"

"Yes, sir. Thank you for making the time."

"Sit down, sit down. How many times have I told you there's no need to be so formal."

Kate selected the chair closest to the door. "Sir, do you remember our conversation after the AP story came out?"

"Of course I do."

"Well, as I told you then, there is a concerted effort going on to discredit me. Today the campaign is going to reach a new low."

"How do you know?" Sampson made a show of looking at his watch. "It's barely seven thirty in the morning."

"I know with a great degree of certainty that the plan is to release Jay's identity as my partner to the tabloids today, sir."

Sampson raised his eyebrows. "And you know this how?"

"I'd rather not say yet, sir. I'd rather focus on what I plan to do about it."

"Kate, I told you once before, I want to know who's responsible for all this. If you know something, I want you to share it with me."

"Is that an order, sir? Because if it is, I will answer you, but I'd rather take care of today's business first, if you don't mind."

The commissioner sighed. "Kate, I'm not going to force you to tell me what you clearly don't want to share, for whatever reason"—he stared at her meaningfully—"but I like to keep control over what goes on in my shop. I'm sure you can understand that?"

"Yes, sir, I do. But I still don't know enough yet to act on anything except heading off today's disaster."

"Okay. Tell me what you have in mind. And, by the way, before you go any further, let me go on the record as saying I'm sorry."

"Sorry for what, sir?" Kate looked puzzled.

"Sorry that Jay is getting dragged into this and that the two of you have to go through such garbage."

"Thank you, sir. Have I told you lately that you're an extraordinary man?"

Sampson laughed. "I think I would have remembered if you had, but feel free."

"Most people wouldn't be as accepting as you and the governor have been, sir," Kate's voice cracked with emotion, "and I can't begin to tell you how much Jay and I appreciate that."

"You're welcome, Kate. Now, tell me what's going on."

Kate filled Sampson in on their plans for the morning. As she did so, he sat watching her intently, his fingers steepled under his chin.

When she finished, he said, "All right. I can understand why you want to get out ahead of the curve. I'll let the governor know—that will be one less thing you have to worry about."

"Are you sure, sir? I mean, it's my responsibility."

"I'll take care of it, Kate. You've got more than enough to worry about without having to do that also. I can assure you right now, though, that his reaction will be much the same as mine. We're behind you one hundred percent."

"Thank you, sir." As she stood and turned to leave, she added, "If you change your mind and we need to reevaluate my position here at DOCS, I'll understand."

"I won't hear of it. Good luck, Kate. You've got a lot of guts. I wish you the best."

"Thank you, sir."

# CHAPTER SEVEN

At 8:00 a.m., Kate and Jay rendezvoused once again at Barbara's office.

"Everything okay, love?" Kate asked, as she shut the door to Barbara's meeting room, where Jay was already seated at the table.

"So far, so good. Trish was very understanding, totally supportive, and willing to go to the managing editor for me to run interference."

"That's great."

"Yeah, but I'm not so sure that Mr. Standislau is going to be quite as accepting and helpful about all this as Trish has been. He's a pretty conservative, by-the-book kind of guy. If this goes down the way we think it will, the magazine's reputation could take a hit for allowing a reporter with close ties to a subject to write the story."

"Maybe. Did he know at the time what happened?"

"I don't know if Trish ever shared that with him or not. For her sake, I hope so. If this comes as a surprise to him—well, I sure don't want to get her in trouble with the big boss on my behalf."

"I'm sure she knows that, honey. She sounds like a tough, smart woman. I'm betting she knows how to handle Standislau." Kate noted Jay's grim expression. "In any event, that's not something we should be dwelling on right now. First things first."

"Right," Jay said with a noticeable lack of enthusiasm. "Today we let the wolves have at both of us. Tomorrow they can pick on my carcass. On day three they can take aim at *Time* for good measure."

Before Kate could respond, there was a knock at the door. Barbara stuck her head in.

"Ashton is here, ladies. She's in the waiting room. Want me to entertain her for a bit?"

They both sighed heavily. "No," Kate said, "I'll be out in a second."

As the door clicked shut once again, Kate crossed to where Jay was sitting and pulled her to her feet and into a hug. "I love you and I would do anything to protect you. You know that, right?"

Jay looked up into Kate's intense eyes. "I know that. It's just one of many things I love about you." She stood on tiptoes and kissed Kate softly on the mouth. Pulling back she added, "I haven't had a chance in all the excitement to say this, but I want you to know how very much I appreciate the fact that you let me be part of the decision-making process this time."

Kate hung her head. "I may be stubborn, Jay, but I'm not stupid."

Jay lifted Kate's chin with two fingers, forcing eye contact. "Hey. That's not what I was trying to say."

"I know."

"I'm only trying to say thank you for overriding your protective reflex so that we could face this monster together. It makes me feel incredibly loved and special."

"You *are* incredibly loved and special, sweetheart." Kate captured Jay's lips in a reverent kiss. "Stay here. I'll be right back with Wendy." At the door, she hesitated and looked back at Jay. "Deep breath, baby. Are you ready?"

Jay straightened up and assumed a no-nonsense pose. "Ready when you are."

"Right. Back in a flash."

Within two minutes, Kate walked back into Barbara's meeting space, followed by the reporter.

"Wendy Ashton, I'd like you to meet the love of my life, Ms. Jamison Parker. Jay, this is the intrepid reporter for the Associated Press, Ms. Wendy Ashton."

Jay stepped forward, her smile radiant, and thrust out her hand for Wendy to shake. "It's a pleasure to meet you, Ms. Ashton. I've heard so much about you."

"None of it good, I'm sure."

"On the contrary," Jay said, "Kate has told me you're fair and honorable. And believe me," she added with a chuckle, "she doesn't say that about every reporter she meets."

Kate, standing aside and observing, smirked. It was clear to her that Jay had already won the reporter over.

"I bet," said Wendy, noticeably more relaxed now than she was when she stepped into the room.

"Why don't we all sit down?" Kate suggested.

When they were settled, Wendy looked from Kate to Jay and back again. "Okay, let's start with an off-the-record question."

Both interviewees raised their eyebrows.

"Why on earth are you willing to step in front of all those reporters today when you've been avoiding them for months?"

As Kate started to open her mouth, Wendy held up a hand. "Don't answer. Not yet, anyway. That was sort of a rhetorical question. You'll ruin my fun if I don't get an opportunity to show your fiancée here how smart I am. Here's my guess—Breathwaite has figured out Jay's identity and you need to head him off at the pass."

Jay glanced to Kate before responding. "Oh, I am suitably impressed, Ms. Ashton."

"Please, if you don't start calling me Wendy I'm going to think I've turned into my mother." She turned to Kate. "What happened?" When Kate didn't immediately answer she added, "Off the record—just ally to ally."

Kate calculated how much she should reveal. She knew that if it hadn't been for the bond they'd developed as a result of recent events, she would never even have considered sharing that information. She also was well aware that Wendy had shown great faith in her, and she should return the favor.

"Breathwaite came to me this morning with Jay's identity and leaned on me to resign. I told him to go to hell, and here we are."

Wendy nodded. "He figured Jay was your weak spot. Well, nothing else has worked for him, I guess he felt like he needed to try a different approach."

"Apparently," Jay said with distaste.

"Obviously," Wendy said, "he was wrong."

Kate looked at Jay meaningfully before answering, "Jay is my strength—she and I will face Breathwaite and any other challenges together." She reached over and took Jay's hand, squeezing it gently.

Jay smiled up at her with tears in her eyes.

Wendy cleared her throat. "If this keeps up, even I'm gonna cry. Okay, let's get down to business then. What exactly are you announcing this morning and why?"

By mutual agreement, Kate took the lead in answering Wendy's questions.

"Jay and I decided to speak out this morning in order to restore some sense of peace and normalcy to our lives. We are proud of our relationship and have nothing to hide. Coming forward, we hope, will bring an end to the incessant questions, rumors, and innuendo about my private life that have swirled around in certain media outlets for the past several months."

"Why haven't you come forward before now?"

"We believed that our personal lives were just that, and that if we ignored the hubbub, perhaps prurient interest in us would die down. It hasn't, so here we are."

"What do you expect the reaction from your bosses will be to your announcement?"

Kate laughed. "I'm fairly confident that my employers are well aware of my preferences, as the matter has been well documented. Fortunately for me, both the governor and the commissioner are fair, open-minded individuals who are more interested in my job performance than they are in my private affairs."

Kate watched Jay out of the corner of her eye, knowing that she was waiting for the reporter to ask her the same thing. Her relief when Wendy moved on to the next question was palpable.

"How do you think this will change your lives from this point forward?"

"I am confident that going out to dinner together won't take quite as much planning," Kate quipped.

"Fair enough. Are you worried about fallout from those who are less, as you put it, open-minded than your employers?"

"We can't worry about things we can't control. We can only live our lives as honestly and truthfully as we can. We'll deal with everything else as it comes along."

The reporter sat back. "Okay, ladies. There's a lot more I should ask, as you both know, but I'm not interested in dragging your personal lives through the mud. I'm sure my colleagues will more than make up for my lack of curiosity in just a little while."

Kate touched Wendy on the sleeve. "Thank you."

Wendy looked at Kate, then at Jay. "No, thank you. Thank you for having the courage to come out like this, and for cheating that jerk out of his thunder. Thank you for paving the way and making it easier for the rest of us, hopefully, to follow in your footsteps. And thank you for your dignity. You both do all of us proud."

Jay spoke up for the first time since the formal interview started. "I can see why Kate has so much respect for you. You earn it."

"Thanks." Wendy winked and smiled. "And I can see why Kate has kept you a jealously guarded secret. She's going to be the envy of every red-blooded lesbian this side of the Mississippi. Now, if you don't mind, I've got a story to get on the wire and, if I'm not mistaken, you've got a date with the horde."

She was gone before either lover could respond.

⊰⊱

As they prepared to enter Meeting Room 6 underneath the Empire State Plaza where the press conference was to take place, Kate turned to

Jay. "Honey, Wendy was very circumspect with her questions. These folks won't be."

Jay tried to smile reassuringly. "I know that, Kate. I trust you to navigate us through this." She grasped Kate's hand and gave it a squeeze. "Whatever happens, I know you'll do your best. That's good enough for me."

"Have I told you lately how much I love you?"

Before Jay could answer, Kate pulled the door open. The flashes from dozens of still cameras, combined with the brightness of the TV klieg lights, blinded them both for an instant before they were able to get their bearings.

Kate led Jay to the front of the room where a podium was set up. On it were more than twenty microphones and handheld tape recorders. The mics all bore the colorful logos, or "flags," of their respective news outfits. As she looked at them, Kate recognized every major radio and television station in the Albany area, plus a few from other nearby media markets and one from New York City.

Kate looked out over the throng of people. There were many familiar faces—some who covered prison issues, others who had been colleagues and acquaintances from her days with WCAP.

She smiled, held out her hands in a gesture encompassing them all, and said, "What? Was it a slow news day today?"

Her comment broke the ice, and the room erupted in laughter.

"I'd like to say I'm surprised to see you all here, but given the number of you who've taken up residence in my back pocket in the last five or six months, I can't."

"Who's the beautiful blonde, Kate?"

"You never did have any patience, Walt, did you? If you wait a second, I'll get to that. First, I want to set a few ground rules." She glared at the tabloid reporters in the front row. "We'll be happy to entertain appropriate questions after I've made a statement. Anything of a purely voyeuristic nature will be ignored. Do we understand each other?"

There were generally grudging murmurs of agreement.

"Okay, then. I'd like you all to meet Ms. Jamison Parker. Jay is my partner, my better half, and, in my humble opinion, one of the brightest, most talented, most beautiful women in the world."

Jay blushed crimson as she looked on.

Kate exercised complete command over the room while working without any notes whatsoever.

"Although this may seem a bit odd to you, Ms. Parker and I have decided to come forward with her identity at this time because we value our privacy." She favored the reporters from some of the more aggressive tabloids with a glacial stare. "For nearly six months we have been subjected to intense media scrutiny, so-called journalists shadowing me at all hours of the day and night, grilling my colleagues and friends, even paying purported 'informed sources' for 'inside scoops.'"

A reporter for the *National Enquirer* piped up, "If you had just answered my questions, I wouldn't have had to get so inventive."

Kate glared daggers at him.

"It is our fervent hope that after standing here together today, answering questions about our personal lives that are so clearly beyond the realm of anything resembling news, you all will find the common decency to let us live our lives in peace." Kate looked over to her left at Jay, who looked for all the world as if she were listening to an interesting lecture. The bunching of her jaw muscles, however, told Kate a different story.

"We'll take appropriate questions now."

"Ms. Parker, you can talk for yourself, can't you?"

Jay stepped up closer to Kate at the podium and smiled engagingly as a new wave of flashes and whirring camera shutters went off. "I'd like to think so."

"How did you and Ms. Kyle meet?"

"We met initially in college."

"Have you been lovers since then?"

"No, as luck would have it, we reconnected earlier this year."

"Ms. Parker, haven't I seen your name before somewhere? Are you the same Jamison Parker whose byline I've seen in *Time* magazine?"

Kate muttered under her breath, "Well, that took all of four questions."

Jay squeezed her lover's hand behind the podium, out of sight of prying eyes and cameras. "Yes, I am a writer for *Time* and have been for several years."

"When you say you met in college, what does that mean? Can you elaborate on that a little?"

Jay, who had been expecting a follow-up question regarding her cover story on Kate, smiled. "Sure. We met for the first time when I was badly injured skiing. Kate was the ski patroller who rescued me."

"Did she steal your heart then?"

"Let's just say she made quite an impression on me."

"How about you, Kate? Were you smitten all the way back then?"

"What's not to love?" She winked.

There were nods of agreement among the male journalists.

Before anyone could ask any more questions, Kate said, "Thanks, folks, but you all have deadlines, and we have work to do ourselves."

She led Jay away from the podium and hustled her out the door.

When they were safely away from the microphones and cameras, Jay leaned close. "That was an interesting turn of events. What happened there?"

Kate, knowing she was referring to the abrupt change in lines of questioning, laughed. "Marcia happened, that's what."

"And who, exactly, is Marcia?"

"Marcia is an old friend of mine from my WCAP days. She's the station's top street reporter."

"So she did that on purpose—to help us out?"

"Mmm-hmm."

Jay looked incredulous.

Kate said, "Did you get a look at who her photographer was?"

"No, I couldn't see anything with all those flashes going off."

"Do you remember Gene, my cameraman?"

"Of course, I got to spend an entire afternoon with him looking at old footage of you when I was working on the story. How could I forget?"

"He was the photog today. He remembers you too."

Realization dawned on Jay. "Ah. As soon as he saw that it was me, he knew where the questions were going to go."

"Sure did. And he tipped his reporter off."

"Great guy."

"Yeah," Kate sighed wistfully, thinking about the way she had been forced to leave her television family behind. "I miss him. Gene is a good man and a loyal friend."

Jay rubbed shoulders with her. "Maybe we could have him over to the house sometime?"

"Maybe," Kate said vaguely.

"You don't think he'll be all right with us?"

"I don't know, love. My sexuality is not something we ever discussed. Plus, he had a pretty big crush on you when he met you."

"No way." Jay gaped at Kate.

"Way. He wanted to ask you out."

"You never told me that."

"I didn't think it was relevant at the time. And I was a little focused on my own attempts to win your heart."

"Aw, you're so sweet."

"Anyway," Kate went on, "I'm not sure how accepting he'd be."

"If he's important to you, Kate, maybe it's worth the risk to find out."

"Perhaps. Oh, and for the record?"

"Yes?"

"Marcia is gay."

"Who?"

"Marcia. The reporter who changed the subject for us."

"Oh." Jay was quiet for a beat. "She is?"

"Yep. I'm sure glad she doesn't hold a grudge."

"What do you mean?"

Kate took Jay by the hand. "I can't count the number of times I turned her down for dates."

Jay chuckled. "Poor girl."

"Nah, she's better off without me."

"Lucky for me."

"There's no contest, sweetheart." Kate looked at Jay lovingly. "By the way, I was very impressed with the way you handled yourself in there."

"Nice change of subject. I'll let you get away with it this time."

"I appreciate your generosity."

"How long do you think it will take before the cover piece becomes the story?"

"Two news cycles."

"Well, that gives us at least until this afternoon, anyway."

"Nah, I mean two *newspaper* cycles."

Jay looked at Kate inquiringly.

"Think about it, Jay—this story isn't really geared for radio and television—it would take too much in-depth research and it's not important enough to their audience."

"That's your area of expertise, so I'll defer to you. Considering the newspapers, then, we've got until at least day after tomorrow for the cover article to become the focus. Tomorrow's editions will be all about my identity and the fact that we came forward."

"Exactly."

Jay stopped walking for a moment and turned to Kate. "If it's not a radio-and-television kind of story, why were they all there?"

"Curiosity, mostly," Kate answered. "And because they couldn't very well ignore the press conference altogether if their print compatriots were covering it."

"Will they run the story?"

"Oh, sure. But it will be old news by noon for the radio folks. The TV guys will air it at noon and again repackaged at six, and that will be the end of it for them."

"Even after round two?"

"Yeah, I'm betting that only the print folks'll latch on to the follow-up story."

"That's some consolation, then."

They had reached Kate's car, which was parked in the visitors' lot underneath the complex of government buildings.

Kate said, "We'll see about that." She kissed Jay on the mouth, lingering long enough to taste her lips and explore a bit, enjoying the freedom of no longer having to care who saw them.

"Mmm," Jay hummed. "What was that for?"

Kate smiled at the slightly dreamy expression on her face. "Just because I could. And because I love you so very much. You really did great today, Jay."

"You did all the hard work. I just came along for the ride."

"And what a ride it's going to be."

At precisely 10:01 a.m. Breathwaite began making phone calls. After the third attempt netted him an answering machine instead of a reporter, he called the general number for the Legislative Correspondents' Association room, where all press releases, advisories, and notices of press conferences got dropped off for reporters to collect.

"LCA room," a bored-sounding voice intoned.

"Hazel? David Breathwaite here." Hazel had been running the LCA room for more than twenty-five years, and Breathwaite knew her from his days as a newspaperman covering the capital beat. She always sounded uninterested, but he knew that she had her finger on everything that went on with the journalists who worked within the bustle of her domain.

"Yeah, what can I do for you on this fine morning?"

"I've tried a few of the guys and I can't seem to get anybody. Where is everyone? Sleeping in this morning?"

"Nope. Out on the job hustling already, as a matter of fact."

"You're kidding. This early? Something big come in?"

"If you like the gossipy side of news, then yeah."

Breathwaite, who was only half paying attention, said dismissively, "I could give a rat's you-know-what, Hazel, but some people like that sort of thing, I suppose."

"This was a big one, smart guy."

"Okay, I can see you're dying to tell, so let's have it."

"Press conference got called all of a sudden-like for nine thirty this morning. Probably still going on. Friend of yours, I think."

Breathwaite stopped reading the document he had in his hand and gave the conversation his full attention. "Really?"

"Yeah. Katherine Kyle. I figure you two run in the same circles, no?"

There was a roaring in his ears that was so loud he thought it might consume him. "Sure. What was the topic of the press conference, Hazel?"

"Got the advisory right here. Want me to fax you a copy?"

"Yes, please."

"Okay, it'll be there in a little bit. Hey, what's a seven letter word for 'one who changes allegiances'?"

It was all he could do not to go through the phone line. "Traitor," he ground out. "Hazel? Could you send my fax, *then* finish your crossword puzzle? I'm kind of in a hurry."

"Aren't we all these days, David? See you around sometime. Don't be a stranger." She hung the phone up in his ear.

By the time the fax arrived twenty minutes later, Breathwaite had already summoned Kirk.

"The bitch went out ahead of us. What the hell?" He rounded on his investigator. "I thought you said you tapped her office phone last night. How could we not have known she was up to this?"

"Probably because there were no outgoing or incoming calls to her line at DOCS before nine thirty-five a.m., and that was some yahoo reporter up in Malone, New York looking for some information on a new inmate."

"How did she set it up, then?"

"I suspect she left the building shortly after you did, but I don't know for sure, since you didn't tell me to tail her."

"Do I have to tell you everything? Damn it all to hell!"

Kirk, as usual, seemed completely unfazed by the tirade.

"Okay. All right." Breathwaite paced as he tried to calm himself down. "We monitor all the news outlets to see how the story is playing, then we go ahead with part two of the plan."

"Which is, what?"

"Outing her girlfriend isn't enough. I want Kyle to suffer. We're going to ruin Parker's career and make sure she never gets a job with another magazine as long as she lives."

"How is that going to further your objective of pushing Kyle out of DOCS?"

"We're just going to keep turning up the heat on all fronts until she folds. Fuck with me, will she? We'll see about that."

When she got home, Jay was surprised to find that she had a message on her office answering machine from Barbara.

"Jay, I wasn't sure you'd pick up the home line at this point, so I thought I'd try reaching you this way. I hope you don't mind. I was wondering if you'd care to join me for lunch? Nothing terribly fancy, I'm afraid, but I could whip us up a couple of nice salads and perhaps some homemade chicken noodle soup. Let me know if you're available. My schedule is somewhat flexible this afternoon."

Jay shook her head. "I'm willing to bet your schedule didn't start out being all that flexible before all hell broke loose this morning, Dr. Jones."

At twelve thirty, Jay knocked on the front door of Barbara's house, a beautiful stone mansion in the heart of a ritzy suburb.

"Jay, I'm so glad you could make it." Barbara enveloped her in a hug.

"Thanks for the invitation, Doc. I appreciate the effort it must have taken to clear your calendar."

"Nonsense. No one was dying to see me today. Get in here."

"Uh-huh." Since she'd come to Albany to live with Kate, Jay had grown to love and cherish Barbara's rapier-sharp wit and wicked sense of humor. They had gotten to know each other well.

They settled at the eating island in the middle of Barbara's gourmet kitchen. The first time she walked into this room, Jay had felt an acute stab of kitchen envy. All of the appliances were stainless steel and commercial grade, the pots and pans rivaled those of top restaurants, and the work surfaces were large and efficiently laid out.

Jay felt the other woman's eyes appraising her.

"What?"

"It's okay to feel a bit undone after the morning you've had, you know."

"Do I look that bad?"

Barbara laughed. "Jamison Parker, I have never seen you look anything less than perfect. But judging by the bulge in your temporomandibular joint, your jaw must be killing you."

Jay smiled. "That's a rather fancy way to say you can see that I'm stressed out."

"Med school had to be good for something. Want to talk about it?"

"What's to talk about? I just outed myself in spectacular fashion in front of a pack of hungry tabloid reporters, Breathwaite wants Kate's head on a platter and figures to get to her through me, and my editor is meeting with the grand poobah at *Time* to discuss what to do about me. My life is completely under control."

Barbara put a comforting hand on her arm. "I can't even begin to imagine what it feels like to be you at the moment. All I can do is listen, offer support, and remind you that tomorrow is another day."

"Yeah," Jay said glumly. "Tomorrow, in addition to putting my personal life under a microscope, the vultures will go after me professionally."

"What makes you so sure they will?"

Jay sighed, looking down at her hands as they methodically shredded a paper napkin. "It's the next logical story. And the door was opened by a reporter this morning who connected me with *Time*. The only reason we managed to dodge the bullet this time was that a reporter friend of Kate's intervened with an unrelated question."

"It's nice to have friends. Have you been monitoring the news?"

"Yes. I listened to the three major radio stations' newscasts at eleven and noon, and I watched the noon newscasts on all three local television stations."

"What's the verdict?"

"About what you'd expect. Everyone except for WCAP rehashed Kate's firing, the *Enquirer* pictures, et cetera, over footage of the two of us coming into the press conference, me standing there listening to Kate talk, and us leaving. Then they all played the sound bite of Kate talking about our reasons for coming forward today. Finally, they closed with a close-up of me. Ugh."

"What did CAP do?"

"They conveniently managed to worm their way around mentioning that Kate had ever worked for them."

"Lovely bunch over there."

"Yeah. Kate never says anything, but I know how hurt she was at the way she was treated."

"I'm sure you're right about that, but your Katherine is a very stoic person."

"Yes, she is." Jay grew pensive. "When I look back now at what happened to her last May, I have a far greater appreciation for the way she handled herself. In the middle of the media circus today," Jay said, almost to herself, "I wanted to run away. Part of that was about wanting to get myself out of the picture so that Breathwaite wouldn't have me to use as ammunition against Kate."

"Jamison," Barbara said sternly, "that is no more the answer for you now than it was for her then."

Jay looked up, startled at the vehemence in her friend's voice. "I know that. I'm not going anywhere, Barbara. You didn't let me finish."

"I'm sorry."

"The other reason I wanted to run was simply because I was scared. I didn't want to have to undergo that kind of media scrutiny. And I hate that I was feeling that way. Kate didn't have the luxury of making a conscious choice when she got outed. At least this was something I could try to prepare for."

"But you weren't really ready, were you?" Barbara asked quietly.

Jay hung her head. "No, I wasn't. I'm just feeling a bit overwhelmed, I guess."

"That's not surprising. Nor is it anything to be ashamed of. Have you talked to Kate about how you feel?"

"She's been flat out since she got back to the office. I planned to talk to her tonight."

"Good idea. The best thing you two can do is keep the lines of communication open. She needs you, Jay. And, just as importantly, you need her."

"Don't I know it." Jay's eyes glistened with tears. "Why is this happening to us? What have we done to deserve this?"

Barbara moved around the island to hug Jay to her. "Nothing, honey. Neither one of you has done anything to deserve this. That's what makes this so incredibly aggravating."

Barbara rubbed Jay's back in circles as she sobbed. "I know, honey. Let it all out. It's okay to cry. I'd be crying too."

After a few moments, Jay pulled back. "I'm so sorry, Barbara. I didn't mean to do that."

"Don't you ever be sorry for letting your feelings show, Jay. Bottling all that up inside will make you sick. I'm your doctor, I ought to know." She winked.

"Here you invited me for a nice lunch, and I've turned it into a pity party."

"No you most certainly have not. I'd like to think I'm your friend too, not just Kate's."

"Of course you are."

"Okay then, supporting each other in the tough times is part of what friends do. It's in the fine print when you sign the contract." She put her fingers underneath Jay's chin to lift it. "Right, friend?"

Jay sniffled and blew her nose in the tissue Barbara supplied. "Right. Thanks, friend."

"Any time."

Kate arrived home just in time to catch the six o'clock news. She hustled into the living room, where Jay was already planted in front of the television.

"Hi, baby," she said, as Jay made room for her on the couch. Kate thought she looked exhausted.

"Hi, sweetheart. You're just in time for the show."

"Yeah, sorry about that. I wanted to be home earlier, but the phone just kept ringing off of the hook."

"Don't worry about it. I understand."

Their conversation trailed off as the anchorman intoned, "In an unusual move today, former local television news anchor Katherine Kyle appeared before a packed news conference to announce the identity of the 'other woman.'"

The picture on-screen was an enlargement of the tabloid pictures of Kate and Jay, whose back was turned to the camera.

"Kyle, who was fired from competitor WCAP after these compromising photos of her and an unidentified female companion turned up on the front page of the *National Enquirer* last May, explained her reason for coming forward at this time..."

In silence, the women watched a clip of Kate talking about their desire to preserve their privacy.

The anchorman continued, "Jamison Parker, the other woman in the *Enquirer* photos who was introduced to the media today, is a writer for *Time* magazine. Kyle is now the spokesperson for the state prison system."

As the camera shifted to the co-anchor for the next story, Kate changed the channel to another network, then the third. In all three instances, the story was the same. When it was over, she turned to Jay and took her hands.

"Are you okay, sweetheart?"

"I've had better days."

"Yeah, I know. Me too."

For a moment, they just sat there, content to be in each other's company.

Jay broke the silence. "You were right. The television and radio stories were pretty basic and mostly benign."

"Jay, the newspapers won't be as superficial. They aren't constrained by thirty-second sound bites."

"I know."

"I'm so sorry about all this."

"Kate, it's not your fault. You didn't ask for any of this to happen."

"Still, I wish we'd had more time to talk through all of the ramifications and your feelings before we acted."

"There was no time. Breathwaite would have done it for us in less than an hour, Kate."

"That doesn't mean I don't wish I could've done something different—found some way to make this less painful for you."

"Let's face it—this isn't what either of us had in mind, but we had no choice. I am glad, in some sense, to have it out in the open. Now we won't have to hide or make an elaborate plan just to go out to dinner together."

"That is the upside." Kate kissed Jay's hand. "The downside is that this isn't going to be just a one-day story. If the reporters don't figure it out themselves, I'm sure Breathwaite will help them find ways to get more mileage out of it."

"Yeah, he pretty much told you that this morning."

"It seems to be his mission in life at the moment to make me as miserable as possible. If that means going after you, then he certainly won't hesitate to do so." The very thought of Breathwaite trying to intentionally hurt Jay made Kate crazy.

"Lucky me."

"It's ironic that the very thing I was most afraid of when I ran away last spring is coming true now, long after the story should have been ancient history."

"Kate," Jay ran her fingers over her lover's cheek, "I understand so much better now why you did what you did. I felt a little bit the same way this morning—I wanted to run to take away Breathwaite's ammunition." Kate's body stiffened perceptibly. "Don't worry, love. I'm not going anywhere."

"You'd better not." Kate turned so that she faced Jay. "I was wrong to leave you then. We've discussed that. I didn't handle that situation very well, and we both paid a steep emotional price for my actions."

"No," Jay interjected, "we both made mistakes."

"Yes, that's true, but the mistakes you made would never have happened if I hadn't run in the first place—if I had stayed and talked to you about how we should have dealt with the situation instead of making unilateral choices."

"It's old news."

"No, Jay, it isn't. Because I feel like I did something equally bad this morning."

"What?" Jay asked.

"I forced you to do something you might not have been ready to do for my own selfish reasons."

"Whoa, wait just a minute here. I made the choice to come out this morning. *I* did. Not you. You gave me options and I made a decision. You didn't put a gun to my head. I knew what I was doing."

"Jay, you made a decision in the heat of the moment because you wanted to help me. That doesn't mean it was the right thing to do for you."

"I'll admit that busting out of the closet in that fashion wasn't the highest thing on my to-do list when I woke up this morning, but I'm not sorry."

"You might be before this is all over."

"Do you remember months ago when I told you that my career meant nothing to me when compared to you? Kate? Look at me."

Kate dragged her eyes from her hands to Jay's face.

"Do you remember that? I told you they could have the job. All I wanted was to be with you."

"Yes, but it was theoretical then, Jay. This is real."

"I realize that, honey. And I'm not going to tell you I'm not scared to death, because I am. But I also know that as long as I have you, nothing else really matters." As if to punctuate the point, Jay pressed her lips to Kate's.

Kate pulled Jay into her arms, surrounding her with love and kissing her tenderly on the mouth and face. "I love you, Jay. More than anything in the world."

"I love you too, Kate. Nothing, and no one, is going to change that or come between us. I won't allow it to happen."

"Me either, baby. Me either."

The *New York Times* ran a small paragraph on the story buried inside the Metro news section. The *Albany Times Union* carried Wendy's AP story on page B2.

The *New York Daily News* ran a teaser on the top of page one, with the full story on page three. There were several quotes from both Kate and Jay, along with a "no comment" from Kate's former news director. Commissioner Sampson was quoted as saying, "Ms. Kyle's personal life is just that. I am very pleased with her performance at DOCS. She is an outstanding spokeswoman and I am lucky to have her." The governor could not be reached for comment. The managing editor of *Time* confirmed that Jamison Parker worked for the magazine, but would say nothing further "at this time."

The *New York Post* also teased the story in a banner across the top of its front page. The story itself appeared on the inside front cover and took up half the page. The headline read, "Disgraced Former News Anchor Outs Girlfriend; It's About *Time*."

Kate, who was reading the newspapers in her office as she did every morning at 6:15, groaned. Truthfully, she didn't want to read any further, given the *Post's* conservative bent.

"Better to read it and get it over with. No sense putting it off."

She ran her hand across her face. Neither she nor Jay had slept particularly well the night before. Kate tried to focus on the page in front of her.

Katherine Kyle, the disgraced television news anchor who appeared on the cover of *Time* magazine as a hero one day and as a lesbian lothario on the front page of the tabloids the very next day, is at it again. Kyle, the current spokesperson for the state prison system, went public yesterday with the identity of her girlfriend, the woman with whom she was photographed in a compromising position on a Caribbean beach last May.

The woman is none other than Jamison Parker, 24, a writer of some repute for *Time* magazine. It was Parker's cover story about her earlier this year that catapulted Kyle to media stardom.

"What makes this so interesting," according to Tom Daigault, a media and ethics expert at New York University, "is the question of the relationship between Ms. Kyle and Ms. Parker at the moment the story was written. If they were an item at the time, it would raise serious ethical questions about the objectivity of the piece."

A careful review of the timeline by the *Post* indicates that the pictures of Kyle and Parker in an intimate pose on the beach were taken prior to the release of the *Time* cover story.

A request for comment from Vander Standislau, managing editor of *Time*, went unanswered.

Governor Charles Hyland, who hired Kyle after the photo scandal, told the *Post*, "Katherine Kyle is among the finest, bravest, most honest people I know. She deserves every accolade she received at the time of the tragic capitol bombing. I read the *Time* magazine story when it came out. I thought it was very accurate, fair, and balanced."

The governor added that he had no intention of asking Kyle for her resignation.

Kate slapped her hand down on top of the paper. "Damn it. Damn it all to hell." She picked up the phone.

"Hello?"

"Hi, Jay."

"Oh, hey. I don't suppose you've gotten to the *Post* yet, have you?" Jay asked.

"'Fraid so."

Jay sighed heavily. "I just got off the phone with Trish. I'm leaving for the city in half an hour. I've got a one o'clock meeting with Trish and Mr. Standislau."

"Oh, Jay. Did Trish give you any indication where things stand?"

"No. She was pretty quiet."

"It'll be all right, honey," Kate said, trying to reassure both of them. "Do you want me to go with you?"

"That's very tempting, sweetheart, but no. I have to do this on my own."

"Are you coming right back here?"

"I guess that depends on how the meeting goes."

"Will you call me afterward?"

"Of course, Kate."

"Okay. Jay?"

"Yeah?"

"I love you. We'll get through this, together."

"I know we will. I love you too, Kate."

Kate held onto the receiver long after Jay hung up. She didn't like the tension and sense of dread in her lover's voice. Furthermore, she *really* didn't like not being able to do anything to make it go away.

# CHAPTER EIGHT

The air in Vander Standislau's penthouse office was chilled, which did not help Jay feel any more relaxed. This was her first trip to the big boss's suite—the first time, in fact, that she had been in his presence for more than a passing moment at a cocktail party.

He was an imposing man, big and burly, with a salt-and-pepper brush cut, coal black eyes, and a moustache. His suit was immaculately tailored, charcoal gray with a white shirt, red tie, and matching diamond cuff links and tie tack.

The office mirrored his stature—larger than life. The walls were papered to resemble a South American rain forest, the trees and birds seemingly lifelike. Jay knew that the managing editor was fascinated with that part of the world—he had taken several trips there just in the few years she had worked for him. There was a picture on his desk of him dressed in camouflage, a huge macaw on his arm, and another of him using a machete to cut his way through dense underbrush. And, to Jay's astonishment, there was a diploma sitting on the credenza from her alma mater.

Jay tried hard not to fidget in the uncomfortably stiff visitor's chair. She stole a glance at Trish, who sat next to her in a similar chair and who looked no more comfortable than she felt. When Jay arrived at the office, Trish had already been upstairs for nearly an hour. The fact that Jay hadn't been able to talk to her editor before this meeting only added to her unease.

"Ms. Parker, I'm afraid you've placed us in an unusual position." His voice was a smooth, rich baritone. "While I am not averse to defending our stories, or our writers, I must say, you've put us in a bit of a bind."

"I'm so sorry, Mr. Standislau, I never intended for this to happen."

He leaned forward suddenly in his chair. "For what to happen, Ms. Parker? To take up with the subject of your story, to write a story about your paramour, or to have it splashed across newspapers everywhere? What exactly," he ground out, "is it that you wished to prevent?"

Jay wanted nothing more at that moment than for the floor to open up and swallow her whole. Trish shifted subtly in her chair and gave her an imperceptible nod, as if to say, "Time to defend yourself, kiddo."

"Sir," Jay said, "I'd like to clear the air about what happened last May and the story I wrote."

"By all means, Ms. Parker, please do."

"Sir," she unconsciously wiped her palms on her skirt, "I first met Katherine Kyle in college, but we were never formally introduced. I had quite lost track of her until I saw her on television the night before the bombings. After the second explosion and the subsequent coverage, I went down to the scene to see if I could find her."

"And you were in Albany for an interview with the governor at the time, correct?"

"Yes, sir. I was supposed to sit down with the governor for a cover piece the day the bombings occurred, but, as you can imagine, the interview was postponed."

"I see. Go on."

Jay found it hard to believe that Trish hadn't already filled Standislau in on all of the details, but she didn't think it appropriate to point that out at that moment.

"I found Ms. Kyle after she finished broadcasting and persuaded her to see a doctor for her injuries. I accompanied her. When the morning news shows wanted her as a guest the next morning, she offered to give me a ride back to the city, where my interview with the governor had been rescheduled for later in the afternoon."

"Very handy."

His tone angered Jay. She sat up a little straighter in her chair and met his gaze unflinchingly.

"I was grateful for the generous offer. I conducted the interview with Governor Hyland, which appeared on the cover, as you know, the week before Ka—Ms. Kyle's story. When I handed in the Hyland story, I was assigned to write a story on the new breed of journalists, focusing specifically on Ms. Kyle."

"And you made no mention, at the time, of your relationship to the subject?"

"Beyond a passing acquaintance, I had no relationship with the subject at the time I was given the assignment." Jay knew she was walking a fine line. What she said was the truth, technically speaking. She also knew, however, that her feelings for Kate ran far deeper than acquaintanceship from the outset. In her mind, though, she had two objectives—protect Trish, and defend her own integrity as a journalist.

Standislau stared at her hard. Then he turned to her editor. "Ms. Stanton, is that your recollection as well?"

"Yes, sir. That is my impression, and I have no reason to think otherwise."

He evaluated her for a moment, his dark eyes boring into her before he returned his attention to Jay.

"Continue."

"Yes, sir. I returned to Albany to conduct the research and interviews necessary to put together the story. I spent a good deal of time with Ms. Kyle, as well as with her associates, colleagues, and friends, trying to get an accurate picture of her personality, her journalistic style, and her philosophy."

"And during that time you became romantically involved with her?"

Jay was annoyed at the interruption and at the assumption.

"No, sir. I did not. Mr. Standislau, I take my responsibilities as a journalist very seriously. I went to Albany to do a job, and that's exactly what I did. I conducted extensive research, interviewed coworkers, bombing victims, Ms. Kyle's superiors, viewed hours of archived footage, and wrote what I think is a very balanced, very fair piece. If you disagree, then I will submit to your judgment. But I imagine that if you hadn't liked the story, or thought it was somehow biased, you would have said so at the time and the piece would have been killed."

There was a stunned silence in the room. Jay's jaw clicked shut, but her eyes remained defiant. Trish gave her a ghost of a smile before her face resumed its neutral expression. Vander Standislau's mouth was set in a grim line.

"You are quite right, Ms. Parker," he said deliberately. "Had I suspected any personal agenda, I most certainly would have pulled the story and disciplined you accordingly. I do not deny that the piece was a brilliant bit of work. In fact, even after rereading it in the current light, I would proudly hold it up to scrutiny as a fine example of journalistic excellence."

Out of the corner of her eye, Jay saw Trish's mouth twitch as she attempted to suppress a smile.

"However, Ms. Parker, that is not the point here." He leveled his intense gaze upon her once again. "You have made us vulnerable to all manner of allegations of impropriety, and in the process, you have called into question our integrity as an impartial source for news and information. That is unacceptable."

"Yes, sir." Jay faced him squarely, prepared for the worst.

"What do you suggest we do about that, Ms. Parker?"

"I would not presume to tell you, sir, how to run your business."

"Yes, I see." Standislau appeared lost in thought for a moment. "All right. This is the way we'll play it for now. I will issue a statement on behalf of the magazine standing by the story and by you."

"Thank you, sir."

He held up a hand. "For now, Ms. Parker."

"Yes, sir."

"I will also indicate that our investigation into the matter continues. That way, if I find that any of what you've told me is not true, or if other facts come to light that do not support your version of events, I have room to maneuver. Do you understand my meaning, Ms. Parker?"

"Yes, sir. I assure you that what I've told you is the truth."

"For your sake, you'd better hope so, Ms. Parker. In the meantime, I suggest you take a couple of weeks off until this whole matter dies a natural death."

"Yes, sir." Jay's voice sounded dejected even to her own ears.

"Cheer up, Ms. Parker, you'll continue to get paid during your absence."

"Yes, sir."

"I want you to understand, Jamison."

She looked up quickly at the use of her first name.

"I think you're a talented journalist. You made a very serious mistake by not coming forward at the outset to explain the nature of your relationship with Katherine Kyle, even if it began after you completed the research for the story."

Jay was unable to hide her surprise at the sudden realization that Standislau had known the truth before she even began to answer his questions.

As if to confirm her thoughts, he said, "I am aware of the fact that you informed Patricia of your relationship after the story was released. The fact that I was not made aware of the circumstances at the time is something Ms. Stanton and I have already discussed."

Jay felt a pang of regret for the tongue-lashing she imagined Trish had already received.

"I also appreciate that you were willing to try to stand on your own and protect your editor. That says a lot to me about who you are as a person. I like that kind of loyalty and nobility."

"Thank you, sir." She tried to keep the agitation out of her voice.

"Jamison, it is not mine to approve or disapprove of your lifestyle. Your choices might not be mine, but your private life should be your own. Having said that, if I ever discover that you have crossed that line and made the personal professional again or vice versa, I'll fire you in a heartbeat. Is that understood?"

"Yes, sir."

His voice gentled somewhat. "Good. I suspect that this whole matter is going to get more difficult for you before it gets easier. I want you to know that my door is always open to you. I've weathered a fair amount in my time, and if I can shed some light or offer some assistance, I'll do that, as long as it doesn't reflect badly on this magazine or its writers. Patricia assures me that you're a quick study and that you are unlikely to make the same mistake twice. I hope she's right about that."

Jay smiled for the first time. "I'll probably make plenty of new ones, sir, but not the same one, and never quite so spectacularly, again. I promise you that."

"Good." Standislau laughed. "I want you to call me once a day while this story is still hot. Where it involves the reputation of the magazine, we'll strategize together. That way, neither one of us will be surprised at what gets printed."

"I can't vouch for what the tabloids might do, sir."

"Can anyone, Jamison? Can anyone?" In dismissing her he added, "Good luck. I have a feeling you're going to need it."

"Thank you, sir." She rose from her chair and, with a fleeting look at Trish, left the office.

It was another twenty minutes before Trish came back downstairs, looking glum and resolute. "I figured you'd still be here, kiddo."

"I am so, so sorry for getting you in trouble."

Trish held up her hand to forestall further apologies. "Don't, Jay. I had choices at the time, and I made them. Perhaps I exercised poor judgment in not sharing what I knew of the situation with Standislau then, but who in the world could've foreseen this mess."

"I should have gone to him myself. Better yet, I should've disclosed that I knew Kate when you assigned me the story in the first place."

"You're going to drive yourself nuts with the should haves. Let it go. There's nothing either one of us can do to change that now. What's important is how we handle what's coming."

"Okay."

"Both Vander and I have already had eight phone calls apiece from news outlets wanting everything from your work history, to a list of every story you've ever written, to comments on *Time*'s ethical standards."

Jay groaned. "And?"

"And we discussed it at length. Vander will issue a statement on behalf of the magazine saying that you have an exemplary record with *Time*. It will state that we are satisfied that you wrote a fair and balanced piece on Katherine Kyle, that a preliminary investigation confirms that you did not have an intimate relationship with your subject at the time you were assigned the piece, and that any relationship began after the research, interviews, and story outline were completed."

Jay contemplated this. It was probably the best she could hope for under the circumstances. "Is that all?"

Trish added gently, "It will also say that you've been suspended for two weeks for failing to disclose a potential conflict of interest."

"Oh." Even though she'd heard Standislau tell her she would not be working the next two weeks, the wording of the statement struck her like a fist in the chest. Jay always prided herself on her journalistic integrity. Now everyone would question her work.

As if reading her mind, Trish said, "Jamison, I want you to know I have complete faith in you and your character. I wouldn't hesitate for a second to give you the most important story on the list, knowing you'd do a great job with it."

"Thanks, Trish. I'm sorry I put you in a situation where you felt you had to say that. It never should have happened in the first place."

"You're right."

Jay's head snapped up in surprise at the bluntness of the comment.

Trish shrugged. "If you had told me up front that you knew Kate, I probably would have questioned you about your relationship to her and maybe assigned the story to someone with no potential personal bias. But that's water under the bridge now. Some lessons are learned the hard way."

"Yeah," Jay answered dejectedly.

"Hey. Chin up. It's not the end of the world. It could've come out much worse."

"It's not over yet."

"No," Trish put her hand on Jay's shoulder, "it's not. But Vander and I agree that you have a great future in front of you with this magazine. We just need to weather this storm."

"That may be easier said than done."

"Maybe. But you can bet that Vander and I are going to do everything we can to make sure we all get through this in good shape."

"I appreciate that, Trish." As if it had just occurred to her, Jay asked, "Did you get suspended too?"

"No, Vander decided that suspending me would raise more questions about who knew what and when."

"He's right about that," Jay murmured. "No one outside of the three of us, and Kate, of course, knows that I told you about what happened immediately after the fact."

"Exactly. So I get to stay on the job. But don't think I didn't get more than an ass chewing. My ears are still ringing, in fact."

"I'm so sorry."

"No. No more apologies from you, kiddo. Let's just move on, okay?"

"Okay. I guess I'll see you in two weeks."

"Jay?"

Jay, who had turned to leave Trish's office, looked back inquiringly.

"I want to hear from you every day to know how you're doing. My heart is with you. You two are going to get through this just fine. You're tough."

"Thanks, Trish. Your support means a lot to me." To Jay's horror, tears sprang to her eyes.

"I'm here for you, Jay."

Unable to say anything more, she merely nodded and fled the office.

Jay aimlessly wandered the streets of New York, trying in vain to process everything that had happened to her in the past twenty-four hours. The task was daunting. Never in her wildest imagination had she envisioned becoming such a public figure, and certainly not for the reason she found herself in the headlines that day. It was her job to chronicle others' lives, not vice versa.

The late October wind was blowing, biting into Jay's exposed skin, but she barely noticed. Her hands jammed into the pockets of her London Fog raincoat, she pushed forward, head bent and eyes on the ground. They were only into day one of the news cycle and already the roof was beginning to cave in. What would happen when the next round of stories appeared?

Trish said that reporters were inquiring about her work history and stories she had written. As a journalist herself, Jay knew the questions wouldn't stop there. Everything in her life would become fair game. Old acquaintances would be interviewed and embarrassing incidents would be dragged out and laid bare for all the world to see. For Jay, this was the ultimate nightmare.

Growing up in her father's house, knowing that the slightest misstep might lead to physical or sexual abuse, Jay strived to call as little attention to herself as possible. As an adult, she recognized that her need to fly below the radar as a child had been a necessary survival instinct. Yet despite her knowledge that she was no longer in danger from her father or anyone else, the drive to do everything just right burned brightly in her still. The idea of having her life examined under a microscope, combined with the forthcoming public reprimand by her employer for showing poor judgment, made Jay wish that the earth would swallow her whole. She wanted desperately to run—to hide from the attention and the shame of having made such a colossal error.

*"You'll never amount to anything."*

She could hear her father's oft-repeated words echoing loudly in her head. For years her silent refrain had been, *"I'll show you."*

She worked so diligently to achieve success, and she made it—or so she thought. At the moment, however, she felt every bit the failure he predicted she would be.

"Stupid, stupid, stupid," she said, not realizing that she had spoken out loud.

She wasn't even able to bring herself to call Kate yet. She knew she needed to do it soon, though—Kate would be worried sick wondering what happened in the meeting. With a heavy sigh, Jay turned and headed for her Greenwich Village apartment.

When she opened the door, she was accosted by a flying dog. Fred weaved his way in and out of her legs, his tail wagging madly. She looked up to see Kate standing there, smiling at the tableau.

Jay was flooded with a sense of relief at the sight of her. Crossing the room, she threw herself into Kate's arms, fresh tears streaming down her face.

"Shh, it's all right, love." Kate stroked her back, rocking gently from side to side. "It's all going to be all right."

Jay continued to sob uncontrollably, all of the pent-up emotion pouring out of her soul.

Kate steered them over to the couch and pulled Jay down to sit on her lap. She stroked her hair, murmuring words of comfort, until it appeared that the tears were all spent.

Jay took the offered Kleenex and tried to catch her breath. "I'm so sorry, sweetheart. I didn't mean for that to happen."

Quietly, Kate said, "That's been coming for a long time, baby. I'm glad you got it out of your system." She tilted Jay's face up to see her eyes more clearly. "Feel better now?"

"Not really." Jay looked up beseechingly. "Kate? Am I a failure?"

"What? Honey, whatever would make you ask a question like that?"

Jay rested her forehead against the side of Kate's neck. "When I was a little girl, my father always told me I'd be a failure—an outcast. And that I was lucky to have him, because no one else would ever want me. Maybe he was right after all."

Kate pulled back so that Jay had to lift her head. "You listen to me, Jamison Parker. You are bright, talented, and remarkably accomplished."

"Kate—"

"No. Don't say anything yet. I'm not finished."

Jay's jaw clicked shut, the words of protest dying on her lips.

"Jay, when you first told me about your father and the abuse, I told you that the things he said when you were young weren't the truth. Baby, he was trying to control you the only way he knew how—by making you think you deserved what he did to you."

Jay nodded, knowing that Kate was right.

"You're not that child anymore. You're a grown, beautiful, successful woman." Kate looked intently into Jay's watery eyes. "I love you, Jamison Parker, and I want you for the rest of my life. So your father can go scratch—he was wrong on all counts."

"I screwed up so badly. I should have known better than to accept the assignment for that cover story. I knew full well that I was in love with you. I ignored every bit of ethics I'd ever learned. I did deserve what I got today."

Kate, seemingly unable to sit still any longer, eased Jay onto the couch and stood up. She balled her fists up, jammed them in her pockets, and shook her head vehemently. "That is not true. I don't ever want to hear you say that again, Jay. The fact is, you were human, and so was I. You might recall, I was the one who invited you to stay at my house instead of a hotel. I was the one who swept you off your feet into a hug when I met you at the train station. You wanted to keep professional distance, remember?"

Jay nodded imperceptibly.

Kate continued. "Your exact words, I believe, were, 'How am I supposed to maintain professional distance with a greeting like that?' Do you remember?"

"Yes."

"Right. So if you're so dead set on assigning blame, then you'd better lay it at my doorstep, because that's where it belongs."

As Jay started to say something, Kate placed two fingers over her mouth.

"What's more, I'm the one who asked you out on a date. I asked you if you would consider staying an extra day, then I plotted a romantic day and evening, hoping I could win your heart. Me, Jay. I did all that, not you."

"I could have said no."

"You were falling in love, and you were human. Give yourself a break."

"I had a job to do."

"And you did it magnificently. Don't you remember me telling you, after I'd read the advance issue of the magazine, how incredibly proud I was of you for that story?"

Jay nodded.

"Honey, that was a perfectly balanced, unbelievably fair piece. No one could have captured the nuances of the story the way you did. It was, frankly, one of the best written stories I'd ever read in that magazine. And I will not stand here and have you apologize for it."

"I got suspended today for exercising poor judgment. Standislau put out a statement telling the world that."

Kate crossed back over to the couch. Using the same two fingers she had used to silence her moments earlier, she lifted Jay's chin to meet her compassionate gaze. "He also told you you were a talented journalist and that he was standing by you and the story."

After a second, Jay's eyes narrowed and focused intently on Kate. "How did you know that? And, while I'm at it, what are you doing here?"

Kate sat down and took Jay's hands in her own. "After you ran out of Trish's office she got worried about you. So she called me and told me what happened."

Jay sat up straighter, indignant. "She shouldn't have done that. She had no business bothering you with my problems while you were at work."

"Jay, she's your friend and she was worried about you. I'm glad she called."

"But you have responsibilities of your own."

Kate pulled Jay into her arms. "There is nothing in the world more important to me than you, love. Your well-being means everything to me. Do you have any idea how badly I wanted to be able to come with you to that meeting? It took all the self-restraint I had not to jump on the next train to the city after you called to tell me you'd been summoned. Besides, by the time I went home and got Fred, the workday was almost over anyway."

Jay looked out the window, surprised to see that it was full dark outside. She hadn't realized she'd been walking that long. "Oh." She didn't know what else to say.

The ringing of the phone forestalled any further conversation.

Jay picked it up on the third ring. "Hello?"

"Jamison?"

Her face went white and her hands started to shake. Kate, who was watching her, was at her side immediately.

"Jamison, is that you?"

"Yes, sir."

Kate mouthed, "Who is it?"

Jay formed the words, "My father."

Kate grabbed her free hand and held it tightly. In the five months they'd been together, Jay never mentioned that she was still in touch with her parents, although she and Kate had briefly discussed her feelings about them.

The gruff voice said, "A friend of mine faxed me something he thought I might be interested in today."

"Yes?"

"I'm sure you can guess what it was."

"No, Dad, I'm sure I have no idea." She rolled her eyes for Kate's benefit.

"It was a copy of today's *New York Post*. What is this garbage about you being...one of *those* people?" The disgust in his voice was plain.

Jay's anger was rising. "If by 'one of those people' you mean a lesbian, then it's true."

"What?"

Jay reflexively recoiled in fear, but cleared her throat and continued, "I said, it's true. I am a lesbian."

"I've never heard such a bunch of hooey in my life."

"Sorry if you don't approve, Dad, but it's not up for debate, and I'm not asking your permission." She had never spoken so boldly to her father before, but the presence of her six-foot, imposing lover gave her courage.

"You will not talk to me like that, young lady."

"Ted, calm down," Jay's mother, who had picked up an extension, interjected.

"Don't tell me to calm down, Edith. This is our daughter we're talking about, and no child of mine is going to be known as some pervert."

"Dad, I am not a pervert, I am a lesbian. I am in love with a wonderful woman, and I have nothing to hide."

"You have no idea what you're talking about. I knew we should never have let you go to college with all those long-haired hippie freaks."

"If you're done, Dad, I've got things to do."

"We'll be finished when I say we are!" he boomed.

As Jay cringed, Kate, who apparently could hear every word from where she was standing, visibly tensed as if to strike at him despite the fact that he was thousands of miles and two time zones away.

"The article questions your ethics," he spat.

"I read the article, Dad."

"What do your bosses say?"

"They are standing by me and the story." Jay had no intention of telling her parents about her suspension.

"That's nice, dear," her mother chimed in.

"Who is this Katherine Kyle, anyway? And what has she done to poison your mind?"

"Kate is everything to me. For the first time in my life, I'm truly happy. So happy, in fact, that we're planning a formal commitment ceremony, which is the closest thing we can have to a wedding."

"Formal commitment ceremony?" He said it with distaste. "What on earth does that really mean? It's not bad enough that you have this perversion? You have to go around and try to pretend that it's normal? I've never heard anything so ridiculous in my life."

"I'm sorry you feel that way, Dad. In that case you won't mind if we don't invite you to the ceremony. Really, this has been a lovely conversation, but I've got to go. Bye."

Jay could still hear her father's rantings as she hung up the receiver. She turned to Kate and buried her face in her chest, seeking comfort for the hurt inside that would never heal.

"I've got you, love. Shh. Don't worry. He can't hurt you anymore. You don't need him."

"I know, Kate. But he's the only father I've got, and, well, every time I talk to him I wish it could be different. I wish I could have a father who could be proud of me, who could love me for who I am and not find fault with everything I do."

"I know, and so you should have. He's not worth your tears, baby."

"You're right. Still, despite everything there's some part of me that still cares what he thinks. And then I hate myself for caring."

"Don't hate yourself, Jay It's natural to want a parent's approval. And it hurts when it's not forthcoming. But you know who and how he is, and he's not likely to change any time soon, is he?"

"No." Jay wiped her eyes with the back of her hand. "And then there's my mother, who just wants to keep the peace. God forbid she should stand up to him on my behalf."

"Maybe she's got her own issues."

"Probably."

"In any case, that doesn't excuse her behavior when you were a child."

Jay sighed heavily. "Can we not talk about this anymore tonight?"

"Of course."

"I just want you to hold me."

Kate pulled Jay tighter to her, effectively wrapping her in a cocoon of safety and security. They stayed like that for a very long time.

Kate held Jay tightly throughout the night, murmuring soft words of love and comfort long after her lover had fallen asleep. She was far too angry to sleep. That anyone would talk to his daughter the way Ted

Parker spoke to Jay was something she simply could not abide. If he had said those things in front of her, Kate wasn't sure that she would've been able to physically restrain herself.

Jay was disconsolate, Kate knew. All she wanted was for her parents to love and cherish her. Instead she was disrespected and made to feel unworthy. Thinking about it, Kate felt a deep hatred well up inside her. It was a foreign and rather unwelcome sensation. She had never hated—truly hated—anyone like she did Ted Parker. What he did to Jay as a child was beyond comprehension, and the fact that he continued bullying her as an adult made Kate angrier than she'd ever been.

At 5:00 a.m. she slipped out of bed to go for a run and pick up the morning newspapers. Jay remained fast asleep, no doubt worn out by the emotional traumas of the previous day. When Kate returned, Jay was still asleep.

Stripping out of her running clothes, Kate stepped into the shower, where she allowed the pounding spray of hot water to help ease some of the tension from her body. When she finished, she felt somewhat better and more in control of her emotions.

As Kate watched Jay sleep, she was overcome by the desire to protect her. She looked so young, so innocent. The depth of pain and suffering she endured at her father's hand had marked her in ways Kate was only just beginning to comprehend, but lying there with her eyes closed she looked like a beautiful angel.

Jay stirred.

"Hi, sweetheart. What are you doing?"

"Looking at you."

"I see that. Come here, gorgeous."

Kate moved across the room, her eyes never leaving those of her lover. When she got within several feet of the bed, she unfastened the towel from around her torso and let it fall to the floor.

Jay beckoned her forward with the crook of a finger. Her eyes conveyed her desire.

Their lips met in a slow dance that was equal parts love and passion. Each savored the taste of the other, both cognizant of the preciousness of their bond. Losing themselves in the wonder of their love, they temporarily shut out the world beyond the borders of their bedroom.

Over breakfast, they examined the newspapers laid out before them. As they predicted, the second round of stories focused heavily on Jay's tenure at *Time*, the stories she covered, the people and events she chronicled. The headlines ranged from the factual to the sensational.

"Magazine Takes Action to Preserve Integrity," said the bold print on page one of *Newsday.*

"*Time* Out for Lesbian Reporter," read the headline in the *Daily News.*

The *New York Post's* front page screamed, "*Time*-ing Is Critical for Parker."

> The nation's top news magazine wasted no time taking action against a reporter whose ethics came into question yesterday in a *Post* exclusive. Jamison Parker, 24, was identified yesterday as the lesbian paramour of Katherine Kyle, the spokesperson for the New York State Department of Correctional Services and subject of a May cover story in *Time* that was written by Parker. It was research by this newspaper that revealed questions about whether Parker had, in fact, written the Kyle piece while she was involved with her romantically.
>
> In a statement released late yesterday, *Time* managing editor Vander Standislau announced that Parker has been suspended for two weeks for "exercising poor judgment."
>
> Although the magazine continues to investigate the matter, Standislau said, "*Time* stands by the Kyle story as written, and by Jamison Parker." Contacted later by the *Post*, Standislau refused to say what Parker's future with the magazine would be.
>
> For months, Kyle had refused to name the unidentified woman in a photograph published nationally in which she and the woman were captured locked in a passionate embrace. Then yesterday, Kyle and Parker inexplicably came forward. Questions raised by the *Post* regarding Parker's obvious conflict of interest in writing the story about her lover were deflected in a press conference held by the two women in Albany. Attempts to reach Parker and Kyle yesterday failed.

When Jay looked up from reading the paper, the pain in her eyes was evident. Kate moved behind her chair, wrapped her arms around her tightly, and kissed her on the side of the neck.

"Well, it could have been worse, right?" Jay's attempt to sound flip failed miserably.

"Yes, it sure could have been, baby."

"Of course, we haven't seen the tabloids yet. And they've got three more days to dig up all kinds of dirt."

"Jay, you and I both know that whatever the tabloids print is going to be garbage."

"Yes, but we also know that people read that stuff, Kate. And they believe it."

There was nothing to say to that, as Kate and Jay were both too familiar with the truth of that statement.

Kate said, "Let's cross that bridge when we get to it. There's nothing we can do about that right now. One day at a time, okay?"

Jay leaned back into her. "Okay."

# CHAPTER NINE

Having just come back from their run, Kate and Jay were sitting in their kitchen in Albany on Monday morning. The *Globe* was out that morning, and they picked up a copy on their way home. Before she started reading, Jay thought she had prepared herself for the worst. She was wrong.

"Maverick Lesbian May Bring Down *Time* Magazine." The headline alone was enough to make her sick to her stomach.

> In what may be the single most damaging scandal ever to hit the venerable magazine, 24-year-old ace reporter Jamison Parker's stunning revelation of an illicit relationship with 27-year-old flak Katherine Kyle has threatened to destroy the credibility *Time* has spent decades building.

"That's a terribly constructed sentence."

"What?"

Kate leaned over Jay's shoulder. "That first sentence. It's too wordy."

Jay looked up at her lover. "You're kidding me, right?"

"Hmm?" Kate continued to read.

"They're tearing me to shreds and you're interested in their grammar?"

"The *Globe* is blowing smoke out its ass. You and I both know it."

"Yes, but the public at large isn't as erudite as that."

"Give them more credit than that, Jay. I think most people understand that tabloids take liberties with the truth."

"Regardless, this is a nightmare."

"I know, honey." Kate kissed Jay on the top of the head and resumed reading.

> "This is the most serious ethical lapse I've ever witnessed by a reporter at a major news magazine," said Ernest

113

Wheatogue, professor of journalism and an expert in ethics and the media. "What Ms. Parker has done—writing a story about someone with whom she was romantically involved— raises questions about every other story the magazine has ever published. Is this the first instance in which a reporter at *Time* has shown such an appalling lack of ethics? How do we, as the reading public, know? The answer is, we don't."

Wheatogue added that the scandal could mushroom, causing the public to lose faith in the information it gets from what has been, to this point, a highly respected news sources.

This is apparently not the first time Parker has brought a news organization to its knees. As a junior at prestigious Middlebury College in Vermont, Parker wrote a scathing editorial that was so controversial it forced administrators to close down the school newspaper, the *Campus*, for two weeks. School officials, contacted for this article, refused to comment.

Jay was beside herself. "Bullshit. We shut down the press so that we could make technological upgrades."

Editors at *Time* are said to be desperate to salvage the magazine's reputation. Sources tell the *Globe* that managing editor Vander Standislau has demanded that every employee sign an oath to adhere to a strict code of ethics. The document was hastily drafted by the magazine's lawyers over the weekend in the wake of the explosive disclosure of the Parker debacle.

Standislau himself is said to be distraught at the potential destruction of *Time*'s credibility. Sources tell the *Globe* that he has been holed up in his penthouse suite, surrounded by loyal editors and reporters, working to come up with a strategy to restore the magazine's good name.

"In truth," said Wheatogue, "I'm not sure anything short of firing Parker outright and disavowing any stories she's written for the magazine will save them."

Calls to Standislau and several editors at *Time* were unanswered at press time.

Jay bowed her head and put her hands over her face.

Kate turned Jay's chair, knelt down before her, and gathered Jay to her. "Sweetheart, you know that's not the truth."

Jay raised her tear-stained face to her lover. "Do I?"

"Yes," Kate answered vehemently. "You talked to Standislau yesterday, remember?"

Jay sighed heavily, "Yeah, right after I read the editorial in the Sunday *Times* calling for my head."

"And what did Standislau say?"

When Jay didn't immediately answer, Kate filled in the silence. "He told you not to worry, that he had no intention of asking for, or accepting, your resignation. He said it would take a lot more than a few bits of adverse publicity and a couple of negative editorials to change his mind. Honey," Kate took Jay's face in her hands, "this is not a man who will be bullied into doing anything."

So quietly Kate wasn't sure she'd heard her at first, Jay said, "Maybe I should resign."

"What?"

"I'm a liability, and the last thing I want to do is to damage the magazine."

"Jamison, you are one of the best writers *Time* has. You have done nothing but turn out masterpiece after masterpiece. Standislau told you so himself."

"If I resign, then the whole story goes away."

"If you resign, Jay, it will lead to speculation that you've done something wrong and lend credence to those questioning your work."

Fresh tears shimmered in Jay's eyes. "I did do something wrong, Kate. And now I have to pay for that mistake."

"Honey, you are paying for that mistake. Look at you. You're eating yourself alive."

Jay glanced at the kitchen clock. "You're going to be late for your Monday-morning briefing."

"Screw the briefing," Kate said.

"No. If you let your job performance slip, then Breathwaite wins and all of this will have been for nothing. You need to be there."

Kate hated that Jay was right. "Okay, but I need you to promise me that you won't do anything without talking to me about it first. Deal?"

After a moment's hesitation Jay said, "Deal."

"I love you, Jay." Kate kissed her on her forehead.

"I love you too."

At the door to the garage Kate turned back. "Don't let them get you, honey. We're going to get through this, together."

Jay simply nodded.

∽ʕ ʔ∾

The meeting in Vander Standislau's office had been going on for nearly an hour. Discarded coffee cups littered the small conference table in the corner. Half-eaten pastries were strewn about on paper napkins.

"Sir, I think this is the best course of action. We have to come out strong on this issue."

The managing editor glared at the young man in the slick suit. Jeffrey Ochs was a capable PR man. He worked for Tandor and Wells, a top public relations firms.

"Ochs, I've been in this business for more years than you've been alive. I've seen things you can't even imagine. You are not going to sit there and tell me that my only course of action is to hang a very gifted reporter out to dry in order to stave off a little bit of crappy press."

"Mr. Standislau, I'm telling you that if we don't take decisive measures right now, in time for the next news cycle, you're going to be facing a potentially insurmountable crisis. The papers are already smelling blood and they're moving in for the kill. If you give them Parker, we can spin it that the magazine does not tolerate even the slightest hint of impropriety. The piranhas will be satisfied feeding on the firing of a reporter who violated *Time*'s high ethical standards, and the story will go away."

Trish, sitting off to the side, thought she had never detested anyone more than she did this brash, arrogant spin doctor. To him, Jay's career was totally expendable, her journalistic integrity just so much chum for the shark-infested waters. The editor stole a glance at her boss. It was clear to her that he was nearing the end of his patience. Trish could see that the other editors around the room sensed the same thing.

"Mr. Ochs," Standislau said, "if every one of us was thrown to the sharks for making an error in judgment, I daresay there would be precious few of us left. The answer is no. I have no intention of firing Ms. Parker to satisfy the press hounds."

Ochs started to say something, then seemed to think better of it.

"However," Standislau raised his voice, "I do agree that we need to take the bull by the horns." He stroked his chin as he appeared to contemplate his options. "Go ahead and book me on the morning shows for tomorrow. Then I want you to set up an interview for Ms. Parker with Wanda Nelson for tonight's *America's Heartbeat*."

"But—"

"Just do it, Mr. Ochs."

"Yes, sir. Do you want me to contact Parker?"

"Heavens no. I'll take care of it."

"But, sir—"

"This might come as a surprise to you, Mr. Ochs, but I actually know a thing or two about publicity and PR. I'll prepare Ms. Parker."

"Yes, sir."

Trish nearly wanted to laugh. The young man's need to object was almost palpable, and she enjoyed watching him have to rein himself in.

"So you don't want me to prepare either one of you?"

"You catch on quickly, Mr. Ochs. Now it seems to me you've got a lot of work to do. You'd best get going."

"Yes, sir." With a fleeting look around the room, he left.

Standislau turned to his editors. "Can you imagine? Yes, let's take every one of our fine writers and nail them to the cross for screwing up. How many reporters would we have left?"

"Vander," said Ivo Norvika, editor of the international desk, "you do realize the threat to the magazine's integrity is real?"

The managing editor sighed. "Yes, Ivo, I am well aware of our situation. I am confident that both *Time* and Ms. Parker can survive this episode intact."

Terri Van Hotten, the lifestyles editor, piped in, "What do you want us to do?"

"I want you to have conference calls with your reporters—tell them to keep their heads down and not to discuss this matter with their colleagues or speculate aloud. The same goes for all of you."

There was a chorus of "Yes, sirs."

"I meant what I said—I am completely convinced that we will emerge from this matter just fine. I expect all of you to convey that confidence to your troops. Let's get back to work."

As they started to file out of the room, Standislau said, "Patricia, can you please spare me a moment?"

"Of course, Vander."

When the rest of the editors had gone, Standislau said, "Sit down, Trish."

He never called her by her nickname, and it unnerved her.

"How is Jamison doing? Have you talked to her this morning?"

"Yes, sir. I talked to her shortly before this meeting."

"And?"

"She's distraught at the thought that her actions have raised questions about the magazine's integrity. She wanted us to know that she would do whatever was necessary to protect us."

"Mmm." Standislau nodded. "I'm not surprised. That woman has a lot of courage, and she's very loyal."

"Vander, Jay Parker is a fine human being. Not to mention the fact that she's a fantastic writer."

"You don't have to convince me, Trish. I'm well aware of her talents. How did you leave it with her?"

"I told her we were meeting and that we'd be in touch in a few hours."

"Okay. Call her and tell her we're sending a car for her." At her raised eyebrow he added, "It's time to fight back."

Trish smiled broadly as she turned to go.

"Oh, and Trish? Tell her to bring Ms. Kyle with her."

∽⌒∾

The limousine trip to New York found Kate and Jay reminiscing about the last time they made a similar journey. It was hard to believe it was only five and a half months ago.

As Kate put her arm around Jay in the back seat, they sighed simultaneously.

"It's amazing how much my life has changed since the last time we took this ride."

Kate smiled. "Mine too." She looked at her thoughtfully. "Are you sorry, Jay?"

"What?"

"Are you sorry for all the upheaval? As stressful as things have been over the past few months, I worry sometimes that you might regret the choices you've made."

Jay turned more fully on the seat to face Kate, reaching out at the same time to link their hands. "Katherine Ann Kyle," her voice broke with emotion, "you have made me happier than I ever thought I could be. My life is so full of love, my heart is bursting. What we have is worth everything that's happened and more. Don't you ever doubt that."

"I wish things could be different, though, Jay. I wish you'd never gotten dragged into this ugliness. I keep trying to think what I could have done to change that."

"Stop it," Jay said. "Stop beating yourself up. I've had choices to make every step of the way, and I've made them. You said it yourself, we'll get through this together. And you're right—we will."

"I know we will, but at what cost? Your privacy, your journalistic integrity, maybe even your career? It's too much."

"Hey." Jay lifted the hands she held to her lips and kissed the backs of each one. "That's my decision to make, not yours, remember? I've told you before—the only thing that matters to me is you, and us. Whatever happens with this scheme, we'll find a way to turn it around. As long as I have you by my side, every thing else pales in significance."

Kate ran her thumbs over the backs of Jay's hands. "Have I told you lately how much I love you, and how incredibly lucky I am to have you in my life?"

Jay pretended to think. "Probably. But feel free to tell me again."

"I love you more than life itself. And I am the luckiest woman alive."

"Good. I like the sound of that." Jay pressed her lips sweetly to Kate's, trying to convey the depth of her love in the essence of her kiss. "Now that we've got that settled, can we discuss our strategy for this meeting with Standislau and then tonight's interview?"

Kate laughed. "Ever the practical one, aren't you?"

"Only when I'm about to be hung out to dry in front of several million people."

"Don't worry, love. You don't really think I'd sit by and let that happen, do you? Over my dead body."

"My protector." Jay laid her head on Kate's shoulder. "Nope. I'm counting on you to bail me out if it comes to that."

"It won't. Wanda is doing the interview. She likes you—she told you so when you met her on the set last May."

"That doesn't count. I wasn't on the hot seat then. She was too busy interviewing journalist and heroine Katherine Kyle."

"As I recall, sweetheart, she told you she was quite taken with your work, and that was apart from anything having to do with me. Don't you remember her saying that she and her husband read your stories and thought they were top-notch?"

"How could I forget? It's not every day an intelligent, gorgeous movie star turned talk-show host pays you a compliment like that."

"Exactly. I can't believe she'd be out for your blood now."

"Just the same, I don't want to take any chances."

"I agree. I've put together a mock interview, trying to anticipate the most troublesome questions she could ask. I thought we could do sort of a dry run. That way there won't be any surprises, and we can refine your answers as we go along. What do you think?"

"I think I love you." Jay kissed Kate again. "Thank you for taking such good care of me. That's perfect."

"I just want you to be as comfortable and confident as possible, Jay. Want to go through this stuff now or wait until after we meet with your boss?"

"Now. I want Standislau to know I'll do a good job tonight."

"If he didn't think you'd do a great job, he wouldn't allow you to give an interview, never mind set it up for you proactively the way he did."

"I'd still rather get drilled now, while we have a couple of uninterrupted hours."

"Okay then, here goes." Kate pulled a reporter's notebook out of the briefcase that rested at her feet and scrolled through several pages of questions and notes she had made.

"Wow, you weren't kidding when you said you'd already given this some thought."

"No, sweetheart, I wasn't. I fully intend for America to know that Jamison Parker is an upright, honest, talented, intelligent, impartial reporter."

Jay laughed. "Is that all?"

Kate smiled. "Well, it's a start." She kissed Jay on the forehead. "Here we go..."

⋙⋘

Trish was waiting in the lobby when they arrived.

"Trish, this is Katherine Kyle. Kate, meet Trish Stanton, editor extraordinaire."

Trish nodded at Kate in acknowledgment before asking, "How are you guys holding up?"

"Okay," Jay answered for them. "How about you?"

"Me? Piece of cake."

"You're a terrible liar, have I ever told you that? Remind me to play poker with you. It'd be like taking candy from a baby."

"You wish, kiddo. Let's go. The boss is waiting for us in his office."

"Is he in a good mood?"

Trish gave Jay a playful shove. "Don't be a chicken." To Kate she said, "Is she this difficult at home?"

"You have no idea."

Moments later they were ushered into the managing editor's suite.

"Hello, Patricia, Jamison."

"Hello, sir. This is—"

"Katherine Kyle, I presume," he finished for Jay as he strode across the room and grasped Kate's hand in a firm grip.

"It's a pleasure to meet you, Mr. Standislau. I only wish it were under different circumstances."

"I'm glad you could make it. Please, sit down, everyone."

When they were seated, Standislau said, "As you know, this has become bigger than any of us anticipated."

"I'm so sor—"

He waved off Jay's apology. "Don't, Jamison. None of us thought this essentially personal matter would rise to this level. What's done is done. The important thing now is to nip this thing in the bud. I'm tired of being on the defensive. It's time to fight back."

Sitting directly across from him, Kate smiled. She'd never met the managing editor before, though his reputation was legendary. He was known as a straight shooter—tough, gruff, fair, and fiercely protective of his magazine and his employees. She could see that the description was well deserved.

"My experts tell me Wanda Nelson is a skilled interviewer. I hear she's not afraid to ask the tough questions, but she's also not obnoxious about belaboring issues ad nauseum. Ms. Kyle, my recollection is that you have some experience with her?"

"Yes, sir. I would say your assessment of Wanda and her style is accurate. I have always found her to be fair. I think we have the added advantage of knowing that she is familiar with, and respects, Jay's work."

Both Standislau and Trish gave her slightly surprised looks.

"Wanda has met Jay once before." Kate didn't want to elaborate any further and was grateful when Jay's bosses simply nodded in understanding.

"Right then," Standislau went on. "That helps."

"If I might, Mr. Standislau," Jay ventured, "Kate and I have taken the liberty of running through the questions we think will likely come up tonight. Is there anything from your perspective you're most concerned about?"

He smiled at Kate. "I knew having a PR expert on hand would come in handy. You two make an impressive team." He turned his attention to Jay. "My focus, as you might imagine, is strictly the integrity of this magazine and its product. I want folks to walk away from your interview and my three torture sessions tomorrow morning having confidence in *Time*, in the news we bring them and the accuracy of the information on our pages. I want the viewers and our readers to trust us."

"Okay," said Jay, "what do you see my role as being?"

"I want to give you a forum to defend yourself and to restore your reputation. I also believe that if the public meets you and gets to know you a little bit, they'll know what we do—that you're an outstanding human being and an excellent reporter with grit and honor."

Jay asked, "Are there any areas you'd like me to specifically avoid?"

Standislau stood and walked over to the large picture windows, gazing out at the city below. Without turning around he said, "I think that you ought to focus narrowly on the accusations being hurled against your character and ethics. Leave the magazine's policies and reputation to me."

"If I'm asked a direct question about who knew what, when, how do you want me to answer it?"

The managing editor turned around to look at Jay, and then at Kate. "How would you have her answer it, Ms. Kyle?"

Looking him directly in the eye, she answered, "Honesty is the best policy, sir." Out of the corner of her eye, she saw Trish shift uncomfortably in her seat. Kate added, "That doesn't mean, however, that you have to say everything you know. It merely means that you should answer the question. As I'm sure you all know, there are many ways to answer a question."

Standislau regarded Kate appreciatively. "Yes, Ms. Kyle, there's certainly a lot of truth in that. I suspect that *Time* and Jamison are in good hands with you."

"Just trying to help out, sir."

"Jamison?"

"Yes, sir?"

"How do you feel about all this? Do you think you can carry this off?"

"I think, Mr. Standislau, that I'm tired of sitting by while everybody takes shots at me and at *Time*. I say you're right. It's time to fight back. I'm happy to have an opportunity to set the record straight and put this behind us."

"I'm glad to hear that, Jamison. Very glad to hear that. Okay, let's reconvene after the interview tonight and see where we are. Then we'll know if we have any specific adjustments we'll need to make to our strategy or any areas on which we need to place particular emphasis. Good luck, ladies. I'll have the car come and get you for the show at six forty-five, all right? I believe my secretary has the address."

"Thank you, sir," Kate and Jay said as they rose to leave.

"Do me proud, ladies. Patricia, can you stay a minute?"

"Of course."

≼δδ≽

When the door closed Standislau said, "Ms. Kyle is quite impressive, isn't she?"

"Yes, sir, she sure is."

"Her looks won't hurt with the viewers, either."

"I think they'll both score well with the public on that count, Vander."

He chuckled. "They will at that. I want you to know I've got pollsters standing by to run numbers after tonight's show. That will give us a good idea what ground we need to cover in the morning." He paused, looking uncomfortable for a moment. "It will also tell us whether or not it will be too much of a liability to hold on to Jamison."

Trish's eyes registered indignation.

"This is a business, Trish," he said, shrugging apologetically. "As much as you and I both like her and have faith in her talents and abilities, I can't keep her to the detriment of the magazine."

"I thought you were of the opinion we could win this battle."

"I am."

"Without casualties," she added bitingly.

"I'd like that to be the case. Patricia, I know you think very highly of Jamison. I do too. But we both have jobs to do and an obligation to the organization. Let's just wait and see what happens tonight. Perhaps she'll acquit herself well and we won't have to worry about next steps."

Trish nodded curtly. "I have work to do."

The studio lights were hot.

"Thanks for insisting that I wear something sleeveless under my jacket," Jay murmured.

"My television experience has to be good for something," Kate said. "Are you okay, Jay?"

They were sitting on the set, waiting for Wanda Nelson to join them. Their lavaliere microphones had not yet been affixed.

"Yeah."

"It's understandable to be nervous. Just remember, I'll be right here with you. Be yourself—you'll win them over in a heartbeat."

"Thanks. I don't know what I'd do without you."

Kate smiled at her affectionately, even as she thought with a pang, *Without me, you wouldn't be in this mess.*

"Good evening, Jamison. It's good to see you again."

Kate and Jay looked up to see Wanda Nelson standing over them. Her tawny skin glowed with good health. Perfect teeth gleamed in a flawless face that had graced many movie screens. After serving as a guest host on the *Today Show* for two years, she had been given her own weekly newsmagazine show two months earlier. The thing that set it apart from all other similar shows was that the interviews were conducted live, not taped for later broadcast.

"Katherine, it's nice to see you again as well."

Both women stood up to shake her hand.

"I thought I'd start by interviewing Jamison first." Wanda looked from one woman to the other. "Then for the last few minutes of the segment we'll bring you in, Katherine, and talk to you as well."

While neither Kate nor Jay was particularly happy with this arrangement, it was clear that Wanda was in charge and there was no room for negotiation.

"Sure," Kate said easily. "Is it all right with you if I just stand in the wings to watch?"

"Absolutely. I'm sure Jamison will be more comfortable that way." Wanda smiled as a production assistant pinned a microphone to her lapel and handed her an earpiece. Another assistant outfitted Jay with a mic as well.

"Two minutes, people," called out a disembodied voice.

With a squeeze to Jay's shoulder and a wink, Kate moved off set, finding a spot that was directly in line with Wanda's head. This would make it possible for Jay to steal glances at her, all the while appearing to be looking at her interviewer.

"Thirty seconds."

Jay rotated her shoulders to relax as Wanda reviewed notes she had placed on the floor next to her chair.

"And five, four, three, two, one...cue the music." A hand behind one of the cameras was raised, and the operator cued the host.

"Good evening, everyone, and welcome to *America's Heartbeat*. I'm Wanda Nelson. In our first segment tonight, we're going to examine a question of journalistic ethics. What happens when a reporter gets too close to her subject? Should a journalist be allowed to write about something, or someone, she knows? We'll get up close and personal with Jamison Parker, a *Time* magazine reporter accused of doing just that, right after this."

The red light on the camera went off, and the host resumed reviewing her notes. Two minutes later, she received the next cue.

"Welcome back. With me in the studio tonight is Jamison Parker, a writer for *Time* magazine who found herself the subject of much discussion this week. Ms. Parker, thank you for being here."

The camera was rolled back to fit both women in the shot.

"Thank you, it's a pleasure to be here."

Kate thought Jay looked relaxed, although she knew otherwise. She had taught Jay a couple of quick techniques for appearing at ease in front of the camera and was glad to see her lover using those to good advantage.

"Ms. Parker—"

"Please, call me Jay." She smiled her most engaging smile.

"Good enough. Jay, let's talk about what happened earlier this week, and then we'll take it from there. At a press conference you took the extraordinary step of openly acknowledging your homosexuality. Why would you do that?"

"As so many people do, Wanda, several months ago I fell in love. Unlike most people, however, I was unable to publicly declare that love. Being a lesbian can be difficult enough under normal circumstances in our society. Add to that a relationship with a high-profile individual, and it becomes nearly impossible. My partner and I finally reached the decision that we no longer wished to be hounded by members of the media, all of whom were inexplicably interested in my identity. It seemed that the best way to reclaim our privacy was to get our relationship out into the open. That is what we did earlier this week."

"For those viewers who are unaware of who Ms. Parker's partner is, she is none other than Katherine Kyle, a former television news anchor who catapulted to fame last May when she became the only reporter on the scene as two explosions rocked the New York state capitol building. Ms. Kyle's coverage was carried all over the world by CNN and other news outlets. The next week, she was featured on the cover of *Time* magazine. And that's where this story gets interesting. Jay, you wrote that cover story on your partner, did you not?"

"At the time I was assigned to write the story, Kate and I were not involved. She was not my partner, no."

"But you knew her?"

"Actually, before the bombing at the capitol, I did not know her name."

The interviewer looked surprised, recalling clearly the chemistry between the two women when they had visited the set of the *Today Show* the morning after the bombing. "No?"

"No. We attended the same college, although Kate was two years ahead of me. Our paths crossed several times back then, but I never knew who she was."

"So you were not an item in college."

Jay smiled. "I'd like to think I wouldn't get involved with someone before at least asking her name." She winked, looking over Wanda's head at Kate, who smiled broadly back at her.

"Good point. When, exactly, did you become romantically involved?"

"We got reacquainted shortly after the bombing. When I saw Kate on television, I finally learned her name. I was in Albany to interview Governor Hyland. When I saw Kate on CNN, I went to the scene of the bombing to see if she was all right. It turned out that we both needed to get to New York City—she was set to appear on the three morning news shows the next morning, and my interview with the governor had gotten rescheduled for his Manhattan office later the same day—so she offered to give me a ride."

"And you became involved then?"

"No. I wrote the story on Governor Hyland, and Kate returned to Albany. When I turned in my piece, I was assigned to write a cover story about the new breed of journalists. My editor wanted the piece to focus on Kate. So I returned to Albany to research the story, interview her colleagues, and talk to some of the victims of the capitol bombing. The fact that she had run back into the capitol after the second explosion to help rescue folks who were trapped was something unique for journalists, who are generally impartial observers. That was one of the major angles of my story. It wasn't until I had completed all of the interviews and research that we started to date."

"So you weren't involved romantically before that, but you did know her."

"Yes, and in retrospect, I should have made that fact plain to my editors."

*Good,* thought Kate as she watched proudly from the wings. *Take responsibility, tell the truth, exonerate the magazine, and control the interview.*

"Your editors didn't know that you had a connection to Kate?"

"No. At the time, I didn't think it was relevant. Should I have told them that I went to college with her but didn't know her name until the bombing? Perhaps, but it just didn't occur to me that it would become significant." Jay leaned forward as Kate had told her to do to convey earnestness. "I set out to write the most objective story possible. In fact, when I wrote the piece, the question I asked myself repeatedly was, would I write this any differently if I didn't know Kate at all? The answer I kept coming back with was no. My intention was to let the bombing victims, her colleagues, and her actions tell the story. I am confident that anyone reading the piece will feel that is the story they got."

Wanda nodded. "I have to say, Jay, I read the story at the time, and I reread it closely several times in preparation for this interview, and I could not find any hint of bias in it."

"I'm glad. I take my job very seriously. I have a responsibility to the public to inform them, to educate them, and to present stories that are well rounded, impartial, and interesting. If I thought for a minute that I had not met those standards in this instance, I would willingly step aside. I have no desire to mislead anyone. Folks fall in love every day with people they meet while working. That's what happened here. If I had it to do again, I would make some different choices, perhaps. I certainly would have told my editors that Kate's and my paths had crossed before, and I might have recused myself from the story if I'd known what would happen later. But I didn't have a crystal ball and couldn't foresee falling in love like that."

Wanda said, chuckling, "I don't know anyone who plans when and where to fall in love. I know that I met my husband while making a movie on which he was a consultant. Falling in love was about the last thing I thought would happen on that set."

There was a momentary pause, then Wanda said. "When we come back, a look back at the stories that made headlines this week."

The disembodied voice called out, "And we're clear."

Wanda rose from her chair and reached out her hand to Jay. "Wow, that went by too quickly." She motioned Kate over. "I'm really sorry I didn't get to talk to you both together, but we just ran out of time."

Kate wasn't sure if Wanda was being sincere or if it had been her intention all along to interview Jay alone. "That's quite all right."

"I want you both to know that I have tremendous respect for what you did by coming out—that took a lot of courage. I understand better than most what it's like to have the paparazzi hounding you day and night. I wish you all the best and hope you find some peace."

"Thank you, Wanda. We appreciate that." Kate waited patiently as a technician stripped Jay of her microphone. Then she placed her hand gently on her partner's back and guided her off the set.

When they were well clear, Kate gave Jay a one-armed hug. "You were fantastic, sweetheart. I am so very, very proud of you."

"Yeah?"

"Yeah. You handled that with grace and style. And you got the interviewer to add to your credibility. That doesn't happen every day, trust me."

"The audience that matters awaits us." Suddenly looking tired, she gestured to the waiting limousine that would take them back to Standislau's office. "I wish we could just go home and curl up together instead."

"Me too, sweetheart. Soon, I promise."

By the time they'd made it through the midtown Manhattan congestion, it was after 10:30 p.m. Standislau and Trish were waiting for them in the managing editor's office.

"Come in, come in you two. Have a seat, you must be exhausted."

"Thanks," Jay said, as she plopped down in the nearest chair. In truth, she was dead tired, but she was also nervous. She was grateful when Kate selected the seat directly next to her, needing that proximity and her lover's quiet strength.

"I'm sure it will come as no surprise to you that I took the liberty of gauging public opinion about your interview."

Jay stiffened imperceptibly, and Kate squeezed her hand surreptitiously before letting go. If Standislau saw the gesture, he gave no indication.

"We asked several questions in the poll—Did you find Ms. Parker credible? Does her explanation of events make you more, or less sympathetic? Would you rate her ethics excellent, good, fair, poor, or unacceptable? Would you trust a story written by Ms. Parker in the future? How much do you trust the stories you read in *Time* magazine: completely, mostly, partially, or not at all? Seeing this interview, are you more, or less likely to trust the information you get in *Time*?"

The managing editor paused for a moment and looked up at Jay. "I have to say, even I was surprised at the numbers."

Jay thought the man would have made a great poker player. It was impossible to tell whether he meant that he'd been pleasantly surprised or horrified by the results.

"I am happy to say that you scored off the charts in almost every instance. Eighty-two percent of respondents said you were credible. Seventy-one percent said your explanation made them more sympathetic. Forty-three percent said your ethics were excellent, and another thirty-one percent said they were good. An overwhelming eighty-seven percent said they would trust a story from you in the future."

Jay relaxed minutely and chanced a glance at Kate, whose eyes twinkled back at her with pride.

"As for the magazine," Standislau continued, "the news was also excellent." He put the poll results down and looked at Jay. "Thank you, by the way, for making a point of letting your editors off the hook. I know we didn't talk about the specifics of what you were going to say ahead of time. That was very classy."

"It was the least I could do, sir."

"Yes, well," he cleared his throat and picked up his sheaf of papers once again, "a combined seventy-four percent of respondents said they would trust the stories in *Time* completely or partially, and an astounding ninety-one percent said they were more likely to trust the information in *Time* as a result of the interview.

"I can't imagine anything I could say tomorrow could acquit us any better than you have tonight. Congratulations, Jamison. I suggest you get some sleep. We'll talk again tomorrow."

The reactions to Vander Standislau's appearances the next morning were equally positive, and his explanation of *Time's* stringent policies and code of ethics more than satisfying to the viewers. Asked about Jay's revelation regarding her personal life, he answered unequivocally that his employees' personal lives were their own business and that he was only interested in the job they did. Jamison Parker, he said, was an outstanding reporter.

# CHAPTER TEN

Breathwaite was beside himself. How in the world had those bitches gotten so damn lucky? What should have been a surefire career ender for Parker had turned out to be a reaffirmation of her worth to the magazine.

"You have got to be kidding me." He threw the editorials down on his desk. The ringing of the phone forestalled the string of expletives he was about to unleash.

"Breathwaite," he barked into the receiver.

"It's time for the next target. It's clear we're not going to get her this way."

"No kidding. I've already begun laying the groundwork. He'll be gone within the week."

"For your sake, you'd better hope so. Sampson's been talking to the big guy about his theories, and that's not good. Patience down south is running in short supply these days."

"I said it would be done, and so it will," Breathwaite snapped at Vendetti. *Hawthorne can kiss my ass,* he thought as he slammed down the phone.

Reaching into his briefcase, he extracted a key. He fitted it into the lock for the file cabinet to his left, slid the drawer back and located the bright yellow folder labeled "BS." Breathwaite had been pleased with himself when he came up with that little name.

He spread the contents of the folder out on his desk, shuffling through photos until he came to the one he wanted. Staring back at him was a younger Brian Sampson, looking dashing in his military uniform, a Vietnamese woman sitting on his lap. Breathwaite combed through more pictures until he came across an image of a beautiful twelve-year-old Amerasian girl, her eyes the same shape and shade of gray as her father's. He smiled coldly. This time there would be no advance warning. Just a well-executed strike that would create a media maelstrom and knock the DOCS commissioner out on his ass. Breathwaite gleefully rubbed his hands together in anticipation.

When the first story hit the *New York Post* as an exclusive, Commissioner Sampson and Kate were in the middle of a swing through the prisons in the westernmost part of the state. As part of the tour, they had invited a select group of reporters to accompany them to Lakeview, one of the state's newest "shock incarceration" camps. The prison, designed mostly for low-level drug offenders, was modeled on military boot camps. For six months, inmates learned discipline, pride, and structure.

At the tail end of the press tour at Lakeview, Gregory Naisbitt, a reporter with the western New York bureau of the Associated Press, raised his hand to ask a question. "Is the *Post* story true, Commissioner Sampson? Did you father a child out of wedlock with a Vietnamese woman twelve years ago while serving a tour of duty over there? And is it a fact that you've been paying her and her mother hush money ever since?"

A tremendous buzz rippled through the throng of reporters. Then a voice shouted, "Does your wife know?"

The commissioner, who clearly had been expecting questions about the shock program, visibly blanched. "W-what?"

Kate, seeing her boss's distress, stepped in and held up her hands for quiet. "Any questions on this tour were to be limited to the exciting, successful, cutting-edge shock program. The fact that recidivism rates have been greatly reduced since the introduction of shock camps is major news. If any of you have any relevant questions about that, we'll entertain them." She paused for a fraction of a second. "No? Have a nice day, folks. The officer," she nodded to a uniformed guard standing rigidly at attention to her right, "will see you out now."

Without further delay, Kate steered her boss into a nearby office and closed the door behind them. When she turned to face Sampson, he was ghostly pale and swaying. She guided him into a nearby chair and poured him a glass of water. The gesture was as much to allow her time to absorb what happened as it was to help the commissioner.

Moving to a phone on the wall, she dialed her office. When her assistant answered, Kate spoke in low tones.

"Why wasn't I made aware that there was a major breaking story in print this morning about the commissioner?"

"I'm sorry, Kate, I was going to tell you when you called."

"Marisa," she ground out with barely controlled fury, "I wear a beeper for a reason. There were reporters accompanying us today, as you well knew. Didn't you think it was important to let me know the commissioner might be blindsided?"

"I guess I didn't think reporters in that part of the state would've heard about it."

"Didn't think would be the operative part of that sentence," Kate hissed. "Send me the story right now. Have there been any calls about it?"

"Three dozen or so."

Kate closed her eyes and willed her tension headache to ease. "Fax me the list of callers with phone numbers and details about what questions they asked. And if there are any more calls, I want to know right away. Am I making myself clear?"

"Yes, ma'am."

Kate slammed down the phone, wondering what could possibly happen next.

"What am I going to tell my wife?"

The words were spoken in something akin to a whisper, as if Sampson didn't realize he'd spoken them aloud.

Kate swallowed the response that sprang to mind, which was that he should have thought of that twelve years ago when he took that woman to bed. Instead, she turned to face her boss.

"Sir, I'm sorry. I should have known about that story and protected you. I—"

He continued as if he hadn't heard her, "I suppose it had to come out sooner or later. I just never thought— Well"—he looked up, seeming to notice Kate's presence for the first time—"I guess it's pretty obvious I didn't think, now, isn't it?" He shook his head with bitter regret.

"Commissioner, we need to decide on a strategy. Please don't say anything more out loud until we determine what our response will be."

He looked at her, uncomprehending.

"I can't answer questions to which I don't know the response," she said. "I can't lie to the media, and if you tell me more, I won't be able to feign ignorance."

"Oh," he said weakly. "Yes, I see."

"Sir? Any idea why this story is coming out now?"

Sampson shrugged and ran his fingers through his thick cap of hair. "I have no idea."

"Where might the *Post* have gotten such a story?"

"The only person who would have had any knowledge of"—he paused, cognizant of Kate's warning about what she knew—"that time in my life would be an old friend of mine who served in my platoon. But I haven't heard from Jack in a long time. We had a bit of a falling out the last time we got together. I was trying to convince him to get some help. It was clear to me that he had a drinking problem."

"How long ago was that, sir?"

"I don't know. A year ago, maybe."

Kate nodded, thinking that alcoholics in the middle of a bender had a penchant for saying things they would normally keep to themselves. "Where were you when you had the argument?"

"Hmm? Oh, we were in The Bleeker. He was in Albany on business so we decided to get together for a drink or two. That was before I realized he had a problem. He was already half in the bag by the time I got there, and it was only four o'clock in the afternoon."

"Did he stay in the bar after the argument?"

"Yeah. When I left he was hurling epithets at me and still sitting at the bar. I remember it like it was yesterday."

"Did you talk about your...situation...during that meeting?"

"Yeah," Sampson said heavily. "He threw in my face that I wasn't exactly perfect either, that I wasn't in a position to be holier-than-thou. I was no better than him, and probably worse, was the gist of his argument. At least he hadn't left a—well, you get the idea."

"Do you remember if there was any one else at the bar at the time? Did anybody overhear you talking?"

"I don't know," Sampson said miserably. "Could have been. God knows we were loud enough."

Kate's mind was working overtime. She was beginning to smell a rat. The Bleeker was Breathwaite's favorite hangout.

"Okay, let's forget about that piece for now. Is there anything more that can come out? Anything else that could hurt you?" Before he could answer, she held up a hand. "Just a yes, or no, please."

Sampson hung his head, tears spilling onto his business suit. "Yes." He looked up at her, his eyes red and pleading. "I never meant to hurt anyone. I was young and far from home. I didn't think I'd ever get back alive."

"Sir," Kate said gently, putting a hand on his arm, "it's not mine to judge you. My only concern is to limit the damage now and help you weather the media storm."

"I can't."

"I'm sorry?"

He looked at her. "I can't, Kate. I won't put my wife through this."

"Commissioner Sampson, I know you're feeling overwhelmed and emotional at the moment. I—"

"No, Kate. I have to step down."

"I don't think—"

"No." He sat up straighter. "No, I need to make her my priority now. It's the right thing to do."

"Sir, has it occurred to you that whoever planted this story is looking for that very reaction? That somebody wants you out?"

He seemed to consider that for a moment. "Perhaps, but it doesn't matter anymore. I'm done. Finished." As if to emphasize the point, he added, "No more."

"Sir," Kate felt her way carefully, "whether you stay or go, a story this sexy won't die. The media will keep after it. Why not stay and fight?"

"Kate, you are brave and courageous. Far more so than I am. I don't have the wherewithal to stand up and have spears thrown at me day after day."

"Respectfully, sir, you do that now."

"Yes, but it's not personal. Never personal," he murmured. He slapped his palms on his knees. "I'd better call the governor. Then I've got to get home to my wife. Prepare a statement for me, Kate, will you?"

"What do you want it to say, sir?"

"That I'm resigning for personal reasons, that I don't want my personal life to be a distraction for this governor and this administration. The extraordinary work that all the fine men and women who work for DOCS do on a daily basis is more important and more worthy of headlines than a mistake their commissioner made a dozen years ago."

"Are you sure you want to do this, sir? We can take the trip home to think about it."

"No, Kate, but thank you for trying. I've got to do this." He looked at her wistfully, "I've been very lucky to have you on board these past few months. I'll miss you."

"And I you, sir. I wish you'd reconsider."

Sampson sighed. "I know, but I must do what's right for my wife and me. She's all I've got." Tears began to roll down his cheeks once again. "I don't know what I'd do without her."

"It may be all right, sir." Kate put her hand on his arm sympathetically.

"Yeah," he sniffed and wiped his eyes on his sleeve, struggling to regain his composure. "Well, I'd better get making some phone calls." As he started to rise, he added, "Oh, and Kate? I'm going to recommend that Bill Redfield take my place. Don't make that public just yet, though. I want to make sure the governor is on board first."

"Yes, sir." For some reason Kate could not explain, the hair on the back of her neck was standing on end.

⇜⇝

"Wow. That's a shocker, huh?"

Kate and Jay were in the kitchen eating a light supper.

"I'll say. I really liked the man. He had integrity and a vision. But Jay, he just rolled over without so much as a whimper. Just threw his hands up and walked away."

"Yeah. That seems sort of out of character, doesn't it?"

"Mmm-hmm. Since he resigned and it doesn't matter what I know anymore, I did a little digging before I left the office for the night. I mean, I felt like I knew the man, and then it was as if I didn't know him at all."

"What'd you find out?"

"He got married right out of college to his sweetheart, then got his M.A. in criminal justice from John Jay College. He and his wife wanted desperately to have children, but for some reason they were never able to. They both got tested, and the problem was never clear. I guess the issue caused some tension in the marriage, but they had worked through that before he was drafted and sent over to Vietnam as part of an intelligence gathering unit."

"Didn't he get a Purple Heart?"

"Yeah. That was apparently around the same time he met the—how shall I say this delicately—mother of his child."

"Hmm." Jay shook her head. "So he and his wife spend years trying to have a kid, then he goes over there and in no time flat he gets a Vietnamese woman pregnant. I can see where that wouldn't go over too well at home."

"To put it mildly." Kate popped a piece of pineapple from a shish kebab in her mouth. "I'm pretty sure he never had any intention of continuing a relationship with this woman, even though he knew she was pregnant before he left to return to the States. So I guess rather than do the honorable thing and tell his wife—"

"The honorable thing would have been if he'd never cheated on his wife in the first place."

"No argument here. But, having already done that, the next course of action might have been to 'fess up to his mistake."

"Right."

"Apparently, he couldn't face telling his wife what he'd done, knowing that they'd been trying to have a child themselves for so long. Ostensibly, he thought she'd feel worse knowing that the problem with conception had to be hers."

Jay snorted.

"Or at least that's the rationalization for his silence."

"That's more like it." Jay started to rise to clear the empty dishes, but Kate put a hand on her arm.

"You cooked, sweetheart. I've got the dishes." She took the plates to the sink. "In any event, after he'd come back stateside, Sampson started feeling guilty about leaving that woman over there with a child to raise on her own."

"Well, bully for him."

"Yeah." Kate shook her head. "None of this sounds like the man I know. Anyway, he managed, through his intelligence contacts in country, to find her. He started sending her money as a means to assuage his guilt."

"Harrumph."

"And," Kate continued, "because the idea of having a daughter appealed to him. I think he thought that somehow he could stay in her life."

"Without his wife being any the wiser, right?"

"Right."

"Jackass."

"Well," Kate said, "it doesn't sound to me like he thought any of this through very logically. So that last part doesn't surprise me."

"What now? Did you talk to him after you got back tonight?"

"Yeah. As you can imagine, it's a mess. She's distraught and spitting bullets. He's beside himself and has no idea how to make it right. They're taking off tonight to get away from the media and to take some time to sort through all of this."

"And you're left holding the bag," Jay said bitterly.

Kate dried her hands on a towel and circled behind Jay, putting her arms around her and kissing her on the cheek.

"It's not that bad, sweetheart. Since he doesn't work for DOCS anymore, I can simply tell the media that they'll have to talk to him if they want answers. It's not within my purview any more."

"What did the governor say?"

"He and Sampson are good friends. I think he was in shock, for starters. He trusts Sampson, so he had no problem following his recommendation for a successor. Redfield was named the new commissioner immediately."

"That's not good for you, right?"

"I don't know. There's something about him that doesn't sit right with me. And then there's the way he blew me off when I wanted to fire Marisa." Kate shrugged.

Jay put her hand on top of Kate's where it rested on her shoulder. "Are you going to be all right in all this?"

"I'd like to think so. I talked to the governor myself. He told me in his discussion with Redfield he made it clear that he wanted me to stay."

"Well, that's good, anyway."

"Yeah, but something's bothering me about all this."

"Yeah? Like all of it."

"No, Jay. I mean something's bothering me about the way this all came about." She sat down at the table again. "Doesn't it strike you as odd that this story should come out right now?"

"What do you mean?"

"Let's look at this." Kate started ticking things off on her fingers. "A series of bullshit stories and editorials blasting me come out. Then we find out that Breathwaite is the source and is using Marisa as a mole—or worse. Redfield refuses to let me do anything about it. Next, it escalates and we get direct proof that Breathwaite isn't just feeding stories to the press anymore but is blackmailing reporters into trashing me. When that doesn't work, he tries the head-on approach, threatening to expose you. We thwart that by coming out ahead of him. And now this." She looked over at Jay.

"You think this is tied in with us."

"It seems awfully coincidental, doesn't it?"

Jay thought for a moment. "Okay, I can agree with that. But what's the angle? Breathwaite wants to come back, but he's certainly not coming back as commissioner. So what's in it for him?"

"Maybe he thinks Redfield will fire me and bring him back."

"He can't do that," Jay huffed indignantly, "he's got no grounds."

"He doesn't need any. I serve 'at the pleasure.' That means he doesn't need a reason to fire me, he just can. Maybe he says he wants his own spokesman in there—somebody he's hired."

"Well, the governor took care of that by telling him he wanted you to stay, right?"

Kate pondered. "So it would appear. The governor has the ultimate authority. I can't imagine Redfield would defy him. After all, you don't bite the hand that feeds you."

"What next?"

"I don't know, Jay. I wish I did. I guess we'll just have to sit tight and see what happens. I can tell you this, though—I don't trust Redfield. It's possible that he's just benefiting from the fallout here and has nothing to do with anything that's come before."

"But you don't believe that."

"I don't know what to believe, but there's something about him that just doesn't sit right with me. That, and his reaction to the Marisa thing."

"Mmm."

"Guess we'll just have to wait and see."

"I hate that part."

Kate laughed. "Yeah, me too."

# CHAPTER ELEVEN

Well, gentlemen, it seems that something good has finally happened." Hawthorne turned to his good friend. "Congratulations, William. Your new position suits you."

"Thank you, Robert."

Breathwaite couldn't stand it. "Oh, no need to thank me," he chimed in. "Never mind that none of that would have happened without me."

Hawthorne smiled thinly. "And thank you, David, for managing to get this one right. I felt certain you wouldn't fail to remind us of your role. I'm glad you didn't disappoint me."

Vendetti snickered.

"Michael," Hawthorne intoned, "it would have been nice if you could have been more helpful here. It seems our boy Charlie is determined to keep the dyke in her current role. What happened there?"

Vendetti straightened up even more rigidly in his chair. "He and Sampson had a conversation before the resignation became public. Apparently, Kyle's status was among the topics of discussion. There was nothing I could do about that."

"That makes our job a bit more difficult. What do you think, Bill?"

"Hyland made it a goddamned condition of employment that I keep her on. I couldn't very well object—he just would have passed me over for someone else. I figured it was better to get in there first, then figure out a way to get it done."

"Agreed." Hawthorne nodded. "But we don't have a long window. What's our boy's social schedule with the witch these days, Michael?"

"It looks like he's got her on his calendar for dinner next week. I've been chatting up his social secretary."

"We have to stop her from getting to him. It's too dangerous. Every single damn time he comes out of one of those dinners he throws out some idea from left field that's bound to jeopardize his position with both moderate and conservative democrats. The friggin' election's going to be close enough without having to worry about him alienating important constituencies."

"I'll take care of it," Vendetti said calmly.

"See that you do." Hawthorne looked at him threateningly.

"Bill, how long before you think you can safely take care of dyke wonder?"

The new DOCS commissioner laughed unpleasantly. "Give me a few weeks."

"A few weeks?" Breathwaite exploded.

Redfield turned to him slowly. "Yes, David," he said patronizingly. "If I move too quickly, it will seem as though I'm defying the governor. And if that happens and I fall out of favor, you have no chance of coming back. Perhaps if you hadn't called so much attention to her in the first place—well, let's just say your lack of subtlety has made the task that much more difficult."

"If it wasn't for me, you two-bit bureaucrat, you wouldn't be sitting in the commissioner's seat right now."

Evidently unconcerned with Breathwaite's outburst, Redfield answered dismissively, "I would have gotten there eventually, and with a lot less scrutiny, I might add."

"Okay, boys. Enough jawing. Bill, let's look at a three-to-four-week horizon. That puts us," Hawthorne consulted a calendar, "just around Thanksgiving or the beginning of December."

On the verge of objecting, Breathwaite thought better of it, and instead sat back in his chair and pressed his fingers together underneath his chin. He tried for calm practicality. "That puts us behind schedule."

"A little bit," Hawthorne admitted grudgingly, "but not fatally so. The nominating convention isn't for another eight months. I think we'll be all right, as long as we can keep her away from Charlie so that he doesn't self-destruct." He looked pointedly at Vendetti.

"I told you," the press secretary said curtly, "I'll take care of it."

"Class dismissed," Hawthorne said breezily. "See you all in a month or so."

⪧⪦

"Where are we going?" Jay was practically bouncing up and down in the passenger seat.

"I'm not telling," Kate said playfully.

"Can I take this blindfold off?"

"Nope."

"What if I get carsick?"

"You won't."

"How do you know?"

"Jay, have you ever gotten carsick before?"

"When I was a little girl," Jay whined.

Kate looked at her lover appraisingly. "You're still little, but you're sure no girl."

Jay didn't need to see her face to know that Kate's blue eyes were dark with desire. "No," she answered in her sultriest tone, "I'm not."

Kate reached over the center console of her BMW and took Jay's hand in hers. "I love you, sweetheart."

"That's it? You're still not going to tell me where we're going?"

Kate laughed. "Nice try, and the seduction almost worked, but no, I'm not telling you anything else."

Jay thumped against her seat, much like a child pitching a fit. "You're no fun at all."

"That's not what you said last night, princess."

"That was then"—Jay pouted—"this is now."

"I promise you're going to like it."

"Why don't you let me be the judge of that?"

"Don't you trust that I know you by now, baby? I'm sure you're going to be thrilled."

In fact, Kate had gone to great lengths to make sure everything was in place. It seemed like forever since they had gotten away, even for a day. Both of them were in desperate need of some unfettered fun. Jay was losing weight and her eyes were shadowed with lack of sleep. Kate was a little worried about her.

"Will I need to keep my coat on where we're going?"

"What is this, twenty questions?"

"Well, nothing else seems to be working, so..."

"You, my curious love, are incorrigible."

"And you, my mysterious brat, are infuriating."

"But you still love me, right, Jay?"

"Sadly, yes. Even though you torture me continually, I still love you with all my heart."

"Good. Then you can wait to find out the answers to your questions."

"Argh! You are the most frustrating woman alive."

"I'm okay with that."

"So I see, or don't see, as the case may be."

"If you keep this up, I'll tie your hands too."

"Why Katherine Ann, I didn't know you were into bondage."

"I didn't either, so don't tempt me."

"You take away all my fun."

"In case you're interested, we're almost there."

"Yeah?"

"Yep. Just a few more minutes."

The sounds of traffic were increasing. And their pace had slowed.

Kate watched her lover as she cocked her head to the side inquisitively. She shook her head. "You are something else, you know that?"

"What do you mean?"

"You're sitting there trying to puzzle out where we're going. I can see it."

"Well, since someone hasn't been particularly helpful—yes, I'm curious. That's what we reporters do, you know, try to solve mysteries."

"Oh, is that what you do? Thank you for clarifying that for me. I feel much better now."

Jay tried to slap Kate playfully on the arm. Kate, however, had the advantage of sight and managed to evade the attempt.

"Hey, where'd you go?"

"Gotta be faster than that, princess."

"Grrr."

"I love it when you make animal noises. It's so sexy."

Jay, who was about to do it again, swallowed hard instead, unwilling to give Kate the satisfaction of making her growl a second time.

Kate simply laughed and steered the car to the left, into the private parking lot where she had arranged to meet a friend of hers.

When it was clear that the car was not going to move again, Jay said excitedly, "Are we here?"

"Uh-huh."

"Yeah?"

"Yep."

"Then why am I still wearing a blindfold?"

"Because I'm not ready to take it off you yet." Kate came around the car and gently helped Jay out.

"Why not? The deal was that I had to wear it until we reached our destination. We're here now, so I should get to take it off."

"Nope."

"When?"

"In another minute." Kate watched as her friend approached, carrying an adorable bundle.

Several seconds later Jay sniffed the air. "What's that smell?"

"Nothing wrong with her nose, I see."

"Nope, that works fine," Kate greeted her friend with a hug. "Hi, Deb. Thanks for doing this."

"Doing *what*?" Jay asked, exasperated.

Kate and Deb laughed, and Deb leaned forward, bringing her close to Jay's face. The bundle she'd been carrying reached forward and removed the blindfold.

Jay blinked and looked delightedly into the face of a very cute, very curious, chimpanzee. "W-wha?"

Kate beamed. "Jamison Parker, meet Zippy. Zippy, this is my friend Jay."

As if he understood the conversation, the chimp stuck out his hand for Jay to shake.

Hesitantly, Jay took the proffered hand. She laughed heartily as Zippy shook it enthusiastically.

"That's enough, Zip. Let's leave her arm intact, okay?"

The chimp let go of Jay's hand and put his arms out instead for a hug.

"Aw." Jay reached out her arms and the chimpanzee jumped into them. "You are just the cutest thing I've ever seen."

"Ahem." Kate cleared her throat.

"You, my dear, are gloriously gorgeous. He," she indicated the chimp she still held, "is adorable."

"Glad we cleared that up," Deb chuckled. "I agree."

"Oh—I..."

"Jamison Parker, this is Deb Nellissen. Deb, meet the love of my life, Jay."

"You have the most endearing blush. Kate is right."

Jay looked from Kate to Deb and back again, obviously confused.

Kate smiled. "I was just describing you, sweetheart, and explaining the many reasons why I fell in love with you, when I wouldn't even give her," she jabbed her thumb in the other woman's direction, "the time of day."

"I'm lost. What am I missing here?"

"Deb and I met a few years ago," Kate explained, "when I was doing a special report on evolution, and whether we humans were any smarter than the apes from which we descended."

Deb picked up the story. "Even though I badgered her incessantly, she wouldn't succumb to my considerable charms. Can you imagine?"

"Hey, I let you be my friend."

Deb slugged her in the arm affectionately. "That was big of you."

"I know."

"Anyway," Kate continued. "When Deb saw on the news that I had a fantastically perfect-looking fiancée, she called to congratulate me."

"And to commiserate."

"Not to mention get the inside scoop."

"Well, there was that too."

"So I talked her into putting this little jaunt together for us, knowing how much you love zoos and animals."

Jay looked around her. "Oh my God. We're at the Bronx Zoo!"

"Very good, Sherlock."

"I thought you said she was smart."

"Normally, she's pretty quick on the uptake. You'll have to excuse her—she's been blindfolded for the last several hours and it seems to have dulled all her senses."

"Grrr."

"And I thought the animals here were bad." Deb shrank back in mock fear.

"Jay, Deb is a handler here. She has kindly moved heaven and earth in order to give us a behind-the-scenes tour of the zoo."

Seeing the light in Jay's eyes was more reward than anything Kate could have asked for. She nodded a silent thanks to her friend, who smiled knowingly.

"Let's get going. We've got a lot to see before the gates open to the general public."

Jay turned to Kate. "Is that why we had to leave so early in the morning?"

"Yep. It would be too hard to do this with all those screaming kids around."

"Although, at this time of year," Deb put in, "it's not so bad." She shrugged. "Only the really hardy types come out in November. Which is a shame, since there's still so much to see."

Kate thrust her hands in her pockets. "As days in late fall go in New York, it's a beautiful day in the neighborhood."

"Okay, Mr. Rogers. Let's go."

❧❦

They spent the better part of the morning peeking into all manner of enclaves—watching the big cats being fed, observing the polar bears at play, and petting the giraffes, who obligingly licked them with their long, black tongues.

When they were done, Jay turned to their hostess. "Deb, I can't thank you enough for this. It's like a little girl's dream come true. I've always been fascinated by all kinds of animals, but I never thought I'd be able to get so close. This was very special."

"The pleasure was all mine, believe me. Seeing Kate happy is a treat, and it's easy to understand why now, having met you. You are both very lucky ladies, and I am insanely jealous."

"Eat your heart out, doll." Kate winked at her, giving her a fierce hug and a kiss on the cheek. In her ear, she murmured, "Thanks, friend. I owe you. That was just what the doctor ordered."

"Happy to help, gorgeous. Take good care of that one. She's a keeper."

"Don't I know it."

"Hey, are you going to unhand my girlfriend sometime today?" Jay tapped her toe in mock impatience.

The two friends laughed and disentangled themselves. Then Deb swept Jay up in a hug as well.

"Oof."

"Didn't want you to feel left out," Deb said. More softly she added, "Be good to my friend. She's one of a kind and I'm rather fond of her."

"I'm a little partial to her myself, so don't worry about that."

Kate broke in. "Hey, are you going to unhand my girlfriend sometime today?"

They all laughed.

When they were in the car, Jay took Kate's hand. "I can't believe you pulled that off—an intimate look inside the Bronx Zoo."

"Yep." Kate was inordinately proud of herself.

Jay narrowed her eyes. "On our first date you finagled a private dinner inside a historic landmark, then you get a reporter to redirect the questioning in a press conference where I'm about to get shish kebabed, now it's a private tour of a famous zoo. All as a result of women who can't say no to you. How many other people that I don't know about yet are lusting after you and falling all over themselves to do favors for you?"

"You have nothing to worry about, Jamison."

"I know." Jay leaned her head on Kate's shoulder. "After all, I was the beneficiary in each case."

"Sweetheart?" Kate turned to face Jay, a quick look of concern causing her brow to furrow, "You don't still worry about..." She flashed back to the terrible phone conversation six months earlier during which Jay, believing a fabricated tabloid report accusing Kate of being a philanderer, had angrily told Kate she never wanted to see her again.

Jay stopped her by putting fingers to her lips. "Shh. No, love, I feel very secure in our relationship. I'm working on feeling equally secure about myself. I look at these other women and I still find myself asking every now and again why it is you chose me."

"That's easy, Jay. You are everything I could ever want in a partner. You're kind, caring, compassionate, warm, fun, passionate, insightful, interested, interesting, highly intelligent—and it's all wrapped up in an incredibly sexy, beautiful package."

Jay laughed. "Is that all?"

"No, but I don't want you to get a swelled head."

"No danger there, love."

"I know. That's what makes you the right one."

Jay twined their fingers together. "I'm so glad you think so. I love you, Kate."

"I love you too, Jay."

⧼⧽

Kate and Peter sat down to lunch at one of Peter's favorite out-of-the-way haunts.

"What's the word, Spinmeister?"

"Hard to say. If Redfield feels the slightest bit of sadness over Sampson's departure, he's certainly not showing it."

"No. Bill tolerated Brian, but I always got the feeling he thought he could do a better job. He was just biding his time."

"And now his time has come."

"Exactly. Is he making any changes?" Peter speared a french fry off Kate's plate, earning him a fork to the back of the hand.

"You know the fries are sacred, Technowiz."

"I know. That's why I want them."

"Try that again and I'll cut off a finger."

"Nothing like the punishment fitting the crime. I'm beginning to think you've been spending too much time with our 'lock 'em up and throw away the key' legislators. What happened to compassion, rehabilitation?"

"I'm all for that when it's deserved. In your case, however, you clearly know you're doing something wrong and your actions are quite deliberate. In such a case, I'm all for sending a message that willful disregard of the laws will be frowned upon and perpetrators will be dealt with harshly."

Peter held up his hands. "Ye gods. You even sound like one of them. You're scaring me."

"Yeah? Good, that was my intent. Now keep your filthy paws off of my plate."

Eyes gleaming, Peter reached across and snagged another fry, studiously ignoring Kate's warning. "That's just to show you that I'm not the least bit afraid of you. Now, can we get back to the topic at hand?"

"Yes, but only if you get your own damn fries," she muttered. "Anyway, Redfield's not doing anything terribly bold, but he is clearly sending the message that he's in charge and it's a new day."

"How's he treating you?"

"You know, it's funny. He's pretty much left me alone. I've seen him come down pretty hard on some other folks, but it's almost as if he's ignoring me. Like I'm a necessary evil."

"From his perspective that's true. The governor made your employment a condition of his promotion, didn't he?"

"I guess you could look at it that way."

"So he knows that, even if he wants to, he can't do anything about you. He doesn't want to antagonize you too much because you clearly have friends in high places. It's too early for him to defy a direct order. He has to build up a track record first."

"Speaking of my friends in high places, something pretty bizarre happened the other day. I was scheduled to have dinner with the governor. At around four o'clock, I got a phone call from his private appointments secretary, who sounded really nervous. She told me that something had come up and the governor regretted that he was going to have to cancel our dinner."

Peter shrugged. "Happens all the time, I'm sure."

Kate nodded. "You're right, except that this time seemed different somehow. I don't know...it was almost as if she was unsure of herself. I've been trying to put my finger on it, and I can't." She paused in thought. "It was like the same feeling you get when you know a kid is telling a white lie."

"Okay. Why would she do that?"

"I'm not sure. It's never happened before. When the governor's had to cancel in the past, this woman has been very matter-of-fact, very efficient and self-assured. She's simply rescheduled for him or told me that she'll get back to me when his schedule clears, and then she has. There was none of that this time—just a simple 'dinner is cancelled.'"

"Any theories?"

"Not yet. I'm trying not to be too paranoid about it. I keep telling myself that not everything that happens has to have a deeper meaning."

"No, but too many coincidences give me a hive."

"Okay then, what's your theory?"

"I don't have one, but I'm going to give it some serious thought," Peter said. "It's just one more thing. By itself, it wouldn't mean anything. But when you piece it together with everything else that's been going on, I have to ask myself if it isn't significant." He looked at Kate meaningfully. "In any event, I don't think we should just dismiss things out of hand at this point."

"I agree with you there."

"Let's add it to the list, and we'll see if it starts to fit with any of the other things that we know, or that have happened." He smiled thinly. "I do love a good jigsaw puzzle every now and again."

"Me too," Kate patted his face as she rose to leave, "but not when the subject is my life."

"I'll be over for dinner tomorrow night. Tell Jay I'm looking forward to some home cooking."

"I'll be sure to pass the message along. After all," she said drolly, "she does live to serve you."

"As all women should," he shot back.

"On that note..." She waved as she walked out the back door to the restaurant, leaving Peter to pay the check.

"Damn her. She did it again," he said when he realized what she had done.

"Did you say something, sir?" the waiter asked as he passed the table.

"Um, check, please."

"Yes, sir, right away."

As he waited, Peter spent more time mulling over the governor's scheduler canceling a dinner. Normally, he wouldn't think it odd in the least. But in this case, he was inclined to wonder if it wasn't somehow connected to what was happening with Breathwaite. He wasn't sure what the link could be, but his gut was tingling. When that happened, it almost always meant something fishy was going on. In his line of work, he couldn't afford to ignore his instincts, and he didn't intend to in this case.

Tapping his fingers on the just-arrived check, he glanced down at it, threw some bills on the table, cursed his friend one more time for sticking him with the tab, and made his way thoughtfully out onto the street.

෴

"Katherine Kyle," she answered the phone absently. She was busy plowing through the thick binder in front of her, trying to decipher the latest statistics on violent crime and average length of prison sentence.

"Kate?"

She was instantly alert. "Governor?"

Charles Hyland laughed. "Only some of the time."

"What can I do for you, sir?"

"I want to apologize."

Kate was puzzled. "For what, sir?"

"It seems our dinner last week got cancelled without any input on my part."

"That's all right, sir."

"It's not all right with me. Can you make it this evening? I know it's short notice."

"Of course, sir."

"Good. I'll see you at eight then."

"I'll be there, sir."

"I'm glad you could come."

"Thanks for the invitation."

Sitting behind his desk in his home office in the mansion on Eagle Street, the governor looked relaxed in a turtleneck and khakis with his strawberry blonde hair slightly mussed. He was a tall, good-looking man, and even at forty-eight, he still had a boyishness about him, an image underlined by the freckles sprinkled across his fair skin.

"Thank you, James." The governor dismissed the state trooper who had escorted Kate from the parking area.

The trooper saluted, turned sharply on his heel, and left the room.

"I want to explain what happened."

"There's no need, sir."

"Kate, how long have you known me?"

"Six years, sir."

"Would you say I was someone who worried excessively about appearances?"

"Sir? I'm afraid I'm not following you."

He laughed. "Well, that would be a first." He sat back in his leather chair and regarded her, a pen twirling in his fingers. "It seems that my social secretary was concerned that, with all the recent publicity you've been receiving, it might not be in my best interests to associate with you right now."

He forestalled her before she could weigh in.

"First of all, I don't give a rat's ass what people say."

"Perhaps you should, sir," she said matter-of-factly.

"Bullshit," he shot back angrily, shoving himself forward in his seat, all evidence of nonchalance gone. "I will not bow to narrow-minded, jelly-spined party bigwigs. I didn't get where I am by being stupid or politically naïve."

Kate was nonplussed. This was a level of intensity she had heard about but never seen personally.

"Second of all, I have no patience for staff members trying to coddle me. It makes me wonder what else I don't know. I want to be able to trust my people, not have to second-guess them."

"Sir, it seems to me your staff was just trying to protect you. That indicates a strong level of loyalty."

"No, Kate, you're wrong. Loyalty is about following instructions and orders, questioning things, perhaps, bringing troublesome issues to my attention, but not making unilateral decisions on my behalf. I deeply resent that."

There was nothing to say to that, so Kate wisely chose to keep her mouth shut.

"In any event, I merely wanted the opportunity to explain to you that I don't care what rumor and innuendo might be swirling around you at the moment. I have full confidence in you, I value your counsel and your company, and I will not be dictated to by outside parties as to whom I might spend my time with. Period."

"I appreciate that, sir."

"Shall we?" He gestured with a sweep of his arm that she should accompany him. "I believe we're having prime rib, potatoes au gratin, salad, and cheesecake for dessert."

"My mouth is watering just listening to the menu."

"Then let's see what we can do about feeding you."

The dining room was stately, with ornate dark cherry china cabinets, matching chairs and table, a very elegant oriental rug, and a solid gold chandelier from Tiffany's. The walls were decorated with original pieces from New York–bred artists.

"This is delicious," Kate said around a mouthful of potatoes.

"Yes, Sandy has really outdone herself tonight." The governor seemed to be having an internal debate. "Kate?"

"Yes, sir?"

He looked her squarely in the eye. "Brian Sampson is a good man. He was a great commissioner. I will miss him."

Unsure where he was going with the conversation, Kate merely nodded agreement.

"I know what he did was inexcusable, and I won't try to justify his behavior. I can't fathom what he could have been thinking in keeping something like that from his wife all this time." He shook his head sadly.

"Those things always have a way of coming to the surface, sir."

"Yes, they do. With the relentlessness of the media these days and the resources available to them, it makes it even less likely that someone can keep secrets of that nature." He paused in thought. "I want to preface the rest of this discussion by saying that you and I have a unique relationship, Kate. As a matter of course, I wouldn't have this conversation about a superior with an employee. But our relationship is such that I rely on you to provide perspective and wise counsel. What we talk about must stay in this room."

"Of course, sir."

"Beyond that, I want to be clear that my remarks and questions tonight are in no way designed to put you in an awkward situation. Bill Redfield is your boss. You report to him."

"Naturally, sir."

He paused another moment before going on. "Brian was, and is, a friend, Kate. He's someone whose advice I trust implicitly. The fact that he thought Bill Redfield should succeed him is the major reason for the rapidity with which I made the decision to promote him. I was more inclined to do a nationwide search."

"Sir, in a situation where there is such upheaval and uncertainty, a drawn-out process might not be the best thing. DOCS is a paramilitary organization. Its employees are used to a sort of regimentation, as are the inmates. A prolonged period of indecision could cause a morale issue among the correction officers and a boldness on the part of inmates."

"Funny, that's exactly what Brian said. Still—I wish I had more time to consider my options." He tapped his temple with his forefinger.

"You could have named an interim commissioner."

"Mmm, and I almost did, except that Brian thought it would indicate a lack of confidence in my final selection if I hired Redfield in the end."

"As if he wasn't your first choice," Kate said.

"Yes. Exactly."

"I'm sure Commissioner Redfield will do a fine job, sir."

He was pensive. "You may be right, Kate, but I just don't feel like I know the man at all. Every conversation I've had with him, I can't seem to get a fix on him."

"He's very different in personality from Commissioner Sampson, that's for sure."

"I wish I knew what makes him tick. Do you have a sense for him yet, Kate?"

"I haven't really spent much time with him, sir." Kate had no intention of sharing her concerns about her new boss with the governor.

"Mmm. Well, he certainly has the background for the position. He worked his way up from correction officer to sergeant, superintendent, assistant commissioner, deputy commissioner, executive deputy commissioner, and now commissioner. There's no doubt that he knows the agency inside and out."

"Yes, sir, he knows every inch of the organization."

The governor nodded and sighed. "On to a different topic. How do you feel about domestic partner benefits?"

"Sir?" Kate was having a hard time keeping up with the abrupt subject change.

"I've been thinking about your situation. Certainly you and Jay are not unique in having to fight bigotry and ignorance."

"No. We may be a bit more high profile at the moment," she winked, "but there are thousands of couples in New York state just like us."

"What acknowledgment do you get officially?"

"Officially, sir?"

"Yes. For instance, can Jay put you on her insurance policy?"

"Are you trying to save the state money on my health insurance coverage, sir?"

"Very funny, Kate. I mean it. Can she?"

"No, sir, *Time* is not that progressive. Nor, might I add, is almost any other public or private entity."

"My point exactly. I think that's wrong, and I want to change it."

"Sir, you realize you're running for president, right?"

He laughed heartily. "That's the rumor."

"Are you sure you'd want to be out front on what will surely be viewed as a liberal issue?"

"Kate, I have no intention of hiding away and sidestepping controversial issues just because I'm running for president. I happen to think a good section of the populace respects a man who stands up for what he believes in, whether or not they agree with his stance."

"I would look at it a bit differently, sir. You are already virtually assured of capturing the liberal vote. It's the moderate and conservative Democratic ballots you should be courting. Creating an environment that encourages domestic partnership benefits is not high on their agenda."

"No, but it should be. They're Democrats, gosh darn it. Our party used to stand for things like that, until we started to behave more like middle-of-the-road vagabonds who couldn't make up our minds whether we wanted to pursue the Democratic agenda or kowtow to the Republicans. That's the problem all across the country, Kate. Democrats everywhere, and particularly in our party's leadership, are scared silly of making policy decisions that might not play in Peoria."

"And you, sir, single-handedly, are going to change that?"

"No, Kate, of course not. But if people like me don't stand up and reassert the principles on which our party is based, who will?" He looked at her oddly. "Kate, are you actually arguing *against* me protecting you?"

She laughed at the almost comical expression on his face. "Heaven forbid, sir. I just want to make sure we examine the issue thoroughly. It certainly wouldn't be in my best interests, or the interests of gays and lesbians everywhere, to have you defeated because you took a strong stand on our behalf as governor."

"Are you convinced that instituting an executive order barring discrimination against you in housing and allowing your partners to be on your insurance policies will lose me the election?"

"I'm convinced that it could."

"I recognize the wisdom of your advice, Kate, as always."

"But you're going to ignore it."

He smiled broadly. "Absolutely. Tomorrow I am going to introduce an executive order allowing gay and lesbian couples who can prove a financial interdependence to have access to each other's health benefits if they work for the state."

She shook her head at him. "You're a troublemaker."

"I prefer to think of myself as a crusader."

"That too. The DNC might not be too pleased."

"Screw 'em. Pardon my French."

"I'm fairly certain that was English, sir." She winked at him.

"Vendetti, what happened? I thought you were going to see to it that the dyke bitch didn't get to our boy?" Bob Hawthorne's voice boomed over the telephone line. "Next thing I know he's out there waving a goddamned rainbow flag!"

"I did take care of it. I convinced his private appointments secretary that it would be detrimental to Charlie's career to allow him to associate with Kyle. She took it off his schedule."

"Apparently it got put back on his schedule, because he had dinner with her last night. And today, he's putting out a friggin' executive order that has my hair standing on end."

"How do you know he had dinner with her last night? It wasn't on his schedule. I checked. There was nothing there. He was supposed to be working at home on a speech to the AFL-CIO."

"Because *somebody* is on the ball. Breathwaite has her office bugged. He heard the call from your boss inviting her over and her accepting. Now he's the poster boy for every flaming liberal in the country, but he's made it impossible for the conservative dems, and next to impossible for the more right-leaning moderates, to support him."

Vendetti was speechless. He was calculating whether or not the appointments secretary would have sold him out to the governor as the one who pushed her to remove the dinner with Kate from the calendar. *Nah,* he thought, *she's too tight lipped for that. Protect your own, that's what she'd do.*

Hawthorne was saying, "Now I have to pay our boy a visit and teach him a lesson or two in teamwork and political strategy. I'll be up there tonight."

"What?" Vendetti struggled to bring his mind back to the conversation at hand.

"Are you deaf now, as well as dumb? I'm stopping in to see the golden boy and remind him how this candidacy works. He needs to understand that he can't just go off and unilaterally piss off the bulk of our constituency. I suggest you stay clear, if you know what's good for you."

Vendetti held the phone out as it was slammed unceremoniously in his ear.

≪ॐ≫

"Charles, it's good to see you." Hawthorne clapped the governor on the back as he shook his hand.

"Bob. I wasn't expecting to see you again so soon. What brings you to our fair state?" The governor, well schooled in keeping his expression neutral, managed to hide his dislike of the DNC chairman. They were standing in the doorway of the governor's New York City office high atop the World Trade Center.

"Well, you know, I like to get out every now and again—see different parts of the country. And I do so love the cold November wind in the Big Apple."

"I can imagine."

"Actually, Charles, I need to tell you—that little stunt you pulled this morning is causing quite a stir, and not in a positive way."

"I'm not sure what you're talking about." Governor Hyland moved back behind his formidable desk and sat down, a subtle reminder to his visitor that he was in a position of power.

Hawthorne dispensed with the niceties. "You know perfectly goddamn well what I'm talking about, so don't play games with me." The spittle was forming at the corners of his mouth.

"All right, Bob. Say your piece. But I want you to remember," Hyland leaned forward in his chair, pointing his forefinger at the DNC chairman's chest, "I'm the candidate here, not you. You seem to have a hard time with that. And I have a state to run. The people of New York chose *me*, Bob. They elected me because they thought I could do the job. And that's exactly what I'm doing. Neither you nor anyone else is going to tell me how to govern my state."

"You little pissant. Without the party you're nothing. You'd be stuck here forever in this backwater if it weren't for me and the party's fund-raising machine. You think you're so important? If we weren't so far along in the process I'd replace you in a heartbeat."

"You and I both know there isn't another Democrat out there who stands a prayer's chance in hell of winning next November. That's why we've got such a great shot at the White House—we're not busy beating the living daylights out of each other before the general election season has even begun. You want me out, go for it."

With apparent effort, Hawthorne put a lid on his temper. "Let's be reasonable here, Charles. I don't want to replace you, and you don't want to be replaced. All I'm asking is that you give a little more consideration to the bigger picture. Polling data taken just hours after your press conference this morning showed a four-percentage-point slip among those identifying themselves as moderates. That's not even the conservatives, Charles. We can't afford to alienate our base."

Hyland, too, reined in his emotions. "The fact is, Bob, what I did this morning helps to solidify our position as traditional Democrats. It sets us apart from our opponents and reenergizes a long-dormant segment of the party faithful that hasn't had a reason to vote in years. We need the core of the Democratic Party to rally around a candidate who stands for their values. Look at the last election. Nearly a third of the most liberal members of the party stayed home. I've just made sure they come to the polls next November."

"From now on, I hope you'll consult with me before you take matters into your own hands. We can do advance polling, feel the voters out, find out where they stand on certain issues. We need to take the guesswork out of our positions. Let us help you, Charles. After all, we're all in this together."

"Of course we are, Bob. But I want to be clear that I will not govern by the polls. I've always been a man who did things because they were the right thing to do. That's how I built my reputation. If I change the way I'm perceived now it will only hurt us a year from now. There's a reason, Bob, why I'm not facing any real opposition within the party. I will not mess with the formula that's gotten me where I am now."

"Just remember, Charles, that without the party behind you, you wouldn't stand a snowball's chance in hell next November."

"Just you remember, Bob, without me the party doesn't stand a snowball's chance in hell next November."

Hawthorne rose from his seat without another word and walked out.

Jay could clearly remember the last time she'd been nervous walking into the massive high-rise in midtown Manhattan that served as headquarters for *Time*—her first day on the job when she was fresh out of college. She had been so intimidated by the building, by the people, and by the idea of going to work for a publication she'd been reading since she was old enough to decipher printed words on a page.

That was three years ago. Now here she was, nervous again. It was her first day back from the suspension. What would her colleagues think? Would they treat her differently? What kind of assignments would she be given? Would she ever get another cover story? And how would the readers react? Would there be more letters to the editor demanding that she resign or be fired? Jay knew from Trish that there had been half a mailbag full of those. But they had been counterbalanced by the half a mailbag full of letters supporting her, deriding the tabloid press for its overzealousness, and expressing respect for the way she handled the situation.

"Good morning," she said to the security guard at the front desk.

"Good morning yourself, Miss Parker. Nice to have you back."

"Thanks. It's nice to be back."

*Perhaps things aren't going to be so bad after all,* she thought as she got on the elevator. The looks she got once she emerged on her floor and made her way to her cubicle were a mixture of amusement, resentment, and benign disinterest.

"Hey, Jay," Warren Jacobs called from across the room. "How does it feel to be a celebrity?" He smiled at her. "Can I have your autograph?"

"Only if you pay for it."

"See, it's always about money with you, blondie."

"Hi. Jay. I'm glad you're back. I've missed that trademark smile." Jessica Howland touched her on the arm as she passed. "Things have been so very dull around here without you. Steve had no one to pick on, Warren was sulking in the corner, Mary couldn't complain about you getting all the choice assignments. Geez, you can't imagine how tough it's been."

As if on cue, Mary skulked around the corner, her face fixed in its usual frown. She looked at Jay with obvious disdain.

Jay made a point of smiling broadly at her. "Hi, Mary. How's everything going?"

In her characteristic monotone she said, "They *were* going fine. I actually had a real story or two to cover in the last two weeks. Imagine that."

"Good for you, Mary," Jay said with as much sincerity as she could muster. "I'm glad."

Mary made a sound somewhere between disbelief and derision before continuing on her way to the elevators.

"She's such a ray of sunshine, isn't she? Just brightens up the place." Jessica walked with Jay over to her desk. "Ignore her, Jay. Most of us are with you. What happened to you could have happened to any of us, and we all know it. I can't say there haven't been times that I've been interviewing some hunk where I haven't wanted to carry the relationship into the personal." She shrugged. "C'est la vie."

"I love it when you speak French. Thanks, Jess. You're the best." Jay smiled at her.

"Parker, get in here!" Trish bellowed, winking.

Jay walked into her editor's office and stood uncertainly inside the doorway.

"Don't just stand there, Jay, come all the way in and sit down."

As Jay settled herself in one of the visitors' chairs, Trish regarded her carefully.

"Welcome back."

"It's good to be here and not upstairs," Jay replied, referring to Standislau's penthouse office.

"Yeah, well, let's try to keep it that way, shall we?"

"No argument from me."

"How do you feel?"

"Honestly, Trish? I'm a little nervous."

"That's understandable. Just remember, Jay, it doesn't matter what a few narrow-minded, two-bit reporters who won't ever rise above writing sidebars think. Standislau and I are behind you one hundred percent, and so are the majority of your colleagues."

"Okay."

Jay got the distinct feeling that Trish was evaluating her.

"What kind of story do you want to do this week, Jay?"

"This is a first. You're asking me what assignment I want?"

"In a manner of speaking. I will, of course, be more than happy to veto any choice you make that I don't like. But I thought I'd at least give you a crack at making a pitch."

"Did someone hit you on the head while I was gone? Who are you and what have you done with Trish? Since when does what a reporter wants to write about enter into the equation?"

Trish laughed. "Look. It's obvious to me that you're uncomfortable, and I can understand that. I might be, too, in your position. I want to give you a chance to shine. Let's show everyone what you can do and why you're one of the best damned writers we have. It seems logical to me that the best way to accomplish that is to let you pick the topic. So what do you want to write about, Jay?"

"You never cease to surprise me, you know that?"

"I like that. Predictability is so boring."

"Uh-huh. Does it have to be a hard news story?"

Trish narrowed her eyes. "Not necessarily."

"Okay." Jay paused to gather her thoughts. "I've been thinking for a while now about doing a piece on Native American medicine."

"Tell me more." The editor sat forward in her chair.

"I want to compare their traditions to our scientific approach. I think there's a lot we could learn from them. Beyond that, there's the mystique of exploring a way of healing that's different from our own. We, as a society, are naturally curious about cultures we've never really understood. The Navajo and Hopi tribes have a large presence out in Arizona and New Mexico near Four Corners. I'd like to spend some time there and come back with something truly special."

"Where in the world did this come from?"

Jay smiled. "I've had two weeks to do a lot of reading. Kate has spent some time out there, and she supplied me with some interesting books chronicling the spirituality of Native American health care. Trish, these people inhabit a fascinating world we haven't taken the time to understand. I want to help change that."

"Let me think about it for a bit. In the meantime, go get yourself squared away." When Jay looked at her for further clarification, Trish added, "I'll admit that I'm intrigued. I'll look at the story board and see if I can clear you to send you out into the middle of nowhere for a week and a half or so."

"Thanks, Trish. You won't regret it."

"Hey, I didn't say it was a done deal, I just said I'd work on it. Now get out of here."

# CHAPTER TWELVE

I heard back from Christine today."

"Who's Christine?" Kate sat on the bed, watching interestedly as Jay stuffed items into a huge suitcase, tossed them back out, then, chewing on her lower lip, reconsidered and repacked them.

"She's the chaplain at Middlebury I was telling you about."

"Ah, the friend who wants to make honest women out of us."

Jay laughed. "I think that's probably beyond her scope, honey, but she did say she was very flattered that we wanted her to officiate at our ceremony."

"Yeah?"

"Yep. Before she can say yes, though, she's got to clear it with the college president, and if he approves, she can check her dates against ours so we can have a meeting of the minds."

"Or in this case, a meeting of the hearts."

Jay paused in her packing frenzy to kiss Kate full on the mouth. "I'm pretty sure we already have that, sweetheart."

"Mmm, I'll give you that. So when will we hear back from her?"

"It should be in the next week or so. In any event, since we were planning the ceremony for early May, we have a little time to play with."

"Does that time frame still work for you, love?"

Jay looked at Kate quizzically. "Of course it does. Why would you ask that?"

"I just want to be sure you don't want it earlier or later than that."

"No, I'm happy with May. It will mark our one-year anniversary, and I like the symmetry of that. Don't you?"

"Yep." Kate peeked into the suitcase. "Are you really taking all that?"

Jay blushed. "I have no idea what I'm going to need there, so I'm bringing a little bit of everything."

"I can tell you what you won't need." Kate reached in and pulled out a business suit that Jay had just packed, holding it up so Jay could see it.

"But I don't want to disrespect them by dressing down."

"Honey, if you wear that, it sets you apart from them and highlights the cultural differences between us. Casual but professional is better, trust me."

"Okay, if you're sure."

"I'm sure. So, are you excited about the assignment?"

"God, yes. Time to spend learning ancient tribal ways, immersing myself in their way of life. It's fascinating. Thank you so much, Kate, for making contact for me and setting this up." Jay zipped the suitcase and placed it on the floor.

"My pleasure. I think you'll find the Hopi and Navajo to be honest, straightforward, wary of the white man, and proud of their heritage."

"The only downside is being away from you for so long. Ten days." Jay wrapped her arms around Kate's shoulders. "I'm going to miss you terribly."

"Me too, love, but it's worth the sacrifice to see you back doing something you enjoy so much."

"I think I was taking my professional life a little bit for granted, you know? This was a heck of a wake-up call for me. How many people get to travel around the world, doing what they love to do all the time and getting paid for it?" Jay shook her head. "I almost lost all that."

Kate put a hand on her arm. "But you didn't."

"No, I didn't. Still, it's not a lesson I'm likely to forget any time soon."

"I suspect not."

Jay sat down on the bed. "I really want to make this story something special, you know? I want to justify Standislau's faith in me."

"You don't owe him anything, Jay. You already paid the price, and you managed to exonerate your bosses in the process. That's a pretty impressive bonus."

"I still feel so bad about the whole thing, though. The magazine and its management would never have come under fire in the first place if it hadn't been for me."

"Just think of all the free publicity they got out of the deal. Appearances on a prime-time news magazine and three network morning shows. That's a viewership of several million. I'm willing to bet subscriptions will go up this month."

"Really?"

"Absolutely. There are a lot of people out there, Jay, who are of the opinion that any publicity, even bad publicity, is good. As someone famous once said, 'Just as long as they spell my name right.'"

"Do you believe that?"

"No. I think that negative notoriety is bad, period. You get name recognition out of it, but name recognition alone isn't sufficient, in my mind, to justify taking a hit."

"I think you're right."

"Well, there are a lot of seasoned PR veterans out there who disagree with us."

"I'll take you over them any day." Jay reached over and tweaked Kate's nose.

"I sincerely hope so, honey, because you're stuck with me."

"I like it that way." Jay's eyes softened, her pupils growing dark with desire, as she regarded her lover. Reaching out with one hand, she ran her fingertips lightly over the chiseled planes of high cheekbones, up over the eyebrows, down the side of Kate's face and along her jawline, her fingers memorizing each smooth inch of skin.

She tangled her hands in luxurious, long strands, the texture reminding her of the finest satin. With a small tug, she pulled Kate to her, exploring the warm wetness of her mouth with reverence.

In a husky voice Jay said, "I am constantly astounded at just how much I want you. I could kiss you a million times, and still, each kiss feels like the first time."

Her mouth returned to Kate's, seeking the softness of her lips, the welcome brush of her tongue, the sensation of coming home that washed over her as it always did when they kissed. She caressed the exposed skin at Kate's throat and collarbones and released the top button of the blue silk blouse to reveal the tantalizing curve of breast beneath. As her mouth continued to explore, her fingers brushed over tender skin.

Jay undid the rest of the buttons, leaving the blouse to fall open completely. She ran her fingers over Kate's warm flesh, stroking and caressing ribs, stomach, back, and navel. With practiced ease she found the clasp on the front of Kate's bra and undid it, moving the material to palm the softness beneath.

Kate's gasp intensified Jay's need to devour, and her fingers closed on hardening nipples. She swept the blouse and bra from Kate's shoulders. The clothing pooled around Kate's waist, her arms still bound by the sleeves. Still without breaking the kiss, Jay pushed her onto her back.

Kate shuddered as Jay peeled off her pants and panties, leaving her naked except for her constricted arms. Jay inserted her jean-clad thigh between her lover's legs and immediately noted the wetness that soaked the denim. She closed her eyes and savored the feeling of power as Kate whimpered in her ear. Rocking forward, Jay ran her tongue down the center of Kate's body, her fingers leaving goose bumps in their wake as they blazed their own path along oversensitized skin. She watched Kate's hands convulsively grasp at the bed coverings and her arms visibly strain against their silk bonds.

When she both heard and felt a deep, plaintive moan, Jay brushed her fingers over Kate's clitoris, paused as Kate arched up off the bed, then stroked her lovingly as she continued to rock against her.

Kate's orgasm, when it came seconds later, was so forceful that it nearly made Jay come without being touched.

Before her breathing even settled, Kate was in motion. She managed to free herself from her sleeves, then used her superior strength to flip Jay over. She tugged off her cotton turtleneck, taking the lace-and-satin bra with it. As she licked and teased already-aroused nipples with her hot mouth, she unfastened Jay's jeans, then pulled them off along with her red lace panties and flung them away from the bed.

With seeming single-minded intent, she pinned Jay's hands to her sides, greedily stroking and biting slick flesh as Jay writhed in anticipation beneath her. She lowered her mouth to Jay's center and tasted her pleasure, allowing her tongue to explore every crevice. Her lips sucked the distended clitoris with a fierce longing.

Jay cried out her release as her body shook with the effort. Pulling Kate up and on top of her body with a strength born of desperation, she wrapped her arms and legs around Kate's long torso and squeezed as tightly as she could.

They stayed like that for a moment, suspended in time, their passion and love for each other boundless and insatiable.

It was a place he didn't have much need for these days, but David Breathwaite continued to lease a dilapidated apartment in Arbor Hill, an area widely considered to be the most crime-infested section of Albany. He didn't rent it himself, naturally—he had it rented for him by one of his many shadowy contacts.

At the moment he was busy pacing across the rotting wooden floorboards, reading from a file he held in his hands. Timothy Rundoon, given the street name "Basher" based on his penchant for bashing late-paying drug customers over the head with blunt objects. Age thirty-six, incarcerated four times since the age of thirteen, when he was sent to a juvenile home for raping his babysitter. He was subsequently bounced from seven foster homes for deviant behavior before being arrested again at sixteen for breaking and entering, burglary, and resisting arrest. He served another two years in juvenile facilities until he was released on his eighteenth birthday. Within two months he was running drugs for the local kingpin. When he was busted, he was carrying five kilos of cocaine and $160,000 cash. That time he served seven years in one of the state's medium-security prisons. He managed to last on the streets for three months before running afoul of the law again; at twenty-five he was convicted of first-degree manslaughter for killing a rival drug dealer. After spending ten years at Attica, he was paroled six months ago.

"Where is he?" Breathwaite asked nervously. There was so much riding on this plan.

"He'll be here." Kirk was leaning against a door frame that had seen better days.

"You're sure you gave him the address and told him seven o'clock."

"I'm positive." Kirk sighed and pushed off from the molding. "Look, he's an ex-con. You really expect him to show up exactly on time?" He shrugged. "For someone who's spent as much time in prisons as you have, you don't know much about the life, do you? If you show up on time it means you're too eager and easy. It's far smarter to wait the meet out a bit, make him sweat." He laughed unkindly. "He's sure got that part taken care of with you."

As Breathwaite spun around to answer him, there was a loud knock. "Yeah," he barked loudly.

"It's Basher," came the muffled reply from the other side of the door.

Breathwaite stalked to the door and threw it open, grabbing the man on the other side of the threshold by the shirt and yanking him inside. The man stumbled and lost his balance temporarily before recovering. He straightened up, intent on teaching Breathwaite a lesson, before Kirk intervened, putting a hand on his chest and shoving him back several steps.

"I didn't come here for this bullshit," he spat.

"When you work for me," Breathwaite snarled menacingly, "you show up on time and straight. You don't come here tripped out and late. Furthermore, you'd better lose the attitude before I change my mind and have your parole revoked for violations."

"Hey, man, you don't hafta get all, like, stressed out or nothin'. I's here, ain't I?"

"Barely," Kirk muttered under his breath. It was clear the man was high on something, most likely crack.

Breathwaite looked at his private investigator accusingly. "What did you do, give him some of the money up front?"

Kirk snapped back, "How else did you think I was going to get him here? He sure didn't come because he wanted to help you in your little crusade."

Breathwaite's face was nearly purple with rage, the urge to strike out almost overwhelming. Didn't these idiots know what was at stake? Couldn't they see? Between clenched teeth he ground out, "I paid for someone who could get the job done. If he's not in any condition to do it, then we've wasted time and money on him."

"I can do whatever you want me to. But you ain't told me nothin' yet."

Breathwaite was struggling with his decision, although he'd been over it a thousand times in the past week. If he gave this junkie any information that could be traced back to him, what was to prevent the ex-con from selling him out? On the other hand, Redfield seemed no closer to firing that dyke bitch than he had been three weeks earlier.

He *had* to get back into his rightful spot at DOCS, whatever it took. He had been exiled to his current, useless position long enough. He was out of the flow and off balance, virtually extraneous to the media whose attention he craved. He needed to be needed by them—needed to control them and the currency of information—and he couldn't from where he was at the moment. It was humiliating when they yanked him out of the hot seat to take a meaningless paper job. It was beneath him. His place was where the action was, in the prime PR seat for criminal justice issues in state government, and Katherine Kyle was standing in his way.

Mind made up, he turned to Basher. "This is what I need. Make it happen for me, and I'll see what I can do about getting your parole supervisor off your ass, in addition to getting you a lifetime supply of crack. Screw up or rat me out and I'll make sure you never see daylight as a free man again. Do you understand me?"

Basher regarded him under droopy lids. "I understand that you's blowin' a lot of hot air and ain't said nothin' real yet. Stop wastin' my time and tell me what you want."

"Very well," Breathwaite said. "For starters, I want you to arrange a riot for me. At Attica. I understand you still have buddies inside."

Basher snorted. "Yeah, I got buddies." Warily he added, "You said for starters. What else you want?"

Breathwaite rubbed his hands together unconsciously. "There's going to be a casualty during the course of the uprising."

"How you know that?"

"Because your buddies are going to make sure it happens. I want the DOCS mouthpiece taken out."

Basher let that statement hang in the air for a minute, obviously stunned. "Lemme see if I got this right. You want to take out a hit on the spokesperson for the main man? That bitchin' broad, what's her name? I seen her on TV. Man, she's one hot piece of merchandise."

"I want her taken hostage and killed as part of the riot. Can you handle it or not?"

"Better question is why would my brothers want to do this for you? Me, I'm square with an endless river of blow, but the bros, man, they ain't fool enough to mess with nothin' that stupid. Most of them hope to get out someday. Pull some damn idiot stunt like that, you might as well kiss your ass good-bye."

"If they complete this assignment successfully, I'll see to it that they'll never be punished. In fact, they'll have commendations in their files for their next parole hearing."

Basher narrowed his already-slitted eyes. "You got the power to do that?"

Breathwaite nodded.

Basher made a whistling sound. "What guarantee do they got? If I's gonna go to them with somethin' like this, they's gonna wanna see a show of good faith, if you know what I's sayin'."

Annoyed, Breathwaite asked, "What would convince them?"

Basher scratched his chin stubble and considered. "Tweety's due for a hearin' day after tomorrow. It's his fifth one in ten years, and he knows he ain't never gettin' out 'til his twenty-five is up. You get the bigwigs to let him walk, and that oughta do it."

"Done," Breathwaite said.

"All right then. I'll go to the bros and tell them to watch what happens with Tweety. Then we'll see what they's wantin' to do."

Two days later they were back in the apartment. Basher's eyes were wide with a mixture of surprise and respect.

"You did it. Man, I ain't never seen nothin' like it. Guy's in for really bad shit and he walks out the front door free as a bird. Tweety's one lucky man. No shit."

"Yeah, yeah," Breathwaite said impatiently. "Are your boys in or not?"

"Shit yeah. Man does somethin' like that with no more than a snap of a finger, yeah they's in."

"Good. Here's how it's going to happen. I want some of your buddies outside in D yard for their rec time just after dinner and others staying behind on the block." Breathwaite pulled out a schematic of the Attica state penitentiary. On it, clearly marked, were cell blocks A, B, C, D, and E. Times Square sat right in the center of blocks A through D and was the one-story area where all four of those blocks intersected. It was highlighted in red. He pointed to where he circled the D block recreation yard and to the floor where Basher had been housed. "I've marked everything clearly."

"Man, you don't hafta tell the bros how to create chaos, they's got that covered. All I needs to know is how you expect them to get to the target, and how you expect me to get that map to the bros."

"Don't worry about the map, my man on the inside will take care of that. As for getting to Kyle, when it becomes clear to the administration that the incident is getting out of hand, they'll send the big guns from headquarters, including her."

"Yeah, but they sure as hell ain't gonna go on the block with four hundred inmates carryin' on."

"No," Breathwaite tried to stay patient, "but the riot will attract the media. She will have to deal with them. In order to do that, she's going to have to walk through Times Square to get out the front door and across the street to an area where the reporters will be standing." He traced the route with his finger on the map. "That's how she'll supply them with updates."

"Yeah? How you know that?"

Breathwaite sighed. "You're just going to have to take my word for it. She'll be unarmed and by herself. Your buddies should take her on one of her trips outside to brief the press, but don't kill her in Times Square—it's too accessible and there are too many chances for something to go wrong. No," he smiled evilly, lost in his own personal fantasy, "let the boys take her back to the unit and have some fun."

Kate's head was pounding. It had been a long day, and it wasn't over yet. She intended to get out and do some Christmas shopping for Jay, but one crisis after another waylaid her until it was too late to shop. The last time she celebrated Christmas was the year before her parents died. Since then, guilt and remorse kept her from allowing herself to enjoy what was once her favorite holiday. Now, with Jay in her life, she was ready to reclaim a tradition she'd lost.

This first Christmas in her house, Kate was determined, would be a grand, fun, and romantic affair just for the two of them. She couldn't wait. As a surprise for Jay, she already bought a huge Douglas fir and decorated it. But she had a lot more work to do to make Christmas everything she thought it should be. Although she hadn't had time to talk to Jay about her plans, she felt sure that Jay would be pleased.

Kate sighed, rubbed her temples, and eyed her briefcase, which was stuffed with memos that she hadn't gotten to review before leaving the office. She missed Jay terribly. Her house, which was once her personal haven and buffer from the rest of the world, now seemed empty and cold without her lover in it. Even Fred was feeling a bit blue. Rather than running around the house with a stuffed toy in his mouth, he was lying on his bed, moping.

As if on cue, the phone rang.

"Hello?"

"Hi, my love."

"Hey, sweetheart. How's it going?" Kate tried to push the pain in her head aside.

"Oh, Kate, it's amazing. I spent the day today talking with a Navajo singer, or medicine woman. So much of their approach to medicine is about healing the spirit. They use sand paintings that take days to produce to help the patient restore harmony and balance with their environment. Then, when the ceremony is done, they destroy the painting! I wasn't allowed to see a completely correct painting, because the Navajo believe that will invite evil spirits, but the singer did show me one being created for artistic purposes."

Although Kate was somewhat familiar with Native American healing rituals, she kept quiet, preferring to let Jay share her excitement.

"Oh, Kate, it's so different from our scientifically based approach."

"Yes, it is." The amusement was clear in Kate's response.

"I'm sorry, love. Here I am, going on and on."

"I love hearing you go on and on when you're excited about something. I'm glad you're enjoying the experience, sweetheart. Sounds like it will make a great story."

"Oh, yes. Over the next few days I'm going to travel with the singer to the various parts of the reservation. It's such an eclectic mix of traditional Navajo ways and western cultural influence. For instance, they may live in a hogan, but they have television. Go figure."

"Mmm-hmm."

Jay paused a beat. "As much as I'm happy to be here learning new things, I miss you, Kate."

"I miss you too, baby. The house seems awfully empty without you. Even Fred is sulking."

"Aw. I'll buy him an extra stuffed toy for Christmas."

"He'll appreciate that."

"Oh my God. I almost forgot. Speaking of Christmas, you'll never believe it. My mother called and left me a message at the office, which she never does. She wants me to come visit so we can have an old-fashioned Christmas like we used to do when I was a kid. It was about the only day I looked forward to all year. This would be the first Christmas I've actually celebrated since I left for college." Jay prattled on excitedly, "Of course, I told her I would never come unless you were invited too, so she agreed. I figured we could fly out there the day before and leave the day after. What do you think?"

Kate thought her head would explode. Her pulse pounded in her ears. "What did you tell her?" Her voice sounded strange and strangled, even to her own ears.

"I told her I would talk to you about it, but that it sounded great."

"You told her what?" Kate was incredulous.

"What's wrong?"

"What's wrong?" Kate got up and began pacing around the living room. When she got to the glittering tree that graced the corner, she turned around angrily and strode in the other direction. "What's wrong? How can you ask me that? You go off and unilaterally commit us to spend Christmas with your parents, a father who abused you for years and a mother who stood by and allowed it to happen, and you want to know what's wrong?"

"They are my parents, the only set I have," Jay answered hotly, "and they are reaching out to me. Why can't you be happy about that?"

"They aren't reaching out to you, Jay, they're trying to get you home so they can talk some sense into you. Don't you get it? They've just found out you're gay and hooked up with some disgraced woman, and they want to get their hands on you to straighten you out again."

"You don't know that."

Kate made a noise of disgust. "It's as obvious as the nose on my face."

"Yeah, because you know my parents so well," Jay retorted sarcastically.

"I don't have to know them to know what they're up to. Do you think they're the first parents to think that if they could just talk to their child they could show her the error of her ways and fix her?"

"Oh, so now let's generalize. You have no idea what my parents are about."

"You're right. I can't fathom a father who would do to his daughter what yours did, and I can't abide a mother who would stand by and do nothing to stop it. I have absolutely zero desire to meet your parents, Jay. None. Zippo. If you want to spend our first Christmas with them, so be it. You'll do it without me."

"Great. Here I thought I could finally go home and feel safe there because I'd have you by my side, and you won't even give me that. Guess I know where I stand."

"If you want to look at it like that, which is ridiculous by the way, then how should I feel about the fact that it's our first Christmas together, and you don't even want to spend it with me alone?"

"You haven't once mentioned Christmas and any plans for us. Now all of a sudden I'm supposed to know you had this big plan? What am I supposed to do, read your mind?"

"No, Jay," Kate said bitterly, "you're supposed to know how much I love you, which might have led you to believe that I had something planned."

"Sorry," Jay said, "the crystal ball's in for repairs and my Vulcan mind meld's a little off. I'll just call my mother and tell her we can't make it."

"Don't bother," Kate said resignedly, "I'll go with you."

"No. I wouldn't want you to have to spend Christmas with the family from hell."

"Jay..."

"Never mind. Anyway, I've got to go. I'll be out of touch for a few days because the reservation is a big place and we'll be traveling around a lot."

"Jay..."

"So I'll talk to you later in the week. Bye, Kate."

Kate sat there, a dial tone buzzing in her ear, wondering how a conversation that started off so well had gone so horribly wrong. Was that her fault? Why couldn't Jay, who was so smart, see what her parents were trying to do? Why did she want to have anything to do with her father, especially? It made no sense to Kate. She looked at the tree, with its shiny balls and tinsel, her dreams for a beautiful, private Christmas shattered, and she cried.

Half a country away, Jay was crying too. Why couldn't Kate understand that her parents were her parents, regardless of their faults and flaws? Once she composed herself, Jay picked up the phone again and dialed Barbara. She wouldn't tell her about the argument—that was too raw, but she needed to talk some things out, and Barbara was about the only person she would consider telling about her past.

When Jay finished disclosing her family history to Barbara, she said, "My feelings about my parents are so muddled. Do you think it's possible to love someone and hate them at the same time?"

"Of course," Barbara said gently.

Jay struggled with her thoughts. "I'm not saying that quite right. I guess what I mean is, is it strange to hate the things that my father did to me but still want to have a normal relationship with my parents?"

"I don't think so. Everyone wants the kind of family they know they should have had growing up. As an adult, you still crave that, and it's natural that you should."

"In spite of everything?"

"Sometimes."

"I've tried to explain it to Kate. You know, how convoluted and complicated my feelings are about my parents—that I love them in a way, and want a relationship with them because they're my folks, but that it doesn't mean I'm okay with the way my father abused me or the way my mother turned a blind eye."

"Mmm."

"She doesn't understand the concept of loving someone who's caused so much damage and pain. To her, he hurt me and he doesn't deserve to have me in his life. Period."

"Knowing Kate and her strong sense of right and wrong, it would be hard for her to get past your parents' actions. Combine that with the fact that we're talking about you—the person she loves most in the world—and I'm not surprised that she feels the way she does. In her mind, she's trying to shield you from further pain, even though you're not asking for her protection."

"Exactly."

"That must make it hard for you."

Jay shrugged. "A little bit. When I do talk to my parents, mostly my mother, I do it from my apartment in New York. The conversations are stilted, and I tell them nothing about my private life, but I can't seem to divorce them entirely. I don't really want to."

"There's nothing wrong with the way you feel, Jay. There are lots of people out there who've been through what you have and feel the same way."

Jay sighed wistfully. "Maybe someday I can introduce Kate to my folks and she can see for herself that they're not complete monsters, just flawed human beings."

"All things are possible, Jay."

"Thanks, Barbara. I've got to go."

"Be safe out there."

Jay hung up the phone and sighed. She had hoped that, with this invitation for Christmas and Kate by her side, seeing her father wouldn't be so difficult. Kate's presence would act like a protective blanket, shielding her from the hurt and fear. Jay wanted to be able to get past those things. Going to see her parents together with her lover, she had hoped, would accomplish that. Now, she was sure she'd never get that chance.

≪⌒≫

"Still haven't heard from Jay?"

"No." Kate sat, looking utterly miserable, in Barbara's kitchen.

"It'll be fine, you'll see."

"That's easy for you to say. You didn't hear how hurt and disappointed she was."

"And she didn't know how much this Christmas meant to you, so you're even." Barbara shook her head. "What a pair."

"Yeah. We sure are."

"When's she due back?"

"I wish I knew. The original time frame was supposed to be ten days, which means she should be coming home the middle of next week."

Barbara put her hand on her friend's arm. "She'll be here. She loves you so much it radiates off her, Kate. You were both out of line. When she gets back you can talk through it. It's a communication thing."

"I was so busy I didn't take the time to tell her what I was thinking about doing for Christmas, and then I just decided I would surprise her. It never occurred to me that there were any other possible scenarios. I knew that she hadn't really celebrated Christmas much in recent years, so I guess I assumed everything would go smoothly."

"The best laid plans and all that. And she assumed that you'd want to meet her family, despite everything."

"Yeah." Kate shook her head at that. "Why would she think that?"

"Because they're her family, Kate, the only one she has. She's proud of you and she wanted to show you off. Plus, there's probably a small part of her that still wants her parents' approval. And given their history, I suspect she thought she'd have an easier time facing her father with you by her side."

"I still can't understand why she would want to have anything to do with them."

"Kate, have you said that to Jay?"

"Probably."

"Every time you tell her how appalled you are that she would want to keep in touch with her parents, you send the message to her that, once again, she's doing something wrong. That was a message her father fed her continually as a child. You don't want to go there, Kate. It leaves Jay torn between a yearning to please you and her desire to maintain some sort of relationship with her parents."

"I hadn't really thought of it that way. All I've been thinking about is what I would do to him if I ever met him. The thought of letting him in the same room with her makes me sick."

"I understand how you feel, but be careful, Kate. He's her father. Whatever else he is, he's still her father."

"An unfortunate act of birth," Kate muttered.

"Do yourself a favor and don't say that to Jay."

Kate grunted.

"You need to eat." Barbara pointed a fork at Kate's mostly uneaten chicken Sorrento. "And when's the last time you had a good night's sleep? You look exhausted."

In truth, Kate hadn't slept well in the two days since the conversation with Jay, and she didn't think she would until she could hold her in her arms again and they could work through things. She spent the previous evening shopping for presents, wrapping them, and putting them under the tree. It was a way to feel closer to Jay.

The sound of her beeper going off startled her. She looked at the clock. Seven p.m. on a Saturday night, six days before Christmas, no less. Didn't it just figure? Getting up and studiously ignoring Barbara's complaints about their interrupted dinner, she went to the phone and dialed the command center.

# CHAPTER THIRTEEN

The incident began an hour and a half earlier. It had started small, with some inmates in the D yard at Attica fighting with each other, but had escalated quickly. By the time Kate arrived at the office, Commissioner Redfield and the other members of the executive team were seated around the big conference table in the command center.

Several speakers were set up in the middle of the table, each connected to a live, dedicated telephone line inside the prison. This arrangement allowed the team around the table in Albany to hear and interact in real time with the prison leadership about everything happening on-site hundreds of miles away at Attica.

"Report," ordered Redfield.

A disembodied voice answered, "There are large numbers of inmates in all four recreation yards setting fire to every flammable surface. Picnic tables, garbage cans, you name it. It's like a giant bonfire. All officers have been ordered out of all yards, and the prisoners are barricading the doors in A yard."

Redfield, whose face was lined with tension, barked, "I don't want to know that there are a large number of inmates, God damn it. I want to know an exact count."

"Yes, sir. I'll get someone on it right away."

"What's the status of getting the rest of D block back to their cells from the mess hall?"

"That is in progress, sir."

"Any issues there?"

"There are some fires being set on the various floors, sir. We're putting those out as quickly as we can."

"Where are we on locking down the rest of the blocks?"

"We're just waiting for dinner to be over, sir."

"Get them back to their cells. Now."

"We're working on that, sir. Right now we're trying to make sure we have enough manpower to supervise."

"Get it done."

"Yes, sir. Sir? I have those yard counts now."

"Let's hear it."

"One hundred twenty-one inmates in A yard, one seventy-nine in B, two hundred twenty-one in C, and one hundred forty-four in D."

Redfield did a quick calculation. "Six hundred sixty-five inmates. Great," he muttered.

For two and a half more hours they sat and listened to the sounds of the disturbance, periodic reports and orders being passed back and forth.

"They're climbing the walls to the second and third floors from outside in the yard, using weight bars to smash in the windows."

"Get the officers off the roofs, except for Times Square."

"Yes, sir. We've got a meeting going on in A yard. They're breaking into the officers' station in D yard."

Kate had received several phone calls from the local media in Buffalo so far about the incident, and minutes ago, news of the riot hit the Associated Press wire, which would no doubt blow the story open nationwide.

Kate expected this, since any time the name Attica came up, reporters took special notice. In September 1971, a deadly riot at the prison made national and international news. That event was very much on her mind as she devised a strategy to handle the media this time.

When she came back from her latest interview, the disembodied voice was saying, "They're breaking windows in Times Square, climbing the walls, attempting to break the window frames to gain access. Right now they're working in groups of ten to twelve at a time, taking turns."

"Are the Elmira, Oneida, Collins, and Auburn CERT teams there yet?"

"Yes, sir."

"Good. Tell them to get the CS gas ready in case they break through into Times Square." Redfield looked around the table. "This is no good. We've got to go out there." He turned to his deputy commissioner for operations, Randy Garston, a middle-aged career corrections man with a no-nonsense face. "Mobilize the Albany CERT team. Kingston and Medford are the leaders on the team, right?"

"Yes."

"Okay. I want them and their two best sharpshooters with us—that way we can strategize on the flight over there. Give the other eight team members a van, and get them on the road ASAP. Request permission to use the governor's plane. I want the following people on board in addition to the four CERT guys—deputy commissioner operations, assistant deputy commissioner operations, assistant commissioner special operations, public information officer, and me. Everybody go home and pack a bag. Bring several changes of clothes since I have no idea how long we'll be there. Meet in the Signature terminal at the airport at 0300."

Heads nodded around the table as the group began to disperse.

Kate made her way to her car. Calling out five correction emergency response teams, or CERTs, meant the commissioner anticipated the possible use of force to end the uprising. The presence of these teams was certain to raise the alarm for reporters. It was going to be a long night. She wished more than anything that she could speak to Jay before leaving, but she still hadn't heard from her and had no way of initiating contact herself.

On her way to the airport, Kate took a quick detour to Peter's house. He was, as she expected, fully awake and dressed when she arrived at his door at 2:35 a.m. with Fred by her side.

He greeted her by saying, "I've talked to some of my contacts. It looks serious."

"It is serious," she answered.

"Albany CERT going out with you?"

"Yes."

He nodded. "Good men. I trained most of them myself."

She smiled thinly. "In that case, maybe I should be worried about my safety."

"Very funny." He looked at her hard. "All kidding aside, Kate, be careful out there. You might be walking right through the middle of everything on your way outside to hold press briefings, depending on where Redfield sets up shop. He tends to like to be near the action, so I suspect he'll hole up in the sergeant's office on B block just off Times Square. I don't like it."

She didn't like it either, but outwardly she made light of the situation. "You know what the sociology professors say. The inmates won't harm the mouthpiece because that's their only means of negotiation."

"We don't negotiate with inmates," Peter answered dryly.

"I know," Kate whispered confidentially, "but the inmates don't know that, which is what keeps me useful and safe."

"So they tell you. Thank you, by the way, for wearing a pantsuit instead of a dress. Trust me, you're the nicest thing those boys have seen in a very long time. No point in tempting them more than they already will be."

"Aw, Peter, they're only murderers, rapists, and robbers. Why would I worry about a silly thing like my safety?"

He chuckled. "I can't imagine."

She looked at her watch. "I've got to get going. Take good care of my boy."

"I always do. Fred and I sit around all day eating bonbons and having belching contests, you know."

"Sounds like fun. I'll be so sorry to miss that."

"I bet. Have you heard from Jay?"

"Not since" —her voice wavered minutely—"the argument about Christmas."

"Don't worry, Kate. She's probably just out of telephone reach. Some of those places on the reservation are pretty remote."

"I know, and I hope with all my heart that's all it is, but—"

"Let it go, Kate. Jay loves you very much. She'll probably already be here when you get back and you'll have a terrific Christmas celebration on Friday."

"If she calls you while I'm out of reach..."

"You have your beeper on, right?"

"Yes."

"I'm sure she'd beep you if she couldn't get you on the phone."

"Yes, but just in case she can't get me and she calls you..." Kate hesitated. "Will you tell her I love her? And that I'll be home just as soon as I can?"

"Of course."

As Kate turned to go, something occurred to her. "Oh, I almost forgot. I've been meaning to give you this." She reached into her briefcase and pulled out an accordion folder filled to bursting.

"What's this?"

"It's all the stuff I've accumulated on the Breathwaite thing. I figure it's safer in your hands than it is in mine. The tapes from his conversation with Wendy Ashton of AP and any physical evidence is in there, along with all of the press clippings, our timeline of events, suspected incidents he might have engineered, and our hypotheses of what he's been up to and why. Also, I've added my own personal notes based on my interactions with the media, the governor, and Commissioner Sampson. Finally, I've included a list of questions I still haven't found answers to that might bring us closer to figuring out the endgame."

"Why are you giving this to me now?"

She shrugged, trying for nonchalance. "Like I said, I've been meaning to give this to you for weeks, I just never got around to it."

"And you happen to get around to it, as you say, as you're on your way to the airport to fly into the middle of a riot? That's convenient."

She shrugged again.

"Kate, I know this is your first riot and you're probably nervous. It's okay. I'd have to have your head examined if you weren't. You're going to do great. Keep your head on your shoulders and don't say more than you need to. You'll be fine."

"It's just that people's lives—potential hostages—could depend on what I say to the media. One wrong word and—"

"You're too good for that, Katherine Kyle. I've seen you in action. I have complete faith in you. If I were a hostage, I'd be confident and comfortable with you out there in front of the microphones."

She kissed him on the cheek. "Thanks, friend. I needed that."

"No charge," he smiled at her. "Now go kick ass, and don't take any prisoners."

"Ha, ha," she said drolly as she bent over to hug Fred one last time before walking out the door.

At 3:00 a.m. on the dot, Kate stood in the Signature Air Terminal at the Albany County Airport waiting to board the governor's small plane that would take them out to Attica. As the group assembled and walked out to the tarmac, she took note of the men around her. The four CERT team members were dressed in full battle gear, CS tear gas canisters in holsters on their hips, silenced MP-5 submachine guns and shotguns in their hands, helmets and masks in their backpacks. Each of them, she knew, had been cross-trained in barricades and hostage rescue in addition to sharpshooting. They looked grim and determined.

The flight was mostly a quiet affair after the brief strategy session, the passengers either lost in thought or dozing in anticipation of the long stretch of sleeplessness that would surely ensue. Kate studied her surroundings. The governor's plane was a small King Air turboprop with a custom blue and gold interior. Twelve seats faced each other, six on each side in the aft section of the plane, with two comfortable captain's chairs up front.

Kate looked at the four men who would, if necessary, put their lives on the line at Attica that day. They were mostly young, all clean shaven, with strong physiques and rugged-looking faces. She thought about the type of mindset it must take to willingly put oneself in extreme danger in the course of doing a job. With a start, she realized that very soon, she would be doing the same thing.

She had instructed the superintendent to have the media cordoned off across the street from the front gate, off prison property and out of harm's way, with state police officers supervising to ensure that none of the reporters entered the facility's grounds. At last report, the number of journalists had tripled, with correspondents from the major networks and CNN being flown in to report live. It would be Kate's job, every half hour, to walk from the sergeant's office in B block that would serve as the command post, through the main cell block intersection at Times Square, down the long A block corridor, through the administration building, out the front gate, and across the street to brief the media. There would be at least one period of time during that trip when she could potentially come into contact with inmates.

Kate blinked. She couldn't worry about that at the moment. She had a job to do, and people's lives, both civilian and inmate, were on the line. The inmates, many of whom had radios and access to televisions, would be watching, listening, and evaluating her every word.

She wished again that she had been able to contact Jay before getting on the plane. She felt so alone and out of sorts. She wanted to know that her lover was okay and to have a chance to talk to her about their argument. She couldn't stand the idea of Jay being mad or disappointed in her.

On impulse, she pulled a pad of paper and a pen out of her briefcase.

*Dear Jay,*

*I know it's silly to be writing this down, since I'll probably talk to you before this could reach you, but it will make me feel better, so here goes.*

*First of all, I want to apologize. I'm sorry if I said some things I shouldn't have. I'm sorry for raising my voice in my exasperation. I'm sorry if my words hurt you in any way. I love you so much, and I ache at the thought of causing you pain.*

*We both made assumptions, and that was wrong. What we really needed to do was to sit down and discuss, together, what we wanted to do about the holiday. I wish I had it to do over again, baby, because I would be far more forthcoming about what I had in mind. I wanted to surprise you, but I see now that I went about that the wrong way.*

*At the end of the day, the only thing that matters is how much we love and respect each other, and our willingness to work through rough spots like this one. I believe we will be made stronger by the experience and the knowledge we take away from it.*

*I love you, Jamison Parker, and I will do whatever you want on December 25th, as long as I can be with you.*

*Kate*

She reread the note, then folded it and put it in her pants pocket. On a clean sheet of paper she wrote:

*Jay,*

*I wish with all my heart I could have talked to you before coming to Attica. I needed to hear your voice, to feel the reassurance of your love, to know that you would be there when I got back, and to tell you how much you mean to me. Unfortunately, I had no way to reach you, so this will have to do.*

*Before you came into my life, my existence was sterile and emotionless. You brought joy, happiness, and love into my world and made me whole. I find myself trying to remember, from time to time, what I did before you came along, stealing my heart and soul as you did with little apparent effort. Each time I reach the same conclusion—whatever I might have valued before pales in comparison to what I have now.*

*Thank you, Jay, for being my light and my life. No matter what else happens, knowing I have you by my side will be enough to carry me through.*

*Every time I close my eyes and see your face in my mind, I know I have come home.*

*I love you, sweetheart, with every fiber of my being, and I will until the end of time and beyond.*

*Kate*

She folded the second note and put it together with the first. After a long moment, she closed her eyes, trying to rest and enjoy the peace and quiet for what she figured would be the last time for at least the next few hours.

Jay stepped out of the medicine woman's truck and brushed the road dust from her khakis. She was tired, having spent the last few days bumping along back roads to remote locations. She had watched, with great interest, parts of ancient rituals and healing ceremonies and had spoken with tribal elders and the next generation of leaders. She had gathered almost all the information and done the interviews she needed to write her story, but when the singer invited her to watch the harvesting of the raw materials for a sand painting, she could hardly turn that down. After all, it could make a great sidebar to her piece, and it would only delay her return to Albany by one more day.

Jay felt a pang of guilt and longing. Over the past several days she'd had plenty of time to think and reflect. She missed Kate so much it was like a physical ache deep in her bones. Her anger over their Christmas discussion had long since dissipated. They would work out the Christmas thing together, as a couple, as it should have been all along. They both bore responsibility for the misunderstanding and would have to work harder at communicating. Jay was committed to making that happen. Being out of synch with Kate left her feeling out of sorts and incomplete.

Spending time in the presence of the Navajo, a spiritually centered people, taught her a thing or two about the importance of staying in harmony with her soul. There was no question in her mind that Kate was the very center of her soul, the other half of her heart.

She couldn't wait to apologize and to share with her lover the valuable lessons she learned on this trip. She considered picking up the phone, now that she was back where there was phone service. She wanted desperately to talk to Kate but didn't want to wake her. It was late in New Mexico, and two hours later still in Albany. The next day, when they were both awake and fresh, would be better. On a Sunday morning Kate would most likely be lazing around, reading the newspaper and doing the *New York Times* crossword puzzle. The vision made Jay smile.

The first thing Kate noticed was the increased number of officers in the wall towers that overlooked each area of the massive facility. The towers were the only places in the prison where correction officers regularly carried guns. She could clearly see the weapons glinting in the moonlight as the officers kept vigil.

The newly arrived group dispersed upon entering the front gate. The members of the CERT team went into the administration building to be briefed by the CERT teams already on-site. The commissioner and the members of his executive team headed for the sergeant's office on B block near Times Square, where Redfield said he wanted to set up a temporary command center. The prison superintendent was waiting for them.

"Commissioner, glad you're here."

"Edgar." Redfield nodded at the paunchy, ruddy-faced man. His hair, what little of it there was, stuck straight up in all directions. He hardly resembled the picture of a prison warden.

"Mr. Garston, Ms. Kyle." The superintendent acknowledged the deputy commissioner for operations, who was his direct boss, and Kate.

"What's the situation, Edgar?"

"Here's where we are right now." He motioned them to chairs around a small makeshift conference table on which he had spread out a schematic of the prison. "There are still four hundred fifty-seven inmates in the yards. The numbers on the color-coded tags indicate how many inmates are in each yard. They have burned pretty much everything there is to burn at this point and destroyed all of the officers' stations. They're still trying to climb the outside of the blocks, breaking windows and attempting to pass weight bars in through the windows. So far, they haven't succeeded, but they're getting closer."

"What's happening in Times Square?"

"Nothing at the moment. Earlier they were trying to get in there by busting the window frames, but they seem to have given up on that for now. We still have a sergeant and two officers on the roof of Times Square, along with two CERT team members from the Collins Correctional Facility."

"Good." Redfield nodded. "Have all of the towers been reinforced?"

"Yes, sir. CERT team members from each of the four teams have been assigned to specific towers. They are already in place."

"All right. How are we doing on the blocks? Everyone back in their cells?"

"The keep-lock inmates, who of course haven't been out of their cells, are getting rambunctious, breaking lights and such. They can hear what's going on, and the other inmates who are coming back onto the tiers from outside are filling them in. There are some fires in isolated pockets on some of the galleries, but we've been able to contain those so far."

"Have you met with the Inmate Liaison Committee yet?"

"Yes, sir. Three inmate representatives from each of the yards met with me an hour ago."

"What do they say?"

"They're convinced that we killed an inmate last night. One of the keep-lock inmates died of natural causes—had a seizure episode and help arrived too late. But they don't see it that way. They want us to take responsibility for the murder, as they call it, and, of course, they want better living conditions. You know, the usual stuff. More pay for their jobs with reduced hours, better health care, more edible food..."

"What did you tell them?"

"I offered to show them the preliminary autopsy report as soon as it becomes available and told them if they want anything else, they need to get their people under control and back in their cells. If they could do that, we could talk about the other items on their list."

"What was their response?"

"Go to hell, or something a bit more colorful."

"I bet. Kate?"

"Yes, sir?" Kate stepped forward.

"Time for the first update. I want you to go out there and tell the media as much of the truth as you need to without delving into causes or demands, understand?"

"Yes, sir."

"Keep them from speculating wildly and making this worse than it already is, all right?"

"Yes, sir."

"Get moving."

Kate pivoted on her heel and headed for Times Square and a date with a pack of crazed reporters. *Maybe facing the inmates wouldn't be so bad after all,* she mused silently.

∽⟨⟩⟪∾

At 5:12 a.m. Kate strode into the rotunda-like area that was Times Square, with its putty-colored cement block walls, highly polished floor, and four steel doors—one leading to each of the cell blocks A through D. The surface was littered with broken glass, and through the barred windows, she could see a number of inmates in the yards milling around burning fires, which shot angry fingers of orange and yellow into the sky. She could hear the pounding of weights against the iron bars that protected the windows and their frames.

She tried to shut out the noise and kept walking, head held high, stride purposeful, nodding to the officer posted inside Times Square who unlocked the door to the A block corridor for her. She made her way down the long corridor to the administration building and knocked on the door. Another officer on the other side of the door viewed her credentials and let her in. He escorted her through the administration building and outside. Along the way, she passed the memorial to the eleven correction officers slain in the 1971 riot and continued across the street to the waiting throng of journalists. The entire trip took less than five minutes, but to Kate it seemed like hours.

"Kate, how bad is it?"

"Kate, is it true that there are hostages?"

"Kate, has anyone been killed yet?"

She held up a hand for quiet, taking a moment to scan the crowd surreptitiously. Two national news reporters from ABC and CBS were present, along with Wanda Nelson from *America's Heartbeat* and an anchor from CNN. By the red light on one of the cameras and the nearby satellite truck, she knew her press conference was being covered live. Wendy Ashton was in the second row of reporters, along with print journalists from the *New York Times*, the *Post*, the *Daily News*, the *Buffalo News*, and *Newsday*. Radio stations like WBEN and WBUF in Buffalo were also represented.

"First of all, let me say that our main concern is for the safety of all individuals involved, both civilian and inmates." She added the last knowing that television sets on the tiers were no doubt tuned to CNN and interested prisoners were watching.

"There are no reports of any casualties at the moment, and we'd like to keep it that way. Nor are there any hostages that we are aware of. Our count of correction officers, administrative personnel, and others is still underway, but so far there is no reason to believe that there are any hostages in this situation."

"Who's unaccounted for?"

"No one is unaccounted for, per se," she answered, "but you have to recognize that there are folks who leave once their shift is over, and we are running a thorough check to make sure that all third-shift personnel have been accounted for.

"Here's the situation as it exists right now. There are a number of inmates in each of the four recreation yards who are congregating, burning materials in the centers of the yards, destroying guard stations. All officers have been safely evacuated from the yards. There are also several small, containable fires burning on several of the galleries—the hallways on some of the tiers inside the blocks."

"Not to ask a stupid question, Kate, but what's a tier?"

"Trust me, I've heard worse." She smiled at the young reporter with a microphone flag she recognized as belonging to a Buffalo radio station. "A tier is a unit within a block. There are five blocks in the prison, lettered A through E. Each inmate is assigned to a block, a tier, and a cell on that tier." She looked at the reporter kindly. "Does that help?"

He nodded gratefully.

"Will you be calling in the national guard? Is this going to be a repeat of 1971?"

"I want to emphasize that the facility is under control. What happened in 1971 was tragic both for those directly involved and the nation as a whole. But this is not 1971, and any comparisons to what transpired on that sad occasion would be completely erroneous and irresponsible."

"Are there talks going on with the inmates? What do they want?"

There would be no negotiations, Kate knew, only the discussions with the Inmate Liaison Committee, or ILC, to try to bring an end to the situation. Actual negotiations, which could include giving in to inmate demands, were tantamount to sending the message that negative behavior would garner positive results. It was against agency policy.

183

The inmates, of course, were unaware of the policy. If they became aware of it, the situation might escalate. So, mindful of that portion of her audience behind bars, Kate answered carefully, "The Hyland administration intends for there to be a peaceful resolution to this situation, and, to that end, all viewpoints are being heard. It would be premature at this time to release any more information than that." She looked at her watch purposefully. "I will be back out to update you at the top and bottom of every hour for as long as it is necessary. It is"—she looked at her watch one more time—"five thirty-four a.m. I'll see you at six."

Jay stretched and rolled over. As tired as she was, she was having difficulty sleeping, even though it was still full dark outside. She looked at her luminescent watch—4:47 a.m. That meant that it was 6:47 at home. She would give Kate another half hour or so to sleep and then call her.

She rolled over herself and fell back into a fitful sleep.

At 5:35 a.m., Jay was awakened by the medicine woman. She was drenched in sweat, and it took her a moment to focus.

"Are you all right, my child?"

Jay felt as though she'd been in a prize fight—her body ached and she felt remnants of an inexplicable fear. She tried to shake off the feeling.

"I'm fine—just a nightmare, that's all." She thought with a pang of Kate, who was always there to soothe her after a bad dream. Perhaps she could call her now.

"If you want to watch the process of refining the materials for the sacred paintings, you need to come."

"Now?" Jay looked longingly at the phone by the side of the bed.

"Yes, right now. Nature waits for no one."

Reluctantly, Jay stumbled out the door, pulling her jacket on as she went.

Kate checked her watch—7:17 a.m. She had only been on-site for a little over two hours, but it felt as though she'd been there for days. As she prepared to go provide the media with a fifth update, Randy Garston strode into the office.

"How's it going?"

"As crises with wide press coverage go, not too badly, I guess. I've been monitoring the coverage on CNN and it looks fairly balanced, not too hysterical."

"Yeah, I've seen some snippets here and there. You're doing a nice job. Not bad for a rookie."

"Gee, better be careful—glowing praise like that could give a girl a swelled head."

"I'll try to tone it down more next time."

"Anything new?"

"Nah, it seems like we're at a stalemate. Don't worry, they'll get hungry and tired eventually and give in."

"Glad to see your confidence."

"Happens every time."

"I'll have to take your word for that." She glanced at her watch again. "I've got to go feed the piranhas. Wish me luck."

"You don't need any luck, Kate. You're a pro. And if I haven't said it before, it's a pleasure working with you."

"Thanks, Randy, I appreciate that. I feel the same way."

✎✎

At roughly the same time Kate was conversing with the deputy commissioner for operations, a large group of inmates was congregating near Times Square in the D block recreation yard. The smallest of the inmates addressed the crowd. "Okay, it's seven twelve. We've got exactly six minutes to accomplish this, so let's get it done quickly and done right. Everybody clear on their instructions?"

"Got it."

"Yeah."

"Let's get to it."

"Go!"

Within seconds, six of the inmates had formed a human stepladder, enabling eight more to climb onto the flat roof of Times Square. A CERT team member in the corner tower of D yard, realizing what was happening, fired a warning shot just as the inmates reached the five men guarding the roof. He aimed to take a second shot, but was forced to hold his fire or risk hitting his own men.

The sergeant, two officers, and two CERT team members were outmanned, overpowered, and knocked unconscious in less than the time it took the tower guards to sound the alarm. One of the inmates relieved the sergeant of a set of keys. The others collected the officers' weapons.

The eight inmates, staying low and using the officers as shields, reached one of the stairwells leading from the roof down into Times

Square. Using the pilfered keys, they unlocked the door and disappeared inside the building.

The next-to-last man in line dragged the sergeant with him toward the stairwell.

"Leave him, Zack. He ain't the target. We don't have time."

As Zack opened his mouth to protest, the inmate in charge called, "Let it be, Zack. We've got to move."

Reaching the bottom of the stairs, the inmates used a separate key from the sergeant's ring to unlock the door that led to the main part of Times Square.

"Wait," one of them hissed, just before they opened the door from the stairwell. Through the narrow glass, they could see the officer on duty unlock the B block corridor door and admit Kate to Times Square.

As she began to make her way over the broken glass, the inmates burst out of the stairwell. Three of them headed directly for the officer, neutralizing him and taking his keys. The other five inmates went directly for their main target.

Before she was even aware what was happening, two of the inmates lunged for her, twisting her arms painfully behind her back and putting her in a headlock. Instinctively, Kate kicked out, nailing a third inmate in the shins with her high-heeled shoe.

"Bitch," he shouted, punching her as hard as he could in the stomach.

The air rushed out of Kate's lungs, leaving her gasping for breath. Still, she bit down fiercely on the arm against her windpipe, prompting a howl from behind her and a momentary loosening of the grip. Desperate to break free, she struggled against the arms that still held hers roughly.

A fist swam into her field of vision, making contact with her face before she had a chance to raise an arm in self-defense. Her eyes watered as bolts of fire lanced through her jaw and cheekbone. Her legs began to buckle, but, stubbornly, she refused to go down.

A second fist, this one as large as a ham, caught her in the temple. Her head felt as if it would explode. Another landed a blow to her other cheek, and her vision blurred. Still, she stayed on her feet, unwilling to give up. One of her assailants used a baton on her midsection, and she felt her ribs crack. Before long, she lost count of how many times she'd been hit, finally surrendering to the pain and going limp.

"I say we finish the bitch right here," said Zack, who was nursing the bite marks in his arm.

"Yeah, right here," echoed Antoine, a strapping mountain of a man who was rubbing his shin.

"No," barked Ahmed Kumar, the leader of the group. "We are to take her back to the tier. Now!"

With a considerable amount of grumbling, one of the inmates used the officer's key to unlock the door to D block.

"Wait!" One of the other inmates stepped forward. "Why don't we just get out of here altogether? We've got the keys to all the blocks—let's use the one for A block. It leads to the admin building. We could get out that way."

"This is probably why you wound up here in the first place, you moron. You can only get as far as the end of the corridor in A block. The entrance to the administration building is controlled by a guard on the other side of the door. You couldn't get through."

"Oh."

"Now let's get moving. We don't have time to waste."

The group proceeded through the entranceway to D block, two of them dragging the semiconscious woman by the arms behind them.

"When we reach the tier," Kumar instructed, "you three will take the lead in neutralizing the guards before we bring her onto the gallery." He pointed at the three largest inmates. "I want the keys to the lock box, and I don't want any screwups. Understand? This has to be timed right. By now they know something's going on, so they'll be scrambling to get extra guards into position. We have to hurry."

The plan went like clockwork. Within three minutes of their exit from Times Square, the inmates managed to disable the three officers on their tier and use their keys to access the lock box that controlled the locks on all forty-two cells on the floor.

"Put the guards in the cell farthest from the go-round. I don't want them anywhere near a way out. We'll throw her in my cell, right in the center of the floor."

"I thought we were supposed to kill her," Antoine said.

"We will do this my way. Got it?" Kumar shouted, wiping sweat from his eyes.

Antoine seemed as though he might argue the point, but instead he threw Kate's limp body over his shoulder and carried her halfway down the tier before throwing her down on the thin mattress in Kumar's cell. When he stepped outside the small space, the door to the cell closed and locked behind him electronically.

The three unconscious officers were unceremoniously tossed into a cell at the end farthest from the one point of entry on the tier.

Randy Garston's walkie-talkie crackled to life less than two minutes after Kate had left the office.

"Attempted breach on Times Square roof. Warning shot fired, can't risk taking a second."

"Officers down, officers down!"

"Subjects are headed for Times Square. Access to stairwells achieved. Building insecure."

Garston whipped the communication device off his belt. "Potential hostage situation. Alert CERT teams to stand by with CS gas to take out Times Square on my order. Is there any answer from the officer in Times Square?"

"No, sir."

On a separate channel he paged the assistant commissioner for operations. "Monroe, I need to know if Kate Kyle is out front briefing the reporters. I want a visual confirmation right away."

He ran his hands through his salt-and-pepper hair, sitting down heavily in a chair at the small conference table. He tried to calculate exactly how much time had passed since Kate had left the room. Perhaps she had made it out front before the inmates arrived.

"Mr. Garston, sir? The PIO has not been seen outside the gate."

"Are you positive?"

"Yes, sir."

"Okay."

He thought for a second, flicked to yet another channel, and keyed the mic. "CERT team leaders, report to the sergeant's office, B block. Stat!"

Before he even finished giving the order, he could hear the sound of footsteps pounding in the hallway outside the small office. The steps stopped abruptly and there was a knock on the door.

"Come."

"Mr. Garston, sir."

Five fully armed, battle-dressed CERT team leaders poured into the room.

"Sit down, everybody, and let's see where we are."

"Yes, sir."

Tense energy and the smell of sweat permeated the close space.

"First, is there anything definitive on Ms. Kyle? Has anyone seen or heard from her?"

"No, sir. We're checking to see who might have seen her last."

Garston suspected he knew the answer to that question—he had.

"What's the status of the officers from the Times Square roof?"

"They are being evaluated presently, sir. Possible concussions and some broken bones. Maybe a dislocated kneecap. Everybody accounted for there."

"What about their weapons?"

"Sir, the eight inmates involved took the keys to the stairwells, two shotguns, two batons, a set of handcuffs, and three sets of flexicuffs."

"Was anybody able to identify the inmates?"

"The CERT guys in the tower were from Elmira, sir. They were unfamiliar with the inmates and thus unable to make an ID."

"Okay. I want a tier-by-tier report from each of the blocks. I want to know where those inmates are, and I want to know it yesterday. Are there any stations that haven't reported in? Do we have anybody other than the PIO and the officer inside Times Square unaccounted for?"

"We're checking now, sir."

Garston bit his lower lip. Every second that went by reduced Kate's and the officer's chances of being safely out of harm's way. He needed answers quickly. Nodding to himself, he said, "I want two teams in position around Times Square. Send the gas in, extricate anyone if there's anyone in there. I also want the videotape from the control room."

"But sir, don't you want to send in the Technical Services Unit first to do reconnaissance?"

Garston was irked at being second-guessed, especially since every moment he spent explaining reduced the hostage's chances of survival. "First of all, Technical Services is en route and not yet on-site. Second, we don't have time to wait. Third, your job is to follow orders, not to question them. Got me?"

"Yes, sir," all five men answered in unison. They snapped to attention, pivoted on their heels, and hustled out of the room.

Commissioner Redfield, who was on his way into the room, had to flatten himself against the doorway in order to save himself from being run over. "What have you got?"

"Kate's missing. I'm next to positive that she's a hostage, or worse, but I don't know where. The inmates breached Times Square as she was passing through, and no one has seen her since. The Times Square duty officer is also unaccounted for."

"Fuck."

"Exactly."

"Has anyone told the press anything?"

"No, sir."

"Okay. If she didn't show up for her regular briefing, they're going to start making up all kinds of stuff. I better go out there and say something."

"Bill, you might want to wait until we get the all clear from Times Square. I've got the boys dropping gas in there now."

"Jesus."

"If neither she, the officer, nor the inmates are in there, we need the videotape to figure out where they went. It's the fastest way. You and I both know that if we don't find Kate and the officer soon, their odds of survival are greatly diminished. I can only get the video from the control room on the other side of Times Square."

"Is Tech Services on the way?"

"Yes, but they're at least forty minutes out yet."

"Okay. Who do we have out with the media?"

"I've got Monroe in the vicinity. He's in the admin building. There are two state troopers out with the journalists making sure they behave."

"Can Monroe handle public speaking?"

"Christ, I don't know. He sure wouldn't be my first choice."

"Let's just have him say that an update will be forthcoming in the very near future and ask the jerks to be patient."

Garston raised the assistant commissioner on the walkie-talkie and explained what he wanted him to do. "And Monroe? Don't take any questions or deviate from the script in any way, okay? Just say your piece and get out of there. Then report back."

Redfield tapped his fingers on the table. "I'd better call the governor and get another spokesman out here. It will have to be Breathwaite—he's the only one familiar enough with everything to step right in."

Garston nodded grimly. "Should we wait to see what Kate's status is first?"

"No. Even if she's fine, which I think we both know is a long shot at this point, it will take Breathwaite an hour or more to get here by plane. If she turns up in the meantime, we'll just send him home."

"Okay. I'll see where we are with the Times Square infiltration." Garston left the room as his boss picked up the phone to dial the governor. He was glad he wasn't the one having to make that call.

# CHAPTER FOURTEEN

Peter sat in his home office studying laboratory reports on trace substances found in a bomb that exploded prematurely, killing two people. He read the same paragraph at least three times. Shoving his chair back from his desk, he keyed the volume control on the television in the corner. It was 7:42 a.m.

He had diligently watched each of Kate's briefings live on CNN. So far, he gave her high marks for grace under fire. When 7:30 had come and gone without an update, he began to get restless. The reporter on the scene was filling air time, recapping what was already known and speculating on the reason for Kate's tardiness.

At 7:49, Peter watched in stunned disbelief as Assistant Commissioner Paul Monroe stepped up to the microphones. The man looked exceedingly uncomfortable in front of the media mob. He held up his hands for silence.

"Katherine Kyle has been unavoidably detained. We hope to get you another update in the very near future. Please bear with us."

He walked away from the microphones as a cascade of shouted questions rained down on him.

Peter thought he would be sick. Monroe's appearance could mean only one thing—Kate was in some sort of trouble. Without a moment's thought, he picked up the phone and called a private number at the airport.

"I need a charter. No, not for this afternoon. I need it right now."

"Where are you going, sir?"

"The town of Attica, New York, or as close as you can get me."

His next call was to Barbara. Without identifying himself he said, "Have you been watching the news?"

"No, why?"

"It's a long story, but suffice it to say there's a situation going on at Attica, Kate is in the middle of it, and I have a horrible feeling that she's in big trouble."

"What can I do?"

"I need you to take Fred, for one thing."

"Done. What else?"

"Kate hadn't heard from Jay before she left. She asked me to pass along a message. Now I'll ask you to do it if you hear from Jay."

"Let me guess, you're going to be out of range yourself."

"Ah, you know me too well. My charter leaves in thirty-five minutes."

"Peter, what do you think is happening out there, really?"

"My guess is Kate's either been incapacitated in some way or she's been taken hostage. I can't fathom any other reason why she wouldn't have done the update at seven thirty and why they would've put an inexperienced assistant commissioner in front of live television cameras. Still, Barbara, I don't want to jump to conclusions until I get out there and see things for myself."

"Okay. If, and I sincerely hope you're wrong, but if she's been taken hostage, what are her chances of survival?"

"It depends."

"On?"

"On who has her, why, and for how long. If they just selected her at random because she happened to be in the wrong place at the wrong time, that's one thing. But if they were targeting her specifically, it means they've got a game plan. Whether she lives or dies depends on what their goal is and how fast the good guys can find and extricate her. The longer the situation drags on, the less likely it is that she'll walk out of it alive."

He knew his words were less than comforting, but Barbara deserved to know the truth. As a doctor, she dealt with life-and-death situations every day. He understood that she didn't want him to sugarcoat the facts.

"Okay. Thanks for being straight with me. When they get her back, and I have to believe they will, she'll need medical attention. Should I come with you?"

He smiled briefly, appreciating her optimism. "I think it's better for you to stay here. Jay is going to need someplace to call and someone to be there for her when she gets the news. I'll try to keep you up to speed as best I can."

"All right, please do. Peter," her voice faltered momentarily, "come home soon and bring Kate back with you."

"You know I'll do everything in my power, Barbara. Everything."

"I know. I just feel so helpless."

"Taking care of Jay is what Kate would want you to do. To her, nothing would be more important than that."

"You're right. Good luck, Peter. I'll be waiting by the phone."

No sooner had he hung up the receiver than the phone rang again.

"Enright? Brian Sampson."

"Yes, Commissioner." The title rolled off Peter's tongue out of long habit. While it was true that the man had resigned in disgrace, that fact did not change who he was to his staff or, in this case, former staff. Peter had always respected and admired him. Despite the circumstances of his ouster, that hadn't changed.

"Have you been watching?"

"Of course. I have a charter leaving in less than half an hour."

"Good. I know you're a friend of Kate's and I figured you weren't likely to sit idly by and wait to see what happens from afar."

"Not my style."

"I know. Governor Hyland called me after he heard from Redfield."

"What's the situation?"

When the ex-commissioner was done outlining the details, Peter whistled. "Sounds like a well-executed strike to me, not some random act."

"I thought the same thing. Do you mind if I tag along?"

"Are you sure?"

"I know I can't have any official role, but the governor called me for a reason. He doesn't know Bill that well, and he said he'd be more comfortable if I wasn't that far away. He wanted to offer me his plane, but it's apparently already out there, and his helicopter has been dispatched to ferry David Breathwaite to the scene to handle the press."

Peter's eyes flashed angrily at the mention of Breathwaite's name, and his gut started to gnaw at him. Aloud, he said, "Yes, the Albany team took the King Air out there at 0300. If you're coming, we'd better get going. I'll meet you at the Signature terminal in twenty minutes."

"I'll be there."

From the air, Breathwaite looked down at the prison, the media across the street, the inmates in the yards, and the officers in their various posts. They resembled little more than dots on a canvas from this height. Everything was going exactly as planned. He expected that if the dyke bitch wasn't already dead, she would be soon. He was very pleased.

Garston informed him while he was waiting for the helicopter that the officer in Times Square had been recovered and taken to the hospital. Also, they were operating on the assumption that Katherine Kyle was a hostage. They were working to confirm this by reviewing the surveillance videotape from the Times Square cameras. The tape was collected by the CERT team that penetrated the area once the tear gas had done its job. They would know more by the time he arrived on scene.

193

At 8:56 a.m. Breathwaite stepped into the makeshift command center on B block. Commissioner Redfield, Deputy Commissioner Garston, the prison superintendent, a staff duty sergeant, and the five CERT team leaders were all hunched over a small TV, watching the videotape shot hours earlier. On it, Kate's struggle with her captors was clearly visible. While the tape had no audio, none was really needed. When the eight inmates disappeared through the door to D block, dragging Kate along with them, Garston turned the tape off.

Breathwaite cleared his throat to announce his presence. "I need to go out and say something to the newshounds, before they make up any more rubbish."

"Hello, David. Thanks for coming." Redfield extended his hand, as if greeting someone he hadn't seen a long time. "Have you been brought up to speed?"

"I believe so. Do you want someone to brief me before I go out there?"

"I'll do it," said Garston.

"No, Randy. I want you to take these guys and the tape and concentrate on identifying the eight inmates and locating the hostage or hostages. I'll fill David in myself."

After the rest of the room's occupants had cleared out, Redfield said, "All right. Let's get down to business. That looked like an orchestrated strike to me and, I'm sure, to everyone else in the room. I don't suppose you know what happened there?"

"I might."

"God damn it, Breathwaite, what the fuck are you playing at?" Redfield's face was contorted with rage.

"We needed to get her out. It wasn't happening. I made it happen."

"You've lost your mind. You have lost your fucking mind! You arranged to have her kidnapped?"

Breathwaite looked at his nails disinterestedly. "No, actually, it's a little more permanent than that."

As his meaning sank in, Redfield stared openmouthed, an expression of horror on his face. "You realize that if she dies, you're an accessory to murder."

"Tsk, tsk, Willy. First of all, that's only if it could be proved that I had anything to do with it, which it can't. Second of all, you're in this just as deeply as I am."

"I most certainly am not."

"Really? You think anyone will believe that when they put two and two together?"

"You've gone too far. You're out of control."

Breathwaite slammed his palms on the table. "I am in complete control, as it happens, and you are going to do exactly as I say."

"Why in the world would I do that?"

"Because if you don't go along with it, or if you try to double-cross me, I'll take you down with me."

"You're crazy."

"No, just ambitious like you. Now here's what we're going to do."

"Sorry, sirs, I forgot something." Max Kingston, the head of the Albany CERT team, poked his head in the office. "I'll just be a sec." He reached under one of the chairs around the opposite side of the conference table and picked up a sheaf of papers. "Thank you, sirs."

When he had left, Breathwaite continued, "As I was saying, here's what we're going to do. When they pinpoint the dyke bitch's exact location, you're going to veto any plan they come up with to rescue her."

"On what grounds?"

"On the grounds that it's too risky and you don't want to chance losing any more men or getting her killed."

"Is she already dead?"

"If she's not, she will be soon. I sent the message that the animals could have some playtime if they so chose."

"How did you get them to do your bidding?"

"I showed them what a powerful man I am and assured them that I could see to it that they wouldn't be punished for this."

"And you intend to make good on that exactly how?"

"I have friends, Willy, in places you can't conceive of. But who says I plan to make good on it?"

"You hired inmates to murder her."

"Don't you go getting holier-than-thou on me, Willy boy. You're in this up to your neck. The plan was to get you installed as commissioner, just like you always wanted, then you were supposed to get rid of Kyle. You weren't able to accomplish that on deadline, and that forced me to take action. If you had just done what you were supposed to do, this whole thing wouldn't have happened."

"You orchestrated the entire riot?"

"Merely a distraction for the main event. The boys will call it off when the goal has been accomplished."

"You've gone over the line, Breathwaite. Not only have you made us accessories to murder, you've put every staff member's safety on the line. What makes you think your boys are going to have enough control over the situation to put an end to it?"

"Stop your whining. It will all work out according to plan. Oh, and if by chance we eventually have to kill those eight inmates, that would be fine too."

"You're sick."

"No, Willy, I'm efficient, and my plans work, unlike yours. Now, if you'll excuse me, I've got a show to put on for the media."

"What are you going to tell them?"

"Why, the truth, of course, Willy." Breathwaite laughed on his way out the door.

⋞⋟

From his own command post in a motel room several miles down the road from the prison, Peter could hear the discussion between Breathwaite and Redfield with surprising clarity. His recording equipment picked up both voices with ease.

When he had landed, he placed a discreet call to a pager number. His call was returned almost immediately. Max Kingston, head of the Albany CERT team, did not even question the order. He simply carried it out. After all, he owed his position and his life to Peter Enright.

⋞⋟

Breathwaite shouted to be heard over the onslaught of questions.

"Where is Katherine Kyle?"

"Has something happened to her?"

"Are there hostages?"

"We're hearing rumors that the violence has escalated. Is that true?"

"*Quiet*, and I'll give you the latest update. If you continue to yell questions, I'm out of here and you'll get nothing."

Two of the more seasoned reporters grumbled, one of them saying under his breath, "I sure didn't miss having to deal with you, asshole."

"I know what you mean," whispered the other. "At least Kyle was aboveboard and fair. This guy never gave us jack and acted like he was doing us a favor."

"This is the situation at the moment." Breathwaite rocked back and forth on his heels. It was good to be home—this was where he belonged. "Several inmates in D yard banded together, overpowering five correction officers on the roof of Times Square, which is the juncture for four of the five blocks. They then breached Times Square itself, knocking an officer unconscious and taking one hostage."

An excited buzz rippled through the crowd. "Is that Kate?"

"One of our specialized teams went in and resecured Times Square."

"Is there only one hostage, and is it Kate?"

Breathwaite continued to ignore the questions. "A videotape of the Times Square incursion was recovered. It clearly shows Katherine Kyle being taken against her will by a group of inmates." He took great glee in breaking one of the cardinal rules of engagement—a spokesperson never, ever gave out the name of a hostage before loved ones had been notified. He thought, *I hope you're watching this, Parker. And I hope you suffer.* Aloud he intoned, "Her whereabouts at this time are unknown. It is unclear if there are any other hostages. We are continuing to check with every duty station to account for all personnel."

"Can we have a copy of the videotape?"

"No."

"Why not?"

"Because I said so. Are there any intelligent questions?"

"Where do you think they've taken her?"

"I believe I already stated that we don't know that yet."

"Did it appear from the tape that she was injured?"

"She was taken against her will."

"Did she know her captors?"

"How should I know?"

"Have you identified the inmates involved?"

"We're working on it."

"Have the inmates made any demands?"

"No comment."

"Do you know if she's alive?"

"If we don't know her whereabouts, how on earth would we know if she is alive? We are assuming that she is, and we are doing everything in our power to rescue her."

Jay was basking in the early morning rays of the desert sun, absorbed in watching the process of natural materials being turned into the vibrant colors that would be used to create a sand painting. Several men and women were working in small groups, harvesting gypsum, yellow ochre, charcoal, and red sandstone. In a practice as ancient as the tribe itself, cornmeal, crushed flower petals, and pollen were also collected to increase the variety of possible color combinations. She had never seen anything like it.

She was just about to ask the singer a question about the significance of certain colors and their placement in the painting when she was overcome by a sharp, stabbing pain in her temple. It was so strong that it nearly knocked her to her knees. She swayed slightly, and the singer put out a hand to steady her.

"Are you all right, my child? You don't seem well."

"No. I—I'm sure it was nothing. Just a bit of a headache."

The healer studied Jay for a moment. "No, I think it is more than that. This is the second time I've seen you suffering today. You know, there are pains that we own ourselves and there are pains that belong to those that are important to us. I have watched you struggle over the past few days with a hurt that comes both from within and from without. You have been troubled by disharmony with one you love. I don't need to be a strong medicine woman to see that. I sense that the discomfort you are feeling right now is something stronger, though, and comes from one who shares your soul. Do you understand what I am saying?"

"Yes." Jay nodded, her head still throbbing painfully. "Yes, I do."

"Do you need to go rest, child?"

"Perhaps that would be a good idea."

"I will come and check on you in a little while."

Jay thanked the healer and retired to her quarters. She thought about what the woman said. A spiritual and potential telepathic connection was something she and Kate discussed before. In their worst times, each of them had felt the other's pain. So was the medicine woman right? Was the headache somehow connected to Kate?

She checked the time—6:59 a.m. That meant it was 8:59 in Albany. She dialed their home number and waited as the phone rang four times. The answering machine picked up.

"Kate? Are you there? Hi, honey. I miss you so much and I'm so sorry about what happened the other day. I just want to talk to you, to tell you how much I love you, and to hold you in my arms. Well, I guess you're not there. I'll try you again in a little while. Bye."

Jay intended to rest for a few minutes, then try Kate again. She noticed the television at the foot of her bed. It was almost a week since she'd had a chance to watch the news. Although her head still throbbed painfully, she felt a need to catch up on the world's happenings. She flipped channels until she found CNN, shaking her head at the incongruity of ancient tribal traditions mixed with the modern conveniences of cable television, heating, and air-conditioning.

Her attention was immediately captured by the urgent tone of the anchor and the flashing crawl across the bottom of the screen that proclaimed coverage of a breaking story. When she heard the word "Attica," she turned up the volume.

Over the next eight minutes she sat shell-shocked as David Breathwaite outlined the situation inside the prison. This couldn't be real. There had to be a mistake. When a picture of Kate flashed across the screen with the word "hostage" below it, Jay gasped and struggled for air. After several moments of stunned inaction, she reached for the phone again, punching in Peter's number from memory. There was no answer.

"Damn it. Somebody tell me something." She jumped up and went to her bag for her address book. "J, J, J...Ah, there it is, Jones." She dialed Barbara's unlisted number.

"Hello?"

"Barbara?" Her voice sounded tight.

"Jay, is that you, honey?"

"Yes."

"Thank God. Where are you?"

"I'm on the Navajo reservation near Four Corners."

"How fast can you get back?"

"It's true, then?"

"Yes, honey, I'm afraid it is."

Jay's hands began to tremble, her legs suddenly unable to support her weight. "When? How? Is she all right?"

"Slow down, honey. It happened around seven thirty our time this morning. Some inmates jumped her while she was on her way out to give a briefing to the media. I just talked to Peter a little while ago. He's out there."

"Thank God."

"He says he's got a copy of the videotape from the control room that shows her being taken. He says she was definitely alive and fighting in the video. But, Jay, she got beat up pretty bad."

Jay gasped, her free hand flying to her temple, which continued to ache. "Oh, Barbara. I've got to get to her."

"I figured you'd say that, and so did the governor. Peter put him in touch with me to coordinate getting you to Attica. We just need to know exactly where you are, Jay. The governor gave me his private number and told me to call him as soon as we located you. He wasn't sure, based on our description of where you were, whether you were going to be in Arizona or New Mexico. He has talked to the governors of both states, and both have agreed, as a favor to him, to make their aircraft available for you."

"The governor did all that?"

"Sure did. Says he has a weak spot for you and Kate. So get me the coordinates, and a helicopter will pick you up and take you to the airport."

"Barbara, did Peter say how badly she was hurt?"

"It was impossible to tell, honey."

"Okay."

"One thing at a time, Jay. Let's just get you out there. Then we'll figure out what happens next."

❧❧

Kate slowly floated toward consciousness. The first thing she noticed was the smell—it was a powerful combination of dried sweat, stale urine, and mustiness. There was a constant din from above, and she tried in vain several times to open her eyelids in order to find the source of the noise. When she finally succeeded, she almost wished she hadn't. The cell in which she was housed was ten feet by eight feet by eight feet, with a stainless steel sink and toilet bolted to the floor. The single mattress on which she lay was thin and threadbare. The concrete floor was dank and cold. The only light she could see was from a window across the gallery. The sound she heard was made by the large heating ducts overhead.

She took stock of her body. Her face felt like it had been used for a punching bag, which, she realized drolly, it had. Her ribs ached and every breath was agony. She tried to shift to a sitting position, but a sharp pain in her left arm made her collapse back onto her side. She looked down. Her wrist was hanging at an odd angle. It could be worse, she told herself.

Gradually, she became aware of voices raised in anger nearby.

"I say we off her now and get it over with. That was the deal we made, we stick with it."

"No way, man, I want to get me a piece of that bitch before we finish it."

"What's to say the man's gonna come through in the end? I don't trust him. Why is we doin' his dirty work, anyway? Why didn't he do her on the outside? I's thinkin' he's gonna welch and we's gonna get stuck with the rap."

"You saw what he did for Tweety. Got him sprung in no time flat. I say we take our chances with him. We ain't getting nowhere on our own."

"You saw what he said on TV…they're coming after her. And when they figure out we've got the three guards, we're done for. He didn't say he'd get us off for that."

"They're for negotiating purposes. We'll let them go as a gesture of goodwill if it comes to that."

"I don't care about the rest of you, I'm gonna get mine."

Footsteps began to approach. Kate could see a shadow fall over the bars.

"Unlock the cell, man, and let me have at her."

A second inmate loomed in the darkness.

"Leave her be."

"There's nothing wrong with a little fun. Lighten up."

"That is not our way."

"Speak for yourself, you self-righteous, Sunni scum."

The second inmate lunged for him.

"Stop!"

A smaller man with a goatee stepped between the two combatants. "Fighting amongst ourselves will serve no purpose. We do not defile her. Until we can see the lay of the land better, she remains unspoiled. Antoine, I will let you know if and when you may, as you so delicately put it, have at her. Now step away, both of you."

Reluctantly, the two shadows receded. The man who seemed to be in charge approached the bars. "Ah, I see that you are awake."

Kate said nothing.

"I want you to know that this is not personal on our part."

"No, of course not." Her words were somewhat mumbled, as she was unable to fully open her swollen jaw.

"This is not our battle, but as it affords us a potential way out, we must proceed."

"By killing me? Fighting other people's battles is considered a coward's way where I come from."

Kumar laughed. "Ah, I see you have some spirit. I cannot disagree with you, but when one is trapped in this land of the forsaken, one sometimes has to make choices and do things that are against one's innate nature."

"That's a very high-minded rationalization for kidnapping and murder. Is it worth it?" She took notice of his appearance. It was obvious to her that he was a Muslim. In the prison population there existed two groups of Muslims—the Sunnis, who adhered to the traditional, more peaceful tenets of the religion and culture, and the more radical, angry Shiites. From his demeanor and choice of words, Kate figured him to be Sunni. "Do your teachings cover this sort of situation?"

"I will leave you now. Rest assured that as long as I am in charge, you shall not be used as a diversion. We will do only what we must. No more."

"Thank you. That's very comforting to know."

Kumar walked away without a backward glance.

*Well, at least I have more information now than I did before. It's clear that someone outside is calling the shots. And that it's someone in a position of power, since he referred to an opportunity to get out of here as being the motivation.* She snorted derisively. *Let's take three guesses who that might be.*

Why on earth would Breathwaite want her dead? Wasn't that a little extreme? Surely there were less drastic ways to accomplish his goal. How did he hope to get away with this? Why was it so vitally important that he come back to DOCS? She wanted to ponder these things further, but her head hurt so much she was having difficulty focusing. As she closed her eyes against the pain and unconsciousness claimed her once again, she thought of Jay, her beautiful face shining brightly like a beacon.

◈◈

The five CERT team leaders, the prison superintendent, Paul Monroe, Randy Garston, David Breathwaite, and William Redfield were packed into the tiny makeshift command center.

"Sir, we've ID'ed all eight inmates. They're all from D block, ten company." Max Kingston handed each man a folder with the eight dossiers in it.

"Wonderful. Four murderers, two rapists, one bank robber, and a kidnapper. Lovely crew."

"We've also identified the three officers on that tier who haven't responded to any radio contact." A second set of folders made the rounds.

There were grim faces as the men looked at three young, fresh-faced officers, all with wives and small children.

"They are all relatively inexperienced. For two of them, this is their first posting."

Redfield glanced once at Breathwaite, contempt and accusation in his eyes.

Garston picked up the briefing. "The Technical Services Unit is on-site. Now that we've narrowed down the hostages' likely location we can send tech in with the fiber optic equipment to pinpoint the exact coordinates, then come up with a course of action."

Unable to muster any good argument against the plan, Redfield gave the go-ahead.

"Report back directly to me at ten bells sharp. We'll reconvene once I have all the facts."

◈◈

Governor Hyland arrived unannounced at 9:17 a.m. He did not go directly to the prison, stopping instead at a nondescript motel some three miles down the road.

"Brian, Peter."

"Governor, sir." Both men stood.

"I know it's a bit unorthodox for me to consult with you two before my own team, but the truth is, this is no time for protocol. What we need are results. Redfield has been on the job for less than a month, and there are lives at stake." He looked from his old friend to the technology expert on whom he had relied so many times during the course of his tenure in office.

Former DOCS Commissioner Sampson said, "Governor, sir, if I step in at this point, it will undermine Bill's authority and add to the tension and confusion."

The governor appeared chagrined. "Understood. I'll ask you to stay here, though, so that I can continue to consult with you as needed." When Sampson looked uncertain, Hyland added, "Brian, I chose you as my commissioner for a reason. That hasn't changed. I trust your knowledge and judgment and I need you with me now."

"I'll be here."

The governor turned to Peter. "My understanding is that you're available for hire as a consultant. Is that not so?"

"It's so."

"In that case, consider yourself hired."

"What is my exact role, sir?"

"I want you in charge of the rescue operation."

"As you wish, sir." To himself Peter added, *Well, that makes things much easier.*

"Let's get going. There's no time to waste."

"I'll be right with you, sir. I just need to gather my gear."

After the governor walked out the door, Sampson asked Peter, "Are you going to tell him about the bug in the command center?"

"Not yet. I'm not convinced we've heard everything we need to hear yet. I'd like to keep that as an ace in the hole—see if there's anything more to be gleaned from future conversations. I have a sneaking suspicion there'll be more to this before it's done."

"In that case, I'll keep listening and recording at this end."

"Thanks, I'd appreciate that. The more evidence, the better. I'll check in with you when I can."

"Peter?"

"Yeah?"

"Bring them all out safely."

"That's my goal."

༺༻

"It's against every policy we have. Absolutely not." Redfield was sitting behind the sergeant's desk in B block.

"You want those three officers out of harm's way or not?" Breathwaite leaned forward, his hands splayed on the opposite side of the desk.

"Of course."

"The object here is to kill Kyle and extract them safely. I'm just giving you a way to get that done."

"It will impact the way DOCS handles hostage situations for years to come."

"At the moment, Willy, we don't care about anything but this specific hostage situation now, do we?"

Redfield chewed his lip. He could not live with himself if those three officers were lost on his watch, but his options were severely limited. He had spent the last half hour trying to come up with some way to extricate them without bringing Kate out. It would look far too suspicious to allow the inmates to keep a member of the management team while letting the others go free.

But what if Breathwaite was right? What if he could position it to appear that the inmates would agree only to let the three guards go in exchange for sending in a reporter with a television camera? Maybe that would be a reasonable explanation.

"Okay. I'll get the Inmate Liaison Committee in here to make it look legitimate. We'll have them present the offer to the eight inmates. Do you have a way of contacting them directly?"

"Don't go through the ILC. I have an ex-inmate I'm working with. I'll have him give them the instructions. I've got him stashed nearby. If he goes in there, they'll know the order is coming from me."

"If I don't use the ILC, it might raise more questions."

"If you do go through them, there's no guarantee the eight will know where the order is coming from. Not only that, but it means involving more inmates in the plan. I don't think that's wise, do you?"

"I haven't liked the plan from the beginning. This was your insane idea."

"Insane or not, you're stuck with it now, Willy. It would behoove you to make the best of it."

❧❧

Kate slowly became aware of her surroundings once again. This time the noise level was much greater. She could hear groups of inmates fighting amongst themselves, and she struggled to make out their words.

"Man, you keep your filthy hands off my shit. If I catch you in my cell again touchin' my props I'll kill you."

"If you was any good at killin', asshole, you wouldn't be in here."

She could make out the clear sound of a skull hitting concrete and other bodies running in the direction of the sound. There was shouting and a loud whistling noise.

"Cut the crap. We don't have time for this."

"Who died and put you in charge, Kumar?"

"Do you forget that it was I who liberated you? I could just as easily have let you rot in your little holes."

"You got a plan for getting us out of this place?"

"I have gotten you this much freedom. The rest, I'm afraid, is up to you."

Kate could hear footsteps coming closer. She closed her eyes and feigned unconsciousness again. The footsteps paused in front of her cell, then moved past and receded in the distance.

After several moments, when she was sure she was alone, she opened her eyes and surveyed her surroundings. Judging by the movement and sounds on either side, it was clear to her that she was in the middle of a tier. She knew from past visits to Attica that each tier had only one exit, located at the end opposite the lock box that controlled access to the cells. The exit, or go-round, was the only way out, as far as she knew, and she imagined the inmates had done something to barricade the door from the inside. It was hard to fathom how, even if she weren't injured, she could get out of her cell, elude forty-two inmates, make it to the go-round, and escape the tier.

She could only hope that help from the outside was on the way. She thought about Redfield. Were she and Peter right? *Was* he working with Breathwaite? It was obvious that Breathwaite was not working alone and that Sampson's coerced resignation was tied to bringing him back to DOCS. Installing Redfield must have been intended to clear the way for that to happen. Add that to the incident with Marisa, and the conclusion seemed a logical one.

Kate sighed. With Redfield and Breathwaite working together, was there any chance that she would be rescued? Or that an attempt would even be made? She thought about Jay, and her heart lurched wildly in her chest. Would an angry conversation be the last memory Jay would have of her? The idea made her nauseous. She would not allow her lover to know the kind of regret and guilt that she herself carried with her every day.

Kate had no concept of time or how much of it passed since she'd been taken hostage. She stared at the shattered watch that hung loosely on her broken wrist. It didn't matter in the end, she supposed. Whatever day it was, it was close to the holiday. If she were murdered during this siege, every Christmas for the rest of Jay's life would be as painful as Kate's had been after her parents were killed.

It was an ache that neither died nor diminished over time. It was a scar that could never heal. Kate could never change what happened, could never reverse the clock and make it all turn out differently, could never bring her parents back, just as Jay would never be able to change the tenor of their heated conversation and would likely blame and punish herself for it for the rest of her life.

Despairing, Kate ran her good hand through her hair. It came away covered in sticky, drying blood. She looked at it for a long moment, turning it over in the dull light from the barred window across the gallery. She would not die here. She could not let Jay carry such a burden with her. She would live to tell Jay how much she loved her and that nothing else mattered. She would find a way out, with or without help.

# CHAPTER FIFTEEN

The Tech Services boys snaked the minuscule cable through the heat ducts, around corners, and through grates. The process was slow, painstaking, and repetitive. Finally, twenty-three minutes and twelve cells after they began, they spotted their first target. Using the shutter, they snapped off several photographs, moving the cable at various angles to be sure they had as much of the environment as they could get without being detected.

When they were satisfied, they carefully removed the cable.

"Three down, one to go."

"Convenient of them to leave all three officers in one cell, don't you think?"

"Yeah, except that, by our calculation, this one is twenty cells away from the go-round."

"Fantastic."

"You didn't think they were going to make it easy for us, did you?"

"It would've been nice, just this once."

"Let's go find the other target."

Another seventeen minutes later they were done and on their way back to the command center.

"What we have here are two insertion points—one in cell one and another in cell eleven." Max Kingston pointed to the enlarged images in the center of the conference table. "The three officers are, fortunately for us, grouped together. The bad news is that they are at the end of the tier farthest from the go-round."

"Gotta give the inmates credit for some brains after all, I guess."

"Ms. Kyle, according to our calculations, is located in cell eleven, right in the middle of the tier. She appears to be by herself."

"Can we get any idea of injuries or conditions on any of the four?"

"Unfortunately, the quality of the pictures is somewhat grainy and we were unable to ascertain anything other than location."

"Commissioner," Randy Garston interjected, "we can mount an exercise using the CS gas—"

"No," Redfield interrupted. "It would be too risky."

"But, sir—"

"No. I want to see what we can do through diplomacy before we rush in there." Noting the stunned faces around the room, he quickly added, "The last thing we want is another 1971 on our hands. I want all the CERT teams standing by on alert. I'll let you know if the situation warrants action once I've exhausted my other possibilities."

Redfield shifted uncomfortably as Randy Garston continued to stare at him in shock.

"Bill—"

"Randy," Redfield snapped. "This is my show, and I'm going to run it my way. Live with it."

"Yes, sir," Garston ground out through gritted teeth as he pivoted and strode from the room, nearly running over Breathwaite on his way out the door. Max Kingston followed after Garston.

"Your boy Randy's not happy with your decisions."

Redfield felt a little sick to his stomach. "Neither am I, David. Where's your contact man?"

"He's ready."

"How are we supposed to send him in with the message?"

"I have an officer who will deliver him."

"We're going to put another officer in jeopardy?"

"No, he's been acting as a go-between for weeks."

"Very clever."

"Thank you, Willy," Breathwaite said smugly. "Not only that, but he'll escort the journalists as well. That way we can be sure there won't be any stupid heroics."

"Just take care of it. I won't be able to hold the CERT teams off forever." He turned his back, effectively dismissing Breathwaite.

⇜⇝

Breathwaite approached the large gathering of reporters, many of whom had been milling around or talking amiably.

"The inmates have agreed to release the three officers they hold hostage in exchange for a televised opportunity to express their demands. They have also consented to letting us film the remaining hostage so that we may determine that she is alive."

There was a chorus of voices. "I'll go in."

"Send us."

"No, we should be the ones."

"Quiet. We'll do this my way. Ashton, you're the one."

"I'm not a television journalist."

"That's obvious," he hissed. "You're going, and you're taking the CNN videographer with you."

There was an uproar of outrage from the journalists who would be left standing on the outside. This was the assignment of a lifetime—the kind that careers were made of.

"Come with me."

"Now?"

"Yes, now, Ashton. Time is wasting and lives are at stake." Breathwaite resisted the urge to smile. It made him giddy to see the fear in the reporter's eyes. While it might be the opportunity that could make a future, it could just as easily end a life. He wished he could accomplish that too. It would have been nice to take out a second dyke bitch in the process. Alas, he would have to satisfy himself with Kyle's death and using Ashton and the cameraman as the vehicle to cause further pain to Kyle's girlfriend.

By all rights he should use a dummy camera—giving the inmates a real live audience would make his life hell later on. But the idea of Parker having to watch her girlfriend's battered face and body on television was too enticing to pass up. He'd deal with the damn consequences later.

≪≫

Jay's limousine pulled up to the tiny motel just as the governor and Peter were leaving. Spotting them from a distance, she was halfway out of the vehicle even before it came to a complete stop.

"Peter," she yelled.

He took three strides forward, catching her as she fell into his outstretched arms.

"Shh, it's okay, Jay. It's all going to be okay." She looked terrible. Her eyes were hollow and swollen from crying, her clothes wrinkled and disheveled.

"Where is she? Is she free yet? Is she hurt?"

"Whoa," he held up a hand to slow her down. "Honey, she's still a hostage, and we don't know her condition."

"You've got to do something. Get her out."

"I'm going to do everything in my power, sweetheart, you know that."

"Me too," the governor added.

Jay straightened up as she remembered that she and Peter weren't alone. "I'm so sorry, sir. Governor Hyland." She grasped his hand in desperation. "I can't tell you how much it means to me that you went to all the trouble you did to help me get here. I don't know how I'll ever repay you."

"No need, Jay. You know how I feel about Kate. That extends to you as well. I give you my word that we will take whatever steps are necessary to bring her home to you."

"Thank you, sir. I know that you will."

"To that end, I've hired your friend Peter here to head the rescue operation. He and I were just on our way to the jail to get started."

"I'm coming with you."

"No, Jay," Peter said gently. "You need to stay here."

"No way. I have to be as close to Kate as I can get."

"Jay, Peter is right," the governor interceded. "If you go to the jail you'll be mobbed by the media outside and it will be a horror show for you. I promise you that we will keep you up to date as soon as we have anything."

Brian Sampson, who had emerged from the motel room at the sound of the commotion, stepped forward. "Hi, Jamison. We've met before. I'm Brian Sampson."

"Yes, I know. Hello." She looked at him quizzically.

"The governor has asked me to be here in case I can be of any service."

"I'm glad."

"Why don't you come in here with me and make yourself at home? Peter's taken the liberty of getting you a room. I'll get you some water and something to eat and we can hold vigil together, okay?"

Jay looked at Peter beseechingly.

"That would be best, honey." He gave her a last hug, saying in her ear, "You know nothing will stand between me and Kate's freedom. I give you my word, Jay, that I will bring her back to you."

"Please, I need her so much. Don't let anything more happen to her."

"I'm going to do my best. See you in a bit."

She stood watching as the governor's car disappeared in a cloud of dust, all of her hopes and dreams for a future riding along with it.

The door to Kate's cell slid open and a couple of inmates appeared in the doorway.

"Get up."

She did not respond.

The two inmates stepped forward and grabbed her under the arms, yanking her unceremoniously to her feet.

"You can walk, or we can carry you."

"Where are we going?" She smelled their fear as it mingled with her own.

"Seems you're going on a field trip."

"Where?"

"To see some of your media scum friends."

Kate breathed a sigh of relief. "I'll walk." Perhaps wherever they were headed would afford her an opportunity to escape.

She exited the cell flanked by the two inmates, both of them carrying batons. Her hands were handcuffed roughly in front of her, the movement and the scrape of metal against her misshapen wrist sending bolts of fire through her arm and down her torso. As they started down the tier they were joined by Kumar.

"When we arrive at the door to Times Square, everyone must put their masks on." He handed each of the inmates a black ski mask. "Antoine, you and Zack will accompany me inside. The rest of you will wait just on the D block side of the door. If anything goes wrong, you will take the guards back to their cell. I will do all the talking."

For the first time, Kate became aware that there were three other hostages. She turned her head slightly, the motion causing a renewed wave of nausea. Walking ten steps behind her were three correction officers, each accompanied by a gargantuan inmate. Behind them were two more inmates, each carrying a shotgun. All three of the hostages wore flexicuffs.

"What's going on?" Kate asked.

"We have a date with a television camera."

Kate was beyond shocked. It was against every rule and regulation—not to mention common sense—to give these men a forum to address the public. Rewarding them for taking hostages and wreaking havoc sent the message to every other miscreant that all he needed to do in order to get attention was to act out. How did this serve Breathwaite's purpose? She was completely baffled.

She measured her position and their location. There really wasn't anywhere for her to go. She focused on Kumar again.

"Am I supposed to say anything?"

"I will allow you to tell the reporter that you are fine and have been treated humanely."

"Have I? I hadn't noticed that."

He regarded her intently. "No one has laid a finger on you since you were taken."

"No, that is true. But I haven't received medical attention, food, or water, either."

"Why would you need those things?"

"Oh, that's right. I'm supposed to be dead, aren't I?"

"Your fate is not your concern."

"That's rich."

"What is meant to be, will be."

"How very fatalistic of you."

Kumar ignored his captive and replayed his conversation with the ex-con named Basher.

*"You gotta turn over the three pigs or the deal's off."*

*"How do you expect us to do that and save face?"*

*"Make it look like a swap. Give up the pigs for the right to say somethin' on national TV."*

*"We don't have anything to say. We made a deal."*

*"Yup. And if you want the man to follow through on the deal, you gotta do this his way."*

*Kumar didn't like it. "What does he want?"*

*"You hafta make it look legit. Make some demands, carry on a bit, then give over the pigs."*

*"Just like that?"*

*"One more thing. You gotta show the bitch so's they know she's alive. She is still alive so far, right? You boys havin' fun?"* Basher *elbowed Kumar in the side knowingly.*

*"Why would we want to show her?"*

*"You wouldn't. But if this were real, they'd want somethin' like that as part of the deal."*

*Kumar shook his head. "I do not understand. They are already getting the three guards."*

*"S'not enough. They wanna see the broad too, before you take her back home."*

*"And he will see to it that we all go free and clear, and that each of us gets out after our first parole hearing?"*

*"Yup."*

*"So be it."*

⤚⤙

They arrived at the door leading from D block to Times Square, and stopped. Kumar called back behind him, "Keep the guards back about five feet. When I give you the sign, you will show them in the window of the door, then take them back to the original position. When I am satisfied and we have had our say, we will turn those three over to their colleagues."

"We should keep 'em."

"No, we do not change the terms of the agreement at this stage. It would jeopardize our position."

*Ah, that answers another question. The other three hostages weren't part of the deal. Breathwaite needed to find a way to take them out of the equation. He must have Redfield by the balls if he's agreeing to that.*

"We will wait until I can see that they have kept their end of the bargain." Several moments later he announced, "Ski masks on, everyone. It is showtime."

Wendy Ashton and Keith Riley, the videographer for CNN, followed the correction officer through the front gate, into the administration building, down the long A block corridor, and into Times Square. There was a faint metallic smell in the air, and something made them squint.

"Sorry, folks, we've fumigated as best we could, but there are trace amounts of CS gas still hanging around. You get used to it after a while."

"What's CS gas?"

"Tear gas."

"Oh." Wendy looked around. Despite obvious efforts to clean up, broken window glass littered the floor in several places, and jagged edges were visible in those panes that were still intact.

Keith began taping, panning the camera around to capture the entire scene. The sound of small bands of inmates shouting in the yards beyond the Times Square walls was barely audible.

As if in answer to the unasked question, their escort offered, "Most of the inmates have gone back inside voluntarily. The yards are under control." Then he realized that he was talking to a reporter and immediately shut his mouth.

"Is the riot over, then?"

"I'm sorry, I'm really not at liberty to say anything at all, and I hope you won't use what I've told you." He thought about what Breathwaite would do to him if he found out he'd offered any information to a reporter.

"I promise not to use your name, okay?"

"I'd really feel more comfortable, ma'am, if you wouldn't use the information at all."

Before Wendy could ask him anything further, the door to the D block corridor was unlocked from the outside. A slight, ski-masked inmate stepped into the space. Directly behind him were two more masked inmates the size of small houses, Kate slumped between them. Keith's camera was trained on all of them.

Wendy gasped. Kate looked worse than any beating victim she had ever seen. Her face was swollen and covered in dried blood, her hair was unkempt and blood-soaked as well. Her left wrist hung at an unnatural angle, and her eyes were dull. The suit she wore was ripped in places and smudged with dirt and grime.

When Kate spied her, she tried to muster a smile. It appeared more like a grimace. Wendy tried to give her what she hoped was a look of encouragement.

The muffled voice belonging to the shortest man announced, "We have asked you here to talk about the appalling conditions in this hellhole and to let you know that we are not monsters."

"If that's true," Wendy found her voice, "then why have you beaten this woman within an inch of her life?"

"She resisted. It was not our wish to cause her harm."

"Then why not let her go?"

"We cannot."

"I don't understand."

"We do not expect you to. Day in and day out we are treated like animals in this place—barely provided the food and water necessary to live and kept in conditions not fit for most beasts. Then you expect to release most of us back into society and have us behave like fine, upstanding citizens—with little job training, no respect, and less assistance."

"You think rioting, acting violently, and taking hostages will get you what? More respect?"

"We think that nothing short of this type of behavior has gotten anyone's attention, and that is unfortunate. We have been forced into this type of action. We have tried other avenues."

"What do you want?"

"We want what all decent human beings want—to be treated with dignity, to get paid fairly for our work, to be taught useful trades, to be well fed. This is not too much to ask."

"And in exchange you will let your hostages go?"

"As you no doubt know, we have already agreed to let three of the hostages go in exchange for this opportunity to explain our position."

"Where are they?"

Kumar motioned to the D block passageway. Loudly, he called, "Show them."

Three faces appeared in the narrow window in the door leading to D block.

"They will be released as soon as we are done here."

"When will you release Ms. Kyle?"

"That depends on the prison leadership. As soon as they meet our demands, we can begin to negotiate her freedom. Until then, she will remain our guest." He began to turn around.

"Wait!" Wendy cried. "I want to talk to her."

"No. It is enough that you can see she is alive."

"She hasn't said anything."

"Say something." Kumar pulled Kate next to him.

"Hello, Wendy."

"Are you all right?"

"Never better."

"That is enough." Kumar yanked on Kate's handcuffs.

She stumbled, falling against Wendy, knocking both of them over. In the reporter's ear Kate whispered desperately, "Take this and give it to Jay. Tell her I love her and always will."

Wendy felt her hand close around something metal. She quickly put it in her pocket.

As the two large inmates roughly pulled Kate to her feet, a folded piece of paper dropped to the floor. Wendy rolled over to stand up, sliding the paper under her shoe in the process.

"Take her back," Kumar instructed Antoine and Zack. "When we have cleared the door without incident, we will allow the others to go free."

The inmates, with Kate between them, disappeared through the door to D block as the three captive officers were shoved unceremoniously into Times Square.

In the confusion, Wendy bent down and spirited the folded paper into her pocket.

The governor's car pulled up to the front gate, where he disembarked and strode purposefully into the administration building. Peter waited a beat and followed inconspicuously with the plainclothes state troopers assigned to guard New York's chief executive.

The group was greeted by a surprised correction officer who barely looked old enough to shave. "Sir." The officer snapped to attention as the governor approached. "I wasn't told you were coming."

"Sometimes life surprises you, son."

"I'll get Commissioner Redfield for you right away. If you'll just come with me."

The officer led the governor and Peter to the empty prison superintendent's office. Peter's eyes were immediately drawn to the television set on the wall.

"What the...?"

The governor, who had been looking out the window at the media gathering across the street, quickly turned his attention to the source of Peter's agitation. On the screen was a shot of Times Square, where an inmate in a black ski mask was being interviewed live on television. The two men watched as Kate was thrust forward, stumbled, fell, and was hauled back up onto her feet.

Peter was out the door and down the A block corridor leading to Times Square before the governor could say a word.

"Sir." An older officer attempted to stop him halfway down the hallway. "Mr. Enright, you can't go down—"

"Get out of my way," Peter ground out.

"I'm sorry, sir. There's a hostage exchange in progress. You can't go in there."

"Come again?"

"Three of the hostages and a news camera will be coming this way any second."

"Explain."

"Commissioner Redfield agreed to let the inmates appear on TV in exchange for their freedom."

Peter tried to clamp down on his anger. This was insanity. "What three?"

"The three officers from D block, ten company, sir."

"What about the PIO?"

"The deal was that we would get to see that she was alive."

"That's it?"

"Yes, sir."

"Where are the CERT teams?"

"Standing by, sir."

"No rescue attempt has been made?"

"No, sir. I talked to one of the CERT guys from Collins and he said their plan to retrieve the packages was vetoed by Commissioner Redfield." The officer paused. "It's okay to tell you that, right, sir? You still have clearance, right?"

"It's a little late for that, but yes, I still have top-level authorization."

There was a tremendous commotion at the end of the corridor, and Peter looked up to see the three ex-hostages being led into a side office, dazed expressions on their dirt-streaked faces, their hands still constrained by the flexicuffs.

Following close behind was a cameraman and the female reporter Peter had seen on the screen moments earlier. They were being led directly toward him.

"Wait." Peter put his hand out to stop them.

"Mr. Enright, sir?"

"I need to talk to the reporter. Alone—in here." He pointed to a cramped, empty office to his right.

"But, sir—"

"Now." Peter's authoritative tone brooked no argument.

"Yes, sir. I'll just wait outside, sir."

Peter steered Wendy into the office and closed the door behind them.

"Do I know you?" she asked.

"All you need to know is that I'm a friend of Kate's. She gave you something in there. What was it?"

The reporter narrowed her eyes, but refused to respond.

"Look. You're Ashton, right?"

"I like to know who I'm talking to."

"My name is Peter Enright. I'm a friend of Kate and Jay's."

"She's never mentioned you."

"To you? You're a reporter."

"Very observant."

"I'm shy."

"I have trouble believing that."

"Look, I don't have time to argue with you. I know Kate gave you something. I need to know what it was. I'm here to help her. Obviously she trusts you, or she wouldn't have given whatever it was to you."

"I'll only give it to Jay."

Peter's patience was running thin. "If this is something that tells us how to help Kate, I need to see it now."

Wendy stared at him defiantly. "I'll deliver it to Jay and Jay alone. I assure you it is nothing that has any impact on Kate's physical well-being."

"You're after an exclusive with Jay."

Wendy actually laughed. "Listen, you may not think much of reporters, and I suppose I should be insulted just on principle, but the fact of the matter is that I have no professional interest at the moment in seeing Jay. I give you my word."

Peter considered the woman in front of him and everything Kate had told him about her, and he made a decision. "All right. I will have a driver take you to Jay on two conditions."

Wendy folded her arms and raised her eyebrows.

"One—you tell no one that Jay is here or that you saw her."

"Done."

"Two—you show me what it is first."

"I told you—"

"I know what you told me. You either want to see Jay and give her whatever you've got—or not."

Wendy blew out a breath in exasperation. "Okay."

"Thank you."

She reached into her pants pocket and found the object. Placing it in the palm of her hand she said, "Here."

Peter gazed down at the diamond-and-sapphire ring Jay had given Kate to symbolize their love. It brought a lump to his throat.

Seeing his emotion, Wendy offered, "She told me to give this to Jay."

"Thank you," he said quietly.

Wendy bit her lip. "There's something else."

"Yes?"

"She dropped this on the ground. I think it was intentional." She held out two pieces of folded paper. "I didn't finish reading them, because they were personal. They're letters to Jay."

"You're a good person, Ashton. I'll get your ride ready."

ॐॐ

Jay was on the phone with her editor. "No, I don't know anything more yet, Trish. I just got here a little while ago."

"I can tell you what's on the wire."

"I've got CNN on." It was like déjà vu for Jay, watching live coverage of a crisis in which Kate featured prominently. Seven months ago it had been her reporting of the capitol bombing that brought them together. On this day—no, she didn't want to think about it.

"If there's anything I can do, Jay—"

"Oh my God," Jay gasped.

"What is it?"

"I've got to go." Jay hung up the phone as Trish was still talking in her ear and turned up the volume on the television. She watched in horror as the camera zoomed in on Kate's battered form. Haltingly, she walked toward the television set, her fingers reaching out to caress her lover's misshapen face. "Oh, Kate. What have they done to you?"

"Jay?" There was a knock on the partially open door. "Jay, can I come in?" Brian Sampson poked his head inside. He approached Jay and put an arm around her shoulders. Softly, he said, "She's alive, Jay. That's a good sign."

Hollowly, Jay asked, "What do you think they've done to her?" Jay couldn't bring herself to formulate the question that was foremost in her mind.

218

"I don't know, Jay, but I don't get the sense that she's in any worse shape than she was when they captured her. The injuries you see are consistent with the struggle she put up when they first took her."

"Okay." Jay tried to get control over her legs, which felt like they had turned to Jell-O. Kate just fell on top of Wendy. Her heart flipped in her chest when the inmates yanked her roughly to her feet and took her away. Jay's fingers followed her lover's retreating image. She sat down heavily on the bed.

"Jay, Peter will do everything in his power to bring Kate out. You know him—he won't let you down."

"What if he can't get to her in time? What if..." she choked, unable to finish the sentence, tears streaming down her face.

"Have faith, Jay. That's all you can do. Peter's the best. He'll get the job done."

≼⌒≽

Some minutes later the phone rang. When Jay made no move to answer it, Sampson did.

"Hello?"

Without preamble Peter said, "The reporter you saw on screen is on her way in an unmarked car. Let her see Jay."

"Wh—"

"It's okay. Trust me. It's not about a story. Still, you might want to make yourself scarce until she's gone. Your presence might raise unnecessary questions."

"Thanks for the warning. Peter, I've got the Breathwaite-Redfield conversation about the TV interview on tape. I just found it. My guess is the conversation took place while we were outside with Jay. The interview was a ploy to get the three officers freed without raising suspicion. Showing Kate was supposed to lend an air of legitimacy to the deal. The officer who accompanied the reporter is Breathwaite's plant. You might want to shut him down. Also, he's got an ex-con communicating the instructions to the inmates. Breathwaite had his inside guy smuggle the scum in disguised as a current inmate."

"That makes sense."

"Randy and the CERT guys had a plan to go in—Redfield vetoed it."

"I know, a helpful officer was nice enough to tell me that just a few minutes ago. I'm going to track down the CERT commanders right now. I want to hear what Tech Services found, then I'm going in there to get her."

"What do you need from me?"

"What the reporter's going to give Jay is going to be tough for her. Can you make sure she's okay?"

"Of course. She saw the dog-and-pony show. She's pretty shook up."

"Wouldn't you be?"

"You bet. She's worried about whether or not Kate's been raped."

"An understandable concern. I don't think so, if it's any consolation."

"I agree with you, and that's what I told her."

"Good. Listen, I've got to go, and you should get out of sight. That reporter should be there any second."

"I'll let Jay know."

❦❦

Jay was standing outside when the car pulled up in the motel parking lot. She waited impatiently as Wendy Ashton slid out of the back seat.

"Hello, Wendy."

"Hi, Jay. I wish we didn't have to meet like this. One of these days, we're just going to get together socially—you, me, and Kate." She smiled wanly.

Jay squeezed her hand. "Come inside."

"Did you see the interview?"

"Yes." Jay's face was tense and drawn, her eyes deeply shadowed.

"I'm sorry, Jay. I took no pleasure in doing that."

"It's okay, Wendy. It's not your fault. I'm glad you were the one who got to see her. I'm glad she got to see..." Jay's voice faltered as a renewed wave of tears threatened. She swallowed hard. "I'm glad she got to see a friendly face."

"She gave me some things for you, and a message to pass along."

"She did?"

"Yep, sure did."

"How on earth could she have done that? Her hands were cuffed and she wasn't allowed to speak to you except for the one or two words."

"Did you see her lose her balance and fall on me?"

"Yeah. They shoved her."

Wendy smiled at the protective tone in Jay's voice. "Yes, but that's not why she fell."

"No?"

Wendy shook her head. "I think she did that intentionally so she could give me this." She held out her hand.

"Oh." Jay's hand flew to her mouth as a sound somewhere between a gasp and a moan escaped her lips. With trembling fingers she took Kate's ring, turning it so that she could read the inscription. *Eternity.*

"She said to tell you she loves you so very much, and that she always will."

Jay could not speak. The tears flowed freely from her eyes, cascading down her face in rivulets. Unaware that she was saying the words out loud, she whispered, "I love you too, sweetheart. So, so very much. Come home to me."

Wendy cleared her throat. "She also dropped these at my feet. I'm pretty sure she meant for me to bring them to you."

Jay took the pieces of folded paper and opened them lovingly. She began to read.

*Dear Jay,*
*I know it's silly to be writing this down, since I'll probably talk to you before this could reach you, but it will make me feel better, so here goes...*

"Um, as soon as I realized they were addressed to you and that they were personal, I stopped reading."

Jay looked up. "Thank you, Wendy. Thank you for these gifts, and thank you for being there for Kate. I can't tell you what these mean to me." She tucked the notes away protectively—she needed to be alone when she read them.

Obviously embarrassed by the strong emotion in the room, Wendy mumbled, "I can just guess."

Jay pulled the hard-boiled reporter into a hug.

"She's going to be all right, Jay. She's tough and resilient. You'll see—this is going to have a happy ending."

"I hope you're right, Wendy."

"I know I am. Well," she continued after an awkward moment of silence, "I've got to be getting back. There's a rumor that the governor's in the jail."

"Good luck, Wendy."

"Godspeed, Jay."

# CHAPTER SIXTEEN

Peter returned to the superintendent's office, where the governor was still waiting to be briefed.

"Governor, do you trust me?"

"I wouldn't have put you in charge of this operation if I didn't, Peter. Why the question?"

"I'm going to ask you to do something extraordinary, and I won't be able to show you supporting evidence until we get out of here."

"I'm listening."

"I can prove beyond a shadow of a doubt that Commissioner Redfield and David Breathwaite are involved in a plot to have Katherine Kyle killed. The uprising is just a sideshow to divert attention and give them an opportunity to make it look like an inmate-driven event."

The governor sat down heavily. "That's a pretty serious accusation."

"Yes, sir, it is. And I wouldn't make it unless I was positive of the facts. I have the two of them on tape discussing the details. Commissioner Sampson is still recording even as we speak. I got a Supreme Court judge in Albany to grant me a warrant to wiretap them based on probable cause before I left."

"How did you manage that?"

"Let's just say I had enough facts and evidence to support the warrant and the judge was willing to listen." Peter had taken the materials Kate gave him just prior to her departure, pored over them for more than an hour after she left for Attica, then made an appointment with a judge as soon as he heard about Breathwaite leaving for the prison. He chose a New York State Supreme Court judge because they had jurisdiction over the entire state. Then it was just a matter of pleading his case and being granted his wiretap on the way to the airport.

"And Brian is aware of what's going on?"

"Yes, sir."

"What is it you want me to do?"

"Have Breathwaite and Redfield relieved of duty and detained in this office until this situation is all over. After that we can determine what the charges will be and some of your troopers can take the two of them into custody."

"Leaving the agency without a leader right now could be a strategic nightmare. What would happen if I brought Brian back to run the show?"

"Your rank and file would be fine. The problem is the media would have a field day and want to know why." *Not to mention the fact that the ex-commissioner still has his own issues.*

"What are the chances that we can keep the situation with Redfield and Breathwaite quiet?"

"I think the media can be distracted."

The governor thought for a moment. "It's time for me to make an appearance, I think. That ought to distract them."

"My sentiments exactly."

"What are you going to do, Peter?"

"Go get Kate."

༄༅

"Max." Peter greeted the head of the Albany CERT team warmly.

"It's good to see you, sir."

"Thanks for taking care of that little matter for me."

"Of course, sir. I don't know what that was all about, but I know you wouldn't have asked me to do that unless you had a good reason."

"I've always appreciated your ability to follow orders."

Max shifted from foot to foot uncomfortably. "Most of the time that isn't a problem."

"Let me guess," Peter said, "you didn't enjoy being told to leave the hostages where they were."

"With all due respect to Commissioner Redfield, sir, I thought we could have gotten them out without having to make any concessions."

"Now we don't know if the target is in the same location. So we have to start from scratch."

"That's correct, sir," Max said miserably.

"Well, we'd best get going, then."

"Sir?"

"Hearing problem, Max?"

"No, sir. It's just that we were given a direct order—"

"And now you're being given another. The governor has put me in charge of the rescue operation. If you'd like to confirm that, I'm sure he'd be happy to tell you that himself."

"There's no need, sir."

"In that case, I want Tech Services back at it, pronto. I want to know the target's exact location and anything else we can find out about the layout and conditions."

"I'm on it, sir."

"Good." Peter looked at his watch, trying to hide his smile at Max's suddenly buoyant attitude. "I want a full briefing in thirty minutes."

"Yes, sir." The CERT team leader hurried from the room.

"Put her back in my cell," Kumar told Antoine and Zack when they arrived back on the tier.

The two inmates virtually picked Kate up and tossed her like excess garbage into cell number eleven.

With her hands still handcuffed in front of her, Kate was unable to regain her balance. She slammed heavily into the metal bed frame before falling to the floor. Behind her she heard the cell door slide closed with a snick. She straightened herself into a sitting position against the bed frame and waited for the pain in her wrist and shoulder to subside.

When her mind cleared sufficiently, she replayed the events of the preceding half hour. She pondered, not for the first time, why none of the CERT teams had attempted a rescue, or perhaps even the correction officer who accompanied Wendy. She was sure Randy Garston would have ordered them in. She was afraid she knew the answer—Redfield must have ordered the CERT teams to stand down, which meant she was on her own.

She closed her eyes and tried to envision Jay's reaction when Wendy gave her the ring and the notes. Kate knew she had taken a chance in dropping the notes on the floor, but she was confident that the sharp reporter would notice them. She tried to comfort herself with the knowledge that Jay would know how she felt in case she died in this godforsaken place. At least Jay wouldn't be saddled with the burden of thinking that Kate had still been angry or disappointed with her.

Kate wondered if her lover was nearby or if she was still on the Navajo reservation somewhere in the middle of New Mexico. She couldn't imagine that Jay hadn't been told what happened by this time. Who had been the one to tell her? Had it been Trish, who might have seen a report on the wire or on television? Or might it have been Peter or Barbara, contacted by Jay when she'd been unable to reach Kate? How would they have broken the news to her? Peter or Barbara, she knew, would have been gentle but honest. She had no idea how Trish would have broken the news.

She tried to put herself in Jay's place. How would she have handled finding out that her lover had been taken hostage? She smiled grimly. She would have torn the place to pieces until she located her. Jay, she knew, although equally determined, would have gone about it a different way. She would have mobilized a team with the expertise and experience to get the job done rather than charging in headlong, without backup.

Kate's musings were interrupted by the sound of a baton reverberating against steel nearby.

"You's crazy, man. What you wanna do dat for?"

"Just 'cuz I can, and 'cuz I have a thing for folks taking what's mine."

"I won that stuff from you fair an' square an' you know it."

"Bullshit."

This time Kate could hear the baton connect with flesh, and the sound made her sick to her stomach. Several pairs of running feet approached from either direction, converging on the spot where the two inmates tussled. There were more shouts, and Kate could see the shadows of struggling inmates. The scene was pure chaos. While it was frightening to witness, Kate understood that the distraction meant the inmates were not focusing on her, a reprieve for which she was grateful.

Above the din a voice shouted, "No! This does not serve our purpose."

"You and your goddamned purpose. I don't see how we're gonna get out of this mess with anything other than more time to serve, in even worse conditions."

There was a chorus of yeahs.

Kumar held up his hands for quiet. "You are all being shortsighted. If we can just stay with the plan, we will be rewarded."

"If that's true, I say we off the bitch now and get it over with."

"No way. I say we turn her over to the authorities and take our chances with them. I don't see how killing her gets us anything but more trouble than we're already in."

Kumar said practically, "So far, the man has delivered on everything he's promised. We have no reason to doubt that he will do so again and keep his word. Enough talk. Let us make the preparations. Ready the TV room. That will serve as the execution chamber."

In her cell scant feet away, Kate gathered her remaining strength and struggled to her feet. If she were going to die, it would not be without a fight. She looked around for anything she might use as a weapon.

⋙⋘

William Redfield strode hurriedly into the prison superintendent's office. "I'm sorry to keep you waiting, Governor Hyland. I wasn't expecting you."

"I bet not."

"Sir?"

"You know, when I hired you as commissioner it was because Brian Sampson thought highly of you. He said you had the experience and know-how to get the job done."

"I appreciate your confidence in me, sir."

"What I'm trying to tell you is that it wasn't my confidence in you at all—it was Brian's. I'm sure after today he's reevaluating his opinion."

Redfield's face turned red with embarrassment. "Sir, I assure you I am doing everything I can to bring about a peaceful resolution to this awful situation."

"Redfield, save it for someone who believes you. I'm not buying your load of BS."

At that moment David Breathwaite entered the room, followed by a state trooper. "You wanted to see me, sir?"

"Actually, I didn't, but I did want you here. You are both hereby relieved of duty and placed in detention until further notice."

Redfield looked miserable.

"What?" Breathwaite asked indignantly. "Do you have any idea what you're doing?"

"Thank you for asking, Mr. Breathwaite. Yes, I do. You will be confined to this office until this situation has been resolved."

"On what grounds?"

The governor's temper flared. "On the grounds that you serve at my pleasure, and this is my pleasure."

"Last I checked, serving at the pleasure didn't include detention. You have no right—"

"On the contrary, Mr. Breathwaite, I have every right. And if I were you, I'd shut my mouth before I incriminated myself any further."

"Incrimina—"

"If you'll excuse me, I have a date with the media. Don't worry, though, I've asked these fine officers to keep you company." Two state troopers stepped inside the room and took up positions on either side of the door.

"Ladies and gentlemen," the governor addressed the members of the press. He looked cool, calm and in complete control. "First, I want to assure you that the three hostages that have been released are in excellent shape, both physically and emotionally. They are being treated for concussions and some minor abrasions and are at this moment being reunited with their families."

"Will we get to talk to them?"

"First things first. There is still a hostage in there. Her safety and well-being are paramount. We are doing everything possible to ensure a positive outcome."

"Will there be a rescue mission?"

"We do not comment on strategy during ongoing situations. All I will say is that this administration and the good people of the state of New York will not be bullied or coerced by unscrupulous felons. In the end, justice will prevail and if need be, I will personally wield the hammer."

꧁꧂

"It will be a much cleaner extrication if we can accomplish it before they move her. Once she's out of the cell, anything can happen."

"I agree, Max." Peter stared at the images in the middle of the table and tried to be objective. He couldn't think about the fact that it was his best friend's life on the line—if he allowed emotion to interfere, he might make the wrong decision. The plan was to get in, neutralize the perpetrators, extract the target, and secure the area—all without getting anybody hurt.

"We're ready when you are, sir," Max and the other four CERT team leaders stood up as one, determination etched on their faces.

"Ready your gear. I'll be giving the order shortly."

Peter exited the briefing room and walked the short distance to the superintendent's office, passing the trooper stationed outside the door. After knocking once, he entered. William Redfield and David Breathwaite were standing at opposite ends of the room, one with his head bowed, the other staring straight ahead defiantly. Two troopers stood just inside the door. The governor was behind the superintendent's desk on the phone.

"Sir, I hate to interrupt your conversation, but I need to talk to you for a moment."

"Oh, thank God." Redfield looked to Peter beseechingly. "Enright, tell the governor he's made a terrible mistake."

"Sir, I'm sorry, there's no time to waste." Peter ignored his former colleague completely.

"Of course." The governor rose quickly, hanging up the receiver as he did so. He accompanied Peter outside and into an empty office across the hall.

"Is your helicopter still on the grounds, sir?"

"As far as I know it is."

"With your permission, I'd like to use it in the rescue operation."

"Of course. Anything you need. I'll tell the pilot to report to you. Are you ready, then?"

"Yes, sir. If we don't move right now, our chances of success are greatly diminished."

"Then by all means, give the order."

"Yes, sir. I will let you know as soon as it's done so that you can give the media the good news."

"I'll look forward to it."

"By the way, sir..."

"Yes?"

"For what it's worth, I think Randy Garston, the current deputy commissioner for operations, would be an excellent choice as the next leader of DOCS."

"That's good to know. Where is he, anyway?"

"At the moment he's overseeing the peaceful resolution of the uprising. Last time I saw him he was in B yard with the members of the Inmate Liaison Committee, supervising the return of the remaining inmates to their cells."

"I'll have a talk with him. Thank you, Peter, and good luck."

When Peter returned to the briefing room, the five CERT team leaders and their top lieutenants were poring over last-minute details.

"Okay, is everybody ready?"

There was a chorus of "yes, sirs."

"Here's the last piece of the plan." Peter pointed to the D block roof on the schematic. "When you bring her up through the roof, the governor's helicopter will be waiting. Max, take the safety harness with you and put it on her. I'll be waiting for you up there to attach a line and lift her into the chopper." He made eye contact with each man in the room. "I'm assuming you've all checked your gear and made sure everything is working. This has to go like clockwork. There's no margin for error." He looked around at the serious faces that looked intently back at him. "You all are the best—that's why you're here. I have every confidence in you. Let's go bring her out safely."

The CERT team members filed out of the room, peeling off in various directions. All were dressed in battle suits, bulletproof Kevlar vests, and helmets, with gas masks and gas canisters attached to their belts. Each man also carried a silenced MP-5 submachine gun, and several carried shotguns. Max and his group headed for the outside fire stairs leading to the D block tiers. When they reached the bottom entrance to the stairs, Max turned to his men. "Okay, this is it. You all know what to do. I have Ms. Kyle's mask and I'll head directly for her. Collins is in charge of breaking down the door. Elmira will take care of the lock box. Auburn will drop the gas and Oneida will secure the tier. We're in charge of the package. She is our only concern." Heads nodded all around him.

Max surveyed the area, looking for the other CERT team leaders, making sure that they were in position and at the ready. At their affirmative signal he tapped his lieutenant on the shoulder, whispering urgently, "Go."

Within seconds they had climbed to the second of D block's three floors. As they waited for the Collins team to overcome the barricade, they donned their gas masks. With a loud crash the door gave way and the Collins team stepped aside to allow the Auburn team to drop the gas. When that was accomplished, Max and his Albany group entered the tier through the go-round.

"Now!" Max yelled the muffled command through his mask as he started down the tier. Each of his eleven team members followed suit, racing through a fog so thick it was difficult to see. All around them they could hear the sounds of people choking and sobbing. As they made their way quickly down the gallery, the cacophony of cries from startled inmates assaulted their ears.

Max tried to count the cells that streaked past him as he ran full tilt down the gallery, one objective in mind. When he reached what he thought should be cell number eleven he stopped, trying to clear the smoke and gas from in front of him enough to see inside. He waited impatiently for the door to slide open. Glancing down the rest of the tier, he tried in vain to spot his counterparts from Elmira who were in charge of the lock box that controlled access to the cells.

Several seconds later, as the cell door began to slide open, he felt a tug from behind. He turned to see a massive inmate reaching for his gas mask. Before Max could make a move to ready his weapon, a second inmate flanked his other side. Max kicked out, landing a blow to the first inmate's solar plexus, doubling him over. As he prepared to strike out at the second inmate, his lieutenant came up alongside and hit the inmate in the head with the butt of his rifle, knocking him unconscious.

Max nodded his gratitude as he slipped into the cell, where Kate lay slumped against the metal sink. He bent down quickly to her and slid the mask over her head, adjusting it until it fit her snugly. It was not immediately clear whether she was breathing, so as soon as he had her mask in place he felt for her pulse and respiration. Her breathing was shallow and her pulse was weak, but it was steady. She appeared to be unconscious.

He whistled twice, loudly, and two of his men appeared in the cell doorway. He motioned to them to watch his back as he lifted Kate over his shoulder and made his way out of the cell. The scene was pure bedlam—inmates and CERT team members were running in all directions. Max pointed to the go-round, indicating his intended path of escape. One of his men moved into the lead, his weapon at the ready. The other officer remained behind him, ensuring a safe retreat. Together, they moved at a jog toward the far end of the tier, back the way they had come.

As they were about to exit through the steel door, Max heard the thwack of a baton cutting through the air, then a single gunshot. He could not see around Kate's slack body, but the man on his flank pushed him forward and off the tier before he could get a sense of what had happened. When they were safely on the landing to the fire stairs, Max laid Kate gently on the ground and turned around. He pulled his mask off. The officer who was behind him was breathing heavily.

"Are you all right, Gary? What happened back there?"

"I got hit. Just give me a second, it hit me in the vest." He leaned against the wall, trying to catch his breath.

"Jason, check him out," Max ordered as he bent over Kate. Carefully he removed her gas mask. Her eyes were closed, her breathing still shallow but steady. He unclipped the spare safety harness from his belt and slid it over her legs, securing it around her hips. Without turning his head he said, "Gary, Jason? Everybody okay?"

"Yeah, boss, just a little bruised."

Jason said, "He's got a nice-size hole in the middle of his vest in back. Lucky guy."

"Can you make it to the roof?"

"No problem."

"Okay, let's move." Max stowed the gas masks in a locked box off to the side of the go-round door and hoisted Kate over his shoulder again. He began to climb upward.

They reached the door to the roof without incident and Max handed the door key to Jason. He unlocked it, holding it open so that Max could carry his burden through, followed by Gary.

Peter was waiting for them when they arrived. He moved quickly to assist Max with Kate. Together they laid her on the roof.

"She's got a weak pulse and her breathing is shallow. She was unconscious when I found her." He started to unlock the handcuffs that still bound her wrists.

Peter, noticing Kate's dangling wrist, stopped him with a hand to the arm. "Don't—her wrist is broken. I don't want to have to worry about her arms flopping free until we can get her stabilized." The sight of his friend's hands restrained left him unsettled. "Thank you, Max—you did a great job." It was hard for Peter to get the words out. Looking at Kate's battered form affected him in a way he'd never experienced before. He'd been in the middle of many battles and seen many of his buddies fall, but this was different. This was Kate. She was not a combatant—just an innocent bystander who was caught up in the middle of an incomprehensible morass.

In an odd way, he felt somewhat responsible. He should have seen the danger for her, should have been able, somehow, to protect her better. She looked so fragile lying there, her face bloodied and swollen, her clothes torn and tattered.

Peter knelt down over her, sweeping the hair back off her face. "I'm so sorry, Spinmeister."

Anything else he might have said was drowned out by the deafening whir of helicopter blades. He stood and waved his arms over his head. The chopper circled once and hovered some thirty feet above them. A door opened in the side and a long cable was lowered until Peter could reach it. He clipped it to his own harness, then yanked on the cable to get more slack in the line. Kneeling, he unhooked the clamp from his harness and attached it to Kate's, then reattached it to his own. He gathered her in his arms tenderly and stood, tugging on the line twice.

Slowly the cable was retracted into the helicopter, pulling Peter and Kate up with it. He cradled her head against his chest, his other arm wrapped securely around her waist. Within a minute, they were being pulled into the helicopter by a state trooper.

"Careful with her," Peter said to the medic who had been hanging over the edge of the chopper watching their progress.

"I've got her," the medic said. He laid her on a stretcher, skillfully evaluated her injuries, and placed an oxygen mask over her face. "Do you have the keys for these?" He pointed to the handcuffs.

Peter produced a key from his pocket and efficiently unlocked the cuffs, careful not to jar Kate's arms. The medic was looking under Kate's lids with a penlight.

"Well?"

"Severe concussion, laceration to the skull, possible fractured cheekbone, displaced fracture of the wrist." He made a slit down the center of her blouse. "Contusions to the abdomen." He palpated her ribs. "Likely fractured ribs."

Peter's mouth was set in a grim line. "What about her lungs? She took in a lot of CS gas."

"We'll flush her system gradually. It will take some time for the gas to work its way completely out of her system, but she'll be okay."

"Why hasn't she regained consciousness?" The concern was obvious in his voice.

"You may not want to hear this, but I suspect she's been drugged." The medic pulled up Kate's sleeve, where a needle mark seemed to confirm his suspicion. "She'll come around."

Peter had to work even harder to contain his emotions. "What kind of drug?"

"It appears to me to be some kind of sedative used to incapacitate her—knock her out."

Although he hated to ask the question, Peter knew the answer would be important not only to him, but to Kate and Jay as well. "Has she been sexually assaulted?"

"I don't see any evidence of that, but a complete rape kit will be done on her at the hospital just in case."

"I don't suppose she can make it to a hospital in Albany?"

The medic considered. "Yes, but I'd like to get her stabilized here, first, before you transport her all that way."

"Okay."

Peter walked to the front of the helicopter and addressed the pilot. "Buffalo General Hospital."

The pilot nodded.

Peter returned to where the medic continued to work on Kate. "Take good care of her."

"Count on it."

Peter leaned over, kissed Kate on the forehead, and reclipped himself to the cable. He gave the trooper, who was standing off to the side, a thumbs-up as he moved to the open door. Slowly, Peter was lowered back to the roof of D block. When he touched down safely, he unclipped himself and waved the chopper off.

"Okay," he said to Max, "let's finish this."

Max turned to his men. "Jason, you're with us. Gary, why don't you wait here?"

"No way. I want the son of a bitch who redecorated my vest."

"Are you sure you're up to it?"

"Yes, sir."

"All right then, let's go."

The four men reentered the stairwell, donning their masks and helmets as they went. They used Max's key to get back through the go-round and onto the tier. The gas had begun to dissipate somewhat, and the scene was less chaotic. Inmates were facedown on the floor with their hands flexicuffed behind their backs, CERT team members standing over them.

Peter motioned to the five team leaders. "Is everybody accounted for?"

"Yes, sir."

"Any casualties?"

"Nothing life-threatening, sir."

"All inmate weapons accounted for and confiscated?"

"It appears so, sir. We have the one weapon that was fired and the inmate who possessed it."

"Okay. I want these scum separated, treated, and interrogated. Then we're going to ship them out."

"Yes, sir."

"I'm going to need a full report within twenty minutes—procedures, weapons fired, force used, injuries sustained, et cetera."

"Yes, sir."

"We'll do a debriefing after that." He paused. "Good job, everybody. Well done."

⋘⋙

"Governor, I'm happy to report that the mission was a success. The hostage was rescued, and no lives were lost in the process."

"Thank you, Peter." The governor looked relieved. "I'd like to meet with your men, if I could."

"Yes, sir, they are just wrapping things up. I should be able to assemble them for you within a half hour."

"Excellent. That ought to leave me just enough time to take care of our friends in the media." He hesitated for a moment. "Peter, did you see her?"

"Yes, sir. I loaded her on the helicopter myself."

"How is she?"

"She's got a number of injuries, and she was unconscious the entire time, but none of the injuries seem to be life-threatening."

"Where is she?"

"They're taking her to Buffalo General Hospital. They have to stabilize her before they can transport her to Albany Medical Center."

"Does Jay know?"

"I'm about to call her now, sir."

"If you don't mind, I'd like to be the one to tell her, and then have you fill her in on the details."

"Of course, sir." Peter picked up the phone, dialed, and handed the receiver to the governor.

∽⋧⋦∾

"Jay? This is Governor Hyland."

"Yes, sir." Jay's heart was beating wildly in her chest, and she sat down on the bed to keep herself from falling down.

"I have some good news for you."

Jay closed her eyes. "Oh, thank God." She had watched the dramatic footage on CNN of a helicopter hovering over the roof of one of the cell blocks, but the camera was unable to zoom in sufficiently to pick out the features of the two figures being lifted into the sky. She didn't dare hope...

"Peter and his men have gotten Kate out safely. She's on her way to a hospital nearby. I'm going to have the car take you there right away. And when she's ready, I'm going to have you accompany her on the chopper ride to Albany Med."

"I don't know how to thank you, Governor, for everything you've done."

"No need, Jay. I'm just sorry it happened in the first place. I'm going to let you talk to Peter now."

"Hey, Half-pint."

"Hey," Jay faltered temporarily at the sound of Peter's familiar, confident voice. "Hey, yourself. Did you see her? Is she okay?"

"I put her on the helicopter myself, honey."

"And?"

"She's had a rough time of it, Jay, there's no question about that. She's got several broken bones, a severe concussion, and she's had a prolonged exposure to tear gas. She was unconscious when I left her. But she's going to be just fine."

Jay was crying, tears of relief mingling with tears of anger and grief. When she could talk she said, "You know I can never repay you for bringing her back to me. I owe you so much—*we* owe you so much. Kate is everything to me." She fingered again the two letters from Kate that Wendy had given her. She had read them so many times the words were indelibly engraved in her mind.

"And you to her, honey. Believe me, Jay, it was my honor and pleasure. You'd better get ready, your ride should be waiting outside. I'll be there just as soon as I can."

"Okay."

"Jay? Put Brian on the phone, will you?"

She handed the receiver to Sampson.

∽⋧⋦∾

"Yes? Good news?"

"The best."

"It was hard to tell from the television images, and Jay and I couldn't listen to their wild speculation anymore. We put the sound on mute. Congratulations."

"Thanks. Any chance you can have that driver courier the tapes over here after he drops Jay off? I'd like the governor to hear them now."

"Consider it done."

"Thanks. I'll see you back in Albany."

"Peter? Good job."

"Score one for the good guys."

ৰ৯

"Ladies and gentlemen of the press, I am very happy to report the success of a rescue mission undertaken a short time ago here at the Attica Correctional Facility. More than that, I am overjoyed to tell you that Katherine Kyle is alive, safe, and undergoing treatment at an undisclosed location."

"What are her injuries?"

"I am not a doctor, and I don't want to speculate. For now I think it is important to focus on the courage that she showed and on the heroic deeds of the professionals who put their lives on the line to save her."

"Can you tell us any of the details?"

"I authorized and personally approved a hostage rescue mission designed to free Ms. Kyle and regain possession of the single tier in D block that remained outside our control. That mission involved five correction emergency response teams from five different regions— Albany, Auburn, Collins, Elmira, and Oneida. Each member of each group showed poise, professionalism, and bravery, and all made me proud today."

"Can you describe what they found in there and how they were able to accomplish the goals you had set for them?"

"I don't want to give too much away because of security concerns, as I'm sure you can all understand. I will say that the mission was accomplished using minimal force and resulted in no life-threatening injuries. The tier is back under control, the uprising is now officially over, and the perpetrators are in custody."

As more questions were shouted at him, the governor turned away from the microphones and waved before he retreated back across the street and into the administration building where Peter was waiting for him with the tapes of the conversations between Breathwaite and Redfield.

By the time he finished listening to them, the governor was standing over the tape recorder, fists clenched in anger and disbelief. "Why? What's this all about, really? You can't convince me that it's all about getting a job. I won't believe it."

Peter answered, "We have no evidence linking them to any motive more sinister than that, sir, although like you, we are rather incredulous."

"How can you order someone's murder just like that? I don't understand."

"Sir, I have to say, I'm glad you don't."

"Where are they now?"

"Breathwaite and Redfield have been moved to separate processing cells in an isolated area of the prison's intake area for the moment, and the correction officer Breathwaite mentioned on the tape as his contact and the ex-inmate who relayed the instructions have been located and taken into custody. The eight inmates we were able to identify from the Times Square videotape have been subdued and arrested and are being transported to separate prisons around the state for interrogation."

"Good. I wonder how long it will be before the media gets a hold of the scope of this mess."

"I would say that, for the moment, we've got a little breathing room. They've got so much to chew on that it may take them a while to figure it out."

"Kate could give us a better, more definitive answer than that if she were here, couldn't she?"

"Yes, sir, she certainly could."

"I don't care what it takes, Peter, let's nail the bastards."

"With pleasure, sir."

# CHAPTER SEVENTEEN

Jay hustled past the guard at the back entrance, following a plainclothes state trooper down the hallway and into the area marked Authorized Personnel Only. They continued down another stretch of corridor, around a corner, and through another set of double doors into the emergency room. The officer led her directly to the farthest cubical from the entrance, where the curtain was drawn and two more plainclothes state troopers stood watch. Jay nodded at them as she parted the curtain and stepped inside.

There on the gurney, covered by a white sheet up to her chin, lay Kate—pale and fragile looking. Jay stood for a moment, frozen in place by the image of her normally vibrant, healthy partner lying beaten and helpless. A doctor who was standing unnoticed off to the side said, "It's all right. You can come closer."

Galvanized to action, Jay walked the last few steps to the bed. Leaning over, she kissed Kate tenderly on the forehead, one of the few places on her face that wasn't swollen or covered with bruises. She reached under the covers and grasped Kate's free hand, which seemed cold and lifeless. It sent chills up her spin. "Is she..."

"She's going to be just fine," the doctor said as he approached Jay and put a hand on her shoulder.

"Then why isn't she conscious?" Jay was unable to tear her eyes away from her lover's face.

"We are still evaluating her situation, but all of her vital signs are satisfactory, given what she's been through. We do know that she was drugged before she was rescued."

Jay looked up sharply at the doctor, an involuntary gasp escaping her lips. She felt the room close in on her and had difficulty formulating her next words. "Did you—" Jay cleared her throat. "Was she sexually assaulted?" She choked on the phrase.

"We collected a rape kit, just to be sure. But no, she was not sexually assaulted."

Unbidden, tears of relief escaped Jay's eyes. "Oh, thank God."

"It appears from our tests that the drug she was given entered her bloodstream not more than five minutes before she was rescued. Its purpose was to render her unconscious. Unfortunately, we have to wait for the drug to run its course naturally and that may take a little while."

"How long?" Jay asked.

"I can't really be sure. But I would say she should be coming around soon."

"What about her other injuries?"

"She suffered several forceful blows to the head, leaving her with a severe concussion. She has a fractured cheekbone, a laceration to the back of her head, three fractured ribs, a displaced fracture of the navicular bone in her wrist, a deep contusion to her abdomen, another to her shoulder, and a variety of other cuts and scratches."

Tears ran freely down Jay's face as the doctor finished reciting the litany of injuries. "Oh, Kate," she sobbed, stroking her lover's hand.

At Jay's touch, Kate's eyelids fluttered open.

"Jay," Kate called weakly. "Is that you, baby? Is it really you?"

Jay leaned over so that she was more in line with Kate's field of vision. "Yes, sweetheart, it's really me." Jay choked on the well of emotion that bubbled to the surface.

"I'm glad," Kate whispered, as she closed her eyes again.

"I love you so very much, Katherine Kyle," Jay said, even though she knew Kate could no longer hear her.

When Kate next awoke, the room was dark. Jay was sitting by her side, slumped forward, her head resting on the bed. It was clear that she was asleep. With effort Kate lifted her good arm and ran her fingers through Jay's hair, reveling in its softness.

The movement awakened Jay. She raised her head and gazed into Kate's eyes.

"Hi there, beautiful girl," Kate murmured.

"Hey there yourself. How are you feeling?"

Kate put her fingers on Jay's lips. "Before we get into that, I want to tell you how very much I love you. You were the only thing that kept me going in there, Jamison Parker. When things got really rough, I closed my eyes, saw your face, and knew that I could survive anything for the chance to see you again."

Jay stood up from the chair and slid onto the bed, gently taking Kate in her arms and kissing the corner of her mouth. "Is this okay, love? Am I hurting you?"

240

"It's perfect. Thank you."

Jay adjusted her position so that she could see Kate's face more clearly. "I love you Katherine Kyle, more than anything in this world or the next. You are my life and my love. Nothing, and no one, will ever change that." She snuggled close to Kate, placing an arm gently across her midsection. Emotionally and physically exhausted, both women promptly fell asleep.

Peter stood in the doorway looking at the tableau in front of him, a smile splitting his face from ear to ear. There on the bed were Kate and Jay, arms wrapped around each other, raven hair and blonde mixing on the pillow. He thought he'd never seen anything that looked so right. Just as he was about to turn around and leave, Kate opened her eyes.

Quietly she whispered, "Hey there, Technowiz. I hear you got to play cowboy."

"Yeah, well, I was getting bored sitting at home—thought I needed a little excitement in my life. God knows I can always count on you for that. A little overdramatic, though, don't you think?"

"I'll keep that in mind for next time."

"Next time?"

Kate smiled. "Well, you never know." She beckoned Peter closer to the bed. Her eyes grew serious as she said, "I don't know how to thank you, friend. I know I wouldn't be here without you. And from the accounts that I've heard, you took fantastic care of Jay too. There are no words to tell you what that means to me."

Peter shrugged. "She's family. Speaking of which, Barbara's on her way here to accompany you on the flight to Albany Med. She wouldn't believe me that they actually have doctors in Buffalo who know what they're doing."

Kate chuckled. "That figures."

Peter touched her hand. "Want to tell me what happened in there?"

Kate glanced down at Jay.

"If you want to wait until later, I'll understand."

At that moment Jay stirred, raising her head at the sound of voices. She looked momentarily dazed as she tried to place her surroundings. Spying Peter standing near the bed, she said groggily, "Hey, when did you get here? I didn't hear you come in."

Kate squeezed her affectionately. "Sweetheart, when you're asleep, an atom bomb could go off and you wouldn't hear it."

"Hey! I resemble that remark."

"Yes, you sure do. But I love you anyway." Kate gave her hair a tweak.

Jay rose up, separating herself from Kate so that she could stretch without causing her pain. She looked from Peter to her lover and back again. "I interrupted something, didn't I?"

Kate said, "Peter was just about to debrief me. You're welcome to stay if you want."

"I don't think I'm really ready for that," Jay said. "How about if I go and grab a quick shower while you two talk?"

Peter looked at her sympathetically. "I'm sorry Jay, but it's best to get her recollections while they're fresh. Time tends to skew the memory."

"I understand," Jay said as she rose, kissed Kate on the forehead, and made her way into the adjoining bathroom.

❧❧

When they could hear the water running, Kate said, "Where do you want me to start?"

"Actually, I'd like you to start at the end and tell me what happened from the time you appeared on television to the time we found you."

"Okay." Kate screwed up her eyes in concentration. Her head continued to throb painfully and the effort of recollection was difficult, but the snapshots of images were as clear in her mind as if they were happening in the present.

"When we got back to the tier, the inmates had pretty much decided it was time to finish the job, although several of them were arguing against killing me. I heard the leader of the group telling others to prepare the TV room." She looked up at him. "I guess that's where they decided I should be executed." She tried to shrug nonchalantly, but the shudder that went through her body was plain to see. "I stood up, trying to think of something, anything, I could do to stop them. I figured with Breathwaite and Redfield calling the shots, I wasn't likely to get much outside assistance."

"You were right about that," Peter mumbled.

Kate continued, "Anyway, I had just started looking around when the cell door slid open and the leader and two of his henchmen came in. One of them had a syringe. As the first inmate came close I kicked out. I think I nailed him in the kneecap. As he was busy screaming, the second goon used my cheekbone for a punching bag. I remember stumbling backward into the sink and all three of them closing in on me. They yanked up my sleeve and jabbed me with the needle. The last thing I remember is them leaving and the cell door closing again. The next thing I knew, I was here and Jay was standing over me. Which, I might add, is the nicest possible way I could have awakened."

Peter said, "Sounds like our timing was excellent. I don't imagine five minutes passed from the time they gave you that shot to the time my guys arrived on that tier." He shook his head. "Sometimes it's good to be lucky."

"And sometimes it's lucky to be good."

"Yes, it is."

Kate fell silent as she considered the implications of what could have happened if events hadn't unfolded precisely as they did.

When Jay reentered the room, the silence was hanging heavy in the air. "Was I too quick?"

"No, sweetheart." Kate's eyes lit up when she saw her lover. "I missed you." She motioned for Jay to join her once again on the bed. She was finding it difficult to let Jay out of her sight, and she imagined Jay felt the same way about her. She looked up at Peter. "So, where are Redfield and Breathwaite?"

"I managed to get the okay for a wiretap and I got them on tape implicating themselves in your kidnapping, not to mention in the plot to kill you."

Kate gripped Jay tighter as she felt her shudder. In her ear, she whispered, "It's okay, love. It's all over now."

Jay put her head down gently on Kate's shoulder.

"That's pretty impressive, Technowiz, getting the goods in their own voices," Kate said.

Peter buffed his nails on his shirt. "Yeah, well, all in a day's work."

Jay chimed in, "You're so modest too."

"Yeah, I'll have to work on that."

Kate snorted.

"With solid proof like that, it was easy to get an arrest warrant for the two of them. The governor relieved them of duty, and they were taken into custody along with an officer they had working on the inside and the eight inmates and one ex-con who were involved in the plot."

"Good," Jay said vehemently. "I hope they all rot in hell."

Peter answered, "I have something worse in mind for them—like a stint in one of their own jails."

"You always did have a wicked streak," Kate said. Then she paused, a thought occurring to her. "So who's in charge of DOCS?"

"The governor's named Randy Garston the new commissioner."

Kate tried to whistle, but the effort was thwarted by the pain in her cheek and jaw. "Wow," she said. "That's a good choice."

"Yeah, I think so too. That's why I recommended it."

"I should have suspected as much," Kate said.

At that moment, there was a knock on the door and the governor stuck his head around the corner. "Can I come in?"

"Of course, sir. Please come in." Jay hopped off the bed.

"You didn't need to move on my account, Jay. You looked comfortable there."

"That's okay, sir."

"Kate. How are you feeling?"

"Much better now, sir."

"I bet. Listen, I want you to know how sorry and appalled I am at what happened."

"It wasn't your fault, sir."

"That may or may not be, but I bear the ultimate responsibility for what goes on under the auspices of my administration. Had I known about the situation, I would have taken action much sooner."

"I know you would have, sir."

"Are you getting good care in here?"

"Yes, sir. It's not exactly a five-star hotel, but it's better than my most recent accommodations."

"I want you to know, Kate, that I have great admiration for you. I always did, but now—well, let's just say I don't know if I could've handled what you did quite as well. You have my deepest respect."

"Thank you, sir. Coming from you, that means a lot."

"If you need anything, anything at all, you just say the word."

There was an awkward moment of silence before the governor said, "I need to get back to Albany. I want you all to know that I will personally see to it that Redfield, Breathwaite, and their accomplices are prosecuted to the fullest extent of the law."

Kate said, "Thank you, sir. And thank you for sending in the best." She nodded slightly in Peter's direction.

"I was lucky he was available."

"Actually, Governor, I was the lucky one."

Michael Vendetti nervously ran his fingers through his hair. "What are we going to do now? What the hell happened? Who authorized that?"

"Nobody, Michael, obviously," Bob Hawthorne replied shortly. "Calm down, you're giving me hives. I would guess Mr. Breathwaite set that up on his own. I can't imagine Bill being a willing party to such an ill-conceived and messy undertaking."

"We've got to cover our tracks, fold the operation."

"Michael, shut up. This unfortunate incident may have accomplished the goal for us. We may not have to do anything more."

Vendetti stared at the chairman as if he'd grown four heads.

"Look," Hawthorne lectured impatiently, "our boy Charlie went out to Attica, presented himself as a tough, no-nonsense governor, and got the hostage out in a daring rescue. We ran polling data immediately afterward—his numbers were through the roof. Very presidential stuff, all agreed." Hawthorne puffed his chest out like a peacock.

Vendetti's color improved from a pasty white to a more normal shade of tan. "Then our work is done, right?"

"For the moment, I think it would behoove us to lay low. If the situation warrants again, we may have to step in."

Vendetti's groan was audible.

"But for now, we'll consider ourselves adjourned." Hawthorne rose and moved to the door. "I would have thought you would have had more stomach for this sort of thing, Michael. You disappoint me." He walked out without waiting for a response.

Kate had fallen back to sleep, her injuries and ordeal getting the best of her.

Jay double-checked to make sure she was in a comfortable position, then got up from the bedside, picked up the phone, and called Trish.

"Hey, boss. I'm sitting at the hospital in Buffalo writing the Native American healing ritual story on a legal pad."

"It can wait, Jay. It's not like it's breaking news. Why don't you take a little time, come back after the holidays rested, refreshed, and ready to go."

"I've just come off two weeks' rest, as you might recall, and I don't want to let any more time pass before I put out a story. I have to get back in the game. Besides, this is a great story and it deserves to be told."

"And it will be. I'm just suggesting it doesn't have to be told today."

"I appreciate the flexibility, Trish, really I do."

"But, stubborn thing that you are, you're going to write it anyway."

"Yep."

Trish sighed in exasperation. "How did I know that? All right, kiddo. The choice is yours. But if you're planning to write it for next week's edition, I'll need it by tomorrow at the latest."

"Thanks, Trish, you're the best."

"Um, Jay?"

"Yes?"

Trish hemmed and hawed uncharacteristically. "I've put Alex on the Attica story. I wanted you to know that we'd be running something on it."

"Oh. I—I guess I got so involved that I never thought about it from a story angle." The idea of her lover's harrowing experience being the fodder for a magazine story made her stomach turn. On the other hand, if she looked at it objectively, if the incident had happened to anyone else, she would have expected it to get ink. "What do you need from me?"

"Nothing. I've instructed Alex to leave you out of it and to treat it like any other story. I promise you he won't come looking for any insider information."

Jay had to smile at the protective tone in her voice. "Alex is very good. I'm sure he'll write a great story. I will give you one thing, though, that nobody else seems to have picked up on yet."

"Oh?"

"The commissioner of DOCS and the former spokesman have been arrested. They're to be arraigned this morning on charges of plotting to have Kate murdered." Sharing that bit of news brought Jay a measure of grim satisfaction.

"You're kidding?"

"Absolutely serious."

"Oh, kiddo. I'm so sorry about this whole horrible mess."

"Yeah, me too. I'm just glad it's over now."

"When are you going back to Albany?"

"They're planning to airlift Kate later today if her vital signs remain normal."

"How's she doing?"

"She's beaten, literally and emotionally, and exhausted. I think she's still in a little bit of shock. She's been having nightmares the last few times she's dozed off, although she won't talk about it."

"Give her time, Jay. Time heals all wounds."

"I hope so, Trish. I guess we'll find out. Talk to you soon. Bye."

Jay hung up the phone and closed her eyes.

"Sleeping sitting up these days?"

"Barbara!" Jay jumped out of her chair and ran to her friend, enveloping her in an emotional hug. "Thank you for coming. I'm so glad you're here." She clung to her as if to a lifeline.

Barbara pulled back slightly to have a good look at Jay. "Hey, it's going to be okay, sweetie. I've already been in touch with the doctors here. They've been doing a great job. Kate's strong and in wonderful physical shape. She'll recover from her injuries quicker than you think."

"I know," Jay sniffled, "but I hate to see her in such pain. I'm afraid to touch her because I don't want to hurt her."

"She's not that fragile, Jay. She needs your touch—it will ground her and remind her she's loved and wanted."

"I woke her once, a little while ago when she was obviously having a nightmare. She flinched and shied away from me."

Barbara nodded sagely. "Honey, she's been through a lot in the past few days. It's going to take her some time to readjust. That wasn't about you—she was still back wherever her nightmare had taken her."

"I don't want to make it harder for her."

"Jay, your presence and your love are the most important ingredients in her healing process. She needs you now, more than ever."

"I was—I was afraid I'd lost her in there, Barbara. I can't imagine my life without her by my side."

"The great thing is, you don't have to."

"It's like every minute with her has become so precious, such a gift."

"Don't tell me that—tell her." Barbara indicated the form in the bed.

"Tell me what?" Kate asked groggily.

"Tell you to get your lazy ass out of bed, you slacker," Barbara rejoined lightly.

"Yeah? Come over here and say that."

"What do you think I am, stupid? I remember exactly how long those arms are. And, with a cast for a club, I'm not getting anywhere near you."

"I always said you were a smart woman."

Barbara looked at Kate with a practiced eye. "You look like hell."

"Flattery will get you nowhere."

"Don't I know it. Okay, sugar, fun time's over. Now let's get down to business."

The doctor proceeded to evaluate Kate thoroughly, making notes on a portable dictation machine she pulled out of a briefcase. When she finished, she gave her friend an affectionate hug. "I don't know how to break this to you, but you're going to outlive us all."

"Good to know."

"How'd you like to go home?"

"Home home?"

Barbara smiled. "No, Albany Med home. We've got some work to do to make you beautiful again."

"Ah, a reclamation project. Sounds like fun."

"Tell me that afterward."

Jay, who was standing quietly in a corner, asked, "What has to happen?"

"They'll have to operate to repair that wrist, and we'll have to see about the cheekbone too. There's not much we can do about the ribs, as long as they're not displaced. The x-rays don't indicate that they are, but we'll do further tests to be sure."

"Sounds like more fun than one woman should be allowed to have."
Kate tried to smile, but the action was just too painful.

"Uh-huh."

"Why don't you guys wait here, and I'll see about checking you out
into my care."

"Have I said thank you yet today, Dr. Jones?"

"I don't believe you have."

"Where are my manners? Thank you, Barbara, for hauling your butt
out here to personally oversee my care."

"I'm just in it for the publicity, babe. I'm going to be able to write a
book about you and your exploits someday, and how I was the one who
got to piece you back together and send you back into battle each time."

"I should have known there was an ulterior motive in there
somewhere."

When Barbara got outside the room, she put her arm against the wall
for support. Even for an experienced doctor like she was, the sight of
someone she cared about so banged up was hard to take. It was obvious
that Kate had been in a fight for her life, and Barbara was worried that
there were scars, both physical and psychological, that would take a very
long time to heal.

"You okay?" Peter came up behind her, placing an arm around her
sympathetically.

Barbara straightened up automatically, years of training kicking in.
"Fine."

"It's hard to see her like that, isn't it? When I laid her down on that
roof, it was all I could do not to scream out loud. She looked so fragile,
so helpless. I just wanted to kill somebody."

"I can understand that."

"Is she going to be all right?"

Barbara sighed heavily. "I think we can fix her physically. Her wrist
may always cause her trouble in bad weather, and her ribs will ache on
occasion. Her cheekbone can be repaired without any noticeable scarring,
and the effects of the concussion will go away in time."

"There's a 'but' in there somewhere. I can hear it in your voice."

"The psychological impact will be harder to gauge. Someone who's
been through something as traumatic as what Kate experienced usually
suffers from post-traumatic stress syndrome. From what Jay has
described and what little I can read in her expressions, I can already see
some issues developing."

"How can we help her?"

"Be supportive, understanding, and don't ignore what happened. She needs to honor what she went through—she'll need to talk about it."

"I can do that."

"You know our Kate. She'll put up a tough front, especially in front of Jay, because she won't want us to worry. It's our job not to let her get away with that, but it's a fine line. She's going to need a sense of normalcy, a sense of purpose—yet none of us can ignore, or wish away, the feelings that are going to keep cropping up at odd times for her."

"What do you suggest?"

"Well, for one thing I'd recommend a good therapist who is well versed with these types of issues."

"Do you think we can get her to go for that?"

"I think if it were positioned as standard DOCS operating procedure in any hostage situation she'd have no choice. I also think making it seem like it's less about her personal frame of mind and more about the situation she was in would allow her to frame it in her head in a way she could live with."

"Actually, counseling is SOP in a hostage situation."

"All the better."

"When do you recommend we break that to her?"

"I don't think we should. She needs to be able to come to us as an escape valve. I would have the governor, or whoever the new commissioner is going to be, do it. She's less likely to give them trouble about it or see it as helpful meddling."

"Done."

"Now let's see what we can do about getting her out of here and fixing her body."

The arraignment was a quiet affair. The defendants, dressed in orange prison jumpsuits, were led into the courtroom in arm and leg shackles by a phalanx of sheriff's deputies. The restraints necessitated their shuffling their feet as they walked. Neither one of them looked at the other. Two reporters in the back of the room recorded the proceedings—Alex Dingle from *Time* and Wendy Ashton of the Associated Press.

Wendy had been beyond flabergasted to receive a phone call in her motel room that morning from Kate, who sounded exhausted and groggy.

*"Wendy?"*

*"You got her."*

*"Kate Kyle."*

*There was a moment of shocked silence on the line. Every reporter covering the story had been trying to find a way to get to the ex-hostage. They had all been told there would be no news conference and that Kate would not speak with the media.*

*"How did you know where to find me?"*

*"I have friends in interesting places."*

*"So I've noticed."*

*"First of all, I can't tell you how much it means to me that you carried my messages and my ring to Jay."*

*Embarrassed, Wendy answered, "It wasn't any big deal."*

*"It was to me."*

*"Are you going to be all right?"*

*"I sure hope so. That's what they tell me."*

*"I'm glad."*

*"Not as glad as I am. Listen, how would you feel about an exclusive?"*

*"When?"*

*Kate laughed. "In a few hours. I'm thinking there's someplace you're going to want to be first."*

Wendy's attention was drawn to the front of the courtroom.

"Gentlemen, I'll make this very brief," the judge intoned from atop a massive wooden platform. "There is more than enough evidence to hold you over for trial, and that's exactly what I'm going to do." He consulted a calendar on his desk. "I'll set the trial date for...let's see...this would be a humdinger to start off a new year, I think. January 3, 1989. A little more than a year ought to give your attorneys enough time to prepare themselves."

He looked down his glasses at Redfield, Breathwaite, and their respective attorneys. "There won't be any bail set in this case. I agree with the prosecutor that you both present a significant flight risk. Enjoy your stay. Court is adjourned."

The sound of the old-fashioned wooden gavel smacking down hard on the desk reverberated through the courtroom. The inmates, numbers 4250 and 4251, were herded out of the courtroom and down to the basement of the courthouse building for transport back to the county jail where they would await trial.

Wendy left the courtroom and drove to the AP satellite office in Buffalo. She filed her story on the arraignment in record time and was on her way to Buffalo General Hospital.

When she arrived on the correct floor, she was greeted by two hefty state troopers. She produced her reporter's credentials and was escorted down the hall to Kate's room.

It was dark inside, long shadows falling lengthwise over the bed where the patient was resting with her eyes closed.

"Hi, Wendy," Jay called softly from a comfortable chair in the corner. Wendy, who hadn't seen her there, jumped. "Hello, Jay. Is this a bad time?"

"No, you're fine. She's in and out. Just give her a few minutes."

Jay stood and crossed the room. With tears in her eyes, she enveloped the startled reporter in a heartfelt hug. "What you did meant so much to both Kate and me. I know I must have said it at the time, but thank you, from the bottom of my heart. You gave me hope and something to hold on to, and you gave Kate a link to the outside world that helped her maintain her sanity."

As she glanced over at the battered form in the bed, tears welled up in Wendy's eyes also. "I wish I could have done more. I kept going over it in my mind, trying to think what I could have done to get her out of that situation."

Kate's voice, rough with sleep, came from the shadows. "You did everything you could, and I am so very grateful."

Jay tugged Wendy toward the bed and indicated the chair next to the side rail.

"How're you feeling, champ?"

"Like I've gone ten or fifteen rounds as a punching dummy."

"I bet. Are you up for some questions?"

"I'll do the best I can."

"Can you recount for me how they captured you, or is that too difficult?"

Kate smiled. "I've never been interviewed by anyone who cared if the question was too painful before. I think I like the kinder, gentler interview."

Wendy smiled too. "Yeah, well, don't get too used to it. Once you're back at the top of your game, I'll show no mercy."

"I'll enjoy the respite while I can get it then." Kate looked over to Jay. "Honey, are you okay being here, or do you want to get a cup of coffee?"

"I'm okay for now, if you don't mind my being here."

"Never." Kate held out her good hand for Jay to take as she recounted the events in Times Square.

"Talk about the conditions you were kept in. It's obvious you were physically beaten."

Kate described her captivity, the hours of uncertainty she'd spent in Kumar's cell, not knowing from one minute to the next what her fate would be. Although Wendy asked for details of things she saw and heard that might implicate either the inmates or Redfield and Breathwaite, Kate declined to answer questions that might jeopardize any legal proceeding.

As it became obvious Kate was tiring, Wendy declared the interview over. "Thank you for granting me this time. I know that wasn't easy for you, and I'm sure reliving that nightmare is the last thing you want to do."

"I owed you," Kate said practically. "This is my way of saying thank you."

"It was my honor to be able to help. What are your plans? Are you going to stay at DOCS?"

"Truthfully, I haven't thought that far. I just want to heal, and then we'll see what happens after that."

"Fair enough. I wish you both much peace and happiness."

"Thanks, Wendy, for everything."

Kate spent three days in the Albany Medical Center, where she underwent surgery to repair her wrist and cheekbone. She was flown there via the governor's helicopter the same day the interview with Wendy hit the newspapers.

While she was healing from her physical injuries, a psychologist worked with her to repair the psychological scars. They spent a long time talking over the course of two days. Despite her reluctance to be shrunk, as she so elegantly put it, Kate seemed to be more settled after the sessions. The psychologist scheduled her for another appointment in her office for the following week.

With much cajoling and a promise from Barbara to personally monitor her, the orthopedic and plastic surgeons released the patient to convalesce at home December twenty-fourth. Although they wanted to keep her another two or three days for observation, it was hard to argue against letting her go home for Christmas.

Jay walked alongside the wheelchair as a nurse's assistant pushed it toward the hospital exit. "I can't wait to get you home, love."

"You're going to show me how much, right?" Kate smiled up at her, although her eyes betrayed a case of nerves.

Jay laughed, intentionally overlooking Kate's anxiety. "Easy there, Tiger. I believe the doctor warned you about overexerting."

Kate pouted. "You know, I remember when you used to be fun."

"Ouch. I'm still fun, baby. I just don't want to wear you out on Christmas Eve. Santa's coming tomorrow and you need to be well rested for that."

"Oh I do, do I?"

"Oh, yeah," Jay purred.

"Do I get a sneak preview?"

"No way. Nice try, though."

Kate shrugged. "Can't blame a girl for trying."

Jay regarded her affectionately. Not having Kate in her bed had been torture, especially the last few days. The few miles that separated the house from the hospital seemed like the Grand Canyon. All Jay wanted to do was to hold Kate in her arms, stroke her hair tenderly, and spend all night wrapped around her.

When they arrived home, Jay helped Kate into bed. Although she argued that she wanted to sit up for a while, it was clear to Jay that just the effort of getting from the car into the house, combined with Fred's enthusiastic greeting, had worn Kate out.

"Are you okay, love?"

Kate mustered a smile. "Better than okay, sweetheart. I'm in my own bed, the woman I love is standing by my bedside, and tonight is Christmas Eve. What could top that?"

"I can."

Jay climbed into bed beside Kate, taking her gently into her arms and kissing her on the temple as they snuggled together.

"Yeah," Kate sighed contentedly. "I guess you can at that." Within seconds she drifted off to sleep, her lover joining her in slumber.

Jay woke first, a smile creasing her face as she felt the slow and steady rhythmic breathing of her lover beside her. She spent long minutes reveling in the scent and feel of her, the texture of Kate's hair and skin sending shivers of pleasure through her body.

Inevitably, her thoughts turned to the unmitigated terror that gripped her as Kate's fate hung in the balance. She couldn't imagine her life without Kate in it. She could no longer fathom what they were arguing about less than a week ago. There was only one thing that mattered— spending the rest of their lives together and making every precious second count.

"Penny for your thoughts, baby?"

"I didn't realize you were awake."

"I didn't want to waste another second asleep alone when I could be spending it awake with you."

"My thoughts exactly."

"Yeah?" Kate snuggled a little closer, pillowing her good cheek on Jay's shoulder.

"Yeah." Jay gave her a small squeeze. "So I was thinking we ought to do something about that."

"What did you have in mind, love?"

"Marriage."

"O-kay. I thought we had that one taken care of."

"Yes, but that's five and a half months away. I don't want to wait that long."

Kate shifted so she could look into her lover's eyes. There was a shadow of desperation there. "What do you mean?"

Jay licked her lips and tried to gather her thoughts. "Honey, I know you wanted a traditional wedding because you're an old-fashioned gal— and so did I..."

"Did, as in past tense?"

Jay took Kate's good hand into her own. "Katherine Ann Kyle, I love you more than life itself. If there is anything I have learned from all this, it's that life is too short to waste a single moment." She brushed her lips against the backs of Kate's fingers. "I don't want to wait until May, I want to marry you now. You are my light, my home, and my life, now and forever. None of the fancy trappings are going to change that. I've been giving it a lot of thought, and I really want to have the ceremony right here, on Christmas Day, with our closest friends on hand to witness it."

Kate hesitated briefly. "Christmas Day, as in tomorrow?"

Jay nodded.

"Are you sure this is what you want? After all, I'm damaged goods." Kate looked away from her, embarrassed.

Both Barbara and the psychologist had warned Jay that Kate might suffer from feelings of deficiency for a time as a result of the psychological trauma, but she had not believed it possible of her normally strong, self-assured lover. She answered hotly, "Katherine Ann Kyle, you are most certainly *not* damaged goods. What you *are* is the woman I love with my entire being and the one with whom I want to spend the rest of my life."

"But honey," Kate licked her lips nervously, "it won't be much of a wedding night or honeymoon." She looked scornfully at her fiberglass-encased wrist and touched her fingers to her bandaged face.

"Sweetheart," Jay smiled at her adoringly, "every day with you is a honeymoon. Besides, we can be pretty imaginative when we put our minds to it." She waggled her eyebrows suggestively.

Still, Kate sat silently, looking unsure of herself.

Jay consciously lightened her tone and batted her eyelashes playfully, "So, what's it going to be? You know you shouldn't keep a girl waiting when she puts her heart on the line."

"So I've heard." Kate arched up and gingerly kissed her. She pulled back and gazed intently into Jay's eyes. "If a wedding tomorrow is what you want, a wedding you shall have, sweetheart. I love you so very much, Jay. I can't think of any better present than being able to formally acknowledge my love for you."

"You are such a gift to me, Kate—the only one I will ever need or want."

"Oh," Kate tweaked Jay's nose playfully, "then I should take all those other things back?"

"Hey, now, don't go getting drastic on me. I didn't say that."

They both laughed, and Kate brushed her lips lightly against her lover's. As the kiss deepened, the women let out twin sighs of relief and contentment, falling back into the soft pillows to celebrate the gift they were to each other.

# CHAPTER EIGHTEEN

The sun, a brilliant orange ball, gilded the two women in bronze as it touched the horizon over the water. The heat of the day had passed, but the fine grains of white sand retained their warmth. The beach on St. John was unchanged from their first visit a little more than a year ago. Kate was resplendent in a white silk pantsuit; a royal blue chemise accented the color of her eyes. Jay had chosen a simple but elegant strapless cocktail dress of the palest green. Both women were barefoot.

"Sweetheart," Kate took Jay's hands in her own as she turned to face her, "I want you to know that this year has been the best year of my life. Being married to you..." Emotions threatened to swamp her. "I never really thought much about settling down before I met you. It didn't occur to me that there could be someone who could mean everything to me, or that I could deserve the kind of love you give me every day. Jay"—her voice faltered—"there are no words to tell you how much I love you."

Jay reached their linked hands up and wiped a tear from her lover's eye.

"Last year at this time," Kate continued, "I was battered and bruised, physically and emotionally. You took me as your wife despite all that." She shook her head in wonder, momentarily unable to go on.

"Kate, I love you with all my heart. I did then and I do—even more— now. I married the woman I've been in love with since my sophomore year in college. You were my hero then, and you still are today." Jay squeezed Kate's hands, kissing her tenderly on the mouth. "Marrying you was the best thing I ever did."

"As special as our wedding day was, I was still too traumatized to remember everything I wanted to give you."

"Kate, you gave me all I ever dreamed of—the promise of a lifetime with the woman I love more than all else."

Kate shook her head. "I want to give you more." She kissed the palms of Jay's hands. "This place, this beach where I first proposed to you...I wish in some small way that we could turn back the clock to that morning—so ripe with innocence and love, before the tabloids changed the course of our lives forever." Fresh tears stained her face.

"I know, love."

Kate swallowed, trying to get a handle on her emotions. The psychologist she'd been working with told her that feeling—really feeling—as uncomfortable as it might be, was a major step toward healing. To Kate, it was just disconcerting.

"I wanted to renew our vows here on our one-year anniversary, to symbolize a new beginning. I know this nightmare won't truly be behind us until the trial is over, but I'm tired of waiting." She reached into her jacket pocket, produced a small velvet box, and handed it to Jay.

"Wha...?"

"Jamison Parker, you make every minute of my life worth living. You bring me joy and happiness. You teach me how to love, and be loved, every single day. I have no idea what I would do without you, and I hope I never have to find out. I vow to love, honor, and cherish you all the days of my life. You are the best part of my heart and the other half of my soul—the answer to every prayer I have ever whispered. I love you, now and forever."

Kate opened the box her lover held loosely in her fingers, slipped out a three-and-a-half carat diamond solitaire ring set in platinum, and slid it on Jay's finger above her wedding ring.

"Oh my God, love."

"Sweetheart, I know this seems kind of backward—after all, one usually gives the engagement ring before the wedding ring—but this ring is very special. It belonged to my mother. I put it away the day I buried her and couldn't bring myself to look at it for many years."

"It's breathtaking."

"Yes, it is, and so was she." Kate looked into Jay's eyes. "Until last year, I hadn't celebrated Christmas since my parents' deaths. I didn't think I deserved to experience a joy that they never would again."

"Oh, honey."

"But you showed me that I was wrong. You gave me back something very precious—something I finally understand my parents would want me to have. Now every Christmas will be special—a day to give thanks for the time I had with them and to celebrate our marriage. This ring symbolized their love. I don't think anything would make my mother happier than to see it symbolize ours. I love you, Jay, with everything that I am and everything that I want to be."

Jay's vision swam as tears filled her eyes. "Katherine Kyle, I never knew genuine, unconditional love until you came into my life. Like you, I never thought I deserved it. Perhaps we were destined to find each other—meant to belong together. You are my family, Kate. You make every day worth living and every night worth sharing. You are everything I could ever have dreamed of in a partner—a passionate, talented lover, a wise and compassionate friend, a beautiful soul."

As she had on their wedding day, Jay repeated Kate's words. "I vow to love, honor, and cherish you all the days of my life. You are the best part of my heart and the other half of my soul—the answer to every prayer I have ever whispered. I love you, now and forever."

From inside her bra, Jay produced something shiny and placed it in her lover's palm. "I wanted to give you something that would be as unique and special as you are. So I designed this necklace."

Winking in Kate's hand was a gorgeous diamond and gold necklace.

"Oh, Jay. This is magnificent."

Jay reached around Kate and stood on her tiptoes to put the necklace on her.

"The diamonds were my grandmother's. I always wished she had been my mother. She was kind and compassionate, and she taught me to strive to be more than I thought I could be. The shape, a crescent moon, symbolizes the beginning of our life together."

"It's a remarkable piece, baby. Incredible."

"Just like you." Jay moved into Kate's arms, capturing her lips in a kiss equal parts love and wonder. "Happy anniversary, darling."

"Merry Christmas, my love."

⋘⋙

"Reality bites, honey."

Kate laughed. "To what do I owe that profound bit of wisdom?"

Jay threw herself on the couch in their rented condo in Alexandria, Virginia and shrugged. "It's a new year. Or it might be that that was probably the last vacation we're going to get for the next eight years."

"Pouting doesn't become you, princess." Kate leaned over and pulled Jay's lower lip into her mouth, savoring the taste.

"Mmm. I'm serious here, love. It's not that I mind being married to the president-elect's press secretary—actually, I think that's kinda hot—but I don't want to share you with every reporter in the world."

Kate sat down in the remaining space on the couch and pulled Jay into her lap. "Honey, we both knew when the governor asked me to be the spokesperson for his presidential election campaign that if he won, I'd be going with him to Washington."

"Yeah, but that was theoretical then, and I didn't want you going back into that DOCS hellhole."

"Any more than I wanted to be there, either, sweetheart. Jay, if you're really serious, I'll step away right now. There are still two and a half weeks to the inauguration. Michael Vendetti reports to work for me in a couple of days as my number-two guy—the president can promote him to my spot."

Jay shifted in Kate's arms and looked at her incredulously. "You're serious? You'd walk away from the greatest PR job in the world just because I wanted you to?"

"Yep."

Jay made a choking sound.

"Jamison, you are the most important thing in my life. No job can hold a candle to you. If it's going to make you that unhappy, I won't do it."

"Katherine Kyle, have I told you lately that you are the most amazing person I have ever known?"

Kate pretended to think. "Hmm. No—no, I don't seem to remember hearing that."

"Brat." Jay punched her lightly in the arm. "That you would even make such an offer is mind-boggling."

"I'm serious about it, Jay."

"I know you are, love. And that makes it all the more incredible." Jay kissed Kate passionately on the mouth.

"Um, before I forget how to think here, tell me what you want me to do. Do you want to go back to Albany? I'm sure I can get something in the private sector. It's not like we don't still have the house there. No harm, no foul."

"Shh. Stop, baby. I want you to be the greatest press secretary in the history of the White House. I want to be married to the most sought after—professionally, of course—woman in Washington."

"Are you sure? The hours are going to be horrendous—worse than anything we lived through at DOCS. And the traveling will take me away often."

"I know all that. I don't care. Sweetheart, you were born for this job. I am so, so very proud of you. We'll make it work. It's not like you haven't already been traveling all over the country with the campaign for the last eleven months."

"Yeah, but now I'll be traveling all over the world."

"Mmm, sounds romantic."

"Not without you there it won't be."

"Aw, you say the sweetest things. Honey, it'll be fine. I'll be able to get away with you some of the time. This is a once-in-a-lifetime opportunity. We've got our whole lives together in front of us. If you don't do this now, we'll both regret it."

"You're really okay with this?"

"Really." Jay brushed her lips along her lover's jawbone. "But what I'd really like right now is..." She undid the buttons on Kate's shirt, slipping her hands inside to cup smooth flesh. When her fingers closed on sensitive nipples, Kate groaned.

"Does that feel good, sweetheart?"

"God, yes."

Jay pulled the shirt from Kate's jeans, kissing her way down the slope of her neck to her shoulders, and below to her collarbones, as her hands continued to make love to Kate's soft, creamy breasts. Using her leverage, Jay pushed Kate onto her back, insinuating a leg between her thighs.

Kate cupped Jay's buttocks with both hands, pulling her tighter against her swollen center. "Too many clothes," she panted. "We've got to lose these clothes."

Duly motivated, she managed to lift them both off the couch. Unfortunately, the move unbalanced Jay, and she fell over backward.

"I've got you, sweetheart," Kate said as she gripped her around the waist, keeping her from hitting the floor by the merest of inches.

"I never doubted it," Jay laughed, as Kate lowered her gently the rest of the way. "Now get down here."

"As you wish, ma'am. First, though..."

Within seconds they were both naked and Kate was lowering herself slowly toward Jay's hungry mouth. Keeping her arms out straight so that only their mouths were touching, Kate teased Jay with her lips and tongue.

Finally, unable to resist the temptation any longer, Jay arched her hips up, bringing their mounds into contact. She ran her fingernails lightly down Kate's back, caressing her, urging her downward.

Kate responded by covering Jay's body with her own. The feel of slick skin sliding on slick skin made her shiver in anticipation. Angling herself to the side, she ran her fingers gently down Jay's midsection, pausing at her hairline.

"I love you so much, Jay."

"I love you too, sweetheart."

With reverence, Kate entered her, her fingers stroking, exploring, electrifying. When she felt her teetering on the edge of orgasm, Kate lowered her mouth to Jay's clit, setting off shock waves so powerful she almost lost her balance. She gathered Jay in her arms, caressing and cooing, until her breathing returned to normal.

"You are the sexiest woman in world." Jay slid a finger into Kate's wetness, withdrew it, and sucked the finger into her mouth. "And you taste delicious." She stared at Kate intently. "I need more of that."

Jay lowered herself until her mouth was positioned over Kate's center. She breathed in the heady scent, ducked her head further, and ran her tongue the length of Kate's clitoris, closing her eyes to savor the taste.

Kate cupped her head, urging her deeper. Jay responded, flattening her tongue and increasing the pressure of her strokes while running her hands up the insides of Kate's thighs. The orgasm was accompanied by a muffled cry, a deep shudder, and a whispered, "I love you, Jay."

Eventually they made it to the bedroom, where they fell into a blissful sleep wrapped tightly around each other.

# CHAPTER NINETEEN

January 3rd, 1989, dawned snowy and bitter cold in Wyoming County, New York, the county within which Attica was located. Kate, who had flown in from Washington that morning, huddled inside her overcoat as she hustled through the assembled reporters and into the courthouse for the trial of David Breathwaite and William Redfield.

She was glad that she had convinced Jay not to come until later in the day. If this morning was any indication, the trial was destined to be a media circus. Although Kate had expected nothing less, the level of noise and the number of microphones being shoved at her unsettled her. The urge to bolt was almost overwhelming.

"Hey, cute stuff, fancy meeting you here." Peter grabbed her by the elbow and shepherded her through the crowd and into the courtroom.

"Thanks, buddy, I owe you one."

"Again," he said, rolling his eyes. "Am I ever going to get to collect?"

"Eventually. Patience is a virtue, you know."

"Yeah, yeah." Peter looked at his best friend critically. "How are you doing, Kate? Are you okay with this?" With a sweeping gesture, he indicated the crowd, the trial, the setting, and her emotional state.

She shrugged. "There are plenty of places I'd rather be, believe me, but this is where I need to be."

He raised an eyebrow at her.

"I need closure. I need to know that the bastards are going to pay for the lives they jeopardized—not just mine, but those three officers on the tier, the five on the roof, all of the CERT guys, you."

"I know." He squeezed her shoulder sympathetically.

"That's not all of it, either. What about Brian Sampson, Wendy Ashton, Jay, and *Time* magazine?" She shook her head sadly. "All of their professional and personal lives were affected. For what? To get me out of a job?" She turned fiery eyes on Peter. "I still don't get it. I've been over this a hundred—no, maybe a thousand times in my mind this past year. It just doesn't add up. I can't help feeling like we're missing something."

Peter nodded. "I agree. It's a pretty thin motivation for all the trouble they went to. I've done some quiet digging, but I haven't come up with a single thing yet. Whatever it is, if there is something more, they've done well to cover their tracks."

"So now what? We wait for the other shoe to drop?"

"My hope, Kate, is that whatever it was has been derailed by their arrests. We'll lock them away for a good, long time, and that will be the end of it."

"I pray that you're right, my friend. I pray that you're right."

At that moment a side door opened and Breathwaite and Redfield were led in. Both wore business suits and were clean shaven. Neither looked at the other or at anyone else in the courtroom.

The buzz, which had risen several decibels, subsided when the no-nonsense Honorable Judge Andrew T. McGovern took the bench. The reporters, who had been stifled by a gag order for the past year, were practically salivating at the opportunity to hear the case against these former high-ranking officials.

"Okay, folks. Let me make it perfectly clear—I don't tolerate any theatrics or any fancy shenanigans in my courtroom. We stick to the facts of the case, we don't try this in the court of public opinion, and we'll all get along just fine. I intend to have this trial over and done with by"—he consulted his calendar—"January twentieth. Any unnecessary delays will be frowned upon. Any questions? No? Good. Let's get down to business. I assume both sides are ready for opening statements?"

"Yes, Your Honor," all three lead attorneys answered.

"Okay, then, we're off and running. Mr. District Attorney, the floor is yours."

"Thank you, Your Honor. Ladies and gentlemen of the jury, good morning. My name is Levon Davis, and I am the lead prosecutor in this case. I won't take up too much of your time. The burden of proof in any criminal case in the United States is on the prosecution, as you no doubt are aware. My team of assistants and I believe that is as it should be. Defendants should be innocent until proven guilty." He paused. "These two gentlemen who sit before you today all sophisticated, spit shined, and polished"—he pointed to Redfield and Breathwaite—"are as guilty as they come."

He stepped from behind his table, approaching the jury of seven men and five women as he buttoned his suit jacket. "I want to remind you before we begin that their motivation is not relevant here. It's hard to fathom, after all, why anyone would conspire to have a colleague killed."

The judge made a warning noise from the bench, which the prosecutor pretended to ignore.

"The real—scratch that—the *only* question here is whether or not these two defendants, William Redfield and David Breathwaite, committed the crimes of which they are accused. Did they, in fact, conspire to have Katherine Kyle, then the spokesperson for the New York State Department of Correctional Services, kidnapped and killed? Further, in David Breathwaite's case, did he conspire to instigate a riot in order to cover up his intentions?"

There was an excited murmur among the crowd of journalists who had not, to this point, been aware of that aspect of the case.

"Ladies and gentlemen, if we were playing a basketball game, this is what would be called a slam dunk. The evidence is so compelling, so overwhelming, there can be no other outcome but to find these two men guilty of kidnapping, conspiracy to commit murder and, in Mr. Breathwaite's case, conspiracy to incite a riot. You will hear the defendants, in their own words, implicate themselves in these crimes. You will hear the testimony of participants in the crimes, eye- and earwitnesses. You will have more proof by the time we rest our case than you could possibly need.

"The defense will try to convince you that everyone is out to get their clients. They want you to believe that the evidence is insufficient, the witnesses unreliable. Hogwash. Let me assure you, when you hear these two gentlemen, in their own words—their voices, in fact—talk about the crimes of which they are accused, it will chill your blood as it did mine.

"Mr. Redfield's lawyer will try to convince you that he didn't know anything about it in advance." The prosecutor shrugged. "Maybe he's right, maybe he's wrong. It makes no difference. The fact of the matter is that, regardless of when he knew what, once he was aware of the scheme, he went along with it, actively participating in the crimes—that is part of the definition of conspiracy. Whether or not he had prior knowledge is immaterial to this case.

"Ladies and gentlemen of the jury, when the day is over and you have heard both sides, I am more than confident that you will, as is your legal duty, find these two defendants guilty of kidnapping and conspiracy to commit murder and, in the case of Mr. Breathwaite, guilty of the additional charge of conspiracy to incite a riot. Thank you for your time."

"Thank you, Mr. Davis." The judge pointed to the defense table. "How about you folks, you ready?"

"Yes, Your Honor." Defense attorneys for both Redfield and Breathwaite responded.

"Who's going first?"

"I am, Your Honor," announced famed defense lawyer Calvin Nepperson.

"Good morning, ladies and gentlemen. I am Calvin Nepperson, and I represent Mr. David Breathwaite in this very serious matter. Mr. Davis is a compelling man—no doubt about that. The problem here is, he's built his case largely on the testimony of convicts and ex-convicts—unsavory characters who would say anything in order to get a reduced sentence or other favorable treatment. But don't take my word for it. All you have to do is pay attention and keep an open mind as the prosecution presents its case. Count the number of convicted criminals and folks with an axe to grind they call to the stand. I want to be honest with you." He leaned on the railing to the jury box. "I'm not going to argue that my client is going to win any nice guy awards—but the fact that he's not always very likeable is not a crime. If it were, imagine how full our jails would be. I'm sure you all could think of a few people in your lives you'd like to see put away. We all have those. The point is, you can't just go locking up folks because you don't like them—it's not the American way. In the end, as you will see, the prosecution simply has no real case. I look forward to proving that to you as soon as the prosecution has finished having its say. Thank you."

When Nepperson sat down, a man in a charcoal pin-striped suit stood up. "Ladies and gentlemen of the jury, my name is Josiah Green, and I represent William Redfield. Despite the rhetoric that you heard earlier from the esteemed prosecutor, I'm here to tell you that Mr. Redfield's only crime is that he happened to be at the head of an agency targeted by one man"—he turned around and pointed to Breathwaite—"with a nefarious agenda."

A collective buzz went through the crowd as Redfield's apparent strategy became clear—separate himself from his alleged co-conspirator and place the blame squarely on Breathwaite. The reporters were madly scribbling in their notebooks—whenever defendants broke ranks with one another it meant a better, more interesting story.

"Mr. Redfield operated according to the best of his ability. He was made aware of a potentially dangerous situation at Attica, he evaluated all options and acted in good faith to secure a positive outcome with a minimum of injuries.

"The evidence will clearly exonerate Mr. Redfield of any knowledge of a plot to do harm to anyone. No one, in fact, was more surprised than he was when Mr. Breathwaite informed him of the scheme. You will clearly hear Mr. Redfield's disgust and you will listen as he authorizes steps designed to rescue the hostages.

"Ladies and gentlemen of the jury, Mr. Redfield is not the bad guy here. He was just an innocent bystander in the wrong place at the wrong time. He was a man with a job to do and a mission to uphold, and that is exactly what he tried to do. But don't believe me—you will hear it for yourselves. Thank you for your time." He looked up at the judge. "That's all I have, Your Honor."

"Splendid. Okay, folks. That's enough for one morning. Let's adjourn for lunch and the prosecution can begin presenting its case this afternoon."

༺ঔৈ

Jay arrived just as the lunch break was announced. She reached Kate at the same moment the prosecution's team exited the courtroom. As Kate started to ask her about her trip, she noticed an odd expression on her lover's face—one she had never seen before.

"Jay? Honey? Are you all right?"

Levon Davis walked past, followed by two assistants. One of them was an attractive, willowy redhead, who, upon reaching them, stopped dead in her tracks. She sported an expression remarkably similar to Jay's.

"Jay? Is that really you?"

"S-Sarah?" Jay's voice quavered.

Kate merely stood to the side, perplexed, watching the scene. The woman seemed somehow familiar to her, like she'd seen her somewhere before. Seconds later, as she was searching her memory banks, she made the connection.

The last time she'd seen the redhead was six years ago in a hospital emergency room. Kate had summoned an ambulance to take Jay there after saving her from an attempted sexual assault. She and Jay barely knew each other then, and she had asked Jay if there was anyone she could call for her. She managed to get Jay to give her the name of her college roommate—*and lover,* Kate reminded herself.

"Wow. Um, Katherine Kyle, this is—"

"Sarah Alexander." When she looked shocked, Kate shrugged. "I remember you from the hospital ER."

"Oh," Sarah remarked, obviously uncomfortable.

"Sarah, Kate and I—"

Sarah touched her on the arm. "It's okay, Jay. I read the papers and watch TV. I guess it just never occurred to me that you'd come to the trial. I don't know why. It should have."

"Hey, so what's your role here? Are you the big-shot attorney?"

Sarah laughed. "No, just a lowly assistant district attorney trying to get some experience."

"I don't believe it," Jay said warmly. "You were the smartest person I knew. I bet you're already sitting in the first assistant's chair, aren't you?"

"Actually," Sarah blushed, "I am. I'll be doing some of the witness questioning in the case." She looked quickly at Kate. "But not with you. I'll have to disclose my relationship to you and Jay and see if I need to recuse myself from the case."

"Geez, Sarah, I hope not. This case could be a big break for you." Jay looked regretful.

"Yeah, but there'll be others, I'm sure."

"If it helps, I'm not going to be testifying."

"That might help a little, since my connection to Kate is so slim. You know, a girlfriend of an ex-college roommate might not count for much."

"Maybe. Hey, can you have lunch with us?"

"No, I'm sorry. We're going to start presenting our case this afternoon and we've got to go over last-minute strategy."

"That's too bad. Maybe another time?"

"Sure. Well, I've got to go. It was nice bumping into you, Jay. You look great."

"You too, Sarah."

"Yeah, I'm actually doing really well."

"That's terrific. I'm really glad to hear that."

As Sarah turned to leave, Jay touched her on the sleeve. "Sare—I really do want to find the time to catch up." She looked at her former girlfriend intently. "I-I'm sorry about…"

"Jay, it's okay, really. I'm fine about what happened. I've moved on. I've got a wonderful partner, and we're very happy together."

"That's great. I'd love to meet her sometime."

Sarah looked at her for a long moment. "Yeah, I think I'd like that. I miss your friendship, Jay."

"Here's my number. Give us a call."

"I might just do that." Sarah tucked it in her skirt pocket as she hurried off.

When she'd gone, Kate said, "You all right, love?"

"Yeah. You?"

"Absolutely. Is it hard to see her?"

"A little." Jay bumped Kate with her hip. "I didn't handle breaking up with her very well."

"She obviously forgives you."

"True, but forgiving myself is another matter." Jay took Kate's hand. "How about we get some lunch and you can tell me all about what I missed this morning."

"Sounds great. Peter will meet us a little later. Naturally, he got beeped in the middle of everything."

"Some things never change."

"Nope, and they likely never will."

It was obvious from the outset that the prosecution had painstakingly built its case. The files and evidence Kate had left with Peter before going to Attica laid the groundwork for proving that Breathwaite intended to have her fired from DOCS. Over the course of eleven days, witness after witness painted a picture of a man who left his position as PIO under a cloud of controversy and became obsessed with ousting his successor, whatever the cost. While the DA handled one or two of the witnesses, it was Sarah who did the bulk of the questioning, the judge having decided that her relationship with Jay did not present a conflict of interest sufficient to warrant her removal from the case.

Marisa, Kate's former assistant, testified under oath that Breathwaite recruited her to spy on Kate and to report back to him. Under Sarah's gentle questioning, she was forced to admit that on several occasions she intentionally misled Kate in an effort to get her to fail at her duties. When asked why she was willing to sell out her boss in such a fashion, the assistant replied that Breathwaite promised her that when he came back to DOCS, she would get a raise and a promotion. She defended her actions by saying she stopped spying when Kate caught her at it.

In a highly unusual move, a couple of reporters took the stand to admit that Breathwaite was the predominant source for several of the negative stories they wrote about Kate. Those reporters subsequently tendered their resignations.

Although Wendy had offered to testify, Kate urged Levon and Sarah to use her only in case of an emergency. Putting her on the stand and introducing the audiotape of her conversation with Breathwaite would have resulted in disclosing details of her personal life that would have caused her great pain and also might have led to her being fired from her job.

Basher, while admitting that he struck a deal for a light sentence in exchange for his testimony, established that he was hired by Breathwaite to have some of his inmate buddies stage the riot, capture Kate, and kill her. His testimony was followed by that of Antoine, Zack, and Kumar, all of whom corroborated his story and added details about the deal to let the three correction officers go at Breathwaite's behest, along with the order to "kill the bitch already."

Jay who, unlike Kate, would not be called to testify in the trial, had sat through every witness since that first day. She was impressed with Sarah's poise and ability to handle the witnesses, and told her so on the one occasion when they bumped into each other in the hallway.

The testimony, itself, however, was occasionally difficult for Jay to stomach. She squirmed and struggled through some of the more graphic descriptions of her lover's captivity, glad that trial rules prevented witnesses from hearing the testimony of other witnesses. As she waited for the prosecution to call its next witness, she thought about her discussion with Kate the previous night.

*"Are you sure you're okay, love?"*

*"Fine, baby, really. I'm more worried about you. I'm not the one sitting through the testimony day after day."*

*"Yeah, but I'm not the one they're talking about."*

*Kate massaged her shoulders. "In some ways, Jay, I think it must have been worse being you—not knowing exactly what was going on and feeling helpless to do anything about it."*

*"I wasn't in any imminent physical danger, though—just in danger of losing the only thing that mattered in my life."*

*Kate kissed the top of her head. "It's over, sweetheart. Here I am, safe, sound, and where I belong—snuggling with the woman I love."*

*"Honey, as much as I appreciate the sentiment, we both know this won't really be over until the jury has had its say and those two morons are locked away for good." She turned around in her lover's arms and kissed her on the shoulder. "Besides, the hardest part comes tomorrow when you have to testify. Are you ready?"*

*"As ready as I'm going to get."*

*"Maybe we could get Levon to agree that you don't need to take the stand."*

*"Jay, if I don't testify, it will throw the whole case into doubt. Everyone will wonder why the woman who is at the heart of the case isn't testifying."*

*Jay pouted. "It doesn't mean I have to like your being put through the experience a second time."*

*"I love your protective side, baby, you know that? The therapist and I have been working on this for a few months. It'll be fine. You'll see."*

*"Just the same, I'm going to be right there with you. All you need to do is look to the first few rows and you'll find me."*

*"I know, sweetheart, and I appreciate that more than words can say. But if we don't get some sleep, I won't be worth anything by the time they get to me."*

Jay was jarred back to the present when Levon Davis announced, "The prosecution calls Ms. Katherine Kyle to the stand."

The buzz rippling through the crowd intensified as the double side doors opened and Kate strode in, confident and beautiful in a perfectly tailored deep navy suit with a sky blue blouse, sheer navy pantyhose, and matching shoes. With no apparent effort, she commanded the attention of every person in the room, with the notable exception of the defendants. Neither of them so much as looked her way.

The district attorney handled the questioning himself, taking Kate through the events of the six months from the time she was offered the job as DOCS public information officer to her rescue and recuperation. She related the incident with Marisa, along with Redfield's refusal to dismiss the assistant. She described the meeting in her office with Breathwaite during which he'd threatened to out Jay. She explained how he told her she didn't know what hell was, but that she would soon.

Finally, just as the DA was about to take her back to the day of the incident, the judge declared a short recess.

"How're you holding up, honey?" Jay asked.

"So far, so good, but the fun is just about to begin."

"I know." Jay rubbed her back soothingly. "It will be over soon, Kate, and then we can get on with our lives."

"I can't wait." Kate smiled lovingly. "Jay, are you sure you want to stay for this next part?"

Jay stiffened.

"I just mean," Kate put her arm around her, "this will be the hardest part for you to hear. I love you, sweetheart, and I'd like to spare you that."

"No," Jay said determinedly. "If you can live through it again, so can I."

"You can be so stubborn. Have I ever told you that?" Kate bumped her with her right hip.

"Maybe once or twice, it's hard to recall."

Kate grew serious. "Thanks, Jay, for being here for me."

"There's nowhere else I'd want to be, love. We'd better head back. I'm pretty sure the ten minutes is up."

They strolled back toward the courtroom from the antechamber where they had been allowed to spend the recess, away from the prying eyes of reporters.

༒

"Ms. Kyle, can you recount for this court the circumstances under which you came to be captured on the morning of December 20, 1987?"

Kate told the story of being paged, going to the office, the decision to go out to Attica, taking the governor's plane, and arriving at the prison. She described her first trip through Times Square to update the media and the three subsequent trips prior to her capture. As she reached that fateful last trip, her posture unconsciously stiffened and her facial expression intensified.

"Ms. Kyle, I know this is very difficult, but could you tell us what happened from the time you entered Times Square just before you were taken to the time you were rescued?"

"I can tell you about the parts of that time that I was conscious, yes."

"Of course."

Kate narrowed her focus, shutting out the courtroom, the people, and the noise. "I had just finished having a conversation with Randy Garston, who was the deputy commissioner for operations. I remember walking into Times Square, stepping on some of the broken glass that littered the floor, and thinking about what I wanted to say to the media." She paused and took a sip of water from a glass the bailiff had thoughtfully placed within her reach.

"I was two, maybe three strides into the room when I was grabbed from behind. I struggled, kicking one man in the shins. Then I remember being punched several times in the face and midsection." She winced. "I felt my ribs break and my cheekbone fracture. I tried to keep fighting..." The action became so real to Kate as she recounted it that she visibly flinched, as if from a blow. She shook her head.

"I have a vague recollection of being dragged through one of the cell block corridors. The next thing I remember is waking in a cell, hearing angry voices nearby." Kate closed her eyes as the sounds of Antoine, Zack, and some of the others arguing over her fate overwhelmed her. With effort, she opened her eyes again. She focused on Jay, who was halfway out of her seat in the first row of spectators, a worried expression on her face. With her eyes, Kate told her it was okay.

"One of them wanted to rape me before they killed me." She tried to keep her voice level—matter-of-fact. She purposely didn't look at Jay, knowing that seeing the expression on her face would be her undoing. "Another just wanted to kill me outright. A third man argued that the man, as he referred to him, should have done his dirty work himself and that perhaps the best course of action was to turn me over to the authorities. A fourth, a man who seemed to be in charge, told them that I would be left alone until it was time to do away with me."

"Do you know who he was?"

"I heard the other inmates call him Kumar. I do not know if that was his first or last name, or perhaps a nickname." Kate took another sip of water before resuming her story. "When the others had dispersed, Kumar came and talked to me. He told me that kidnapping and murdering me was not their choice, but that it, as he said, afforded them an opportunity and they had to take it."

"What happened then?"

Kate screwed up her face in concentration. "I'm not really sure. I lapsed in and out of consciousness for a period of time."

"You had a severe concussion, in addition to your broken bones."

"Yes, I was hit in the head a number of times, hard. My vision blurred occasionally and my head throbbed."

"But you are sure of the conversations you have related?"

"Positive." She nodded. "The next thing I remember is waking to hear the inmates fighting amongst themselves. I pretended to be asleep or unconscious when one of them came by to check on me."

"How much time had passed?"

"It's hard to say—the concept of time in there was measured simply by the moments I managed to stay alive." She could hear Jay gasp from the spectator's section. She tried to send her a reassuring look.

"Understandable. What's the next thing you remember?"

"There was a commotion, and three men appeared in my cell. They handcuffed me with my hands in front of me."

"Your wrist was broken?"

"Yes. The pressure of the handcuffs was excruciating."

"I'm sorry, go on."

"They shoved me out of the cell. I asked where we were going. I was told that we were going to talk to the media. I looked for a means of escape but couldn't find one. Along the way, one of the inmates argued to keep the other three hostages."

"The three correction officers?"

"Yes, they were also taken to the media."

"Did you talk to them?"

"No, I did not have the opportunity. In fact, that was the first time I was even aware that there were any other hostages."

"Okay, go on."

"When the one inmate argued for keeping the three correction officers, Kumar answered that it would jeopardize their position to do so—they were not part of the deal."

"So he indicated that the other three hostages weren't supposed to be kidnapped and killed?"

"Right."

"Is that why they let them go?"

"Objection, Your Honor!" Breathwaite's attorney was on his feet. "Calls for speculation."

"Sustained. Do not answer that question, Ms. Kyle."

"Kate," the prosecutor began again, "what happened next?"

"Kumar, two of the other inmates, and I entered Times Square, while the others stayed behind with the three correction officers. I was allowed to answer one or two questions from the reporter, then I was taken back to my—back to the cell they were keeping me in." Kate experienced once again the feeling of helplessness that had enveloped her when the cell door slammed shut with her inside again. She fought against the tears that threatened.

"It's okay, Kate. Take a minute. It was a traumatic time."

"They began arguing amongst themselves again about whether they should kill me right away or turn me over to the authorities and beg forgiveness. I guess killing me must have won out," she shrugged, "because someone—Kumar, I think—gave the order to ready the TV room."

"Why the TV room?"

"That is where they planned to execute me." Her heart ached at the terror etched on Jay's face. She looked away.

"Did they try to execute you?"

"They injected me with a drug that I guess was supposed to knock me out so that I wouldn't struggle. I fought with them, trying to keep them from putting the needle in me." She was back in the cell, fighting for her life, twisting, turning, scrapping. She used every bit of remaining strength she had left trying to fight them off. She was sure that this was the end. But it couldn't be. She wouldn't leave Jay this way—she couldn't. "Jay, I'm so sorry," she whispered brokenly, just before she lost consciousness.

"What? Kate? Did you say something? Are you all right?" The prosecutor approached the witness stand. "Your Honor, may we have a moment?"

"Of course."

"No," Kate said, returning to the present. "I'm fine. Let me finish."

"Are you sure?"

"Yes. After the drugs took effect, the next thing I remember is waking up in the hospital, with friends and family by my side." She smiled lovingly at Jay, who still looked pale and shaken.

"Very well, Kate. Thank you. No further questions, Your Honor."

"Mr. Nepperson, Mr. Green?"

Breathwaite's attorney stood. "Ms. Kyle, first, let me say how very sorry I am for your ordeal."

*The only thing you're sorry for is that your client got caught.*

"Ms. Kyle, did you ever, at any time, hear any of your captors refer to my client by name?"

"No."

"Excuse me, what was that? No?" Nepperson nodded, as if this were a revelation. "In that case, you really have no way of knowing whether or not it was Mr. Breathwaite to whom they were referring, now do you?"

Kate didn't answer.

"I'm sorry, I'm afraid I didn't hear your answer."

"No."

"So they could have been talking about anybody?"

"They were talking about your client."

"But you don't know that for a fact, now, do you? Let me ask you again. Did they ever refer to this mysterious man on the outside by name?"

"No."

"Thank you. No further questions, Your Honor."

"Mr. Green, any questions for the witness?"

Redfield's attorney looked up. "No, Your Honor."

The judge turned to Kate. "You may step down now. Court is adjourned until tomorrow at nine a.m." He gaveled the session to a close.

Kate was standing in the antechamber when Jay came running in. She hugged her tightly, both of them dissolving into tears.

"I'm so sorry, baby. I'm so, so sorry for what you went through."

"It's okay, Jay. It's over now. I'm sorry you had to relive it with me."

"No, I needed to know."

"Well, now you do."

"It helps explain some of your nightmares to me."

"Oh."

"It's a good thing, Kate," Jay said, trying to reassure her. "I feel better knowing."

"Okay."

"Are you all right? You want to go home?"

Kate sighed. "Let's let the media clear out, then get out of here. I'd like to stay in town for the rest of the trial, though, especially now that I can sit in and listen."

"Okay, love. Let's see the rest of this through together."

The prosecution rested the next day after calling Peter and Max Kingston to the stand to introduce the explosive audiotape of Breathwaite and Redfield's conversations in the makeshift command center.

The prosecutor smiled triumphantly when Breathwaite's voice boomed throughout the courtroom.

"Don't you go getting holier-than-thou on me, Willy boy. You're in this up to your neck. The plan was to get you installed as commissioner, just like you always wanted, then you were supposed to get rid of Kyle. You weren't able to accomplish that on deadline, and that forced me to take action. If you had just done what you were supposed to do, this whole thing wouldn't have happened."

"You orchestrated the entire riot?"

"Merely a distraction for the main event. The boys will call it off when the goal has been accomplished."

The tape of the second conversation was even more damning, as Breathwaite fumed, "You want those three officers out of harm's way or not?"

"Of course."

"The object here is to kill Kyle, and extract them safely. I'm just giving you a way to get that done."

Sitting in the audience and listening to the tapes, Kate was thunderstruck. The venom in Breathwaite's voice sliced through her like razor blades. It was unfathomable that the man had coldly, cruelly calculated to kill her. *For what? Because I was standing between him and a job. It doesn't make any sense.*

A piece of the puzzle fell into place when Breathwaite reminded Redfield in the tape of the first conversation that what he had wanted out of the deal was to be made DOCS commissioner. Another piece clicked when Breathwaite said that it was Redfield's job, once in place, to get rid of Kate. She supposed he hadn't been able to do that because she had the governor's support. So Breathwaite had apparently taken matters into his own hands.

Kate was convinced that there were still pieces missing.

Beyond that, she worried that there would be insufficient evidence to convict Redfield—until the prosecutor played the sections where he took an active part in the plot, his voice caught on tape helping to advance the plan.

"Okay." Redfield's voice could clearly be heard. "I'll get the Inmate Liaison Committee in here to make it look legitimate. We'll have them present the offer to the eight inmates. Do you have a way of contacting them directly?"

"Don't go through the ILC. I have an ex-inmate I'm working with. I'll have him give them the instructions. I've got him stashed nearby. If he goes in there, they'll know the order is coming from me."

"If I don't use the ILC, it might raise more questions."

"If you do go through them, there's no guarantee the eight will know where the order is coming from. Not only that, but it means involving more inmates in the plan. I don't think that's wise, do you?"

"I haven't liked the plan from the beginning. This was your insane idea."

"Insane or not, you're stuck with it now, Willy. It would behoove you to make the best of it."

In Kate's mind, though, the final nail in Redfield's coffin came when he admitted that he had deliberately ordered the CERT teams not to rescue her, despite Randy Garston's wanting to send them in.

Breathwaite said, "Your boy Randy's not happy with your decisions."

"Neither am I, David. Where's your contact man?"

"He's ready."

"How are we supposed to send him in with the message?"

"I have an officer who will deliver him."

"We're going to put another officer in jeopardy?"

"No, he's been acting as a go-between for weeks."

"Very clever."

"Thank you, Willy. Not only that, but he'll escort the journalists as well. That way we can be sure there won't be any stupid heroics."

"Just take care of it. I won't be able to hold the CERT teams off forever."

Knowing with certainty that Redfield could have saved her but didn't, instead going along with Breathwaite's twisted plan, made Kate furious. She had never liked William Redfield, but she had never picked him as an accessory to kidnapping and murder. She was glad the evidence was clearly there to convict him. *May he rot in hell,* she thought, as the prosecutor sat down for the last time.

Breathwaite's defense lasted exactly three minutes. As he had already browbeaten the inmates and ex-con on cross-examination as to their credibility, Breathwaite's attorney didn't bother going through that again. His portrayal of them as pond scum with an axe to grind against anyone in a position of authority in his mind sufficiently eliminated them as reliable witnesses. Instead, in a surprise move, he recalled Peter to the stand.

"Mr. Enright, is it not true that, when you obtained the warrant for a wiretap, you were furious at Mr. Breathwaite for what you perceived to be poor treatment of Ms. Kyle, a personal friend of yours?"

"Objection, Your Honor!" Levon Davis was on his feet before Nepperson had even finished his question. "The question of whether or not the wiretap was obtained legally and its admissibility was argued and settled during the preliminary hearings when he made a motion to suppress. This line of questioning should be disallowed."

The judge nodded. "Agreed. Mr. Nepperson, unless you have something unrelated to the wiretap issue to ask of this witness, I suggest you move on." He glared at the attorney. "Ladies and gentlemen of the jury, I would ask you to disregard the previous exchange."

"Your Honor, I was simply—"

"That's enough, Mr. Nepperson." The judge pointed a finger in warning at the attorney. "I won't hear another word about the wiretap or anything related to it."

"I rest my case, Your Honor," Nepperson said smugly, having accomplished his goal of making the jury think about the circumstances of the wiretap.

"Scumbag," Jay said heatedly under her breath.

"Easy, girl," Kate patted her knee. "He's just doing his job, disgusting as that may be."

In truth, Nepperson had spent the better part of the night before, as he had on one previous occasion, trying to convince his client to plead guilty to a lesser charge. Breathwaite, however, had vehemently refused. Nepperson sighed as he turned the floor over to Josiah Green. *Well, I took my best shot.*

Redfield's attorney called his client to the stand and asked him, "Were you aware in any way of Mr. Breathwaite's plan?"

"Objection, Your Honor!" This time it was Nepperson who was on his feet. "My client has not been found guilty of having involvement with any plan."

"Sustained. Counselor, you're going to have to rephrase that question."

"Of course, Your Honor. Bill, did you know anything about the alleged plot to kidnap and kill Ms. Kyle?"

"No, sir."

"Did you condone such a plot?"

"No, sir."

"In fact, did you not act to save the lives you thought you could?"

"Yes, sir, I did. That is why I authorized the exchange for the three correction officers."

"Why did you not try to save Ms. Kyle, Bill?"

"In my professional judgment, more lives would have been endangered by a rescue mission than would have been saved."

"So you didn't send the teams in, not because you were trying to have her killed, but because you were trying not to jeopardize the lives of the rescue team?"

"That is correct."

"Naturally," Kate mumbled under her breath.

"What a noble guy," Jay answered behind her hand.

"Thank you, Bill. That's all."

The judge looked at all parties. "Any further witnesses?"

There was a chorus of "no, Your Honor."

"Very well. Closing arguments begin tomorrow morning at nine a.m. sharp. Adjourned."

"What do you think, love?"

"I don't know what to think, Jay. I didn't get to see the whole trial the way you did. I should probably be the one asking you. What do you think?"

"I think I'd like to personally fry their butts."

Kate laughed. "Unfortunately, honey, they're not eligible for the death penalty, even if there were one in New York at this stage, which there isn't."

"In that case, I'll settle for having them be some great, big badass's concubine for the next eighty or ninety years."

Kate kissed her on the temple. "That's what I love about you, honey. Not an ounce of vindictiveness in you."

"Oh," Jay said sheepishly. "Were you looking for my objective reporter's assessment of the case against them?"

"Nah, I kind of like what I got instead. We'll leave that objective stuff to the jury tomorrow."

"Sweetheart?"

"Yes?" Kate drew the word out.

"You do realize the inauguration is the day after tomorrow, right?"

"Mmm-hmm."

"That means that you'll have to be in D.C. before noon that day."

"Correction, Scoop—it means *we'll* have to be in D.C. before noon. If you think I'm going to experience this once-in-a-lifetime thrill without you by my side, you're crazy. Besides, I'm counting on dancing the night away with you at a minimum of eight inaugural balls."

"Eight? Why stop there?"

"You're right. Let's shoot for ten."

"That's better. You scared me for a minute there, Stretch—I thought you might be slowing down."

"You wish." Kate bumped Jay with her hip.

"No, actually, that's about the last thing I'd wish for." Jay smiled mischievously.

 ぐろ

Kate and Jay shielded themselves as best they could from the elements—snow, wind, bitter cold, and the paparazzi—as they made their way into the courthouse the next morning.

"I'll tell you this much—I sure won't miss this weather."

"You got that right. Washington is supposed to be a more moderate climate, right?"

"Yes, you delicate flower, it is."

Jay gave her lover a mock glare. "Didn't you just finish complaining about the weather?"

"Yep."

"Then how is it that I'm the one who's a delicate flower?"

"The description just suits you better than it suits me."

Jay seemed to consider for a moment. "Yeah, I suppose it does, at that."

"I knew you'd see it my way."

"That is not a capitulation. I want to be clear about that."

"Oh, no, you didn't give in at all." Kate nodded agreeably.

"I don't like the way you said that."

"What? I was agreeing with you."

"It wasn't *that* you agreed with me—it was *how* you agreed with me."

"Ah, I wasn't aware that there was a protocol for such things."

"Well, there is. Now please familiarize yourself with the handbook before you go agreeing with me again."

Kate laughed easily. "I'll be sure to do that."

They reached the front row and sat down just as the bailiff called the court to order.

The closing arguments were predictable and echoed the themes spelled out by the attorneys in the opening statements. Redfield's attorney went first, painting his client as a hard-working, responsible public servant who was only doing his job. Commissioner Redfield, he said, used his best judgment as to the course of action to be taken. He managed to secure the release of three of the four hostages and kept as many as sixty CERT team members and another forty-two inmates from being hurt in the process. He should not be held criminally responsible for doing his job.

Nepperson stood before the jury next, reiterating his assertion that the prosecution's case relied on the word of inmates, ex-convicts, and others who had an axe to grind with his client. Just because, he asserted, David Breathwaite was not the nicest guy on the block did not make him a criminal.

Levon Davis delivered the closing remarks for the prosecution, taking the jurors back through the parade of witnesses and mountains of evidence he said proved beyond a reasonable doubt that David Breathwaite and William Redfield were guilty of the crimes with which they were charged. He pointed out that, even if the jurors wanted to discount the word of the inmates, there were Kate, Marisa, the reporters, and the two defendants themselves to consider. The defense attorneys were right, he added, to say that convictions should be based on actual facts. The facts, he concluded, more than supported guilty verdicts on all counts.

At 3:34 p.m., the jury retired to the jury room to begin deliberations.

Josiah Green and William Redfield met in a side room off the main courtroom.

"What do you think?" Redfield asked nervously.

"I don't know. It will depend on how much weight the jury gives those audiotapes and how carefully they pick them apart. I think we made a strong argument." He looked at his client carefully as Redfield shredded a piece of legal paper in front of him. "Look, I don't think they have any basis on which to convict you of kidnapping. After all, as we explained to them and as was made clear on the tapes, you didn't know that Breathwaite had arranged for the kidnapping. The only wild card is the conspiracy to commit murder count."

"Great," Redfield mumbled glumly. "That charge only carries a twenty-five year sentence."

"That's a maximum—the judge could give you less. Let's just wait and see—you may well get off scot-free."

David Breathwaite and Calvin Nepperson were sequestered in another room on the other side of the judge's chambers.

"Calvin, sit down—you're making me nervous."

The lawyer was pacing around the room as his client sat doodling on a legal pad. "This is our last chance to work out a deal."

Breathwaite jumped up and stormed over to Nepperson, getting right in his face. "I've already told you—twice now, in fact—that I will not make any deals. Don't bring it up again."

Nepperson backed off a little, holding his hands up in front of him. "Okay, okay. Your choice." He sat down heavily and began drumming his fingers on the conference table.

"Stop that and make yourself useful. I want to see Kirk. Can you get him in here without a hundred people seeing him?"

Nepperson gave his client a murderous glare and left the room, slamming the door behind him. He returned twenty minutes later with the private investigator in tow.

"You might not want to be here, Calvin. Wouldn't want to offend your delicate sensibilities." Breathwaite smiled unpleasantly.

When the lawyer had shut the door behind him, Breathwaite said, "Is everything in place?"

"Yes, boss."

"Are you sure?"

"I said yes, didn't I?" Kirk snapped.

"If this goes down wrong, I don't want any mistakes. I want that bitch to suffer for the rest of her life."

"So you've said on more than one occasion." Kirk buffed his nails on his shirt.

"Damn it! Look at me when I talk to you."

Kirk glanced up, and then back down at his fingernails with apparent disdain.

Breathwaite began to pace. "If I get convicted, Kyle gets to find out that you just don't fuck with David Breathwaite." He laughed delightedly. "Understand?"

"Got it." Kirk got up from the table and left the room.

Kate and Jay were standing in a conference room in the district attorney's office, looking out the window at the wintry scene below.

"What do you think will happen?"

Kate shrugged, "Hard to say. I think Breathwaite should be a two-minute decision, but I'm not as sure about Redfield. It's hard to prove the guy knew of, and approved, the kidnapping based on his reactions on the tapes. In fact, I would say it's pretty clear he didn't know. The conspiracy to commit murder charge, though..." She shrugged again. "In the end, it will depend on whether the jury bought the 'he was just doing his job' defense or whether they put more weight on his statement to Breathwaite that he could only hold the CERT guys off for so long."

Jay nodded. "Yeah, that's the way I've got it figured too."

Kate came up behind Jay and put her arms around her. "Either way, sweetheart, once we have the verdicts, we have closure. Tomorrow we start a brand-new life."

Jay turned around in her lover's arms. "Boy, that sounds good."

Sarah Alexander appeared in the open doorway and surveyed the scene. A momentary pang of regret surfaced before she shoved it away. She thought about walking back out, but decided against it. Instead she cleared her throat. Kate and Jay turned at the same time, arms still linked around each other. "I'm sorry to interrupt, but I thought you'd like to know the jury has asked the judge a question."

Although Jay flushed bright red, she did not move away from her lover. She turned slowly to face her ex-girlfriend, sliding her hand down to grasp Kate's. "Thanks, Sare. What is it and what does it mean?"

They moved to the conference table. "They wanted to know if there was a lesser charge than conspiracy to commit murder that they could consider for Redfield."

"Ah." Kate nodded knowingly. "I'm not altogether surprised by that."

"What do you make of it, Sare?" Jay asked.

"I think it means that they're done with Breathwaite and probably with the kidnapping charge for Redfield too. I would guess they got the easy ones out of the way first. I suspect they're stuck over whether or not what Redfield did or didn't do constitutes conspiracy."

"What did the judge tell them?"

"He told them that, since he hadn't given it to them in their instructions, there was no lesser charge they could consider."

"What do you think they'll do? Any guesses?" Kate asked.

Sarah shook her head. "I honestly don't know. This was a hard jury to read. They haven't been out very long, and if they're seriously deadlocked it could be a long time. The best I can say is get comfortable—it could be a long wait."

At 9:36 a.m. the jury shuffled back into the courtroom after six hours of deliberations over two days. The defendants were already standing at their respective tables with their attorneys. Kate and Jay were standing in the front row. The remaining spectator seats were filled with reporters who, excited about the forthcoming verdict, radiated energy.

The judge addressed the jury. "You have reached your decisions?"

"We have, Your Honor," said the jury foreman.

"With regard to Mr. Redfield, on the count of kidnapping, how do you find?"

"We find the defendant not guilty."

Redfield nearly collapsed in relief.

"Again with regard to Mr. Redfield, on the count of conspiracy to commit murder, how do you find?"

"We find the defendant guilty."

Redfield dropped his head into his hands and sobbed.

"With regard to Mr. Breathwaite, on the count of kidnapping, how do you find?"

"We find the defendant guilty."

A buzz went through the throng of reporters, but Breathwaite showed no emotion.

"On the count of conspiracy to commit murder, how do you find?"

"We find the defendant guilty."

The noise in the room increased, and still Breathwaite made no move.

"On the count of conspiracy to incite a riot, how do you find?"

"We find the defendant guilty."

"Ladies and gentlemen of the jury, thank you for your service. You are dismissed. The defendants are to be remanded to custody for a sentencing hearing. Court is adjourned."

As he was being led away, Breathwaite spotted Kirk standing in the back corner. He nodded once in Jay's direction and back to Kirk before he was swept out the door.

✑✎

Kate and Jay embraced each other, smiling.

"Is it really over?" Jay asked.

"Yeah," Kate responded, "it really is."

As they turned to leave the courtroom they were surrounded by a mob of reporters.

"Kate, how do you feel?"

"Kate, was justice served today?"

"Kate—"

She held up her hands for quiet. "The jury has spoken. Honestly, if I were given a choice, I would prefer that none of this had been necessary." She gestured to the courtroom behind her. "I wish I could turn back the clock and rewrite the story of those events at Attica, but I can't. For me and my family," she glanced at Jay, who was standing at her side, "this has been a long and very painful chapter. I am very relieved to see it ended so that we may move on. Tomorrow is a new day, ladies and gentlemen."

She guided Jay through the crowd as reporters continued to shout questions at them.

◦⋧◦

The ballroom was awash in gold glitter; men and women in formalwear crowded the dance floor, and a popular ballad singer belted out a well-known tune. When the song was finished, an announcer intoned, "Ladies and gentlemen, the President of the United States, Charles Hyland."

The room broke out in thunderous applause. The president made his way down the steps from a balcony above, his wife on his arm, flanked by a dozen Secret Service agents. He waved at the crowd, stopping to shake hands and receive compliments on his inaugural speech.

Kate and Jay stood in the center of the room, looking happy and relaxed. "He does look good in a tux."

"Yep, I'll give him that," Jay agreed. "Very presidential."

"Mmm."

The president mounted the stage and took the proffered microphone. He held up his hands to quell the applause so that he could speak.

"Ladies and gentlemen, I want to thank you all for coming tonight. Without you, I wouldn't be standing here. I just want to say that I intend for this to be the start of a new beginning—a brighter day—a time we can all look back on and be proud of. Enjoy yourselves tonight, as I will, because I've got a lot of work to do come tomorrow."

The room erupted in cheers once again as the president handed the microphone back to the singer and invited him to continue his performance.

As the strains of a familiar ballad washed over the room, the president stepped down from the stage, walked unerringly to the middle of the room, and stopped in front of Kate and Jay.

"Ladies, might I say that you look positively radiant tonight."

"Thank you, sir," they said in unison.

"I didn't get a chance to call you this morning before the inauguration, but I wanted to tell you how glad I am that the ordeal with Redfield and Breathwaite is over with. I know you'll never be able to forget, but I do hope you'll find some peace now."

"Thank you, sir. I think we're both happy to close that chapter of our lives."

"I'm sure. Speaking of new chapters," he looked at Jay, "are you sure I can't lure you away from *Time*? I have a great position with your name on it. The pay is okay, the hours are awful, and the boss is a tyrant, but other than that it's a great job."

Jay laughed. "You make it sound so attractive. Thank you, sir, but I think I'll stick with the lousy pay, irregular hours, and demanding boss that I already have. In fact, I leave tomorrow for a story in Arizona."

"Well, if you ever change your mind, my door will always be open to you."

"Thank you, sir. I'm honored."

∽∂∾

As the trio stood talking, a tuxedoed figure standing just off to the side in the shadows listened intently. It was amazing, Kirk noted, what a fancy set of clothes and a hefty campaign contribution could buy you. He had no difficulty getting an invitation to the inaugural ball, despite the tight security, and even less trouble getting to his target. Having heard what he needed to, he slipped away. "Arizona," he muttered to himself. "Perfect."

∽∂∾

The president continued talking. "Ms. Kyle, I'll see you bright and early tomorrow morning in the Oval Office."

Kate groaned. "Remind me why I agreed to take this job?"

Together, the president and Jay said, "Because the pay is okay, the hours are awful, and the boss is a tyrant."

"Oh," Kate laughed, "now I remember."

The president took his leave, having spotted the chairman of the Democratic National Committee standing close by.

"Bob, it's good to see you."

"Congratulations, Mr. President."

President Hyland considered. "It has a nice ring to it, doesn't it?"

"It sure does, sir."

The singer announced, "This is for all you lovebirds out there. Grab that special someone and hold them tight, because when you find the right one, you should never let go."

As he began singing a love ballad, Kate took Jay into her arms, staring into the face she adored. "I've got that special someone right here," she lowered her head and kissed her lover on the mouth, "and you can be sure I'll never let her go."

"I love you, Kate."

"I love you too, Jay, and I always will."

The two women proceeded to dance the night away, savoring the moment and the beginning of the next chapter in their lives.

**THE END**

# About the Author

An award-winning former broadcast journalist, former press secretary to the New York state senate minority leader, former public information officer for the nation's third largest prison system, and former editor of a national art magazine, Lynn Ames is a nationally recognized speaker and CEO of a public relations firm with a particular expertise in image, crisis communications planning, and crisis management.

Ms. Ames's other works include *The Price of Fame* (Book One in the Kate & Jay trilogy), *The Value of Valor* (winner of the 2007 Arizona Book Award and Book Three in the Kate & Jay trilogy), *One ~ Love* (formerly published as *The Flip Side of Desire*), *Heartsong*, and *Outsiders*.

More about the author, including contact information, other writings, news about sequels and other original upcoming works, pictures of locations mentioned in this novel, links to resources related to issues raised in this book, author and character interviews, and purchasing assistance can be found at www.lynnames.com.

You can purchase other Phoenix Rising Press books online at www.phoenixrisingpress.com or at your local bookstore.

Published by
**Phoenix Rising Press**
**Phoenix, AZ**

Visit us on the Web: **www.phoenixrisingpress.com**

CPSIA information can be obtained at www.ICGtesting.com
Printed in the USA
BVOW040019270911

272075BV00004B/10/P

9 780984 052158